Kindle

THE

GARDEN

of

PROMISES

and LIES

ALSO BY PAULA BRACKSTON

Secrets of the Chocolate House

The Little Shop of Found Things

The Return of the Witch

The Silver Witch

Lamp Black, Wolf Grey

The Midnight Witch

The Winter Witch

The Witch's Daughter

THE
GARDEN
OF
PROMISES
AND LIES

Paula Brackston

ST. MARTIN'S PRESS
NEW YORK

First published in the United States by St. Martin's Press, an imprint of St. Martin's Publishing Group

THE GARDEN OF PROMISES AND LIES. Copyright © 2020 by Paula Brackston. All rights reserved. Printed in the United States of America. For information, address St. Martin's Publishing Group, 120 Broadway, New York, NY 10271.

www.stmartins.com

Library of Congress Cataloging-in-Publication Data

Names: Brackston, Paula, author.
Title: The garden of promises and lies / Paula Brackston.
Description: First edition. | New York : St. Martin's Press, 2020. |
    Series: Found things ; 3 |
Identifiers: LCCN 2020028412 | ISBN 9781250072450 (hardcover) |
    ISBN 9781466884120 (ebook)
Subjects: LCSH: Paranormal romance stories. | GSAFD: Fantasy fiction.
Classification: LCC PR6102.R325 G37 2020 | DDC 823/.92—dc23
LC record available at https://lccn.loc.gov/2020028412

Our books may be purchased in bulk for promotional, educational, or business use. Please contact your local bookseller or the Macmillan Corporate and Premium Sales Department at 1-800-221-7945, extension 5442, or by email at MacmillanSpecialMarkets@macmillan.com.

First Edition: 2020

10 9 8 7 6 5 4 3 2 I

FOR DEE.

WHO IS MOST DEFINITELY NOT A WICKED STEPMOTHER,

AND WHO KNOWS A THING OR TWO ABOUT GARDENS AND ANTIQUES.

HERE'S TO ENJOYING LOTS OF BOTH IN HAPPIER TIMES.

This above all: to thine own self be true,
And it must follow, as the night the day,
Thou canst not then be false to any man.

—WILLIAM SHAKESPEARE

THE MOON SHADOWS IN THE GARDEN CREATED UNFAMILIAR SHAPES BENEATH THE tumbling climbers and chaotic shrubs. From the window seat of her attic bedroom, Xanthe had a clear view of the muddle of borders and the barely tamed lawn as they began to emerge from the chill of winter. The roof-scape of the sleeping town beyond the redbrick garden boundary glistened under a light frost. She thought of how quickly the weeks had passed. Christmas and New Year had come and gone in a blur of activity in the antique shop and extra bookings for the band. Then there had been January sales to organize, and work on the room of mirrors in order to accommodate the new vintage clothing venture. And now it was the first day of March, and their first spring in Marlborough, with the slumbering garden at last beginning to properly reveal itself again after the bare winter months.

In the corner, the grey stone of the little blind house stood without the softening cover of its deciduous rambling dog-roses and honeysuckle, so that it appeared all the more solid, aged, and humble. There was nothing about its size, nor its proportions, nor its worn, heavy door to give a hint of the magic that it contained. There was nothing to suggest that within those damp, bleak stones lay the secrets of the past and the means for some people—a few, special people—to journey back to times gone by. Not for the first time, Xanthe felt a sense of wonder at what had happened to her since she and her mother had opened The Little Shop of Found Things. What had begun as a new home and a new business for both of them in a quiet Wiltshire market town had turned into the greatest adventure of her life. On the first few occasions she had traveled back down the centuries she had done so without control, falling through time as if pushed from the top of a cliff of immeasurable height. Her trips to the era where she had faced danger and found love had been the floundering actions of a beginner in the art of time travel. Now though, after many more journeys, she knew that she did have some control over what she did. And now she had the book of the Spinners. To discover that she was part of a group who shared her ability to move through time and to hold their collected wisdom in her hands had given her courage. There were others like her and she could learn from them, and she was hungry for that knowledge. Slowly, she was starting to uncover their secrets. To understand who and what she truly was. However dangerous her journeys to the past had been, she was no longer afraid. That early fear of what she had been doing, and of all the possible perils, had been replaced by an excitement, a thrill, a deep, precious joy at the thought of what she now knew herself to be. Nothing, however, had prepared her for the shock of seeing her nemesis, Benedict Fairfax, standing at the top of her street, in *her* time. She had used her skills as a Spinner to send him away from Samuel, and in doing so, somehow, she had enabled him to travel forward to the present day. However he had achieved this feat, she had to accept some responsibility for it. She was the one who had helped him get the astrolabe. It was she who had tricked him into traveling to a time not his own to ensure Samuel's safety. She could not, however hard she tried, shake the belief that it was her own actions that had led him to appear so close to her home, to her mother, to everything that now mattered to her. It was up to her, then, to hone her skills, to be better able to protect those she loved. In short, to become what Mistress Flyte had told her it was her destiny to become: a true Spinner of time.

What was it that Fairfax wanted? Why had he come? Still she did not know, for since that first brief, heart-stopping glimpse of him standing at the end of the alleyway, she had not seen him again. She had attempted to convince herself, at first, that she had imagined seeing him. That the vision was simply the product of a tired mind, an overactive imagination, and a confusion brought about by the tumultuous events of her life at that time. But she knew, truly *knew*, that she had seen him, and that he had really been there. Flesh and blood, not a ghost or shadow of a person long dead. Real and calm and cold and dangerous as he had ever been. And knowing Fairfax as she did, she could be certain that he had not chosen to appear in front of her without good reason. He had meant her to see him. He had wanted her to know that he was close. That he could choose when to confront her. And yet, so far, after so many weeks, he had not. She had been watchful, nervously checking she was not followed if she went out at night, vigilantly locking the doors of the shop, taking care not to leave her mother alone for longer than was absolutely necessary. But she had not seen him again. What was his plan, she wondered. Did he want revenge for what she had done, for how she had tricked him? She couldn't be sure. As time went by she wished he would show himself so that she could face him, once and for all. The waiting and wondering had become intolerable, and she knew that she had begun to let her guard down. It was impossible to stay alert to the danger forever. And the not knowing when or where he would show himself again was taking its toll. The only thing she felt with absolute certainty was that he would come again. One day. And that he was capable of anything.

She pulled her woolen shawl tighter around her shoulders and got up from the window seat. Morning would come soon enough, there was work to be done and nothing to be gained by hours spent worrying over things she could not change. When Fairfax made his move she would have to be ready for him; losing sleep in the meantime was pointless.

❖ ❖ ❖

Having at last fallen into a deep slumber, it was after eight the next morning when Xanthe descended the stairs from her attic bedroom to the kitchen on the first floor of the tall narrow apartment that sat on top of the shop. She could hear her mother singing along to the radio, raising her voice to compete with the sound of the whistling kettle.

"Ah, there you are. I was going to give you a shout. Coffee's nearly made. Sit down and help yourself to breakfast. We don't want to keep Gerri waiting when she gets here. Can't have been easy finding someone to man the tea shop." Flora pivoted on one of her crutches as she reached for the jar of ground coffee, deftly snatching a spoon from the draining board as she did so. She had become so adept at managing the restrictions her arthritis placed upon her that most of the time Xanthe forgot how she had been before it had encroached upon her health. Before she had needed sticks for support and painkillers to sleep. "It's going to be such a help, having her input on this. I can't think of anyone better placed to advise us on buying vintage clothing," Flora went on, waving the spoon at her daughter. "Apart from you, love, of course."

"I think of myself more of an enthusiast than an expert." She gestured at her own seventies floral dress and sleeveless shetland jersey. "I can't hold a candle to Gerri. How she always manages to look so perfectly turned out with two small children and a business to run single-handedly amazes me."

"Not to mention her scarlet lipstick," said Flora, pouring water into the coffeepot. "Never a smudge in sight. How come it always ends up on my teeth if I try it?"

She smiled, taking in her mother's fine, fluffy hair which was even now escaping from the random bit of scarf she had tied around it. She glanced down at the plate of food on the table in front of her. "Another experiment, Mum?"

"There's nothing particularly outlandish about crumpets."

"Crumpets, no. Crumpets covered in avocado and—is that broc-coli?"

"We had some left over from last night. I've added some grated cheese. It'll be fine. Come on, eat up. Green food is healthy, isn't it?" She sat down opposite her daughter and squeezed brown sauce from a plastic bottle onto her own breakfast. Xanthe poured coffee for them both, grateful for its aroma and hopeful it would make the food more palatable. Despite the twice-weekly food markets in Marlborough high street which her mother enjoyed browsing, Flora still preferred to cook whatever she found in the fridge, almost regardless of the end result.

"And don't forget," she said, sipping the hot coffee, "you've got the sale at Corsham tomorrow. We need to get as much done to the new room today as possible. If I'm manning the shop and finishing that escritoire in the workshop I'll have my hands full."

"Still can't believe you're letting me go and do the buying at a sale like that on my own. Stately home clearances are your favorite."

"I can't be in two places at once. And besides," Flora beamed, "we had a good Christmas, and now is the perfect time to invest in stock. A sale like that could yield all sorts of treasures. You know what you're doing, most of the time."

"Thanks. I think."

"But if something sings to you . . ."

"I know, don't go mad."

"Of course you will have to get whatever it is. Just don't blow the whole budget, is all I ask. We have made so much progress with the shop."

"Proved the doubters wrong, eh?"

Flora nodded. "Your father among them. Not that I care, of course."

She chose not to pick up on the reference to the man she now thought of simply as her mother's ex-husband. Instead she stayed on safer ground. "Like I did with the chatelaine, you mean? We did get a good price for it in the end, you know."

Flora smiled. They both knew that when something sang to Xanthe, when it triggered her gift of psychometry, she wouldn't be able to resist it, whatever the cost. The ability to detect information about an object—its past, its origins, its story—was a rare thing and unheard of by many, but to the Westlake family it was simply a part of their daughter. Nothing would change that. "We need saleable items, love. Preferably small things. A little more jewelry wouldn't go amiss. Seems popular. And if you see a little dresser for me to paint, or a pair of decent bedroom chairs . . ."

"I will keep my eye out. Don't worry. Business head firmly screwed on, Mum."

"Why don't you see if Liam is free to go with you?"

"You think he's a sensible influence?"

"I just thought it would be nice."

"Mum . . . he has his own business to run."

"He likes helping you. Spending time with you."

"I'll see him soon at band practice. We spend plenty of time together already." She shook her head at her mother's shameless attempts to encourage her relationship with Liam. It was nice that Flora liked him, of course, but she refused to be rushed. Since the medieval weekend—since that kiss—they had agreed to take things slowly. In truth, Xanthe had insisted upon it and given him little choice. She valued their friendship too much to risk it. She knew she was still on the rebound from Samuel. And now that she was a full-time member of Tin Lid, her closeness to Liam had several aspects to it, all of which were woven into her new life. She didn't want to jeopardize a possible future they might have together. As friends. As band members. As lovers. She gulped down her coffee. "Come on, Mum, eat up. I need to unlock and let Gerri in. We've work to do."

The room that the previous owner, Mr. Morris, had used to house his collection of mirrors was behind the main shop, and had only a small window. Xanthe had thought it rather dark and cramped, but since they had removed what turned out to be over fifty mirrors, the space had grown. They had ripped up the old carpet, sanded and polished the floorboards, applied pale gold paint to the walls and white gloss to the woodwork. The window had been left without curtains to make the most of the natural light, and three vintage standard lamps had been carefully placed to give the room a warm glow. Some of the mirrors had been a useful part of the transformation. A full-length rectangular one had been given a makeover by Flora, its pine frame painted and decoupaged with roses in soft greens and pinks. Two smaller mirrors, one elaborate French gilt, the other a smooth white plaster, had been hung to reflect the daylight and allow customers to view themselves from several angles when trying on the vintage clothing. The tasks that remained included setting up new rails and a hatstand, positioning and filling the glass-fronted display case, and unpacking the stock they had amassed over the preceding few months.

"Right," said Xanthe, rubbing her hands together. "Let's start with these boxes."

Gerri, who had arrived on the dot of nine o'clock and was dressed as a land army girl in dungarees, hair expertly twisted under a gingham scarf, lipstick perfectly applied, started to pull garments from the nearest crate, handing them out for inspection. "What have we here? A houndstooth-check winter coat—good and roomy. A suede jacket with tassels . . ."

Flora gasped. "Oh dear . . . does anyone actually wear tassels anymore?"

"Mum," she took it from Gerri and gently smoothed the fringed sleeves, "don't be so quick to judge. It's all about putting a look together. You'd be surprised what some people would do with that."

"Xanthe's right." Gerri held up a Laura Ashley dress. "It's a matter of seeing the potential in things."

"Well, I'm very glad I've got you two to do that," Flora said. "To me it all looks like jumble. All thrown out for good reason."

Xanthe shook the folds out of a maxi skirt. "Some of it's a bit down-market, I grant you, but fans of vintage stuff know what works. We just need to make sure we have some high-end items too."

"Yes, designer pieces!" Gerri's eyes lit up at the thought. "I bought an original Biba blouse the other day. It wasn't cheap, but it'll hold its value."

Flora tried on a dusty bowler hat, peering at herself in the gilt-framed mirror. "Hmmm, I think it's a bad idea to wear vintage if you yourself are vintage," she decided, making the others laugh.

"The trick is," Gerri said, minutely adjusting Flora's hat to a more flattering angle, "to always choose clothes that suit your own shape and coloring. That's the secret to avoiding giving the impression you're in fancy dress." She thought for a moment, removed the bowler hat, and replaced it with a beret, artfully positioned.

Flora grinned at the result. "As long as you agree to be my personal dresser, Gerri, I'll give it a go."

Xanthe started slipping blouses onto hangers. "The challenge is going to be locating the fine, expensive items. We want to get known for quality as well as range."

"Can't we find things on the internet?" asked Flora.

"If only," said Gerri, frowning at a lurid green skirt before dropping it into the rejections box for recycling. "People are much more clued up about the value of things nowadays. Good pieces are in demand. You can end up paying over the odds."

"I'm going to the dispersal sale tomorrow," Xanthe told her. "Corsham Hall, out toward Bath. Do you know it?"

"Oh, that was the house of the Wilcox family. They were fabulously rich, once upon a time."

"Let's hope the late owner secretly hoarded all her ancestors' clothes."

"There might be flapper dresses in the attic!"

"Well, if there are, I'll snaffle them. That's exactly what we need to elevate this little lot."

They worked on, steadily sorting the wheat from the chaff, ignoring some of the faces Flora pulled at the more outlandish items. Xanthe was happy to have Gerri's support for their new room. She knew her mother had agreed to it to please her, and it helped to have the input of a person whose taste they both trusted. Even though they were no longer in the financial difficulty they had been when they first bought the shop, every space in it still had to earn its keep. Mr. Morris's mirrors had been taking up too much space and moving too slowly. She had been forced to swallow her pride and call Theo Hamilton again. She did not enjoy having to contact her rival antique dealer and offer him the pieces after turning him away the first time, but needs must. Fortunately he had still wanted the mirrors as a job lot, though he had not been above making her work at getting his forgiveness for his previous wasted journey when she had changed her mind about selling them. In the end his eye for a bargain had won out and they had agreed on a fair price. Her hope was that the vintage clothes would attract new browsers, extra shoppers who might not otherwise visit an antique shop. Once over the threshold, who knew what they might be tempted to buy?

"Oh, look at this, love." Flora held up a black sequined dress. "You could wear it for your next performance with Tin Lid."

Xanthe laughed. "Not unless we start booking gigs in a jazz club, Mum!"

"I think you'd look lovely in it," she insisted. "I bet Liam would agree with me."

"He usually does."

"Such a nice boy."

"He's smart enough to know how to get around you," she said, taking the dress from her mother and hanging it on the rail. "Anyway, he doesn't really notice what I wear."

Gerri raised her eyebrows. "From what I've seen, he notices every little thing about you."

"We're just good friends."

"With benefits?" Flora asked, giving a pantomime wink.

"Mum! You know full well what that means. Don't pretend you don't."

"I'm assuming friends who help and support each other?" she replied innocently, while Gerri tried not to laugh. "He's been so good, running you around when your car broke down, driving the van to pick up bigger pieces of furniture...."

"Right, firstly *please* don't ever use that expression again. Secondly, Liam and I are perfectly happy with the way things are between us, thank you very much."

Flora and Gerri pointedly exchanged looks that clearly told her they thought otherwise.

Later, after she had shut the shop for the day, Xanthe said goodbye to her mother and headed for The Feathers. Her irregular but increasingly frequent chats with Harley had become an important feature of her week. While Benedict Fairfax might not have shown himself again, he was still ever on her mind, and her determination to be ready for him next time she saw him occupied her thoughts whenever she was alone. However, between the shop, Flora, the band, and of course, Liam, it was difficult to find clear time to focus on the madness of what she had experienced since moving to Marlborough. Sometimes the pull of normality and the wish to believe all was safe and sensible prevented her from facing what she knew, in her heart, had to be faced. The fact that Fairfax never did anything without a reason. The fact that he was not a man to give up on something he wanted.

The fact that he had proved himself capable of doing anything in order to further his own interests. Which was why she felt blessed to have Harley—publican, local historian, hairy biker, and true friend—as a confidant. He alone knew the truth of where, and more important *when*, Xanthe went when she was away from Marlborough. He knew about the Spinners; she had shared their secrets and their precious book with him and no one else. And she had told him about Fairfax. Speaking with Harley about so many impossible things made her feel just a tiny bit less crazy, and a tiny bit more in control of what was happening. And now that she had decided to properly study the Spinners' writings she was eager to test her theories about its contents with him.

She found Harley fixing new window boxes to the sills of the pub. He was a burly man, big rather than fat, but not in the best of shape. She heard him puff a little and curse quietly in his endearing Scottish lilt as he wrestled the heavy, soil-filled boxes into position.

"I've never thought of you as a gardener, Harley. Will you be arranging flowers next?"

"You are so bloody funny. Don't just stand there, hen, hand me that hammer, would ye?" He gestured at the pile of tools on the pavement. Passersby were forced to step into the street to avoid the muddle.

"Must be spring," said Xanthe, passing him the hammer. "Window boxes going up, Harley sighted out from behind the bar."

"Not for long," he said, taking a large staple from the pocket of his biker's leather jacket, placing it through the flower box stay, and bashing it into place. She watched him work for another five minutes. At last he was satisfied, brushed mud from his hands, and picked up his tool kit. "Right, that's me done. I'll leave the tending of the plants to Annie. Come away inside. Winter might be over but it's still cold enough to freeze a man's ears off, if ye ask me."

The pub was in its late-afternoon lull: lunch service over, evening meals not yet started, and no live music scheduled. Harley grabbed two bottles of Henge beer from behind the bar, removing their tops with practiced ease, signaling to his wife and the young man working with her that he was going upstairs. Xanthe, after pausing to say hello to Annie, followed him up the slightly wonky staircase to the apartment on the floor above. The sitting room was warm, comfortable, and in its customary state of barely contained chaos. Harley moved a stack of motorbike magazines from one of the worn leather sofas and subsided onto it, handing her a beer as she joined him.

"Did you bring the time travel manual with you?" Harley asked with the now familiar note of awe that crept into his voice when he spoke about the *Spinners* tome.

She nodded, taking the old leather volume from her bag and passing it to him.

Harley took a swig of ale and wiped his beard with the back of his hand, then wiped his hands on his trousers before carefully, almost reverently, taking the book from her. "This is an incredible thing you have in your possession, hen."

"I read a little every day and still there is so much to learn. It's not just the stories; there are maps, drawings, poems, recipes, spells even. It's crammed full of stuff. The tricky thing is working out what's real. I mean, what's instructions, and what's just, I don't know, cautionary tales?"

"Aye, it's not your straightforward user's manual, that's true enough."

"Sometimes I feel stupid not being able to properly understand what I'm reading. Some pages make more sense only because I've been back in time. I can relate parts of what is written to my experiences but, well," she gave a shrug, "it's easy being wise after the event. What I need is clues for what I do next. How to use what I've learned to travel better. Safer. With more control."

Harley smiled. "I'm just pleased I can see anything written there at all," he said, referring to the fact that *Spinners* did not reveal its contents to everyone. Xanthe had wondered about this fact since they had first discovered it. The book could not be copied, nor could it be read by just anyone. Why had it chosen to let Harley see its secrets? He did not have her gift of psychometry, nor did he ever glimpse the past. No objects sang to him, and when she had taken him to see the blind house in the garden he had detected nothing strange or magical about it at all. In the end, she had concluded that *Spinners* wanted him to be able to help her. It shared its wisdom and stories with him just enough for him to be able to give her his support and input. The subtlety of the way the book guarded its knowledge astonished her. It also made her feel all the more privileged. It was as Mistress Flyte had told her. She was a Spinner. Her journeys through the centuries had not been random experiences, caused by stumbling upon powerful objects and coming to live near the blind house. It was all meant to be. She was learning who she was, or at least, what she could become. She briefly entertained the thought that one day she might be able to travel back and visit her friend and mentor, and the thought of having such control and such freedom thrilled her.

"Do you think it's what your man is after?" Harley's question broke into her thoughts.

"*Spinners?*"

"Aye. Is that why he's found his way here, to this time?"

"He wants something, there's no doubt about that. And I'm actually rather hoping it is the book he's come for. Because if it's not, then the only other reason he would go to the trouble and the risk of spinning time to get here is . . ."

". . . for you," Harley finished her sentence.

"It's not a pleasant thought."

Harley gave a snort. "You're right about that, hen. From what you've told me the man's a right bastard." He took another long gulp of his beer, his expression thoughtful. "Way I look at it is, whether it's the book he's after or taking his revenge on you for tricking him the way you did, well . . . one way or another he's trouble. But you've not seen him again?"

"No, still just the one time, standing at the top of our street. But I know he's close."

"You sure you're not imagining that? I mean, it's understandable you're spooked, but if he hasn't turned up again maybe it was just a one-off and he's gone back to wherever—whenever—he came from."

"I wish I believed that, but I don't. I *know* he's still around. I can sense his presence, sometimes really strongly. I think he's waiting for something. And then . . ."

". . . and then?"

Xanthe drank deeply from her beer bottle. She paused, taking a breath. "Mistress Flyte was right. He's not a fit person to have something so powerful. A Spinner should respect the order of things, the way things are meant to be. They shouldn't change them to suit their own purposes."

"No pressure then." Harley shifted his not inconsiderable weight, making the leather sofa creak. "In the meantime, you've plenty on your plate with the band. Annie says we're lucky to book you now!"

She smiled. "I'll always find time for The Feathers, you know that. Actually, it's Liam who's elusive at the moment. He's been really busy with work. He's up in Oxford today delivering a recent restoration. A beautiful blue Jaguar."

"Hell's teeth! Has he won you over to classic cars too? He must be even more bloody charming than he looks."

Xanthe recalled the first time she had seen Liam and how his good looks had made her wary of him, her experience of beautiful men up to that point not having been entirely positive. He had worn his hair cropped short then, giving an edge to his appearance. Lately he had grown it out a little, causing her to tease him about being a secret surfer. The truth was, he'd look highly appealing either way. "I'm just quoting him," she said. "He's been so passionate about the thing it would be hard not to remember what it was. Anyway, he's doing a second one for the same enthusiast. He said it'll take another few weeks. He should be more available for gigs after that."

"Let's hope so. We miss your singing, lassie."

"Trust me, the other members of Tin Lid won't let him get away with much more shirking."

As always after her chats with Harley, Xanthe felt reassured. She was not dealing with everything on her own anymore. Whatever her future as a Spinner held, she had a confidant. A part of her was sorry it wasn't Liam. Their friendship mattered to her and they had become closer since Christmas, so she was increasingly uncomfortable about keeping secrets from him. And time travel was a pretty big secret. She wondered, briefly, what would happen if she allowed herself to truly care for him. If she let herself fall for him she knew he would be waiting with open arms to catch her, but would she ever be able to tell him about the Spinners? Could he understand? Would he even be able to believe her? It was a lot to ask. And then there was Flora to consider. The more people who knew about her other life, the greater the chance that her mother would find out. Would she be terrified at the thought of what her daughter had been doing, and would, Xanthe knew, continue to do? Would she beg her never to step through the blind house again? If coming to terms with her own abilities and true identity was challenging, sharing it with people who cared about her seemed one of the biggest challenges. And yet increasingly she was drawn to the idea that she should tell her mother everything. In fact, there were days when she came close to doing so, when her excitement about being a Spinner came close to making her blurt it all out. Flora had long accepted that Xanthe had the gift of psychometry; surely she of all people would be the most accepting, even of something so incredible.

By the time she left the pub it was nearly seven, properly dark, and cold enough to remind her that spring was still in its infant days. The peal of the church bells sounded through the thickening air of the evening, seemingly suspended in the damp chill that was descending. Not for the first time she was reminded that Flora had her own life outside the shop now, her own friends, her own interests. Her joining the Marlborough bell ringers had been a significant step toward that. As the ancient iron bells pealed on Xanthe allowed herself to take comfort from this. There would, one way or another, she believed, come a time when her mother would have to do without her. It was good that she was establishing herself in the community of Marlborough, slowly but surely. It lifted a little of the weight of responsibility from Xanthe's shoulders. As she walked she fancied she detected an urgent note to the tolling of the bells. Their usual celebratory pealing appeared to have been replaced with something more like a warning.

In the wide main street the daytime bustle had been replaced by the early evening crowd. There were workers heading home, some pausing to take advantage of happy hour in their favorite pub or a glass of wine in a lively bar to signify the switch from business to leisure time. Others were on their way out, striding purposefully to the supermarket for their shopping, or arm in arm, destined for one of the many quality eating places. All was happily familiar and quietly lovely. And yet Xanthe could not shake off a feeling of unease. Her stomach tightened, and she was aware of a nervousness in her posture. However safe and normal things were around her she could not rid herself of the thought of Fairfax and the feeling that he was somehow watching her, whether from the shadows in the doorways of the old shops and houses, or via a vision granted him by some device even though he might have been centuries distant. Either way, she felt his presence. She quickened her step, wishing only to be home talking to Flora, enjoying light conversation and sharing simple food. It was as she turned down the narrow cobbled street in which their shop was situated that she became convinced she was being followed. She dared not look around; did not want to see who might be there. She strode on, resisting the urge to run, telling herself there was no real danger with so many other people about. She reached the shop door and fumbled in her bag for the key. As she tried to wriggle it into the lock she felt the unmistakable sensation of warm breath upon the back of her neck. With a half-suppressed shout she wheeled around, the bunch of keys held high ready, to strike.

Liam raised his hands in supplication. "Hey! No need for violence."

"Oh, for God's sake, Liam!" She felt relief surging through her, and yet fear remained, real and powerful. For an instant, Liam's features were clouded, indistinct, as if shadowed by something, and a fierce sense of peril emanated from him. It made no sense. She shook away the unwelcome emotions, telling herself she was simply reacting to a moment of panic and to being startled. "You scared me half to death, creeping up like that. What were you thinking?"

"That I'd surprise you? That you'd be pleased to see me?" He dropped his hands and laid them gently on her shoulders. "I'm sorry, I didn't mean to scare you."

"I thought you were in Oxford," said Xanthe, the sound of her galloping heart still pounding in her ears, taking its time to settle.

"I was. The guy was thrilled skinny with the car. All done and dusted really early so I hurried on home to see you. Thought I could take you out to dinner to celebrate getting paid for the work on the car." He smiled, his pale blue eyes catching the light from the street lamp, the warmth in his expression hard to resist.

She smiled back, allowing herself to be pulled into a hug, breathing in the familiar smell of his leather jacket, happy to feel close and safe. She looked up at him.

"Seeing as you nearly gave me a heart attack I'll let you pay," she said. "But first, come up and see Mum. You can tell her you're taking me out."

"Will she be fed up being left on her own?" he asked, pushing open the shop door, causing the battered brass bell to announce their arrival.

"Trust me," Xanthe smiled, "she'll be delighted."

{ 2 }

AS SHE HAD PREDICTED, FLORA WAS PLEASED TO SEE LIAM AND MORE THAN HAPPY TO forego having her company for dinner if it meant she was going on a date with him. Xanthe was still a little too shaken to be bothered by her mother's shameless matchmaking. Shaken and perplexed. It wasn't just the scare about being followed, or her irritation at Liam being thoughtless enough to creep up on a woman walking home alone in the dark. It wasn't even her ever-present state of alert regarding Fairfax. What continued to rattle her was that moment when she had turned, seen Liam, known it was him, known she was safe, and yet still felt filled with dread. It was that glimpse of a darkness about him that she could not easily dismiss. Was it perhaps a premonition? Was he in danger? The thought that Fairfax might use her loved ones to get at her was not new. After all, was that not precisely what he had done with Samuel?

After a brief chat and a couple of phone calls, Liam booked them a table at the Italian restaurant down by the river. Half an hour later they were seated at a table in the window overlooking the early spring bulbs lit by fairy lights, the moon on the narrow water glinting in the background. Liam hungrily scanned the menu.

"I love Italian food. Proper portions. Bring on those carbs!"

"There's a man immune to fashionable diets." She was relieved to find that her own appetite was returning at the sound of all the tempting dishes on offer.

"I plow my own furrow," he said.

"Happily, red wine is now thought to be essential for long life."

"Is one bottle enough?" He signaled to the waiter and ordered some Chianti.

Xanthe wished she could just relax, forget about complicated, impossible things, forget even about *Spinners*, ignore the constant pull she felt from it, and simply enjoy the moment, putting all else from her mind. She became aware of Liam studying her. "What?" she asked, meeting his gaze.

"You look thoughtful."

"And that's a bad thing?"

"Depends what you're thinking about."

"Pasta."

"And?"

"Garlic bread?"

He frowned at her. She made a point of closely examining the menu again but knew he was too perceptive to move on without questioning her further. He had noticed her demeanor and wouldn't be so easily convinced that nothing was the matter.

"Hey, I'm sorry about earlier," he said, "scaring you like that . . ."

"It's fine, forget it."

"I was an idiot."

"Granted."

"I aim to make it up to you with fabulous food, fine wine, and erudite conversation."

"Good luck with that."

He hesitated before reaching across the table and touching her arm. "Seriously, what's up?"

She knew him well enough to be sure he wouldn't let it go. What could she tell him? That she had been scared because she thought a ruthless, violent man from four centuries ago was stalking her? That she was worried because she had experienced a premonition of something bad happening to someone close to her, quite possibly Liam himself? She steered for safer ground.

"I saw Harley earlier. We were talking about booking the band for performances at The Feathers. Made me realize how . . . unavailable you've been lately, when it comes to Tin Lid."

"The workshop has been hectic, you know that."

"I do, but that doesn't really matter to people who book us, does it? They want to feel we are serious, committed, you know . . ."

"Has anyone else said anything? Mike? Any of the others?"

"I haven't discussed it with anyone else. Why would I do that?"

"You discussed it with Harley," he said, sitting up a little straighter and withdrawing his hand.

"Because Annie asked him to see if we could fill a slot Friday week," she explained, beginning to wish she hadn't brought it up. There was a moment's silence during which she allowed herself to be happy that Liam had accepted her reason for being distracted. At the same time she felt a niggling regret at somehow making him be the cause of it. "It doesn't matter." She tried a smile. "You're right: It's a temporary thing. Once you're less busy with work we can pick up the pace a bit."

"Actually, I'd been meaning to tell you I got a call from Sharon at The Bull, out at Laybrook. She's interested in booking us some time over Easter."

Xanthe experienced a jolt at hearing the name of the village. Laybrook was where so many things had happened. It was where she had first encountered Fairfax. It was where she had lost her locket and almost become stranded in the seventeenth century. It was where she had met Samuel's fiancée and accepted that he and she could never be together. And, most poignantly of all, it was in the churchyard of St. Cyrian's in Laybrook that Samuel had his grave. She silently chided herself for being so sensitive. In her own time Laybrook was one of the prettiest villages in the county and home to some extremely popular pubs which would be perfect venues for band performances. Even so . . . "Maybe we shouldn't book any new gigs until we're back in the swing of things again," she suggested. "Once you've got more time we need to spend some sessions working on new material, don't you think?"

He gave a shrug and a nod. "OK, if that's what you reckon. I'll have a chat with the lads on Sunday. Now, I refuse to talk business any more until I get some food!"

The following morning was a thoroughly convincing spring day. The garden behind the shop was filled with birdsong and sunshine fell through the long windows of the first-floor living room, shedding beams of light in which dust motes danced. Flora put down the phone as Xanthe came to stand in the doorway.

"Well," she said, hands on hips, a surprised expression on her face, "a voice from the past."

"Oh?"

"Do you remember Helga Graham?"

"Your old school friend? Hard to forget her."

"Is it the copper red hair or the rattling laugh that makes her stick in the mind, d'you think?"

"Both. And her habit of smoking French cigarettes. How did she even get this number?"

"Your father gave it to her."

"Uncharacteristically helpful of him."

"Not really. He couldn't stand her. Probably put her in touch to spite me. But I liked her. She has character. When we shared a student flat a hundred years ago she was fun."

"So why has she turned up now? You haven't seen her for years."

"She wants to come and stay!"

"Really? What prompted that?"

Flora gave a shrug. "She just said she'd heard about me and Philip splitting up, that you and I had moved . . . wants to come and see our new home . . . sort of thing. We have exchanged Christmas cards over the years."

"Still, seems a bit out of the blue. And we haven't got a spare room."

"That doesn't matter." Flora smiled. "She can sleep in here. The sofa's perfectly comfortable for one person."

Xanthe took in the muddle that was their living room. Even though nine months had passed since they had moved in there were still boxes in corners, chairs stacked up, and all manner of office chaos littering the space. Her mother saw the look on her face.

"She'll be fine," she assured her. "Helga's not the fussy type, and it'll only be for a couple of nights."

"Well, she can't smoke in here. She'd set fire to something for certain. When does she want to come?"

"The day after tomorrow."

"Blimey, that doesn't give us long to get this lot sorted out."

Flora pointedly fluffed up the cushions on the sofa. "She wouldn't want any fuss. I think it will be rather nice, catching up with an old friend. Especially without your father to roll his eyes at her like he used to."

Flora showed no sign of finding discussing her ex-husband painful anymore. The divorce settlement had at last been agreed on and all but completed. The first part of the divorce decree had been granted; a significant legal step in the process. Xanthe recalled the day the paperwork had arrived from the solicitor and remembered how subdued Flora had been for the entire weekend. Now though, it felt as if she was properly moving on, putting her marriage behind her. Perhaps she was right. An old friend visiting their new place was another step away from the difficult bits of her old life while holding on to some of the better bits. There was surely more room for friendships now. Old connections being reforged with their new life.

"You're right," she said, pulling her hair back to secure it into a band. "It will do us good. The two of you can have a good catch-up and we can take her out a bit. Somewhere nice to eat, perhaps. Maybe a walk up by the white horse. Does she like walking?"

Flora frowned. "Can't picture it, somehow, but who knows. It's been years." The clock on the mantelpiece struck the hour. "Shouldn't you be on your way? You'll need a bit of time to look around the sale before it starts."

"Don't worry, I've studied the catalogue and planned my campaign. And Gerri's given me her thoughts on what to look out for. I've even put together a packed lunch to keep me going. I have a feeling this one will attract the trade in numbers."

"I hate the way the London dealers only venture out for the high-end sales and then swan around snapping up all the best pieces because they plan to charge city prices."

"Do swans snap?"

"You know what I mean." Flora threw one of the scatter cushions at her.

Xanthe caught it, brushing off the small puff of dust it sent up. "I will beat them at their own game."

"Just don't . . ."

". . . blow the budget. I know, I know."

However well planned she thought her day had been, the drive to the sale venue took longer than she had expected. Her trusty black cab was running smoothly after having spent some time in Liam's workshop, but it made no difference to the journey time. The traffic farther west was heavy, with lorries making their way to the motorway and the first holidaymakers of the season adding to the lines of cars and caravans filling the roads. By the time she turned through the charming gate-houses and sped along the tree-lined drive of the big house it was already nearly ten o'clock. As she had feared, there were lots of vehicles in the car park that had the look of dealers' wheels. She would have to choose her stock with care. No point bidding on the obvious, safe sellers; they would likely reach higher prices than was sensible with so many traders chasing the same lots. She parked between a large van and a jeep with a trailer, which did nothing to allay her fears.

The car park was in fact a small field near the stables, a little way apart from the main house. This was a private property, not owned by the National Trust nor opened to the public, so it wasn't set up for hordes of visitors, as the temporary signs put up for the sale attested. The route took Xanthe across a spotlessly clean and beautifully maintained stable yard. There were no horses in residence, but it wasn't hard to imagine how impressive the place would have looked filled with carriages and the horses to pull them, liveried footmen and ostlers and grooms hurrying with quiet efficiency about their work. There was an archway through which the carriages must once have entered, having allowed their passengers to alight at the house. It was only once she had passed under the creamy stone of this portal that she got her first view of Corsham Hall itself. It was splendid enough to make her stop in her tracks, shielding her eyes against the sharp morning sun to better take in the grandeur and scale of the building in front of her. It struck her in that moment that what she was looking at was the quintessential example of a fine Georgian mansion. Its proportions were classically perfect, with three stories of long windows, balanced by a porticoed main entrance sporting fine Doric columns, approached by a flight of broad steps. It was constructed of flawless pale golden stone which showed no signs of weather, no crumbling or distressing, just a smooth beauty that had withstood time and the elements wonderfully well. As she gazed up at the impressive facade a woman with a soft French accent paused behind her, commenting on the loveliness of the place. Her companion's reply was to point out the impossible cost of the upkeep of such a place; the maintenance of the buildings, the heating bills, the work and staff needed to keep up a house of such size and importance. Xanthe wondered that the house had remained so long in private ownership, as most stately homes of its ilk that she had come across had long ago been taken up by trusts or preservation organizations. That or turned into luxury hotels. The thought made her wonder how the family—she recalled Gerri saying their name was Wilcox—had succeeded in hanging on to it as long as they had. And what had brought the current owner to this point? There was an inescapable sadness to selling off the entire contents of such a historic and significant home. She always sensed a different feel to sales that followed the death of the last inhabitant of a place compared to sales that were to disperse goods and raise money while members of the family still lived. What, she wondered, had made them give up such a heritage?

She followed the crowd of buyers and browsers up the wide steps and through the imposing double doors. Her mind kept traveling to times past, imagining the footmen and butlers and maids scurrying about as the upper classes, dressed in their finery, went about their glamorous lives. How many important aristocrats had visited this house? How many giggling girls had swept out of the entrance in rustling silk gowns, hurrying down the steps to waiting carriages that would whisk them away to grand balls in other equally grand houses? How many messengers had hammered on those very doors bearing news from the Napoleonic Wars, or details of the Crimean campaign, or updates on the health of the king or queen of the day? So much history was held within those fabulous walls. So many lives lived to the rhythms of bygone eras, so many hearts beating to times spent and gone. She realized that she was experiencing more than a pleasant bit of daydreaming; she was yearning for the past. It was as if her Spinner self craved it. As if the past were a long-lost lover and she felt the separation keenly. Xanthe knew, if she was completely honest with herself, that she was hoping something at the sale would sing to her. More than hoping, she was praying for it, to whatever deity watched over Spinners and their journeys. She needed a found thing to call her back. She accepted that she was no longer waiting for something to find her; she was actively, fervently seeking it out.

The entrance hall was no less jaw-droppingly splendid than the exterior of the house. She tried to take it all in: the grand staircase, the larger than life-sized portraits, the marble floors . . . she made herself dizzy twisting her head this way and that, trying to see everything while still moving on toward the ballroom where the auction would take place. She felt annoyed with herself for not having come to the viewing day, which would have allowed her plenty of time to examine the lots before the bidding started. She had thought that studying the catalogue would be good enough, but now she began to doubt the wisdom of that. The house was vast. There would be so many interesting things to see, and little time in which to examine them properly. And now that she had arrived late she had put herself at a further disadvantage. She moved to a corner of the hallway and pulled the catalogue from her bag, flicking to the second page to remind herself of the most imminent lots that she had marked out. She was interrupted by a familiar voice at her shoulder.

"Ah, the lovely Xanthe Westlake. Such prettiness in such sublime surroundings, dear heart. My morning is complete." Theo Hamilton greeted her with his customary effusiveness. On this occasion he sported a mustard velvet jacket with polka-dot cravat at his throat.

"Looking dapper as ever, Theo." She put on her best smile. "Are you here for something in particular or just hunting for the unexpected?"

"A little of both. I confess I am in love with a Louis XIV chiffonier. Alas, I fear it will be hotly contested." He turned to wave pointedly to another dealer on the far side of the hall. "So I must allow myself to be the plaything of serendipity. I will go where I am sent."

She smiled at how flippantly Theo threw out the idea of chance leading him to the best buys when she herself was the one who could be pulled irresistibly to certain items. It was as she formed this thought that she became aware of a slight dizziness and the sound of distant bells ringing. The dizziness could be explained by an insufficient breakfast, or it could be the start of an object singing to her. The bells were a surprise, not only because she had never been called by such a sound before, but because she now realized they were the same bells she had heard when leaving The Feathers. The pealing she had taken for her mother and her friends practicing at St. Mark's had in fact been an aural glimpse of something that was singing to her. It made sense, now, that they had sounded odd on that occasion. Something in that great house, about to be auctioned. But what? And where? She needed to shake off Theo and start searching.

"Well, don't let me keep you from those happy discoveries," she told him, moving toward the ballroom.

Theo was not to be so easily got rid of. "But tell me, darling girl, how is your mother? The shop still afloat?" Without waiting for an answer he went on. "I bumped into your father the other day. I must say his auction house goes from strength to strength. I paid a ruinous price for a chaise. He must be fair raking it in. I mentioned how I had run into you at Great Chalfield and found you buying such charmingly girlish things. A chatelaine, wasn't it? How much did you part with for that piece? Remind me."

"More than I should have," said Xanthe without missing a beat. "Luckily for me we sold it for a seriously masculine profit. Now, I'm sorry, Theo, but I have other soppy purchases to make."

"Bon chance!" he called after her as she strode away.

She ground her teeth, determined not to let the man provoke her into a bad mood. The bells in her head were now accompanied by a high-pitched buzzing, and the dizziness had increased. At the entrance to the ballroom she paused at the pop-up desk to get her bidding number and paddle, before hurrying to the far side of the enormous room, which was already filled with eager auction goers. She cast about frantically for a sign of what could be calling to her, but there were too many people to see much, apart from the lots which were being taken up onto the temporary stage where the auctioneer sat. She found a spot against the wall and opened her catalogue again, flicking through to see if there was something that could be triggering such a strong response. She was relieved that at least this time, despite the unusual sounds, there did not seem to be the awful fear and dread attached to the object as there had been to the chatelaine. Nor was there even the urgency with which the chocolate pot had sung to her. This found thing, whatever it was, appeared to be announcing its presence with strength, importance, clarity, and insistence, as the sensations and sounds were growing more powerful by the moment.

Xanthe found the mysterious object in the catalogue at the exact moment the auctioneer announced it, so that he appeared to be reading over her shoulder, causing her to shiver. There was no photograph with this particular lot, which was why she had not noticed it when she had first gone through the listings. She looked up as the auctioneer spoke.

"Ladies and gentlemen, a beautiful lot here," he intoned in his calm, professional voice. He pointed his gavel to the right as the assistant held up the item. There was a collective gasp in the room. Even the stony hearts of the dealers could not fail to be moved by the delicate beauty of the antique wedding dress in front of them. "An Edwardian wedding gown, believed to date around 1908. The lace is still in fair condition, showing some repairs. The embroidered bodice is particularly fine . . . what am I bid? Who'll start me at 300 pounds? Anyone?"

In the pause that followed, Xanthe's head was filled with a cacophony of bells, along with the more familiar high notes in which her found things usually sang to her. The dizziness continued and was accompanied by a slight blurring of her vision, into which fragments of images danced. She glimpsed a face, flowers, a swirl of water, a sweep of lawn, each snatched vision tumbling one upon the other in just that brief moment.

The auctioneer continued.

"I have 275 pounds on the internet, who'll give me 300 pounds? Thank you, 300 pounds I have. And fifty. 400 pounds. And fifty . . ."

Xanthe craned her neck to try to spot the bidder. It seemed to be a two-way tussle between a buyer on the net and another in the room. The piece was climbing with alarming speed. She held her nerve, waiting until the first bidder dropped out. At £500 she made her move.

"A new bidder," declared the auctioneer, acknowledging her bid.

As always, she felt a thrill at entering the fray, pitched against another keen buyer, both of them hoping to secure a quality item and a good price. For her though, this was personal. An object that sang to her could not be missed. It had its story to share with her, and though part of her feared what it might reveal, what it might ask of her, the greater part knew she could not turn away. This was a part of her. Her as she always had been, with her gift showing itself when she was only a child. And her as she was now; a Spinner. The two things could never be separated, and she could never be separated from either of them.

"575 pounds," she heard the auctioneer say as the bidding slowed slightly.

Across the room her competition made himself obvious, stepping forward just enough for her to see him. It was a deliberate move. She knew the man, and knew him to be the owner of a high-end interior design business who bought choice pieces for discerning clients. No doubt he had someone specific in mind who would pay handsomely for such a rare antique gown, perhaps to dress a bedroom, or as part of a display in a hotel or restaurant, or even a boutique. Xanthe told herself better to be matched against a dealer than a private buyer for such a romantic lot. A person might fall in love with the dress and pay silly money for it; a dealer would, ultimately, only part with as much as would leave room for a profit on his investment.

She held up her hand for the auctioneer to see, signaling clearly she would go to £650. The auction room was quiet now, all attention focused on the dueling bidders. The dealer hesitated, narrowing his

eyes at Xanthe. Would pride push him to go further? Just as it seemed
he would go again he shook his head, turning back to his catalogue,
both her and the dress dismissed. She was so relieved she barely heard
the auctioneer's gavel descend with a smart rap upon his desk. A little
dazed, she held up her buyer's paddle so he could see her number and
watched as the wedding dress was taken down. After a few steadying
breaths she forced herself to concentrate on the following lots. She
had already parted with a chunk of money. To redeem herself she
must find things her mother would approve of. Things that would sit
well in the shop, sell well, and raise their own profits, and build on the
success they had already achieved.

The remainder of the morning passed swiftly. The Wilcox family
had amassed an impressive trove of wonderful things down the generations. There were splendid collections of fine bone china, often
consisting of 24 place settings; richly colored Persian rugs; glorious
damask curtains to fit windows far too big for most people's houses;
handsome chests of drawers in glowing mahogany; ebony sideboards;
faded but still beautiful oil paintings and watercolors; enough silverware to stock a small hotel; chairs, beds, stools and whatnots, and a
heartbreaking collection of teddy bears. It was nearly three o'clock
by the time Xanthe was able to step out of the auction room and
find a quiet spot at the rear of the house in which to sit and eat her
packed lunch. She settled on an iron bench set into the outside wall
of the enormous kitchen garden. The stones had been warmed by the
sunshine and she leaned back against them, enjoying her sandwich,
able at last to think about the wedding dress that had sung to her. It
was a beautiful thing, and would look marvelous in their new vintage
clothing room. She thought she might even dress the window with
it to advertise their new collection. But she knew, of course, that
first, before it could become simply another found thing to be admired and ultimately sold, it had its story to tell her. Its secrets to
share. And, more than likely, something to ask of her. She found her

hands were trembling as she held her sandwich now. And this time she knew this was not caused by anxiety but by excitement. Of course the dress needed her. Of course it was calling her not to itself now, in the present, in her time, but back to *then*, where and when its story had its heart. And when was that? The auctioneer had described it as Edwardian, and its style did seem to fit with that. It had a high waist, a fitted bodice, and a long, slim silhouette. The details in the fine needle-work of the bodice were exquisitely worked, with tiny silver beads threaded into the embroidery. The sleeves were long and sheer with more lacework at the cuffs. The fabric, from what Xanthe could tell from where she had been sitting, had survived in very good condition. It had evidently been looked after exceedingly well in the generations that followed its original owner. She wondered who the young bride had been, and whether or not others had worn it too. It was likely to have belonged to a member of the Wilcox family, so the wedding must have taken place in the great house. Was that a glamorous and lavish event, or had the unfortunate bride married at the start of the First World War, perhaps, in a quiet, poignant family ceremony? She realized that she wanted to know, and that what she was feeling now was the thrill of anticipation of what lay ahead. Was this what it meant to be a Spinner? Did this shift from apprehension to thrill signify that she had truly accepted her new purpose?

"Mind if we join you?"

She looked up to see a plump, middle-aged woman in a colorful anorak standing in front of her, a frailer, pink-cheeked friend at her side.

"Not at all," she replied, scooting along the bench to make room.

"Here we are, Sandra, ooh, lovely to rest our feet. A marvelous sale, but my word, so much walking, and so many stairs!"

After exchanging pleasantries the women turned their attention to their picnic lunches and Xanthe was left in peace. The interruption to her thoughts brought her back to the task in hand. She was there for stock, first and foremost. She was a businesswoman. The Little Shop of Found Things needed her too. She picked up her catalogue and her pen and worked through it making notes next to the lots she had successfully bid for. Whatever lay ahead for her as a Spinner, she had to prioritize business right now. Some of her purchases had been made with Flora very much in mind. She had found a pair of bedside tables that would be greatly improved by painting; a glazed corner display cupboard missing a hinge; a tapestry footstool in need of re-upholstering; and a Georgian silver creamer with a sizeable dent in it. She knew Flora would happily work her magic on all these treasures. She had also secured a box of silk scarves, some of which looked rather promising; a small trunk full of clothes that appeared to date around World War II; a porcelain vase with an attractive thistle pattern on it; two silver berry serving spoons; a Chinese fan; two velvet cushions, and a box of assorted 1930s costume jewelry. Not a bad haul.

The sun disappeared behind an unhelpfully dense cloud, causing the temperature to drop, reminding Xanthe that spring had not yet properly arrived. She got up, dusting crumbs from her lap, and said goodbye to her fellow antiquers. Even in the flatter light of the afternoon, the garden was lovely. The area the public had been allowed access to for the sale was limited to that immediately behind the main part of the house. There was a sweeping lawn, accessed by broad steps, which led to an impressive planting of topiary, which had been roped off for the day. The wall against which the bench was placed formed the end of the vast walled garden that would have provided fruit, vegetables, and flowers for the great house in its heyday. Its boundaries were made of the same creamy stone as the house, tall and capped with flat, pale coping stones. Xanthe noticed an entrance to it a little way off and could not resist a peek. The wrought iron gate was securely locked. As she reached forward and touched the dark, expertly worked metal she felt it vibrate very slightly. The cool bars warmed suddenly beneath her hand. She leaned forward for a better view of the enclosure and was astonished to see the garden transform in an instant. What had only seconds before been a dormant, largely bare collection of flower beds and planters, with leafless espaliered pear trees and empty glasshouses, became a verdant, floriferous, blossom-filled spectacle of color and blooms and abundant plants. She gasped, seeing at that moment a young woman standing among the roses, a wooden trug basket hanging from her arm as she snipped some choice buds. The woman was wearing a broad straw hat, her dark hair tucked up under it, and a long primrose yellow dress. Suddenly she raised her head and then, seeing Xanthe watching her, smiled brightly. She was a remarkably beautiful girl, and it was such a warm, spontaneous expression that Xanthe found herself smiling back as a reflex. And then, in a heartbeat, things changed. The sky darkened and the woman, surprised by the sudden alteration, pricked her finger on a rose thorn. She exclaimed, pulling her hand back, glossy droplets of blood falling onto the bodice of her dress as she did so.

"What a lovely garden," said a now familiar voice behind her.

She whipped around to see her lunchtime companions had also come to peer in through the iron gate.

Sandra nodded. "I bet it will be pretty as a picture in the summer," she added.

Xanthe turned back to look again. The woman had gone. As had all the blooms and summer abundance. Once again the garden was bare and slumbering. She felt her grip on the gate tighten as she heard the unmistakable high-pitched humming of a found thing singing to her. The wedding dress was calling to her, and it had to be connected to the vision she had just glimpsed. Connected to the lone figure with her vulnerable openness to strangers, and the dark, somber warning of blood that had been spilled.

{ 3 }

AS XANTHE HAD HOPED, FLORA APPROVED OF HER FINDS AND WAS EXCITED ABOUT setting to work on them. Together they shifted things around in the workshop to make way for the new projects, conjuring up space where none had been before, taking care to allow Flora to work, as her crutches meant she required extra elbow room. They decided she would prioritize the smaller pieces, which could be quickly done and then moved into the shop. The costume jewelry would not turn much of a profit, but it had been bought at a low price and a little bit of bling went a long way to brightening up displays. The velvet cushions needed careful cleaning and would then sit nicely on the Victorian chairs Flora had already repaired. She was particularly impressed with the silver jug, happy to rise to the challenge of painstakingly knocking out the dent to restore it to its former glory.

"Excellent selections, Xanthe, love. I should let you go off on your own more often. Lovely things, and all within budget."

"See, I am to be trusted."

"Yes, well, I wonder what would have happened if the bidding had gone mad on that wedding dress, hmmm?" her mother teased.

"It will be the perfect feature for our vintage clothing display, Mum, and ..."

"Stop," she said, holding up a hand, "you don't have to convince me. I know the drill. You keep the object until it stops singing to you and then it goes on sale with everything else. I actually think you got it for a bit of a bargain, so it will more than wash its face. Eventually."

She smiled at her mother's use of the phrase so well known in the antiques trade, meant to suggest that a sale item would at least cover its costs and turn a modest profit.

Xanthe had planned to sort through the box of jewelry when she was manning the shop through the remainder of the afternoon, but instead she was kept busy with customers.

"Don't complain about that," he mother laughed when they finally turned the CLOSED sign on the door. "It's great that business is picking up so soon after the winter lull. Must mean our reputation is spreading. And it's a surer sign of spring than any amount of cuckoos calling. Come on, time to knock off. I'll be kind to you and let you cook."

She gave her a wry smile. "Supper will have to wait a bit. I need to get this lot sorted and priced up," she said, indicating the box of strung beads, jet brooches, paste bracelets, and assorted rings. "And I really want to take a closer look at that wedding dress."

Her mother looked at her knowingly. "OK, new plan. Give me that," she insisted, taking the box of jewelry from her and tucking it under one arm in the awkward but effective way she had of carrying such a thing while using her sticks. "I'll sit upstairs and sift through it for half an hour, then I'm ordering pizza. When it arrives, you have to stop and come up and eat it. Deal?"

"Deal. Thanks, Mum."

Xanthe needed no further prompting to hurry into the second room of the shop. As soon as she stepped over the threshold she could hear the gown singing to her. She took it from the box in which the auction staff had expertly packed it, and slowly removed the layers of tissue paper encasing it. The light in the little room had yet to be perfected, and dusk had already descended outside, but even so, the tiny silver and translucent beads on the dress seemed to glint and gleam. With great care, she unfolded the precious garment, aware of it almost trembling as she held it up. She thought it to be around a British size ten, made for someone with slim shoulders and long legs. It was thrilling to think of a bride walking down the aisle in it, and she was greatly relieved that there wasn't the heavy sadness attached to it that she felt with some of her found things. She found a padded hanger and slipped the dress onto it before hooking it onto the top of the door. She stood back to take it all in. There was a fairly high neckline, modest and trimmed with lace, with sleeves set to sit on the points of the shoulders. The sleeves themselves were long enough to cover the backs of the hands and made of very sheer fabric, possibly some manner of voile, embroidered with tiny roses here and there. The bodice of the dress was richly worked with the beautiful beads that she now realized were also stitched to form patterns of tiny tumbling roses. The dress was cinched in tightly below the bust, a broad ribbon of doubled lace forming the shape, and then the skirts fell in a beautiful, flowing sweep to the floor. It occurred to Xanthe that there were signs the dress had been altered in places. Could these have been repairs or adjustments made to accommodate a second bride who chose to wear the dress? Perhaps more than one daughter in the lofty Wilcox family had been married in it. She reached out and touched the delicate fabric of the sleeves, listening to the high notes only she could hear, wondering what it was the dress had to tell her. As she did so the sound shifted and then became bells ringing, clear and bold. She gasped as a realization came to her.

"Those bells," she muttered to herself, remembering again how she had heard pealing the other evening as she had left The Feathers. Even then, even at that distance, the dress had been calling to her, drawing her closer, waiting for her to find it. She had longed for something to call her back to the past, and now she had something with a particularly powerful connection emanating from it.

Excitement mounting, she renewed her examination of the beautiful object. The style did seem to be Edwardian, but there was something unusual about the neckline, and the way the bodice was attached to the skirt. She tried to recall what she knew about fashions in that time but could picture only leg of mutton sleeves and high collars. She recalled the Queen Mother's wedding dress, and could see similarities. The intricate lacework. The slender silhouette. It struck her then how different wedding dresses of the day were to what people were wearing in general. In fact, they seemed to hark back to the style at the beginning of the previous century, with its elegant Empire lines. She was aware that the Arts and Crafts movement of the late 1800s drew upon medieval styles and shapes for its inspiration. But that didn't seem to fit with this garment either. At least, not quite.

She leaned closer, searching for clues. Could it be that part of the dress was in fact older than the rest of it? The lace of the bodice, she decided, was the thing that didn't seem to quite fall easily into a style she could put a date to. It was then, when she was at her closest to the thing, that she became aware of a wonderful scent. She inhaled carefully, trying to place it, wondering if it were possible that perfume could stay in the fabric for over a hundred years. Of course she knew it could not. The glorious scent of roses that she was now experiencing was simply another way of the treasure calling to her, provoking her senses, trying to connect with her. She thought of the girl she had glimpsed in the walled garden of Corsham Hall standing in the rose beds, and felt with a fierce certainty that this dress and that young woman were indeed inextricably linked.

The arrival of Helga had slightly more of an impact than either Xanthe or Flora could have anticipated. This was in part due to the fact that she turned up much earlier than they were expecting, so that they were eating breakfast, with Flora still in her pajamas, but mostly because she brought with her a small, wiry, exuberant bundle of energy that was her pet whippet, Pie.

"Don't mind her," Helga said, pausing for a burst of her trademark laughter as the dog tore through the upstairs rooms, a black-and-white blur. "She'll settle down in a bit. Just exploring her new surroundings."

"She's very lively," said Flora, moving back against the fridge to allow the careening creature to fly past.

Xanthe couldn't decide if their visitor was genuinely oblivious to the extreme nature of her dog's behavior, and the very real hazard it presented to her mother, or if ignoring it was just her way of coping with the fact that she couldn't control the dog. Helga sat heavily on one of the pine kitchen chairs, giving a sigh of relief as she did so.

"The traffic between me and you was ghastly," she told them. "Not what I was expecting at all."

"We don't have a commute so we've never really noticed," Xanthe pointed out, fetching an extra cup and pouring coffee. "It's generally better after the school run is over, I expect. Would you like some breakfast?"

"Heavens, yes! I'm famished," she said, spooning sugar into her drink. "Don't worry, I'm the least fussy eater you could ever find. I'll eat anything. So will Pie."

Xanthe and Flora exchanged glances. Happily, there was fresh bread and locally made honey, so they were able to offer something less startling than some of Flora's more usual meals.

Helga was a large woman, not fat, but sturdy, with broad shoulders upon which, according to Flora, many troubles had been placed. She had weathered a difficult childhood, a bad marriage, needy children who grew into problematic adults, and the loss of both her elderly parents in the same year. Through it all she had remained determined and positive, refusing to ever give in to self-pity. She was, Xanthe decided, a woman for whom the word "stoic" could have been invented. She appeared to favor clothes chosen for comfort rather than style, and wore no makeup. Her short, almost bristly hair was worn in a choppy pixie cut that many women her age might have shied away from. On her it looked right, somehow. Practical, and more than a little peculiar. After a bit of clearing space, moving breakable things out of the dog's way, and finding another plate, the three were able to enjoy a pleasant breakfast. As promised, the whippet did calm down and sat beside Flora, gazing up at her with soulful eyes.

"She's very friendly," Flora said, reaching down to stroke her velvety ears.

"Don't be fooled by that face," said Helga through a mouthful of toast, "it's your food she's after. You could bribe her to do just about anything with the right treat."

"She doesn't look like a big eater," said Xanthe, taking in her sinuous shape.

"Burns it all off tearing about the place. Loves to run. You don't have a cat, do you?" she asked suddenly, an anxious note creeping into her normally confident voice.

Xanthe shook her head. "Doesn't she like them?"

"Oh, she likes them well enough, as long as they're running and she's chasing them. This really is the most delicious honey. I'll bet you have a splendid farmers' market out here."

"We do!" Flora said, offering a long-handled spoon which Helga ignored, preferring to upend the honey pot over her toast instead. "It's on tomorrow. I'll take you. There are lots of lovely stalls. And lots of good walks nearby too."

Having drawn a blank on treats from Flora, the dog moved on to Xanthe, who fed her a crust. "She's very pretty, with those smart black-and-white markings. Did you name her after a magpie?"

"The moment I saw her I thought of one of those darling pied wagtails that flit about near water. Dear little birds. There, I told you she'd settle."

As they watched, Pie turned a circle three times and then lowered herself into a tight knot, eyes shut, ready for a snooze, on top of Xanthe's left foot.

"Like a baby," Helga crooned. "I don't suppose the real thing will be half as appealing, though of course I'm not allowed to say that, not when I'm about to become a grandmother."

"Congratulations," said Flora. "Isn't Penny living in Australia?"

"She is, and I'm not happy about it but what can I do? She must live her life, and I must embrace long-haul flights. But there, enough about me. Your life is far more interesting." She took a large gulp of coffee. "Let me see if I've got this right: You've ditched the odious, cheating Philip, turned your back on London, and headed west for a new business and a new life. Do tell all!"

Xanthe noticed her mother smiling as she answered and thought how it would do her good to have someone she knew so well to talk to for a while. A friend rather than a daughter. Perhaps it would allow her the chance to dip deep into *Spinners* again to see if anything presented itself as connected to the wedding dress in some way. For the most part the book was silent, revealing its contents on the page to her so that she could slowly sift through them, gleaning what wisdom she could. The memory of the way the book had whispered to her when she had been at Mistress Flyte's chocolate house was still vivid. She knew the book would only behave in such a way when it chose to; when the time was right. Perhaps, she thought, it would only do so when she was back in the time of the found thing that was singing to her. Maybe if she took the dress out to the blind house—just near it, not inside—maybe that would prompt it to speak to her again. She was wary of heading back to the past without knowing to when she was headed. Also, although the gown was clearly singing, and indeed chiming, there did not seem to be any great danger or urgency attached to it. How could she justify the risk of returning to the past if it wasn't absolutely necessary? The risk, and the lies. While she was growing in confidence in her ability as a Spinner, she had not yet found a way of disappearing for days at a time without constructing elaborate lies to explain her absence. Lies that she had to tell again and again to the people who mattered most to her, which now included Liam. And Liam was not a person to be easily fobbed off with a half-baked story. The closer they became, the more difficult it would get. Was that one of the sacrifices of being a Spinner, she wondered. Would it be impossible to have a meaningful relationship ever again? Unless, of course, she shared her secret. It had been such a relief to Xanthe when she had told Harley about how she time-traveled. It had stopped her feeling quite so crazy, and given her another mind to put to all the complex questions and dilemmas she faced. She looked across the table at Flora and wished she had the courage to take her into her confidence too. *One day*, she promised herself. *One day.*

She left Helga and her mother to catch up and went downstairs to open the shop. The weather was warm enough for her to decide to prop the door open. She stood a moment on the threshold, taking in the day. The fresh spring air brought with it the distant sounds of the town coming to life, birdsong, and the smell of the burgeoning blooms in the hanging baskets outside. Xanthe felt at once more connected with her fellow shopkeepers, most of whom had also thrown wide their doors. Gerri was busy wiping dew from the wrought iron tables and chairs outside her tea shop. The woman who ran the print and framing business a little farther along the cobbled street was putting out a new wooden sign, searching for stones flat enough to stand it on. The newly opened traditional sweet shop at the end of the alleyway was already serving eager children who had evidently made a detour on their way to school. She promised herself she would visit it later and treat herself and Flora to a bag or two of old-fashioned sweets. She heard bells ringing and for a moment thought the wedding dress was calling to her again, but then realized it was only the town clock chiming the hour. She went back inside and turned her attention to the shop, arming herself with a feather duster, methodically working her way around the displays, rearranging items that had been put back in the wrong place, trying to decide where new stock could go, working out which pieces needed to be discounted, and what might make an eye-catching window display.

She was so absorbed in what she was doing she didn't notice Gerri come into the shop until she spoke.

"You can come and give the tearooms a good dusting next, if you like," she said.

"I can't imagine there is a single speck of dust in there," Xanthe replied, climbing down from the small set of steps that had enabled her to reach the top of one of Mr. Morris's remaining over-mantel mirrors. "Unless it's icing sugar, possibly."

"You'd be surprised. Sometimes I feel I'm barely keeping on top of everything."

She caught a rare glimpse of strain on her friend's face. However well Gerri presented a perfectly turned-out image to the world, managing as a single parent with a business to run would surely challenge even the most capable of women.

"Come and see what I found at the auction," she said, leading the way to the second room. She knew Gerri well enough to be certain she would be cheered up by her new acquisitions for the vintage clothes collection. "Here," she said, dragging a large cardboard box to the center of the floor space and opening the lid. "How's that for a cracking little job lot?"

Gerri gasped as she pulled out the first two of the silk scarves. "Oh! These are gorgeous. Some excellent silk here. And they're in really good shape, most of them," she added, digging deeper into the hoard. "Look! This one's Yves Saint Laurent. Imagine throwing it in a box . . . and that's a lovely chiffon one."

Xanthe folded her arms and leaned back against the doorjamb. "You like them, then?"

"I want to take half of them home myself right now! How do you resist keeping the best things you find for yourself?" she asked, hugging tight a shocking pink silk square.

"Being hungry and having bills to pay makes you ruthless. There's more. Look," she said, stepping aside to reveal the trunk. This time she let Gerri open the lid.

"Oh! You hit the jackpot here. I know you like older stuff, but nineteen forties is the most popular era for vintage stuff bar none, I promise you. Just look at this little suit! Let's make a window display with them, shall we?"

Xanthe thought then of how she had imagined the wedding gown one day gracing the shop window. She was keenly aware of the fact that she had deliberately kept the dress a secret from Gerri. Her mum understood her need to spend time with the things that sang to her, even if she only knew a fraction of the reason why. It seemed simpler just to wait. She would share the dress with Gerri once she had discovered its story. One way or another. In the meantime, a new window display trumpeting the arrival of the vintage clothing room was a great idea.

"We'll need more than the clothes . . . what shall we put with them?" she asked as Gerri ran the silk through her fingers, releasing the faintest aroma of old perfume and mothballs.

"How about we do a forties and fifties mixed themed display? Most of these seem to date from around that time, not that they all have to. It'll give you a slightly wider reach with other things to make the display. Have you got some stock in the shop that would fit?"

"Ooh, there might be one or two things. Let's have a quick look." She grinned. She enjoyed Gerri's delight as she showed her a table lamp, two leather suitcases, a small collection of enamel signs, some biscuit tins, and a Lloyd Loom wicker chair. They went to stand as far into the bay window as they could, given the Victorian display that was already in it.

"Yes," Gerri put her hands on her hips, her face serious and focused, "we can do something really clever with this. Almost a corner
of a bedroom with the cases open, as if a glamorous young woman is
about to go on holiday. I'll have another look through our stock and
find a dress. Oh, and a swimsuit! Wish I could stay and do it now but
I'm late opening up as it is. I'll come back after closing. Is that OK
with you?"

But Xanthe heard little of Gerri's excited chatter. Her attention
had been taken up entirely by what she had seen through the small
panes of the old window. There, sitting cross-legged and relaxed, leaning back on one of Gerri's terrace chairs, sat Benedict Fairfax.

4

"XANTHE? ARE YOU ALL RIGHT?" GERRI COULD NOT HELP BUT NOTICE THE LOOK OF shock on her friend's face.

"I . . . just a minute," she said, pushing past and running out of the doorway. However much she had dreaded this moment, she had to face him. This time, she wouldn't let him melt away before she had the chance to confront him. As she drew closer to him she felt anger growing inside her. Anger which overcame any alarm she might justifiably have felt. This was the man who had tried to send Samuel to his death. The man who had shown himself to be utterly ruthless in the pursuit of whatever it was he wanted. She let the memory of what he had done, of how he had behaved, lend her determination. She was a Spinner now. She was a match for him.

Fairfax was dressed in a curious ensemble, as if his clothes had been snatched from different places at different times. While there was nothing particularly outlandish about his long woolen coat or slim worsted trousers or wing-collared white shirt, they just looked odd together. It was an uncomfortable reminder for Xanthe of how unconvincing her own period costume must have been during her travels back to the seventeenth century. Small wonder people had been suspicious of her. Fairfax's own disguise was further undermined by the fact that he was wearing a black broad-brimmed hat, and sporting a leather eye patch. She shuddered at the thought of how she had inflicted the wound on him that had resulted in him losing the sight in his eye. It had been in self-defense, but the violence of the moment would never leave her.

"Good morning to you, Mistress Westlake," he said in a voice as level and light as the day itself, giving no trace at all of the significance of his being there. He did not stand, but lifted his hat in a gesture of respect that was at once both out of place and unwelcome. Xanthe was glad that at that moment there was no one else in the little street and tried to put from her mind what Gerri would be making of the strange encounter she must certainly be watching.

"This is . . . unexpected," she said, determined not to let slip how disturbed she was by his presence, hoping he would reveal his intentions without her having to give away anything of herself; of how much she hated having him so close to her own home and those she loved.

Fairfax tilted his head a little. "You surely cannot have believed that I was to be so easily cast aside?"

Xanthe experienced a flashback to the moment she had crouched hidden beneath the scaffold upon which Fairfax had stood, listening to the jeers of the crowd as the hangman placed the noose around his neck and then the astonished gasps as the condemned man had vanished while they watched. "I don't recall anything being particularly easy for either of us," she said.

"And yet you succeeded. You secured the continued safety of Appleby and his family. Thanks to your trickery, he escaped his due as a traitor to the crown."

"I gave you the astrolabe. That was the deal."

At last a flash of anger fractured Fairfax's previously inscrutable expression and he sat upright, his tone sharper now. "You speak to me of bargains struck! Were you not the one who broke our agreement? Where in it did you pledge to send me to a time not my own, certain in the knowledge I would be adrift, requiring time and practice to master the device? No matter," he said, composing himself once more. "Happily, I have learned my lessons well. As you see." He spread wide his arms, indicating his own solid, real presence there in Xanthe's time. The very last place she would ever have wanted him to reach.

"Why are you here?" she demanded. "Why now? What more do you want from me? It doesn't look like you need my help to go wherever—whenever—you want."

He turned away from her then, evasive, not yet willing to reveal precisely what it was he had come for. The effect was unnerving. "I am not a man to limit my reach when it can be so very expansive," he said slowly.

She tried to work out for herself what his most likely goal could be. Had he come for revenge? To punish her for tricking him? Or was it the book of the Spinners that had tempted him and made him risk so much?

"I have nothing to give you," she said with a shrug. "This is not your time, Fairfax. You will be found out here, exposed as a fraud. This is my world."

"Indeed. Thus far," he added, cryptically. "Oh, I have no power here, in this chaotic, modern era of yours, I grant you that. I have not established myself in this time. It is not here that I wish to reside. No, I have settled well in a period more fitting, a time that offers more opportunity and will not demand questions of me which I am not able to answer. It is there, in my chosen moment, that I require your allegiance."

"You still expect me to want to be with you? To what? Marry you? Work with you? Trust me, neither thing is going to happen. Ever."

"Xanthe?" Gerri's voice interrupted their conversation. "Everything OK?"

Xanthe turned to see her standing in the shop doorway, her hand shielding the morning sun from her eyes. "I'm fine, Gerri. I'll be right there," she called back.

Fairfax got to his feet. He tugged his jacket straight and picked up the silver-topped cane that he had laid upon the table beside him.

"I made the mistake of underestimating you once, mistress. I am not in the habit of repeating my missteps. I am aware, also, that you are a woman of strong opinions and a willful disposition. I have considered these ... shortcomings. They present a temporary hindrance to my plans, nothing more. They simply mean I must do my utmost to convince you of the wisdom of complying with my wishes and the unfavorable consequences of refusing me. For the moment, I bid you good day."

So saying he brushed past her, close enough that she could smell his heavy cologne, and feel the warmth of his body. This was no phantom. Fairfax was very real and presented a very real threat, though precisely to what end she was not yet certain. She watched him stride up the street, waiting until he had gone and her jangling nerves had steadied before going back to the shop. Gerri greeted her with raised eyebrows.

"Another ex-boyfriend?" she asked.

"Good grief, no!" Xanthe busied herself adjusting a stack of leather-bound volumes in the window. "An old friend of my father's. A business acquaintance," she added somewhat lamely.

Gerri's momentary silence suggested she was unconvinced. At last, obviously accepting that Xanthe did not want to talk about the stranger further, she commented, "If you don't mind me saying so, you do know some rather peculiar-looking people."

When Xanthe merely shrugged, the conversation turned back to the planned display before Gerri noticed a customer heading for the tea shop and hurried off.

However much she tried to concentrate on running the shop it was impossible not to dwell on Fairfax's threat. For threat it was, even though he had neither told her specifically what he wanted from her nor what he would do if she refused. Beyond him demanding she travel back through time with him, he had given nothing away. Now she was back to waiting. Her first thought was to talk to Harley about the fact that he had shown up again. She needed to say aloud all the possible things that were going round and round in her head. Like the danger her mother might be in. Or Liam. Or even Harley himself. How much did Fairfax know about her life? How closely had he been watching her, and what was he planning? She felt if she didn't get a chance to thrash it all out with Harley very soon she would drive herself mad with thinking and wondering. Flora and Helga had taken the dog out for a walk by the river and Xanthe found herself checking the grandfather clock in the shop, wondering where they had got to. Her mother enjoyed getting out for a stroll but her crutches meant she couldn't go far. They had been hours. What if something had happened? What if Fairfax had already got to Flora? She was soon distracted, however, by the busyness of the shop. There was nothing approaching a pattern to the number of customers who came in to browse in the months between Christmas and spring. Randomly hectic days happened, and this, it turned out, was one of them. She sold a set of wine goblets, an occasional table, two pieces of militaria, and a travel clock all in the space of an hour. A pair of teenagers came in, which were not the usual type of customers she had come to expect. They giggled a lot and looked at the antiques in astonishment as if they had never been in such a shop before. She kept a close eye on them, wondering if they might be a little light-fingered. A tall woman in a full-length tweedy coat came in at the same time.

"I understand you have vintage clothing for sale," she said, her manner rather formal.

"We certainly do. It's through here," said Xanthe, leading her to the entrance of the second room. She was reluctant to leave the teenagers unsupervised. The woman proceeded to examine the clothes on the rail, picking up one and then another, inspecting them minutely. "If you're happy to browse I'll leave you to it," she said. "Any questions, please do give me a shout. There's a changing room behind that curtain if you'd like to try something on."

"Thank you," the woman replied without looking at her. "I shall be quite content here."

Xanthe stepped back into the main shop just in time to hear the sound of shattering china. She hurried to the young couple, who were looking suitably shamefaced. The girl stooped down and picked up the pieces of what had been a Wedgwood plate.

"Oh my God," she said, "I am *so* sorry. It just slipped out of my hand."

Xanthe took the pieces from her. "Well, that's beyond repair..." she said, beginning to impart the bad news that breakages must be paid for, prepared to point out the sign to this effect that was on the wall. The boy interrupted her, however.

"We'll pay for it," he said, pulling some folded notes from the pocket of his jeans. "How much is it?"

It looked like a lot of money for a youngster to have, and he was surprisingly happy to pay up. Xanthe couldn't help thinking that something did not quite add up.

"Eighteen pounds," she said simply, taking a twenty from him and then giving him his change. All the while the pair kept apologizing, making rather more of the whole event than was necessary. "It's fine," she told them. "These things happen."

With even more words of regret and thanks, the pair slowly left, reverting to giggles once they were outside the shop. Xanthe did a quick check but could see nothing missing. She was on the point of returning to help the customer in the clothing room when the woman emerged.

"Find anything you liked?"

"Not today. But thank you," the woman spoke as she walked toward the door. "You have some rather fine pieces."

"Come again," Xanthe called after her as she left.

With the shop empty once again her mind returned to fretting about her mother's safety.

She was relieved when the old doorbell clanged again a little after three o'clock and Flora and Helga came smiling and laughing into the shop, Pie panting from the fun of the outing.

"Mum, where did you get to? You've been ages."

"Sorry, love, has the shop been really busy?"

"What? No, not especially. I was just . . . a bit worried, that's all."

Helga unclipped the lead from Pie's collar and the whippet bounced around Xanthe in joyful circles. "My fault entirely," she said. "We found a darling café on the very bank of the Kennett and I begged Flora to agree to lunch there. Such a pretty spot. And delicious food."

"It was." Flora nodded. "And we were able to sit outside and eat."

"Which allowed me to smoke without feeling like a pariah. Such a treat!" Helga laughed heartily again. "And it was better for Pie," Flora put in. "She was so well behaved. Until she saw the ducks."

"Ducks?" Xanthe was moving from relief her mother was unharmed to slight annoyance that while she had been worried, they had just been having an extended lunch and messing about with the dog.

"She's never liked them," Helga explained. "Good thing we had her lead tied firmly to the leg of the table."

"Would have been better if the table had been heavier!" Flora laughed at the memory. "I thought she was going to drag it, lunch, wineglasses, and all, into the river at one point."

Helga noticed Xanthe's less than amused expression and looked a little sheepish. "No harm done. Why don't I pop up and put the kettle on. Tea and biscuits? We must fuel the worker!" she announced before heading for the kitchen.

After watching her go, Flora turned and said, "I'm sorry if I made you worry. Helga can be pretty persuasive, and it was lovely to sit out in the sunshine for a bit."

"It's fine, Mum. I'm happy you were enjoying yourself. You've surely earned a bit of time off."

"I actually rather enjoyed having a dog to walk too," she said.

Xanthe crouched down and made a fuss of Pie, who responded by wagging her tail happily. "She is a funny little thing. Strangely appealing. Not sure if it's the velvety ears or the way she looks at you with those bright eyes. As if she's smiling, somehow."

"I'm glad you like her," Flora said carefully, leaning on one stick and tugging the scrunchie from her hair, "because she's going to be staying a bit longer than we'd expected."

"Oh? Have Helga's plans changed?"

"Not exactly. The thing is, you know her daughter is about to have her first child?"

"The one in Australia, yes, Helga has mentioned it. More than once."

"Well, she wants to go out there to be with her before the baby's born, spend some time, first grandchild and all that . . . only the woman she had lined up to look after Pie now says she can't do it. The date of her hip replacement op has been brought forward. Of course she can't turn it down, and Helga wouldn't want her to. If she goes back on the waiting list it could be next year before she gets it done. . . ."

"Wait a minute . . . is that the reason she suddenly wanted to come and stay? To ask you to look after her dog?" Xanthe stood up again, frowning down at Pie, who rolled over exposing her tummy in what she evidently thought was a winsome manner.

"No, of course not. Well, partly, yes, in fact."

"Some friend."

"She's desperate."

"Even so."

"I don't mind, honestly." She reached over and obligingly rubbed Pie's tummy with one of her crutches. "I like having her around. And she'll get me out of the house a bit more. As long as we steer clear of ducks and cats she doesn't pull at all on the lead, so I just loop it over my wrist. And you could take her with you when you go for your hikes up to the white horse, couldn't you?"

Xanthe looked from the dog to her mother and found they were both wearing the same hopeful expression. How could she say no? And anyway, it might be good for her mother to get out of the work-shop now and again. Not to mention have a companion when Xanthe was away. That thought reminded her of Fairfax and set her wondering about Pie's abilities as a guard dog.

"So long as she doesn't chew anything . . ."

"Oh, I don't think she's the type. Are you, Pie?" Flora fell to chatting to the dog and Xanthe realized that, in fact, there had never been any question of the animal being turned away. Pie, as if sensing her new position in the household, righted herself, ran a quick circuit of the shop, narrowly avoiding knocking over an umbrella stand, and then disappeared upstairs in a scramble of claws on wooden floorboards.

"See"—Flora smiled—"she's settled in already."

That night Xanthe found another use for their new boarder. Under the guise of taking Pie for an evening trot around the quiet streets, she planned to call in at The Feathers and try to snatch a moment's conversation with Harley. She still badly wanted to tell him about Fairfax's reappearance. When she had first shared the secret of her time travel with him she had quickly realized that she would never dare send a text speaking of it. The thought of writing something down about what she did, with the possibility that someone other than the two of them could read it, made her uneasy. Likewise, she never could bring herself to phone him, for phone calls could be overheard, both ends. It was ten o'clock when she set off up the high street, an eager yet cooperative dog stepping out smartly beside her. Where the little hound could be a wild, racing creature when loose, once on the lead she behaved beautifully, as long as there weren't any ducks around to trigger her drive instinct. There had been a light fall of soft rain which had left the pavements shimmering beneath the street lamps. Pie picked up her feet as if the wetness was offensive to her dainty paws. Xanthe thought about going straight into the pub—dogs were allowed in, after all—but it would be impossible to talk privately with Harley at the bar. Better to go around the back, using the entrance through the rear yard. She could ask for Harley at the door and he could come out to talk with her there, if only briefly. She turned down the narrow road that ran along the side of the pub. Looking up, at the bottom of the street, she could see that Liam's flat above his workshop was in darkness, with no lights at the windows. She remembered he had been visiting his parents for the day. At that moment, as if thinking of him had summoned him up, the familiar red sports car swung off the high street. Liam stopped the car when he drew level with Xanthe and lowered the window.

"Who's your friend?" he asked, smiling at the dog.

"Our new lodger. Her name's Pie."

"Chicken or beef?"

She groaned. "She was named after the black-and-white birds."

"I didn't know you were getting a dog."

"Neither did I." Xanthe stroked the dog's head as she spoke. "She belongs to my mum's friend. She's just staying for a couple of weeks."

"Cool. Were you coming to see me?" he asked.

"Oh, well, I was taking her out for her evening walk. Apparently she's used to having one. Just ten minutes. We were about to head back." Seeing his slight disappointment she added, "I'd forgotten you'd be out. Helga will worry if we're out much longer. I think she's testing us as suitable dog carers. But I thought I might take her up to the white horse for a run tomorrow morning. D'you want to come with us?"

"Sure. Maybe she'll catch us a rabbit for lunch."

"God, I hope not!" She started to walk away, giving a friendly wave as she went. "See you early. Seven-thirty?"

He blew her a kiss. "Bright-eyed and bushy-tailed," he promised.

As she made her way home, she wished she had not allowed herself to be diverted from talking to Harley. She would just have to look again at *Spinners* alone. The answers to everything were in there, some-where. Discussing things with Harley might be reassuring, but it was up to her to find out what she needed to know. She should turn to other Spinners for knowledge and guidance. At that moment a black cat trotted across the road in front of them. Seeing Pie it paused to hiss, causing the little dog to let out a sudden and uncharacteristic yap. The sound echoed off the walls of the narrow alley they were in, causing Xanthe to jump. Suddenly she was wary, jolted back to the thought that Fairfax had been watching her for weeks. Was he watch-ing her still? At that very moment? She whipped around, scanning the shadows and dark doorways of the shuttered shops. From the open window of a nearby restaurant the hubbub of happy chatter felt at odds with her own nervousness.

"Come on, pooch," she said to the dog with forced cheerfulness. "Let's get home."

Even after sharing a bottle of heavy red wine with Flora and Helga, sleep proved impossible for Xanthe that night. When she closed her eyes all she saw was Fairfax's gaunt face, the brim of his hat casting a shadow across it, but his eye patch still clearly visible, a reminder of all that had gone before. What disturbed her even more, however, was the now constant singing of the wedding dress. She had it hanging in her room on a quilted satin hanger. The light from the bright moon and the streetlights falling through the fabric of her lightweight curtains cast upon the gown a cool glow, the tiny pearls and beads upon the bodice glinting as all the while distant church bells rang, accompanied by a persistent high note that vibrated through her mind. She sat up in bed, watching the dress, half expecting it to leap into life, so insistent was its singing. It was as she did so, with her encounter with Fairfax playing out in her mind's eye, that she came to the realization that the two were indeed bound together in some way. Of course they were connected by the facts that Xanthe time-traveled, that she was bound to history as a Spinner, and through those bonds to Fairfax because he had been part of both Alice's and Samuel's stories. But she decided it was more than that. It was as if the dress was responding to her preoccupation with him. Was it warning her, or summoning her? That was impossible to tell. There was no doubt that its song had become more urgent since Fairfax had reappeared. Whereas before she had felt only that it wished to tell its story, now she felt it was agitated, demanding her attention, demanding, in fact, her action. And it was action that was needed, she could see that now. She could not simply sit about and wait for Fairfax to carry out his threat. She got up, taking a warm woolen shawl from the back of her bedroom chair and wrapping it around her shoulders. She took *Spinners* from its place on her bedside cupboard, switched on the lamp on her table at the window, pulled back the curtains, and curled up on the window seat. Outside more light rain had started to fall, feeding the burgeoning spring plants while they slept, keeping noisy cats and hungry owls silent for the time being.

Each time she opened *Spinners* up she felt a thrill of anticipation run through her, for she could never be certain what she would find. The book held between its worn leather covers its own special kind of magic. Only a Spinner or someone chosen to help them could see anything at all. Only a rare type of Spinner could hear what the pages had to say. On this occasion, as Xanthe leafed slowly through the ancient pages, she became aware of a clamor of whispers, growing in volume, urgent voices seeking her attention in the way they did when she stepped into the blind house to begin her journey through time. The sounds from the wedding dress were still strong, so that her head was soon filled with a cacophonous tangle of noise. She did not attempt to make sense of it but simply let it wash over her, a wave of sound, allowing it to urge her on to seek the wisdom of the work without trying to listen to a particular voice or pick out the thread of a particular story. She had already learned to be patient when it came to asking the book for answers. It worked in its own way and at its own pace. She let her fingers glide over the surface of the thick vellum pages. Certain sections of the book, certain tales or images, were beginning to become familiar to her now. There was the story of the girl running through the woods carrying a baby in her arms. There were the cautionary words she had heard back in Mistress Flyte's chocolate house. And there was the faded map of the English countryside with sharply straight ley lines drawn upon it. Another page showed a portrait of a stern-looking woman, though it had no caption to identify her. There was a sketch of a tall town house with long windows and steps leading to the front door. Another page had a recipe for a balm to cure skin infections. Toward the middle of the tome there were several pages of poetry. The whole thing was a collection of wise words, stories, recipes, images, and what looked like songs or possibly spells. Xanthe's skin tingled at the thought that these were not random tales written to entertain, but real histories, or records of events or practices of people who had died possibly centuries before.

"Who is it who needs me?" she muttered. "And while we're at it, what is it you can tell me about Fairfax? Tell me what I should do."

She continued turning the pages and the clamoring voices continued to grow louder and more insistent. And then, abruptly, there was silence. Even the gown ceased its music. The cessation of sound was startling, it was so sudden, and the emptiness it left was in vivid contrast to what had surrounded her only seconds before. She examined the page she had reached, feeling sure the silence must indicate something important had been found. Like a game of musical chairs, the whispers and bells had pushed her toward the point where she must stop and take her place. Where she must read. Where she must listen.

The blankness in front of her blurred with swirling ink and then words began to appear, as if written by some unseen hand. And though the calligraphy was fine, she knew the storyteller to be a young man, not much more than a boy, for she could hear his breathy voice in her ear, so that he spoke the tale as it bloomed upon the page before her.

I did not slow my step until I reached the cover of the narrower streets. Here the lamps were fewer, their pulsing light dimming at the edges, fading into the gloom. Here I could be concealed. I glanced over my shoulder, searching the damp night for that bulky, familiar figure. As I retreated further into the cover of a doorway I trod in an acrid pool, still warm, its stench reaching my nostrils just as its wetness found its way through the worn stitches and cracked leather of my boots. I was accustomed to such privations and paid them no heed; poverty having been my companion since birth. The sounds of the city dwellers going about their nightly deeds had ever been my lullaby. The rattle of cartwheels over cobbles and the cries of the hawkers and poppsies the music of my childhood. I knew well every snicket and alleyway and had countless times darted through the labyrinth of the borough to evade capture after snatching an apple or a small loaf from a stall. Now I waited, listening for another sound. For the ragged breathing of the one that I knew I could evade no longer. This night would see an end to running, and only one of us would survive to see another. This certainty yet gave me pause. That it should come to this. Now, from the distance of age, I see that it was my tender years that made me hesitate, for I was but a boy, on the cusp of manhood. I had been cut loose from my mother's apron strings cruelly young by the swift intervention of typhoid fever. My experience of care thereafter had been loveless and lacking and brutal. Even so, I clung to the belief that grown men were the protectors of the innocent, defenders of those in need, with honor and integrity their watchwords. How, then, my fantasy was to be dissolved before my innocent eyes that night. As I cloaked myself in the shadows, in my heart I knew this. Knew that my moment of transformation had come. I gasped as the lamplight glanced off that blade, a flash of danger cutting through the caliginosity. I dared not move. I could hear those familiar heavy footfalls so near, but I was lighter, more nimble, more driven, I believed, than my foe. This was what gave me strength, while fear lent me patience and caution.

A startling shout cut the damp air, but it was merely a street vendor plying his wares. Roast chestnuts, hot and rich. Hunger gnawed at my belly provoked by that sound and that sweet smell as it reached me. But I would not be diverted from my fate. Could not be.

Again, I broke cover, sprinted across the gritty cobbles, hurrying to flatten myself against the shadows on the far wall, moving with stealth and guile, my breath all but held, my chest tight with it. He was broader at the shoulders than me, weightier, certainly, though no longer taller. As the distance between us shrank, so his presence grew. It took all my courage not to bolt. The proximity to one who had caused me such suffering for so long continued to urge my flight, however hopeless. And yet, I knew, I could run no more.

So deep was the darkness in the alley, save for slivers of candlelight through the gaps between the planks of the oak door beside us, that I could not see his face, nor he mine. This was no hindrance to identification, however, for I knew the bitterness of his odor and he the sweetness of mine. I could calculate the weight of his bulk by the manner in which it blocked those fractured lines of light, and he could assess mine by the way in which they fell upon me. He looked at me squarely then, and I could sense his grim smile, detect the subtle movement of his features, the wetness of his lips as they parted, the minute alteration in the sound of his breathing as his fetid mouth opened.

If he was intent on speaking I did not permit him the time to do so. The blade was long, and yet I plunged it to the hilt. I felt it cut through the thick cloth of his coat, glancing off a tortoiseshell button on his waistcoat, pressing through the yielding flesh of his stomach, the upward thrust finding its mark beneath his ribs. The shock of it preceded the agony, so that his in breath sucked the air from the space between us. He slumped forward, into my arms, his weight threatening to topple me as I braced myself against him. I would not have him die pinning me to the rough street. I would not ever suffer under his cruelty again.

As the life started to ebb from him and we moved in a small dance of death, a shard of light fell across my face and he found it in him to spit an oath at me one last time. "Curse you!" he hissed. "I say curse you to hell, Erasmus Balmoral!"

I let him slide to the ground, withdrawing my knife as he descended. I wiped the blade upon his coat, watching him a moment more to check that no further cry would come from him. At last I was convinced the deed was done. My persecutor was dead. My childhood finished along with him. I straightened, pushing my hair back off my face with a shaking hand, sheathing my knife at my belt. It was the first time I had used it to kill a man. It would not be the last.

Both the writing and the whispering stopped. The story came to an abrupt end. Xanthe leaned back against the wall of the window seat and gazed out through the darkened panes, as if hoping the stars might provide sufficient illumination to see how what she had just read related to her own situation. It was, as she had come to expect of *Spinners*, anything but straightforward. A young man in danger killing his tormentor, the setting unhelpfully vague. A town, certainly, and at least a hundred and fifty years ago, judging by the language used and the descriptions of carts rather than cars. Beyond that . . . what? It could be seen as a warning of danger, particularly from someone she already knew. It might be directing her to a particular place, but where? There were no landmarks. The Spinner had given no real clues as to his location. She had his name to go on. Erasmus Balmoral. She leaned over, picked up her phone, and quickly googled him. Nothing. A complete blank, which in itself was quite unusual. As if it had been waiting for her to finish reading, the wedding dress struck up its singing again. She frowned at it.

"I'm trying, OK? I'm trying." Feeling more than a little exasperated, she climbed back into bed, wrapped the pillow over her ears, and willed herself to go to sleep.

{ 5 }

IT FELT AS IF SHE HAD ONLY BEEN ASLEEP A MATTER OF MOMENTS WHEN XANTHE WAS disturbed by a curious wailing noise. It took her a little while to real-ize she was not dreaming, and that the sound was coming from the landing outside her bedroom door. As she surfaced more fully from the depths of her sleep, she began to make out voices, urgent and agi-tated. They carried a similar tone of fear and distress to the sounds of those calling to her when she approached the blind house. The differ-ence was that these cries were of the here and now. These voices were of people living and close to her.

"Xanthe!" At last she clearly heard her mother calling her name. It was in that instant that she smelled the smoke.

Throwing back the covers she jumped from her bed, running to the door, which opened as she reached it, Flora, Helga, and Pie all tum-bling into the room.

"Oh, love, there's a fire! The stairway is full of smoke!"

"We can't go down!" Helga confirmed.

Xanthe helped her mother to the bed, acutely aware of the fact that she did not have her crutches. She would never have tried to walk without them, not unless she had been too terrified to take the time to pick them up.

Helga grabbed her dog as it ran by, clutching the trembling animal against her chest. "It was Pie who woke me! She was crying and pawing the door. Dear God, if she hadn't, the smoke might have got us all while we slept!"

"It's below the sitting room then?" Xanthe asked, wanting to know exactly what they were facing.

Helga nodded. "I shouted up, thinking we must get down through it, but the smoke was already too thick. I ran up to wake Flora. . . ."

"Mum, use my phone, call the fire brigade," she said as she hurried out of the room to the top of the stairs and peered down, ignoring the shouts of protestation of the two women behind her. "I'll be right back," she called to them, already beginning to cough because of the thickness of the smoke that billowed up the narrow stairwell. She cursed the fact that the only fire extinguisher in the house was in the kitchen. There was no chance she could get down to it; although the fire itself might be on the ground floor, the smoke was too thick, the heat too intense. Quickly, she dived into the bathroom, grabbing the nearest towels, jamming them beneath the cold taps, which she turned on fully. The seconds it took for the towels to soak up water passed as if in slow motion, with Flora all the while calling her with increasing anguish in her voice. At last, Xanthe lifted the towels, leaving the taps running, and raced back into the bedroom. She slammed shut the door and placed the largest towel along the gap at the bottom of it. Helga helped her move the narrow wardrobe against the door and pin another of the wet towels against the jamb in an attempt to hold back the smoke. That done, she joined her mother on the bed. "Did you get through?"

Flora nodded. "They are on their way." She took her daughter's hands in hers and the two women exchanged looks that were a mixture of fear and determination. Each was, in truth, terrified. Both were, as an instinct, set on helping the other.

"The fire station is close by," Xanthe said, more for Helga's benefit than her mother's. "It'll be OK. They'll be here any minute."

"I hope you're right," said Helga with great control, her voice giving nothing away, but her anxiously tight grip on her dog making it wriggle. "Because I for one am too large to fit through that," she said, pointing at the tiny dormer window set into the slope of the roof.

Xanthe knew she was right. If the firemen couldn't get up the stairs they would have to go back out onto the landing and try the slightly bigger window there, which was at the front of the building. Her mind raced to figure out how such an escape could be possible. Even assuming they could help her mother climb out, it would be difficult for the firemen to get a ladder to it, as the fire engine could never fit down the narrow street to the shop. Sensing rising despair in the others she sought to reassure them.

"They'll get through the front door. You know it will give with a good enough shove. They can take hoses in that way. The fire is at the bottom of the house somewhere. They can put it out. I don't think we'll need to climb out of any windows."

Flora mustered a smile. "And here was me looking forward to being carried down a ladder by a hunky firefighter."

A sudden loud crack followed by a judder that seemed to shake the whole house startled everyone. Into that moment of held breath came the wailing of the engine siren.

"They're here!" Xanthe grabbed the bedclothes and piled them up against the bottom of the door, determined to keep back the smoke that had started to work its way through the defenses. "We just have to sit tight. They'll soon have it under control." As she spoke she could hear shouts and then a repeated slow banging.

Helga gasped. "They are breaking through the front door. We should let them know we're here."

Flora dialed the emergency services again and told the operator they were staying put unless instructed to do otherwise.

As they waited, more smoke began to crawl through the cracks in the door, creeping through Xanthe's barricades, even seeping through chinks in the plaster where the wall met the sloping attic roof. Pie began to whine again and Helga fell to a bout of coughing. In that tense moment, the smell of the burning building filling her senses, Xanthe was taken back to the time she had arrived in the hayloft at Great Chalfield when it was on fire. She recalled the familiar rush of adrenaline, the tightness of her chest as she had breathed in the smoke, the heat from the flames as they had begun to devour the boards beneath her feet. She had been lucky to survive that time. This time, she told herself, help was on its way.

The shouts from below became louder.

Flora listened to the operator on the phone, then told the others, "They've reached the bottom of the stairs! There's no fire in the shop. She says they already have it under control and we are not to move."

There came the noise of water pouring onto the fire, causing the floorboards to crack and pop, a wet hissing sound continuing as the flames were doused. The discordant sounds signaled the moment of danger had passed. Whatever mess and destruction awaited them downstairs, their lives were no longer in peril.

"I don't understand what caught fire," said Xanthe. "I mean, if it started on the ground floor, it's none of the appliances in the kitchen . . . were you using something volatile in the workshop today, Mum?"

"Not especially. I always keep white spirit and varnish under the sink. There's nothing that could make a spark. I never have any naked flames in there."

The same thought occurred to Xanthe and her mother in the same moment. They turned to look at Helga, who had already guessed what they were thinking.

"I swear I have not had a single cigarette in the house! I always go out into the garden, I promise you."

"It's OK, Helga." Xanthe put a hand on the older woman's arm and found she was trembling more than the whippet. She felt for her then, admiring the way in which she had hidden her own very real terror. "No one's saying the fire had anything to do with you. We're just trying to work out what could have happened."

"Hello! Everyone all right up there?" The shouted questions reached them through the sounds of the hose and the hissing fire. "How many of you are there?"

"Three of us here!" Xanthe yelled back. "We are all good, and better for hearing you!"

"Be with you in a minute, ladies. Wait for us to get to you," came the instruction.

Flora got up from the bed and helped herself to one of Xanthe's oversize cardigans, shrugging it on over her pajamas.

"Are you cold, Mum," Xanthe asked, helping her into the sleeves.

"These pjs are really not fit to be seen. If the room's about to be filled with strange men I'd rather not meet them looking like an orphan." She ran her fingers through her hair and smiled, posing, doing her best to relieve the tension in the room. "What do you think? Got any good pink lippie handy?"

"Stunning even without the lipstick," Xanthe said, rolling her eyes and slipping her arm around her mother's shoulders. She knew how Flora preferred to cope with things that frightened her, and playing the whole thing down, remaining matter-of-fact, was crucial. She had learned, years earlier, how her mother dealt with her illness in the same way. Giving in to self-pity or voicing her darkest fears just wasn't her way. It didn't mean she was never frightened. Didn't mean she never doubted that all would be well. It was simply her way of coping, and Xanthe loved her all the more for it.

Two firemen came walking in with surprisingly light steps in heavy boots. They gave reassurances that the stairs, though badly damaged, were now navigable.

"There are several treads missing and the whole staircase will need to be properly assessed," said the taller of the two men. "What's important now is that we get you out of the building so that we can carry out a proper check, make sure there are no hot spots left, make a report of where the blaze has affected the integrity of the building. . . ."

Seeing the alarm on Flora's face he went on. "The damage isn't significant. There was a lot of smoke, but the fire itself seems to have been limited to the stairwell."

"But why would the stairs catch fire in the first place? Was it a bit of faulty wiring in the electrical system, perhaps?"

The fireman wouldn't be drawn further on possible causes. "As soon as we've done our inspection we'll let you have our findings. Now, let's get you ladies out into the fresh air, shall we?"

"My mum needs her crutches. They're in here," Xanthe said, moving toward her mother's bedroom.

"I can't allow you to go in there yet, miss."

"They're just beside her bed. I can get them really quickly."

The fireman shook his head. "The floor could well be unsafe."

"She needs them."

"It's all right, Xanthe, love, I'm not in a hurry to go anywhere."

"Leave it to us," the second firefighter insisted. Cautiously, with practiced focus, testing each floorboard with a gentle tap from his fire ax, he moved into the bedroom and retrieved the sticks.

With great care, the men helped the three women down the stairs. Another firefighter joined them so that two were able to carry Flora without difficulty, while Xanthe and Helga, who was still clutching Pie, managed to clamber down by themselves. The firemen had already put ladders in place to bridge gaps where the fire had consumed some of the old wooden steps. As they made their slow descent the men warned them which bits were still hot, which bits were too damaged to stand on, and how to safely use the ladders. Xanthe felt her stomach lurch at the thought of how close they had come to disaster. If the smoke had got to them before they had woken up, or the fire had burned a little quicker, they might not have got out at all. As they reached the ground floor she heard Flora making the point that they still hadn't got around to checking the smoke alarms, and Helga insisting to anyone who would listen that she absolutely had not smoked a single cigarette in the house during her stay. All the time Xanthe could not shake off a growing sense of dread. How could a fire have started in a place with no volatile substances, no electrical appliances, not even a plug socket? Wooden stairs did not simply burst into flames on their own. On the other hand, old wood, with years of polish worked into it, each plank as dry as bone, would burn very well if someone set light to it. She thought of Fairfax. Of how he had left the threat of danger hanging over her. Could he have broken into the shop and set the fire?

When they reached the foot of the stairs they were assailed by the acrid smell of wet ash, sodden plasterwork, and saturated soot. Flora was unable to suppress a small, heartfelt wail at the sight of the mess.

"I don't know which has done more damage: the fire or the water," she said, causing a slightly defensive firefighter to point out that without the water the fire would have consumed the whole building. "I know, I'm sorry," she said. "It's just . . ." She raised an arm and let it drop to her side in a gesture of defeat.

Xanthe put an arm around her mother's shoulders. "Come on, Mum. It's not as bad as it looks. Most of the stock has escaped being either burned or soaked. We can wash off the smoke and get someone in to repair the stairs." Even as she said it she feared for the vintage clothes. Smoke would spell disaster for most of the delicate fabrics. She couldn't bring herself to look and was at least thankful to think of the wedding dress safely upstairs in her own room.

"Oh, love, it'll take such a lot of work," Flora muttered.

At last Helga set Pie down, looping her dressing gown belt through the dog's collar so that she wouldn't get in the way or trample wet soot further through the shop. "I feel bad giving you something else to do," she said. "Last thing you need is a dog to look after on top of everything else."

Xanthe leaned down to stroke Pie's silky ears. "If it wasn't for this little one things might have been much worse. She raised the alarm. If her barking hadn't woken you up . . ."

Helga nodded. "She certainly knew we were in danger, but she didn't bark."

"No?"

"She squeaked and whined and scrabbled at the bedclothes. Once she was certain she had woken me up she ran about in circles, but she never barked, not once. She's not really very vocal. That's typical of sight hounds. She only ever barks at a person if she doesn't know them, or if they frighten her badly."

Xanthe looked at her. "So, if someone had broken into the shop, if she'd heard somebody on the stairs, that would have made her bark?"

"A stranger in the house at night? Definitely. You'd have found your voice then, wouldn't you, little Piecrust?"

Xanthe processed this information. If what Helga said was reliable, the dog hadn't barked, which meant nobody had broken into the shop or the flat and started the fire. Not a random arsonist. Not Fairfax. She turned to the firefighter who was at that moment pulling up some of the loose floorboards in the hallway.

"Any clues as to what could have started it?" she asked.

"Not so far. Your wiring looks blameless; nothing suspicious there. Was anything left switched on downstairs? A cash register, maybe? Or spotlights?"

"We keep the money in a tin in a drawer. The lights are switched off at the door. I do use standard lamps in displays sometimes, but not at the moment."

"Any smokers in the house?"

She glanced at Helga who was at the front of the shop and busy recounting Pie's heroism to another firefighter.

"A guest, but she's adamant she hasn't been smoking indoors. Why, have you found anything to suggest . . . ?"

"No. Just trying to get all the information that could help us. Not pointing the finger of blame at anyone. Not yet." He went back to scrutinizing the site of the worst of the damage. "What's mysterious," he said, almost to himself, "is that there appear to have been other pieces of wood here. Did you have some antiques on the stairs, perhaps? Old wooden boxes or decorative bits and pieces?"

"What? No, nothing like that. The stairs are quite narrow and Mum uses her crutches to get up and down them. We'd never put stuff where she might trip over it."

The man straightened up, his demeanor subtly altered. He was suddenly a little less friendly and a little more professional. "You're recently come to the town, I understand. This is a new business."

"That's right."

"Going well, is it?"

It was a simple enough question, but she knew exactly what lay behind it. Had they deliberately started the fire in an attempt to make a hefty insurance claim because the business was struggling?

"It's going just fine," she told him. "I know you are only doing your job, and I'm sure you've met some desperate people, but is anyone crazy enough to start a fire that's likely to trap themselves and their family above it?"

The fireman made no comment, but turned back to his task. Xanthe took a deep breath. She knew she was still shaken by what had happened. She didn't need anger at unjust accusations making her feel worse. She went to join her mother, who was being told it would be at least an hour before they could go upstairs and get their clothes.

"They think we should find somewhere else to wait," Flora said. "I suppose we are only in the way here." Her mother's eyes filled with tears.

"Hey, Mum. It'll be OK. Look, this room's just a bit grubby, and the door to the vintage clothing was shut, so it shouldn't be too bad in there. I'll ring Gerri, see if she can come into town and open up early. We can have some breakfast while we're waiting."

Flora mustered a smile. "Cake for breakfast could go a long way to making us feel better. Oh, look! Liam's here."

Xanthe glanced at the ormolu clock. In all the drama she had forgotten she had invited Liam to join her for an early morning dog walk. As he hurried through the door and saw her he let out a breath he had clearly been holding since finding the fire engine parked at the top of the alley.

"For God's sake, what happened?" he asked, pulling her into a warm hug and holding her tight. She let herself be held, resting her head on his shoulder, comforted by the feel of his strong arms around her and his calm, reassuring presence.

"There was a fire," she mumbled.

He pulled back so that he could study her face. "That much I worked out for myself."

Flora tried to explain. "Pie smelled the smoke and woke Helga."

"Such a good girl!" Helga patted the whippet with pride. "We might all have been burned to a crisp in our beds if she hadn't raised the alarm."

"But what started the fire?" Liam asked, still holding Xanthe's arms, his expression suggesting he had not quite yet recovered from discovering she might have been injured or worse.

She took his hand in hers. "Can we go to your flat while we wait for the firemen to do their bit? They won't let us back upstairs yet. I was going to ring Gerri, but . . ."

"No need. Come on." He let go of Xanthe at last and took Flora's arm. "I can't promise catering at Gerri's level, but I do have coffee and brandy."

"Lead the way!" said Helga.

Liam took off his leather jacket and gave it to Xanthe. After a little persuading, one of the firefighters fetched a random selection of footwear and coats from Flora's bedroom, so that they were able to walk to Liam's flat.

The rooms he inhabited were set above his workshop, the smell of petrol and engine oil growing fainter as they climbed the stairs.

He patiently helped Flora to the top, and ushered them all into the kitchen. Pie was excited at yet another new place to explore and insisted on doing reckless circuits of the room for a full minute before settling down.

"I'm most impressed," Helga announced.

"Really? My flat is nothing special," Liam said, filling the kettle while the women took seats around the little kitchen table.

"I'm impressed by how respectable and tidy the place is. Most young men would be horrified at the thought of a surprise visit sprung upon them at such an hour. No chance to clear away signs of youthful high jinks."

"Oh, Helga," Flora laughed at her friend, "you're making daft assumptions. Not everyone under the age of thirty lives a wild existence."

"I try," Liam insisted.

Xanthe helped him make a *cafetière* of coffee. He set sugar, milk, and brandy on the table, along with the biscuit tin, which yielded gingersnaps and shortbread.

"A feast!" Flora declared, spooning sugar into her mug.

"So," Liam unscrewed the brandy and began sloshing it into the coffee cups, "who's going to tell me exactly why Marlborough's finest firefighting team are, as I speak, stomping up and down what is left of your stairs?"

No one was able to give a satisfactory answer. They went around in circles, dismissing each possible cause for the fire, becoming increasingly baffled by what had happened. All the time, Xanthe had her own silent ideas about the origins of the blaze, none of which she could share with the others, and most of which put Fairfax squarely in the picture. Somehow. And yet he hadn't been in the building. Or at least, she realized, he hadn't been in it a few hours ago. Not in her own time. Could he have done something in a past time that somehow caused the fire? As the thought occurred to her it seemed more possible and more terrifying. What if Fairfax had been able to set the fire in the stairwell decades ago? Centuries ago? Would that result in a fire in the present? Surely if he'd done that the *results* of the fire would become evident, but not the actual fire itself. It didn't quite add up, and yet nor could she completely dismiss it as a theory. And if it was possible, what else could he do from a remote time, safely out of harm's way himself? And how would she be able to stop him starting another fire, or somehow else damaging the shop? Her head started to ache with the effort of trying to make sense of the impossible. She gulped her brandy-laced coffee and immediately wished she hadn't as the caffeine and alcohol only worsened the pain in her temples.

"I'll give you a hand with the cleaning up," Liam was saying to Flora.

"That's sweet of you, Liam. I don't suppose you know a reliable carpenter who could come and fix the stairs?" she asked.

"Leave it with me. It's finding one that can do it at short notice that will be the tricky bit."

Helga pointed out that Flora wouldn't be able to get up and down to the flat from the shop until they were repaired. "Unless the lovely firemen are going to come and carry you up and down like the Queen of Sheba every day," she added, laughing loudly at the thought.

"You can stay here until it's mended," Liam offered. "I can kip on the couch."

"Thank you." Flora helped herself to another biscuit. "I'm sure we'll sort something out at the shop, but it's good to have a backup plan. Don't you think so, Xanthe?"

"Sure, Mum. That's a great idea," she answered, but her mind was elsewhere. The stairs were easy enough to repair. The smoke and water damage to the rest of the building and the stock could, with hard work, be made good. None of it was worth doing, however, if Fairfax remained able to rain chaos upon them whenever and however it suited him. She had to find him. She had to stop him. And she needed Harley's help to do it.

{ 6 }

THE BEER CELLAR BENEATH THE FEATHERS WAS SEVERAL DEGREES COOLER THAN WAS comfortable without a coat. Xanthe perched on an upturned mixers crate and pulled her old tweed jacket a little tighter around her. The air was so heavy with the smell of hops and ale she could almost taste it. The many pipes which fed the different beers from carefully positioned barrels up to the bar above ran along the walls and arced across the low-slung ceiling, making the space feel like the ribcage of some giant creature. There were soft hissing and bubbling sounds as the levers upstairs were worked by the bartender pulling pints. On the other side of this singular space, Harley manhandled a new barrel into position and swapped the connecting pipes to it with practiced ease, before rolling the empty one out of the way.

"So, tell me again, hen, how that nasty piece of work sat calm as you like outside your shop just waiting for you to notice him. That guy has some brass balls right there."

Xanthe had given him only the briefest summary of recent events, wanting to update him, but eager to get to the main point of her visit. Once again, she needed Harley's cooperation if she was to travel back in time. She had spent most of the day back at the shop, sweeping up debris, washing walls, sorting items into damaged or not damaged, and generally putting the place back together again. In fact, although the fire had been frightening and the heat intense, it had been mainly confined to the stairwell, with less damage elsewhere than she had first feared. An electrician had already been summoned up by the fire service and made good any wiring that had been affected. Liam struck gold with a sympathetic carpenter who had turned up within the hour, assessed the situation, measured up, gone to fetch materials, and returned to start work, all before lunchtime. Flora's spirits had been lifted by the realization that they would be back in the flat the same day. She set up a repair station in her workshop with Helga helping, including popping out to fetch snacks and lunch from Gerri. With everything being so swiftly put right, Xanthe had been able to slip away to see Harley without feeling as if she was abandoning them.

"Fairfax seems to pick his moments very well," she told Harley. "It was as if he knows exactly where I'll be at any given time. As if he is watching me."

"Not a pleasant thought."

"It isn't. Nor is the fact that he hasn't yet said what it is he wants from me. Just made threats."

Harley paused in his work, straightening up to look at her, his brow furrowed in concentration. "So, do you think that the wedding dress you found is in some way connected to him? It's singing away, you tell me, and now he reappears. Coincidence, or more than that, d'you reckon?"

"Honestly, I'm not sure. The dress is supposed to be Edwardian, and it's possible that is the time he's now inhabiting. He was wearing a shirt with a starched wing collar, so that would fit the fashion of the era." She pushed her hair back off her face, weary from lack of sleep, the drama of the fire, and the challenge that lay ahead. "It's not much to go on, though. He could be hopping back and fore, picking up clothes from any time. Who knows."

"Trouble is, hen, if Fairfax isn't connected to the dress and you answer the call, well, you'll be spinning off to deal with that, meanwhile yon man could be somewhen else, so you'd not be dealing with him at all."

"Worse than that, I'd be leaving Mum unprotected. Apart from Pie."

"I'd want something a wee bit more than a skinny hound between me and that bastard, if you don't mind me saying so."

"I know. I wish I could be sure. I tried to find an answer in the *Spinners* book."

"Oh aye. Any joy?"

"Hard to tell. It showed the story of a young man killing someone who had evidently been tormenting him for years. I couldn't work out what time period the events took place in. And what his story has to do with the wedding dress or with Fairfax I have absolutely no idea. It really doesn't make any difference, not to what I have to do next," she said firmly.

"I know that look. You've decided then? You're definitely going back?"

"I have to. It's the only way I'll find out if the dress and Fairfax are connected. Its singing does seem to have got more urgent since he reappeared. And . . . I hate to ask, but I need your help. With Mum."

"And here was me thinking you'd come to ask my advice as the ally of a Spinner, an expert on all things weird and downright peculiar hereabouts, a man of multiple and invaluable talents. . . ."

"Could you invite her round to dinner again? Please?"

"And which night would you like me to wine and dine and lie to your lovely wee mother?"

"Preferably the same night you've sent me to London to sing at your friend's pub. Again."

"Oh aye, that'll be the friend who doesn't exist in his ever-so-popular fictitious pub?"

"I'm sorry."

Harley walked over to her and put his bear paw of a hand gently on her shoulder. "Tell me where to go, hen, but in my opinion, you are going to have to tell your mother the truth."

She nodded. "One of these days," she agreed. "But not today."

"Today," Harley insisted. "You said yourself, she's in real danger. She has a right to know."

"I think she'll believe me. I hope so."

"The daughter who's been listening to singing antiques all her life? I should say so."

"What if she tries to stop me traveling . . . ?"

"Hen, she'll be able to see how you have no choice in the matter. Even if it wasn't for Fairfax . . . this . . . this spinning . . . it's what you have to do. It's who you are." He squeezed her shoulder gently. "Tell me to bugger off and mind my own business if I'm wrong, but . . ."

"You're not wrong. I've wanted to tell her for ages, really. I mean, it is a wonderful thing. . . . A crazy, beautiful thing. And I feel honored that I've been chosen, that I have this fantastic gift. . . ."

"There, that expression on your face right now, the one you get when you talk about it, that's what'll convince her, lassie."

Back at the shop there was much to be done, and Xanthe had to be creative to engineer getting her mother on her own so that she could talk to her. She took Helga briefly to one side and spoke quietly to her, telling her she was worried Flora was struggling with the work the fire had caused and would Helga mind if she took her off for a quiet tea somewhere, just the two of them? Helga had proved herself a true friend, immediately volunteering to get on with some of the clearing up herself, so that Flora wouldn't feel compelled to do it on her return. Xanthe had brushed off her mother's initial resistance to the idea, letting her know she needed to talk to her on her own. As soon as Flora realized her own health was not, in fact, the issue she fetched her coat and bag and followed Xanthe out to her car. They set off in silence, driving through the afternoon countryside as long shadows fringed the rolling fields. At last the tension was broken by Flora spotting two hares standing in the center of a swath of plowed land, paws raised at each other.

"Oh, would you look at that! Stop the car, let's watch. I don't think I've ever seen hares properly boxing before."

Xanthe pulled over onto the grass verge and switched off the engine. "There is something magical about them."

"Now I know it's properly spring."

"They say hares are witches in disguise," she told her, casting about for a way into talking about the impossible.

"Really? I didn't know that. I knew they heralded spring, and that there's nothing madder than a March hare."

"Except possibly your daughter."

Flora turned and studied her face closely. "OK, let's have it, love. You can tell me anything, you know that, don't you?"

"It's hard to choose where to start . . . are you sure you wouldn't rather we go and find a café? Do you want tea?"

"I want you to tell me what's troubling you. What's been troubling you for some time."

"Is it that obvious?"

"Xanthe, I'm your mum. Just because I don't ask, doesn't mean I don't notice. . . ."

"I hate that you might worry."

"I'm not a child. It's not your job to keep things from me because you think I might not like them. Is it . . . something to do with Liam?"

"Liam? No, no, not him."

"To do with the fire, then?"

"No, well, yes, in a way."

Flora raised her hands and then let them drop on her lap. "OK, I'm not going to play this game. Love your taxi as I do, it's not the warmest place to sit, and no, I don't want to go somewhere else. Just tell me, right here, right now: What's wrong?"

"Well, actually . . . it's not all bad. That is, there's something quite wonderful that I've wanted to tell you about for a while now. Something even more magical, even madder than those hares. The thing is, Mum, I haven't been entirely honest with you. When I said I was going to London, to do gigs for Harley's friend, well, I went somewhere else."

"You made it up? There were no gigs? I don't understand. . . ."

"There was no pub. No friend of Harley's, either. I had to come up with an explanation for my absence."

"It was all lies? But why?"

She watched her mother's expression change from angry to hurt and she thought her heart might break.

"Mum, I'm so sorry. I didn't want to hide things from you. . . ."

"No, Xanthe, you didn't just *not* tell me things, you made things up. You lied to me. More than once, by the sound of it. Why would you not trust me? Don't you know you can tell me anything? Surely, after everything that happened with Marcus, after all we've been through together . . . why did you feel you couldn't talk to me?"

"I wanted to, *so* badly . . . I—I suppose I was trying to protect you."

"Do you know how patronizing that sounds?"

"And, well, that you might think I'd lost my mind."

"Anything would be better than Marcus."

"I might have to remind you that you said that."

There was a pause, a small silence filled with confusion and hurt on Flora's side, guilt and regret on Xanthe's.

"OK," she said at last, switching on the car engine so that they could benefit from the heater, "however crazy this sounds, here goes."

And so she told her. She told her how, since moving to Marlborough, the objects that sang to her had done so more clearly, more urgently, more persistently than ever before. She told her how the blind house in the garden sat on an intersection between two powerful ley lines. She told her how those three things combined to allow her to travel back in time. She told her how she had been called by the chatelaine to save Alice. She told her how she used the locket Flora herself had given her as a talisman to draw her back home again. She told her how she had found a book that held all the secrets of the Spinners, and that this what was she had discovered herself to be. And she told her about Benedict Fairfax and how she had unwittingly brought danger back to their home. To her.

Flora listened. At first she made small exclamations or put in questioning words, but as Xanthe's story unfolded she fell completely silent, patiently hearing what her daughter had to say, waiting until at last she stopped and waited for a reaction.

"That is quite a lot to take in," she said.

"I know."

"Just to be clear, you've done this . . . time traveling . . . several times?"

"Quite a few."

"And each time you spun a web of lies to cover your tracks."

"Mum, I'm sorry, but . . ."

"Which is understandable, I suppose, given what you've told me. Even so, I can't pretend it doesn't hurt; the fact that you didn't want to share all of this with me in the first place."

"I know it will take you time to forgive me, but right now we don't have time to get stuck on that. We . . . I have to deal with Fairfax. And I need to keep you safe. Which is why I wanted to tell you now. It wasn't fair to keep you in the dark any longer."

"This man, you think he will do something here? To me, perhaps?"

"The fire, Mum. I think that was him."

Flora gasped. "How can you know that? Even the firemen couldn't figure out what started it."

"That's because people starting fires in another century is probably not something they've come across before."

"Is that what you think happened?"

"I'm not sure. I hope not, but I have an awful feeling it might be. I am a long way from having all the answers, but it's my best guess."

"No wonder the poor firemen were stumped. It sounds so . . . huge."

"It's a terrifying idea. I need you to believe me."

"Says the person who has been lying to me for months."

"You know things sing to me, Mum. They always have."

"It's quite a step from sensing things in a solid here-and-now object to you being whisked off to another century."

"It happened, all of it, just as I've told you."

Flora opened her mouth to speak, then changed her mind. She looked away from Xanthe now, gazing out through the car window at the fading day. "You should have told me sooner. I might have been able to help. I am not, as you well know, completely useless."

"Of course not! But, well, it's not an easy story to believe."

"You know I love you. I will always be on your side. If you need someone to talk to, someone professional . . ."

"You think I'm crazy? You think I'm, what, imagining all this stuff?"

"I didn't say that. . . ."

"It's OK. To be honest, I'm not sure I'd believe me either. Here, this might help a bit." She reached down to her bag and pulled out *Spinners*. She handed it to Flora.

"This is it?" her mother asked. "The special book of how to time-travel?"

"This is it. Take a look."

Flora set the heavy book on her lap and carefully opened it. She sifted through the old, dry pages.

"But, it's all blank. There's nothing written here at all."

"The book's magic, Mum. It only reveals its contents to some people. Watch." She leaned over and pulled it a little nearer herself, turning it so that it was more directly facing her. She placed a finger at the top of the blank page and slowly ran it along. Instantly, flowing handwriting in dark brown ink appeared, following her finger.

Flora gasped, watching as the words continued to appear. They flashed up only for a few seconds, disappearing again as Xanthe's finger moved on.

"I can hear them too," she explained. "You won't be able to, but I can hear someone whispering the story in my ear."

"That's . . . astonishing! What a marvelous thing!"

"You don't know how badly I've wanted to show you this before. To tell you everything. You do believe me now, don't you?" Xanthe lifted her hand from the page and pushed the book back to her mother. Immediately all the writing vanished.

Flora gave a small laugh. "It's pretty convincing. . . . But it must be dangerous, love, surely? Traveling through time, pretending to be someone, some*thing* you're not. What if you got into trouble, who would help you? What if you got, I dunno, stuck in a different time?"

"People do help me. Ordinary people, and other Spinners. And, well, this is something I have to do. Like when things sing to me. This is what all that has been about, all these years, do you see? Being here, in Marlborough, having the blind house, finding this, it's all led me to where I need to be. To what I need to be doing. And now, now that Fairfax is threatening us . . . I have to go back again, Mum. He and the wedding dress are connected somehow, I'm pretty sure of that. I won't know how, or what it is I have to do to stop him until I go there. Go then."

"But, you said yourself he's a ruthless person. What does he want from you?"

"I'm not sure, but I think it might be *Spinners*."

"Would it really matter if you gave it to him? He might leave us alone then."

"That is not an option. He can never have it. He's not a good person, Mum. If he is able to see what's inside the book, to read its secrets, well, it would make him more powerful. And he's not a man to use that sort of power morally. Justly. Spinners are supposed to keep the order of things, to protect the way things are meant to be. But not him. He's just in it for what he can get out of it."

Flora rubbed her temples with her fingers and Xanthe saw her breath forming in front of her. Despite the taxi's heater, the temperature was dropping. Outside the hares had long ago loped away to their grassy nests. The sky had bruised purple as dusk descended.

"Come on, Mum. Enough for now. Let's get you home and in the warm."

"There's so much to take in, so much to process."

"I know. We'll talk more." She switched on the headlights and fastened her seatbelt again. As she was about to turn the car around Flora put a hand on her arm.

"Thank you, for telling me."

"Do you forgive me for lying to you?"

"I . . . understand why you did. I'm just very glad that now I know everything. Now I can help you."

"I am so happy to be able to share this with you, Mum." She smiled in the half-light of the car interior. "It is a wonderful thing, isn't it?"

Flora smiled back. "It's bloody fantastic!" she said, making them both laugh.

Once back at the shop all conversation about time travel had to be put on hold while Helga was still there. Xanthe and Flora had agreed they would talk more once she had gone the next day, and before she made her next trip back. Which would have to be soon. They decided to get as much of the cleaning and repairing of the shop and stairs done as possible and then prepare for Xanthe's trip once Helga had left.

On the day of her planned departure, despite everyone's efforts, there was still a deal of work to be done. Xanthe had forced herself to check the vintage clothing collection the day before and had been hugely relieved to find it, for the most part, undamaged. Smoke had seeped beneath the door so that everything smelled of it and would have to be washed. A slow job, but doable and not costly to fix. Some water had also got into the room, bringing down some of the ceiling plasterwork, which would eventually have to be replaced, but the room was still usable. Gerri had come over to inspect the stock and offer support, leaving with all the silk scarves, blouses, and dresses, which she volunteered to launder by hand at home. When Xanthe found a moment on her own with the clothes, she pulled out a few garments she considered workable for her next journey back in time, though it was hard to be specific, not knowing the exact date of origin of the dress.

Aside from the general washing of walls and cleaning grit and grime off surfaces, the downstairs floors would take a while to dry out. At least floorboards would recover more quickly than carpet. Xanthe and Flora decided to put up a CLOSED sign for a couple of days while they dried things out. They couldn't risk having customers slip or trip over something, and the smell of smoke was rather off-putting.

Helga came into her own, lifting things that were too difficult for Flora, scrubbing floorboards and beams without complaint, and generally being an all-round good egg. Xanthe secretly wished she would stay longer; she seemed the ideal companion for her mother. Leaving her would have been so much easier knowing Helga was there. But her ticket to Australia was booked, so that was that. She would be leaving at teatime. Unexpectedly, she became quite tearful at the thought of leaving Pie. Xanthe did her best to reassure her that the dog was very welcome to stay and would be fine with them. In the end it was agreed that she and Liam would take their postponed walk up to the white horse that afternoon, so that Pie would not see her owner leaving.

Liam was happy with the new plan and picked Xanthe up in his cherished vintage red sports car at four o'clock. Now that the days had at last begun to properly lengthen, a cheerful March sun hung low in the sky as they sped out of Marlborough. On either side the sweeping fields were hemmed by hedges grown fuzzy with seasonal buds and new growth. There was no wind, but a freshness to the day that balanced the sweetness of that light, warning that winter had not yet departed the landscape, frosts were still likely, and icy mornings would catch out unwary travelers and nascent crops. In the open-topped car, Xanthe sat with Pie held firmly on her lap. The little dog's ears streamed behind her in the wind as she poked her nose up in the air. Liam laughed at her.

"She's definitely a classic car enthusiast. It's obvious," he said, steering the car easily along the narrow, winding road.

Xanthe's hair fought against the loose plait she had worked it into. She put on sunglasses, leaning back against the worn leather of the seat, enjoying the feel of freedom and speed that came with the open-top car.

"It's just like it is in the movies," she said. "Though possibly colder. I'm not sure we live in the right country for soft-tops."

He grinned. "I know a guy could convert your taxi. Give you a roll-back lid on the thing, what d'you reckon?"

"You keep your hands off my cab! I love her as she is, thank you very much. No, any time I want to feel like a film star I'll give you a call." She grinned.

The road followed the incline of the landscape until they reached the top of the broad hill above the town. The little car park was empty, so that once they had stopped Pie was allowed to hop out and trot around, sniffing enthusiastically at everything. After a short struggle to put the roof up—during which Xanthe made strong points in favor of her own vehicle—they left the car and followed the path up onto the chalk hill figure. As always, being close to the ancient horse made her feel even more strongly connected to the past. What times the great steed had witnessed from its lofty viewpoint. What events. Civil war. The fall of one royal house and the rise of another. The invention of the railway system. The birth of the internal combustion engine. And still it stood, steady and proud, the watcher on the mountain.

As they reached the part of the path that passed close to the giant horse's head, she stopped, not wanting to move away from it. Visitors were discouraged from treading too near the figure itself to protect it from eroding footsteps. There were many occasions when walking there alone that Xanthe had crept onto the hallowed chalk, to place her hand on the ancient gouges, to feel the mythical heartbeat of the animal. But today was not about her. She turned to look at Liam and was both alarmed and surprised to feel her heart respond to him. Was she really ready for that? She did not entirely trust her feelings yet, knowing herself to be vulnerable after Samuel.

Liam became aware he was being stared at. He smiled at her and took her hand.

"Penny for your thoughts," he said.

"That's a low offer."

"Mates' rates." When she said nothing he squeezed her hand. "Something's bothering you, isn't it?"

"You mean aside from me and my mum nearly being turned to toast in our own home?"

"Aside from that," he said and nodded.

"It's complicated." She felt his hand on hers tense and saw at once how she had carelessly used an expression that seemed always to point to affairs of the heart. "I mean, I've got lots to think about, to do with work, and Mum, and the business, and the band . . ."

The look he gave her suggested he wasn't convinced by this answer.

"I'm going to have to go away for a couple of days," she explained, "and the timing is really bad. My friend in Milton Keynes, you remember?"

"The one with boyfriend trouble? I thought that was sorted out last time you went."

"It's . . . ongoing. Thing is, I promised I'd go before the fire. She wouldn't ask if she wasn't really desperate."

"Well, if you've got to go . . ."

She stuffed her hands into the pockets of her jacket and walked on. "Come on," she said. "Let's walk the loop of the hill and get home before the sun disappears. Gets cold quickly up here this time of year."

"Could you perhaps slow down a bit?" He struggled to match her pace as she strode on and his awkward gait caused her to smile despite herself. He stumbled, for a moment almost toppling off the ridge and threatening to pitch down the steep slope. Instinctively she grabbed his arm. He righted himself, smiling ruefully. "Where would I be without you?" he asked.

"At the bottom of the hill?"

"With only myself to blame. But, seeing as I am still up here, and you are up here too . . ." He pulled her gently into a warm hug and murmured into her hair. "Lovely girl. You know I only want to help."

"I know," she said, glad to be with him, enjoying the comfort of the moment. Pie, with little respect for anyone's feelings, chose that instant and that spot on the path to take a long, steaming pee.

Liam laughed loudly. "Upstaged by a pooch. OK, I give up." He held up his hands.

Xanthe turned on her heel. "And she's quick too," she called over her shoulder. "Last one back to the car buys the beers!"

They drove home in companionable silence, Liam having closed the roof of the car. Pie curled up on Xanthe's lap, too tired to look out of the window at the dusk-covered landscape as they headed back to Marlborough. They returned to Liam's yard to safely park the car, picked up some beers from the supermarket—paid for by Liam, who had stood no chance of catching up to the others after a slow start—and went back to the shop. They found the stairs sufficiently repaired to be usable, most of the clearing done, and Flora happily sitting up-stairs in the living room, surrounded by odd bits of stock that had got shifted during the cleanup.

"You three look healthy," she said, bracing herself as Pie flew onto her lap. "All that fresh air must have done you good." She reached up and gave her daughter's hand a squeeze and the two exchanged conspiratorial glances. Xanthe recognized excitement in her mother's expression and was heartened to think that in the time she had had to mull over all that she had shared with her about being a Spinner, her reaction was still one of wonder, first and foremost. It meant so much to be able to share everything with her at last.

"We bring beer," Liam told her, holding up six bottles of Henge Ale.

"Did Helga get away OK?" Xanthe asked, taking off her jacket and dropping it over the back of a chair.

"Just about. We were so engrossed in our mission to get the place livable again we almost forgot the time. Will you miss your mistress, little Piecrust?" she asked the dog, stroking its ears.

"She'll be fine with us," said Xanthe. "Oooh, where did these prints come from?" She stooped to examine a small collection of pictures stacked against the wall.

"Helga found them. She said they were in the hallway, which they must have been because they are quite sooty and a bit wet. Most of them are glazed, luckily, so they escaped too much damage. Strange thing is I have no recollection of them being there before the fire, do you?"

Xanthe shook her head. "We never left things there. Perhaps they were hidden in a corner of the shop and the firemen moved them."

"Well, either way we didn't buy them. They must have been in the original stock, most likely stuff old Mr. Morris bought in a job lot. The majority are hunting, shooting, or fishing prints. Quite saleable but nothing special. One or two look like water colors, though. Victorian,

I think." She pointed at the stack. "The one at the back looks like where you went to for the auction."

"Corsham Hall?" Xanthe put down the one she was looking at and lifted the watercolor up to the light. It was unmistakably the grand house she had so recently visited. The original home of the wedding dress. The painting was called *Arriving for the Ball* and showed carriages drawing up to the front of the house and finely dressed guests making their way through the magnificent front doors. She studied the shape of the gowns, the high waists, the low, square-cut necklines, the long sweep of fine fabric in the skirts. Here was the shape of the wedding dress, no doubt about it. "Is this dated?" she asked her mother, turning the picture over to check the back for clues.

"Not that I could find. The scene looks Regency. Of course it might have been painted later, but my money's on it being contemporary with the setting."

Liam peered over Xanthe's shoulder. "Isn't it popular now, though, that sort of thing? I mean, it could have been painted a hundred years after it was set. People still like Jane Austen stories well enough for films to be made of the books, don't they?"

Xanthe and Flora looked at Liam and exchanged surprised glances. Flora laughed, "I didn't have you down as a lover of costume dramas, Liam!" she said.

He pretended to look hurt. "Don't you know that I am a multi-faceted modern man?"

Xanthe ran her fingers over the join between the frame and the back of the painting. "I agree with Mum; I think it's definitely nineteenth century. Probably quite early. Feels old."

"Oh, very scientific," Liam teased.

"It just does," she insisted. "Which means it wasn't anything to do with Jane Austen, who is a lot more widely known now than she was then. So the question you have to ask is, *why* was it painted? It's not a particularly important house. It's big, yes, but there are lots of grand mansions in the area that are about the same age and style. No, this was most likely commissioned by someone connected to the house."

"What was the family name?" Flora asked. "Gerri mentioned it."

"Wilcox," said Xanthe. "If we only knew what any of them looked like. . . ." She squinted at the faces of the figures. "Can't see anyone dressed like royalty. Just a bunch of well-heeled aristos at the start of a classy and expensive social event. Plenty of young women looking for a good husband. A fair amount of handsome young men and . . ." What she saw then made her stop without finishing the sentence.

"And . . . ?" Liam prompted.

Xanthe, flustered, muttered something about there being lots of footmen and valets but she found it difficult to form a sensible reply. Her attention was entirely taken by the figure standing to one side of the front door. He was tall and lean and immaculately attired in evening dress of the period with tailed jacket, broad silk cummerbund, perfectly cut breeches, and starched wing collar. What marked him out was the light color of his hair, the paleness of his sharp features, and the black leather patch that he wore over his left eye. "Fairfax!" she said to herself, half in astonishment, half in triumph. Now she knew beyond doubt that he and the wedding dress had at least once been located at the same place in the same point in time. Corsham Hall in the early 1800s. That was where and when the gown was pulling her toward. That was where and when she would find Fairfax, she was certain of it. That was where and when she had to go.

$$\{ 7 \}$$

WITH A MORE SPECIFIC DATE IN MIND XANTHE FOUND IT EASIER TO PREPARE FOR HER journey. Later that night, she went downstairs to the vintage clothing room. After thirty minutes' rummaging and searching, the stock yielded a pale blue striped cotton maxi dress with smocking at the top which more or less conformed to Empire lines in its shape. She found a pair of laced leather ankle boots, wincing at the narrowness of them compared to her preferred Dr. Martens, but satisfied that they looked right enough. A navy shrug of felted wool worked surprisingly well. What proved harder was knowing what to do with her hair. She wrestled it into two plaits and coiled them one over each ear. The effect was without argument the least flattering hairdo she had ever worn, but it was silly to be vain when it would be under a hat anyway. Finding the headgear to hide it was more problematic. What she actually needed was something that could pass as a bonnet. There were any number of cloth caps, bowlers, and top hats, but none of those would do. In the end she took a straw sun hat with a wide brim and tied a broad pink ribbon over the top of it so that it held down the sides, securing it with a bow beneath her chin. Looking in the mirror it was hard not to laugh out loud at her reflection, and yet she was confident she had more or less achieved the look she needed. Having no idea what time of year or what weather she would meet she picked out a woolen wrap that would work as a shawl and a handbag with a brass clasp into which she dropped a drawstring bag containing coins of the right era, a silver-backed mirror which had some value and might work in a trading situation, a box of painkillers, and a small folding knife with a mother-of-pearl handle without any clear idea of what she would do with it beyond perhaps using it to escape from somewhere as it might stand in for a screwdriver or jimmy if necessary.

Xanthe took the clothes upstairs to her room. It was such a relief not to be having to hide everything she was doing from Flora. She didn't want to wake her, as she knew she was struggling to sleep well after the fire, but in the morning she would show her what she had done to prepare for the journey. She hung her outfit up on the back of her bedroom door and then checked the wedding dress next to it. The beautiful lace of the bodice minutely vibrated beneath her fingers. As she climbed into bed the song of the gown grew louder, as if it sensed something was about to happen at last.

After a day of returning the shop to a state good enough to be opened, she felt slightly better about leaving Flora. It would only be for one night, she had promised herself that. She was so much more sure of what she was doing with the found things and the blind house now. This time would be different. This time Flora would know what was happening. This time, Xanthe would be in control. She would let the wedding dress lead her to its story and to Fairfax; she would find out what she could about what he was doing there, what people thought of him, what he was trying to achieve, and, vitally, where his vulnerability lay. She was painfully aware of the fact that she could do little to rid herself of him on this occasion. She would not face him head-on. Not yet. She knew he would be aware of her presence when she arrived in his time. All Spinners were able to detect others when they drew near. She must not allow frustration and anger to get the better of her. She must view this trip as a fact-finding mission, staying only long enough to arm herself with the information she needed to deal with him, and to see how doing so answered the call of the wedding dress.

Then she would come home and she, Flora, and Harley would put their heads together and form a plan. The whole process was much slower than Xanthe would have liked. She wished *Spinners* would show her something more helpful, some way of getting to Fairfax. Some way of removing the threat that he posed to herself, her home, and those she cared about. But however much time she spent poring over it, studying its pages, willing it to reveal something more to her, all she got was the same story of the young Spinner who killed his abuser. And precisely what use that was she was yet to determine.

On the evening of her departure, Harley arrived to collect Flora, who had happily accepted Annie's invitation to supper. Xanthe had thought Flora might resist the idea of being out of the house when her daughter was about to vanish through the portal in the garden, but Flora explained she would find it easier to be with friends and be busy. As her mother finished getting herself ready in her room upstairs, Harley drew Xanthe to one side in the kitchen, his voice low as he spoke to her.

"I confess I'm not happy with what you're doing here, hen. Are you sure you've thought this through properly?"

"We've talked about this, Harley. I know the dangers. I'm ready for them."

"The dangers of your actual time travel, aye, but what of your man Fairfax? He's a nasty piece of work, lass. And he's not above hurting people to get what he wants."

"Yes, I know. It was my home he set fire to, remember?"

"So what do you think you're going to do? Just march up to him and say 'Excuse me, Mr. Time-Spinning Psychopath, would you mind handing over that astrolabe of yours so I know you'll stop messing with the way of things, be a good boy, and leave me in peace? Oh, thank ye kindly!' I can't see that ending well, I'll be honest with you," he said, his bushy brows meeting in a deep frown.

"I'm not going to confront him, not if I can help it. I need to know what he's doing in his own time. That way I can find out what he wants from me."

"You still think it's the book?" he asked, glancing in the direction of the cheerful singing coming from Flora's room. "He risked losing it in that fire. . . ."

"I don't think he meant to kill me, or destroy the shop. Not this time, at least."

"Nothing you're saying right now is making me feel even a wee bit better."

She put her hand on his. "Don't worry about me. Honestly, I'll be careful."

"I'd sleep a whole lot easier in my bed the night if you weren't on your own. I feel pretty useless staying here while you go . . . back there," he gestured toward the blind house.

"Actually, I think I do have someone helping me," she told him.

"Oh? How so?"

"The picture of the ball."

"The one with Funtime Fairfax in it?"

"I've been trying to work out how it got there. I mean, I know it wasn't there before the fire. Mum thinks it was part of Mr. Morris's stock and we missed it but I *know* it wasn't there. We found it, or it found me, exactly when I needed it. When I needed to be sure following the call of the wedding dress was the right thing. It's the most straightforward clue I've been given yet."

"From another Spinner, d'you mean? But how?"

She shook her head. "I'm not going to drive myself crazy trying to work that out. But it does make sense, if you think about it. After all, if Fairfax can watch me from his time, if he can turn up here when it suits him but have his life somewhere else, well, why couldn't another Spinner?"

"A friendly one? Aye, it's a comforting thought, hen. You're right about that."

"There's something else . . ."

"Oh? Should I brace myself here, lassie?"

"You'll be pleased. . . . I've told my mum."

"You have? Everything?"

"Pretty much."

"A good decision, hen. How did she take it?"

"She was amazing. She is amazing, after all. I . . . I haven't told her that you already know, though. I hope it doesn't upset her that I told you first."

"She'll understand," Harley assured her. "It's your safety that's the most important thing to her. She'll get that I was helping you."

Xanthe nodded, wanting to believe he was right. "Here, I want you to have this," she said, dropping a spare key to the shop into his hand. "Just in case you need to, you know, help Mum."

He closed his fingers around it, nodding, as they heard Flora returning.

"Here I am," she called as she stick-stepped her way down the stairs, a fresh application of pink lipstick and a pair of oversized daisy earrings straight out of the sixties making her look younger and more upbeat than Xanthe had seen her in quite a while.

"You look lovely, Mum," she told her, leaning in for a quick kiss and a hug. "Have a great evening."

Flora leaned in for a hug. "I know there's no point in my telling you to be careful, but . . . be careful, OK?"

"I will," she promised.

"You sure you don't want me to stay and help you get ready?"

"I'm better doing it on my own, I think. Staying focused, without goodbyes."

"Fair enough," her mother said with a slightly forced cheerfulness.

"Just be on your guard, Mum. Anything odd, talk to Harley."

He offered Flora his arm. "Away with us, then. Annie'll skin me alive if I get you there late for one of her famous salmon soufflé starters," he said, steering her down the patched stairs, pausing to turn and give Xanthe an enthusiastic thumbs-up.

As soon as they had gone she hurried upstairs to her room, Pie at her heel. Excitement was mounting inside her, her stomach beginning to churn. It was as though she had been waiting for this moment, the moment to time-travel again, for such a long time. The thought of it, the thrill of it, the wonder of it, grew more intense with each occasion. She began her transformation into a nineteenth-century young woman. As she plaited her hair she noticed her hands had started to shake. As if aware of her nervousness, Pie jumped up to sit next to her on the bed, nudging her arm with her long, delicate nose.

"It's OK, pooch. You're going to stay here, safe and sound. Don't worry about me. I've got this. I know what I'm doing," she added, as much to give herself courage as to reassure the somewhat puzzled dog. She succeeded in working her hair into its coils, securing it with an abundance of pins to guard against collapse. She wriggled out of her clothes and into the outfit, trying not to give in to the niggling worry that it wasn't as convincing as she had first thought. After tying the bonnet ribbon she decided against looking in the mirror. This was no time to feel ridiculous. She double-checked the contents of her bag. Satisfied she had everything she needed, she moved to her bedside table and picked up *Spinners*. The thought of being parted from it caused her physical pain. For a moment she held it close to her heart, before wrapping it in a fine shawl and tucking it under a floorboard beneath her bed. Finally, she took the wedding dress down, draping it over her arm, noticing at once the smell of roses. She paused, breathing in the scent.

"OK," she murmured. "I'm on my way."

As she descended the stairs the pitter-patter of small paws alerted her to the fact that the dog was following her again.

"Oh no, you can't come with me, girl. Come on, I'll get you a biscuit." She put her things down and nipped into the kitchen for one of Pie's favorite dog chews and a handful of treats. "Pie?" she called. "Here, look . . ." She showed her the goodies and tempted her into the sitting room and onto the velvet sofa. "There you go," she said, stroking her head and putting the treats in front of her. "You stay here. Flora will be home soon." She waited until Pie was busy chewing and then tiptoed out of the room.

The back door was still propped ajar to help rid the hallway of the smell of smoke. Xanthe slipped out into the cool night, the garden a collection of shadows and soft pools of light where the clouds parted to allow moonbeams to fall. Although the shrubs and flowers were only just showing signs of spring, the sweet smell of roses grew stronger as she carried the dress across the lawn toward the stone shed. Soon she could hear the whispered entreaties of long-lost souls, clamoring to be heard above the high singing of the antique find and the ringing of church bells which were not miles but centuries distant. Unlike on previous occasions, she was prepared for all these things. She expected them. She accepted them as part of the process. She remembered the first time she had discovered the power of the blind house and had experienced the menacing presence of Mistress Merton. She recalled the force with which she had made her return journey after answering the call of the silver chatelaine, when she had been knocked unconscious, bruised and confused, unable to drag herself from the place for several hours. This time she did not feel afraid. She felt determined, focused, able. She knew now that the slight trembling of her hands and the racing of her pulse was not due to fear but excitement. She was a Spinner. This was her calling and her gift. It was what she was meant to do.

She pulled at the handle of the heavy oak door. Winter frosts and rain had seeped into the wood, causing it to swell, so that it took some effort to drag it open. From within came the aroma of damp earth and wet stone. Xanthe held the wedding dress close against her as she stepped inside, allowing the dark interior of the humble building to cloak her, not resisting it but choosing it. She closed her eyes, focusing all her thoughts on the dress, on the vision of the girl she had seen in the gardens of Corsham Hall, willing it to take her to the right place; to a place of safe landing. To where she needed to be. Just as the myriad voices crying out to her rose to maddening levels she felt herself beginning to fall, having the sensation that the ground under her feet was melting away. And as she let herself fall she was aware of a different energy in the space. It was not threatening, nor sad, but possessed of a vigor and spirit that seemed somehow at odds with the more somber mood that usually accompanied her as she traveled back through the centuries. She had no more time to question this curious aspect of her journey as she sped through nothingness, her senses swimming, descending ultimately into the full dark of swift and brief unconsciousness.

As she steadied herself, taking a breath, sensing firm ground beneath her boots once more, Xanthe struggled with the one aspect of time spinning she had yet to gain more accurate control over, namely the location of her arrival. She was still, for the most part, at the mercy of the found thing, it seemed to her. It would always take her to a place of importance for its story, but it would not be entirely of her choosing. As she blinked away the bleariness of unconsciousness, she decided that clues to the ability to determine her arrival point must lie within the pages of the Spinners book and she promised herself that she would discover them. She quickly realized that she was in a small street, an alleyway, roughly paved, narrow, and mercifully empty, given that it was daytime. Her sudden appearance would have been easily spotted by anyone had they been nearby, and extremely difficult to explain. As it was, there were no men or women to terrify with her ghostlike manifestation. What there was, however, was a small black dog with white paws.

"Pie!" Xanthe instinctively shouted the whippet's name, causing it to bound over to her, tail wagging excitedly, apparently having suffered no ill effects during its unexpected spot of time traveling. "My God, what are you doing here?" Even as she formed the question she understood what had happened. The unaccustomed, agitated presence in the blind house now made sense. The dog must have abandoned its treats to follow her, wriggling through the slightly open door to the garden, and running into the stone shed at the last moment. The enormity of what had just happened was hard for her to process. She had taken objects with her back in time on each occasion without difficulty, but the fact that another living thing could travel with her was a revelation. It meant that it wasn't necessary to be a Spinner to make the journey, so long as you were with one, in the blind house, and being called by a found thing that was singing. More pressingly, she knew that Flora would miss the dog as soon as she returned home after her supper with Annie and Harley. She would be frantic. A search would be set up. With mounting frustration, Xanthe saw that she would have to cut her trip short, or at least keep it as short as possible. She silently cursed herself for not making sure the back door of the house was shut. Pie, as if sensing she was in trouble, flattened her ears against her head and gazed up at Xanthe in a way that was hard to resist.

"It's OK," she said with a sigh, stroking the dog gently, "it's not your fault. I should have been more careful. Looks like I'm going to have your invaluable help this time, eh? I can't wait to tell Harley about this!" As she said the words another consequence of Pie having followed her hit home. She could bring someone with her! The dog had suffered no ill effects, so surely it would be safe to bring a human. "Mum!" she murmured to herself, excitement growing at the thought that she could actually show Flora what it was she did. Suddenly Pie's impulsive behavior seemed like less of a nuisance and more of a blessing. Having no lead, she had no choice but to trust to the dog's desire to be with her. She straightened her bonnet and smoothed down her skirts before addressing her unexpected companion. "Come along, then. Stay close, little one. At least there won't be any traffic."

When they emerged from the quiet of the alleyway into the broad, busy street, Xanthe realized the inaccuracy of this statement. It was true, there were no cars of course, but there were carriages of all shapes and sizes, flying up and down the cobbled road without any apparent system, whizzing past elderly pedestrians, and hawkers with hand-carts, and darting small children, and striding businessmen, at dangerous speeds. No one else seemed in the least perturbed by what looked to her to be a highly dangerous situation. Pie was alarmed by the horses and started to bark at them, causing a passing couple to turn and mutter their disapproval. Xanthe scooped up the dog, tucking it under her arm, and set off with a purposeful stride along the edge of the street. She reasoned that if she looked confident and as if she were going about her legitimate business she would appear less suspicious and out of place, even if her clothes were not as perfectly in keeping as she would have wished. As she walked she looked about her, searching for what it was the wedding dress wanted her to notice. On her previous trips she had always arrived within sight of something significant, but that significance had not always been immediately obvious. She had hoped to turn up in the garden of Corsham Hall, but here she was in a small town. It looked familiar and yet not. She reminded herself that if this was indeed the early 1800s there would have been a great deal of changes and new building before her own time, so it was not surprising that it was hard to place. She scoured the street. For most of the length of it there were buildings of pale golden stone on either side, most of which were shops, some were inns, others offices of some sort. Halfway down, the buildings of the far side gave way to railings which first enclosed a small park and then the edge of a churchyard, with the imposing church set back among tall yew trees. The evergreens gave no indications as to the time of year, but the fullness of the blossom on the flowering rhododendrons suggested late spring or early summer. It was certainly quite warm. Xanthe's felted shrug began to make her feel clammy. She slowed her pace a little, breathing in the aroma of warm bread from the bakery, and pausing outside a silversmith to read the name of the proprietor and study the pretty pieces on display. Nothing spoke to her. Nothing seemed connected to the dress. Or to Fairfax. Pie wriggled in her arms as they approached a butchers' shop.

"This is no time for snacking," Xanthe told her. As she glanced at the sausages that were the focus of the dog's attention she saw, reflected in the windowpane, the shop on the opposite side of the street. Its name was reversed, so difficult to read, but what it sold was so beautifully arranged in its bowfronted window it caused her to gasp. Clutching Pie tightly, she turned and dashed across the street, dodging a smart gig pulled by a wild-eyed chestnut horse, and avoiding a cart laden with potatoes. She reached the shop a little breathless and stood gazing at the display. This was clearly a dress shop of great elegance and no doubt expense. There were two mannequins clothed in summer outfits of muslin and cotton and voile, one accessorized with a parasol, the other sporting an elaborate straw bonnet. They were beautiful, exquisitely detailed, and finely worked, but what had caught Xanthe's eye, what now made her smile broadly, was the bolt of fine white organza, partly unrolled, the fabric spilling prettily beneath a small sample of the most delicate, most intricately patterned lace. The exact same lace of the Corsham Hall wedding dress.

She took a step back and looked up at the sign above the shop, tweaking the brim of her bonnet to shield her eyes against the strong sunshine. PINKERTON'S FINE FASHIONS AND HABERDASHERY was inscribed in flowing letters, sophisticated gilding making the words look every bit as important as they sounded. Xanthe pushed the door and went inside.

The interior of the shop more than lived up to the promise of its facade. Tasteful use had been made of the space so that while there was plenty of tempting stock on display, the room felt refined and uncluttered. A broad, high counter of burnished walnut ran across the back of the shop, and behind it a wall of small cupboards, each with brass handles and label plates bearing cursive descriptions of the contents: buttons, tortoiseshell; fasteners, silk; binding, one inch; hooks, small; and so on. The underneath of the counter was glass-fronted and housed a splendid collection of ribbon of all widths, colors, and textures. These had been ordered by hue, so that they presented the whole spectrum of vibrant colors and their more subtle pastel cousins. The left wall was taken up with bolts of fabric lain horizontally on shelving that appeared to slide out when required. The far side of the shop was given over to three more beautifully dressed mannequins. Two wore day summer dresses of muslin of powder blue and palest mint green, one with a full-length open-fronted pelisse as a layer against chills. The third displayed a silk gown that looked suitable for a ball, perhaps for a more mature lady, with a voile insert, or chemisette, which adapted what would otherwise have been a revealing neckline. Beside these exquisite outfits there was a regal blue-and-gilt chaise. Xanthe imagined highborn and wealthy customers sitting there having dresses brought to them, choosing fabric and designs, the cost of which must have been considerable.

"May I be of assistance?" A man's voice, low and soothing, alerted her to the fact that she was not alone. Her improvised bonnet effectively blinkered her, so that she had to turn around to see the chicly dressed figure who had bobbed up from behind the counter. She watched him take in her imperfect ensemble and the dog she was holding and saw his expression harden from one of obsequious welcome to displeasure.

"Good morning to you," she said, attempting to rediscover the patterns of speech that sounded overly formal to her own ears but that she hoped would pass for authentic in the time she was now inhabiting. It was only after she had uttered her greeting that she wondered if it was, in fact, morning. The man did not react so she pressed on. "There was an item in the window which caught my eye. You have a sample of particularly fine lace in your display."

The shop owner's pride in his wares overcame his snobbery so that his face was transformed by a smile of excitement. "Ah yes! The Flemish lace. There is none finer to be found, even in the London establishments. Indeed, they clamor for it, as do all ladies of refinement and good taste. And naturally, since the news that none other than Petronella Wilcox has chosen our lace for her wedding gown... it goes without saying, demand is far outstripping supply."

"The Wilcox family of Corsham Hall?"

"It could be no other."

Xanthe moved closer to the window and leaned toward the lace, listening to the high notes of its song as it sensed her presence. The shopkeeper sprinted from his place behind the counter in a flash, placing himself between her and the fabric as if he feared her touch might somehow contaminate it.

"I must tell you that such workmanship commands a high price." He paused, apparently not wishing to give offense, yet willing to risk it to protect his precious lace and no doubt the superior reputation of his shop. Xanthe evidently did not look like the sort of woman who could afford to buy anything more than a yard of ribbon.

"I would expect nothing less than the best of everything for the Wilcox family," she told him. "Which is of course why the bride-to-be came to Pinkerton's for her wedding dress." As he beamed at the compliment she asked, "Remind me, if you would be so kind, what is the date of the wedding?"

Here his professionalism reasserted itself. "I fear I am not at liberty to divulge details of a client's account. You must surely understand that Pinkerton's prides itself on its unfailing discretion."

"Of course, I merely..."

But he had made his judgment of Xanthe. He held up his hand.

"I believe there are other establishments to be found in Bradford-on-Avon which might be better suited to your . . . requirements," he told her.

"Bradford? This is Bradford-on-Avon?" She could not stop herself asking. She needed to be certain.

The shopkeeper, understandably, viewed Xanthe as if she had taken leave of her senses, for why would she not know where she was? Wordlessly he opened the door and stood holding it open. Clearly, their conversation was at an end.

Xanthe bobbed him a shallow curtsey and hurried outside. She looked at the street anew, trying to see in it buildings that were familiar to her. But she had only ever seen the small town in the seventeenth century. She wished now she had been there in her own time, as it was known for its graceful Georgian houses and streets. And its river. She strode out, heading down the hill, which must surely mean toward the Avon. Two more turns and she could smell the water and then see the bridge. The bridge with the domed blind house, the cruel little jail, built into it. The blind house that had, briefly, held Samuel. Now it was all so clearly the same place she wondered she had not spotted it at once. If she had arrived within sight of that bridge she would have known instantly. It was a reminder of how much building had gone on in the intervening centuries that the little town had grown almost beyond recognition. Pie had become tired of being carried and leapt from her arms, trotting off down the cobbles in the direction of the bridge.

"Pie, wait!" Xanthe ran after her. The sunshine had brought out more people so that she had to utter beg-pardons and excuse-mes as she weaved her way through the couples and families intent on taking in all that Bradford had to offer. Pie came to a halt at the blind house, pushing her nose through the heavy bars of the door, wagging her tail as if responding to someone inside. Xanthe grabbed her collar.

"I can't cope with you running off like that. Here, keep still." She untied the ribbon that was keeping her hat on her head, bending down to secure it to Pie's collar. Unfortunately, the ribbon was a major part of what transformed a modern straw hat into a bonnet, so that it now flapped with its wide brim unfashionably shady and broad. Trying not to dwell on how she looked, Xanthe peered inside the lockup. She was surprised to see that it was in fact empty. She looked at the dog in a new light. Was she too somehow sensitive to things that had gone before? To people who were no longer there? She picked her up again and turned on her heel, eager to see the other building that had played such an important part in her life. There it stood. The pretty chocolate house looked almost completely unchanged. The heavy stone tiles of the swaybacked roof still sat low over the honey-colored walls. The small square windows, two up two down, were slightly more dipped at the top and their frames painted with thick black paint, but otherwise looked as they had done when Xanthe first found the place. There were baskets of flowers on the windowsills and at the wooden and glass front door. She experienced a pang of sadness, and recognized it as a nostalgia, a slight longing, for her friend and mentor, Lydia Flyte. How much she had learned from the old woman. How close she had come to losing her. If it hadn't been for her the Spinners would have been even more of a mystery to Xanthe. And, of course, she would not have learned the very best way to make the perfect hot chocolate, seventeenth-century style. It was then that she noticed the words on the sign hanging above the door and her heart skipped a beat. She kissed Pie's head in celebration.

"Well, girl, looks like you are about to meet someone very special," she said, before walking briskly in the direction of the place that now declared itself to be THE BRIDGE TEAROOMS—PROPRIETOR: MISS LYDIA FLYTE.

{ 8 }

THE ALTERATIONS INSIDE THE BUILDING WERE MORE MARKED. THE SMELL OF TOBACCO smoke and brandy and spiced chocolate had melted away. Breathing in, Xanthe detected only lavender from the floral displays, and cinnamon and lemons from the cakes on offer. Gone was the rustic furniture, the copper pots, plain painted walls, curtain-less windows, and simple decor. The workaday humble interior had been transformed into a place of delicate prettiness and charm. Gaily patterned fabrics were draped at the windows. Fresh white tablecloths covered the small, slender-legged tables. The settles had been replaced with elegant chairs, cushioned with embroidered linen. The fireplaces were still important features, even on a summer's day, making the space warm and aired and dry, but their mantels were no longer simply oak shelves. Instead they now sported carved wooden or marble surrounds, with artfully placed pieces of decorative china, such as chintz plates or graceful figurines. The counter was taller, rebuilt in burnished mahogany, with a spotless glass cabinet set into it the better to display an impressive variety of cakes and pastries, all set upon fine bone china. But the most noticeable difference between the seventeenth-century chocolate house Xanthe had first found and this eighteenth-century tearoom was the ambience. Gone were the men who had patronized the original establishment, and with them the air of secrecy and tension that had flavored their meetings and discussions. Here now were almost exclusively women, mostly from the higher-ranking classes, turned out to be noticed in polite local society, enjoying the company of their friends. No longer was this little building a home to political intrigue and ferment, but instead it seemed to be a respectable place of simple pleasures for well-to-do ladies, where the most dangerous topic of conversation might be barbed gossip.

As striking as these changes were, Xanthe paid them little attention. She scanned the room, taking in the refined women seated at the tables, searching for the person she hoped to see, only half daring to believe that she was right; that Mistress Flyte herself would be the same, unchanged and recognizable. And that she would know Xanthe. There was not time to process all the possible permutations of time spinning that could have brought her friend to this moment, for suddenly there she stood, only a few paces away, as real and full of life and vibrant presence as Xanthe had always known her. For an instant she was not sure the old woman recognized her, for she showed no sign of surprise at her being there. But then she recalled how she had always known when Xanthe was near. Always expected her. As would any Spinner who sensed the close proximity of another. As would, no doubt, Benedict Fairfax.

Before either of them had a chance to speak, a young woman possessed of a bright energy ran toward Xanthe, flapping a linen cloth at Pie, an expression of undisguised disgust on her face.

"Shoo! Out with it! Such animals are not permitted here, no, no, no!" The girl looked to be in her teens, little more than five feet tall, with tight black curls pinned beneath a spotless white cap, her cheeks flushed with exertion and alarm at the sight of the dog.

"Never mind, Polly," Mistress Flyte addressed the waitress. "My good friend will not allow the hound to set its paws upon your clean floor. Is that not so, Miss Westlake?" She smiled at Xanthe now, genuine affection showing on her elegant face.

Xanthe turned to the girl. "Have no fear on that score, Polly. I will keep her well behaved and well away from the cakes. I wish only to talk to your mistress a short moment."

"Come," Mistress Flyte beckoned, "let us step to my rooms and leave Polly to her work." So saying she turned for the stairs and Xanthe followed, the serving girl frowning after her as she went, evidently not entirely trusting the word of this curious stranger with the outlandish hat.

The small sitting room had changed less than the downstairs and it occurred to Xanthe that this was because some of the things it contained had been out of place when she had first seen it. She remembered thinking that certain pieces of furniture, certain decorative items, had looked as if they didn't quite fit, somehow. They had been too fine, too delicate, and too expensive for the era and the level of society which their owner had then inhabited. Now that disconnect made sense. The gentle curve to the legs of the Georgian chairs, fitting at the start of the nineteenth century, had jarred even to her eye in 1605 precisely because they were out of their own time. George the Third would not come to the throne for another century and a half. The style of furniture associated with his reign had not, during the time of the chocolate house, been dreamt of. There were small additions and changes. The colors of the room were lighter, the fabrics more delicate and more expensive. Pale blues replaced the indigos, silk damask replaced the tapestry upholstery on the chairs and chaise. Mistress Flyte sat straight-backed, hands in her lap, on one of the fireside seats, indicating that Xanthe should take the other.

"You may set your companion down here," the old woman told her. "I am fonder of such dogs than is Polly."

As soon as she was free to do so, Pie moved as close to the fire as she could get and curled up into a tight ball for a nap. "It's her first go at time traveling," Xanthe explained. "She wasn't supposed to come with me. I'll have to take her back."

"She will come to no harm, so long as she is with you."

"I didn't realize I could bring, well, somebody who isn't a Spinner with me."

"Keep her close, particularly as you travel home. One not able to spin time may accompany you on your journey, but should they become separated they are cast adrift, unable to control their own direction. They do not spin time, they merely . . . fall through it."

"I'll remember that. My mother will be searching for her."

"Tell me, then, what has brought you here this time?"

"I was called here by a wedding dress, but, beyond that, I came because of Fairfax."

"I thought as much. Indeed, I have been waiting for you."

"He came to my home! To my time! I never imagined he would do that. *Could* do that."

"You yourself traveled forward in time with him. You know a Spinner can do this."

"Yes, but I was helping him then. This he's done on his own, and so far into the future. And to be so specific, to come to my home . . . it must have been a huge risk."

"No doubt he had a purpose."

"To frighten me, I know that much. And he's succeeded."

"Yes."

"He caused a fire in our house. Without being there. At least, not in my time. I don't know how he did it, but I'm certain it was him."

"It is as I feared. Yet again he is using his gift as a Spinner to confuse the order of things; to bend the will of time to his own ends. And you have come in search of him to do what, precisely?"

"Stop him. From ever coming near me or my family again. Which would be easier if I knew what exactly it is he wants from me."

"He has yet to reveal his hand? He was ever a man who held his cards close to his chest. The time of revelation will be of his choosing. And, it is true that at present he is much occupied with other matters.

Yet, evidently, there is something darker that drives him, beyond his more obvious goals."

"He's definitely here, then? This place? This time?" When the old woman nodded Xanthe questioned her further. "Is that why *you* are here? Wait a minute, the picture...the one that showed Fairfax at Corsham Hall, do you know anything about that? Is it you who has been watching over me? I really hope it is because, I have to tell you, it's spooky enough having Fairfax watching me. If there is someone else, even someone who wants to help me, well, I would feel easier knowing who it is."

Mistress Flyte leaned toward the fire and used the shiny brass tongs to place more coals atop the embers. For a moment pungent smoke plumed up the chimney before the vapors ignited and fresh flames danced in the hearth, their shadows playing upon the elderly Spinner's face. As she spoke she continued to gaze into those leaping tongues of fire.

"I traveled as a Spinner a great deal, in my youth. As you know, I no longer answer the call. However, as you will learn, there are advantages to being able to move through the centuries as one pleases, whatever one's aims or desires. Let us merely say that it suits me to be here, at this time. As I knew it would. So long as one is careful to place at least a lifetime's distance between one existence and the next there is no bar to it."

"A lifetime?"

She sat back in her seat, turning to look at her visitor again. "It would not do to be recognized. The child of a contemporary, themselves grown to old age, would be shocked to find someone they had known as a child reappear now younger than they are. Do you see? As to who watches over you, have you not learned? Have you not understood? To be a Spinner is to belong to an ancient order. You are no longer alone, child. For better or worse, the path you tread is well worn with the footprints of others. Some have gone before, some will follow after. Others step beside you."

"That's reassuring. I think. Though to be honest, I have to stop myself thinking about the details of how all this works when I'm actually doing it. I'll save that for when I'm studying the Spinners' stories. Right now I have to save my focus for Fairfax. What is he doing in this time? Why has he chosen it? What is it that he thinks I can give him now that he does not already have?"

"It may be that only Fairfax himself can provide you with answers to these questions. What is more important is that he has overstepped his role as a Spinner and is abusing his talents."

"More important for who?"

"He cannot be allowed to continue."

"Well, we are agreed on that, at least."

"He is in a far better position now than when first you encountered him. He has acquired wealth, I know not how, and now is to set himself up in society by marrying into a family of high regard and good standing."

"The wedding dress is for his bride? No wonder it sang to me so clearly. The dressmaker in the high street said it was to be the wedding of the year, pretty much."

"His allegiance to such a family will establish him as respectable, acceptable, a man of good repute and with allies at the highest level."

"So what does he need from me?"

"You may not have long to wait for the answer to that question. It must surely have been his wish to confront you here, in his time, and you have spun time, it seems, to grant him that wish."

"I couldn't just wait to see what he would do next. Not now he's started attacking my home. I wanted the dress to lead me to him. I hoped it would, though I hadn't guessed the connection."

"'Twould have been better had you faced him at the place of your choosing."

"Don't worry, I've learned my lesson. I'm not about to go rushing in. This trip is to find out what I can, so that I can figure out the best way to get rid of him. The best way to make sure he can't threaten me or anyone close to me again. I need to find what it is he needs so badly that he's bothered to seek me out like this. But I won't just march up to him and confront him. He's not the only one who likes to play things at his own pace, on his own terms."

"You may not have the luxury of choosing the time and place. Do you forget, he will know you are here? He will have detected your arrival. Even now, he might be making his way toward you." She narrowed her eyes, studying her closely. "Can you detect his presence, child? Do you feel his proximity?"

Xanthe focused, listening with her Spinner's acute sense, searching with her mind's eye. She experienced a shadowy vision, a blur of darkness moving toward her. It was not clear, yet it was most definitely a glimpse of the man. "Yes. Yes, I can sense him. He knows I'm here, precisely here."

"It will be hard for you to take one step without his knowledge of it. A Spinner of limited talent he may be, yet he will know of your arrival. Not least because he will be expecting it. Hoping for it. Working toward it."

"So far all I know is I have to get the astrolabe from him, that's a start. And to do that I will need to get close to him."

"You cannot simply invite yourself to his home, take what you want, and expect he will permit you to leave. You cannot face him so alone. You must be cleverer than that, child. Cleverer than your adversary. You cannot afford a misstep of a foolish girl." Her tone was sharper than her customary restrained voice allowed, making Xanthe wonder just how badly Mistress Flyte wanted Fairfax dealt with. She remembered that it was most likely he who had been responsible for her being beaten near to death, so she should not be surprised if the old woman wanted him gone, once and for all.

Xanthe got to her feet, leaning down to loop the hat ribbon back through Pie's collar. "But I'm not alone, am I? You're here," she pointed out with a small smile. "And I'm truly glad about that."

"So, young Spinner, what will you do now?"

"As you say, I need to choose the time and place of facing Fairfax. And I have no wish to bring him to your home. Now I will take this naughty thing home," she said, patting the quickly wide-awake dog's wagging rump. "Equip myself with what I need to gain an introduction to the Wilcox family. If I get to Fairfax via Corsham Hall I won't be alone, and he will be wary of doing anything to me if I have gained the friendship of his bride-to-be."

"And how do you propose doing that? Minstrels are not in such high demand this century as they were upon your last visit."

"Maybe not, but every event worth going to has singing at it."

"Singing by the young ladies of the households, not, alas, by passing strangers."

"Then I'd better make sure my new identity fits the bill, hadn't I?"

Mistress Flyte stood. "I believe you will succeed in that. You have shown yourself to be resourceful. Only do not underestimate your foe," she warned, smoothing the long skirts of her fine linen dress with her elegant hands.

Xanthe noticed that the broken fingers she had herself set for her friend only a few months before had mended well enough, though not as perfectly straight as she would have liked. She felt a pang of remorse that she had not been a better nurse but reminded herself the old woman would almost certainly not have survived her injuries had she not been there to help her. A thought formed itself in her mind, something she wanted further clarification on. If she was ever to properly make sense of her supernatural travels she needed loose ends tied up and people's motives clearly revealed wherever possible. As she reached the door she paused and asked, "That night you were attacked, did you ever discover who it was who beat you so terribly?"

"It was a very long time ago and I was, as you rightly recall, sorely injured."

"I remember you said you'd heard someone calling your name. Someone you recognized?"

"Alas, the blows to my head ruined my memory of that night. We can only assume Fairfax sent a henchman to do his vile work."

This seemed to Xanthe an unsatisfactory answer and gave her the impression Mistress Flyte was not being entirely truthful with her.

"You should not tarry, child." The old woman's face was inscrutable.

"You'll be here when I come back?"

"I will. I am well suited to this time and find Bradford agreeable. Besides, this is where I am needed." She held out a hand. "Until your return, then," she said.

Xanthe took her hand and gently squeezed it, uncertain of the convention but pleased to be able to express her gratitude. Whatever Mistress Flyte was not telling her, she knew she needed the wisdom and experience of the aged Spinner, now more than ever.

"Thank you," she said, and then left quickly, trotting Pie smartly through the tearooms before Polly had the opportunity to protest.

The summer sunshine outside was in stark contrast to the snow she had encountered on her previous visit to the town. She made a mental note to be sure to find summer clothes for her next trip. She would need to up her game where her outfit was concerned, if she was going to pass herself off as a young lady from a good family. Someone the young Wilcox girl could acceptably befriend. She was so busy turning over in her mind the whys and wherefores of her plan that she was barely two strides from Fairfax when she recognized him. They both came to a sharp halt halfway across the bridge, almost exactly level with the blind house. Pie squirmed on the end of her improvised leash, eager to continue their walk. Xanthe looked Fairfax square in the face as he spoke, for once not caring that the eye patch he still wore was a result of what she had done to him. Here was the man who had set fire to her home. She would never feel sorry for him again.

"Good morning to you, Miss Westlake. How well the sunshine suits you."

Xanthe was keenly aware of how many people were out and about. On the one hand she felt safer because they were observed; Fairfax wouldn't try anything where there were so many witnesses. On the other, she was reluctant to use her locket and spin back to her own time. Vanishing in plain sight would definitely cause a stir, and would not help her cause if she was recognized on her return. She played for time, slowly stepping closer to the entrance to the blind house. As she had hoped, Fairfax was both surprised and distracted by the fact that she chose to walk toward him rather than run away.

"Not all of us choose to hide in the shadows, Mr. Fairfax."

He made a small bow, indicating to any who cared to observe them that they were acquaintances exchanging polite pleasantries, nothing more. "I have looked forward to your arrival greatly," he said. "I trust you are now willing to listen to my proposal?"

"Now that you have shown what you are capable of?" She was able to lower her voice as she now stood almost toe-to-toe with the man. "You must think I scare easily," she added, stooping to pick up Pie, tucking the little dog securely under one arm.

In the instant Fairfax formed his answer she made her move. She stepped sideways so that she was suddenly not on the broad paving slabs of the bridge but standing in the entrance to the jail, the iron door helpfully set back just enough to allow her to be obscured from the view of passersby. As she leaned close against the wall, feeling the worn stones warm from the sun against her back, she plucked the gold locket from beneath the neck of her blouse, clasped it firmly in her hand, closed her eyes, and summoned a clear vision of home in her mind. The last thing she heard as she made the leap from one century to another was Fairfax's exasperated curse.

{ 9 }

WHEN XANTHE STEPPED OUT OF HER OWN BLIND HOUSE INTO HER OWN GARDEN SHE was reassured to see it was still dark but cautious about making assumptions. The time-speed differential between her time and the one she traveled to had already shown itself to be variable and irregular. The only factor that remained constant was that time in the past moved more quickly than in the modern day. By that reasoning, as she had spent barely a couple of hours in bygone Bradford, scarcely any time at all should have elapsed at home. She put her bag and the wedding dress in a snug bundle just behind the little stone building and then made her way into the house. The back door was still as she had left it, ajar and unlocked. As she took hold of the doorknob she felt rather than heard a disturbance somewhere above her. Somewhere up on the roof of the house. Instinctively she yelled at Pie, who bounded through the open door ahead of her. Within seconds there came a loud rumble. It was a sound out of place and curious but its origin was definitely above her. She looked up just in time to see the chimney toppling from the roof and falling toward her. She cried out as she leapt across the threshold, flattening herself against the wall in the hallway, a mere heartbeat before a crushing weight of bricks and ancient masonry crashed onto the lawn at the exact spot where she had been standing only moments before. As the noise faded, the dirty plume of dust spread and fell, coating a large area of grass and path. Her heart was pounding. From upstairs came the sound of Pie whining in fear. Beyond the garden wall two car alarms had been set off by the impact. Xanthe felt unable to move. The thought of what would have happened if she hadn't looked up, hadn't taken that swift step forward . . . there was no possibility she could have survived being underneath the ruined chimney. She peered upward, searching for whatever it was that had caused the stack to fall, but even as she did so she knew she would find nothing. She knew what had toppled the chimney at that exact moment. Or rather, she knew *who* had toppled it. She had the sensation of an earwig descending her spine at the realization that yet again, Fairfax was watching her, observing her every move, witnessing all her plans and preparations. She had come within a few short paces of being killed.

She continued cautiously down the hallway and listened. Nothing. The house was in silence, save for the ticking of the ormolu clock in the shop and Pie's whimpering upstairs. Xanthe stepped quickly along the narrow passageway and peered into the shop, the low streetlight sufficiently illuminating the interior to allow her to read the clockface. It showed ten minutes to eight. After negotiating the repaired staircase and settling Pie in the sitting room with a small feed, Xanthe made doubly sure the door to that room was shut. The dog was, understandably, exhausted after its adventures, so that after a token protest of five minutes of squeaking she gave in to fatigue and went to sleep. When Xanthe looked in on her carefully a little later she was sprawled upside down on the sofa, snoring softly.

"Right!" she said, as much to herself as to the lurking, menacing presence of her unseen voyeur. "Enough of this. You think you're the one dictating things here?" she called out to Fairfax. "You think you can scare me into giving you what you want?" She shook her head, anger and determination driving her now. "You said you wouldn't make the mistake of underestimating me again, well, guess what? You just did!" She grabbed an anorak off a peg in the hallway and shrugged it on over her costume before marching through the shop.

Within minutes, she was pushing open the doors of The Feathers. Ignoring the somewhat surprised hellos from the temporary barmaid, she went straight to the door to the apartment on the floor above, took the stairs two at a time, and burst into the kitchen. It was hard to say who, of the three people seated at the table enjoying their supper, was the most surprised to see her. Annie got to her feet at once. Harley froze, a forkful of food held up, mouth agape. Flora breathed her daughter's name in shock. Only then, catching a glimpse of her reflection in the darkened window of the kitchen, did Xanthe realize how she must look. As if it wasn't enough that she was not in London, not singing with a band, and had charged into the room as if being chased, a fine layer of brick dust coated her clothes and face, making her look for all the world like a ghost of herself.

Harley found his voice.

"What the hell, hen?!"

Annie moved toward her, her expression full of concern. "Are you all right? Come and sit down."

Flora started to get up. "Xanthe, love, what on earth has happened? I thought you were . . . what are you doing here? You're covered in . . . what happened?" she repeated.

She went to her mother and put a reassuring hand on her shoulder. "It's OK, I'm fine. Honestly. This is just . . . brick dust."

"What?" Flora remained puzzled.

Annie pulled out a chair. "You look a bit shaken. Why don't you sit down and tell us what's happened?"

When Xanthe shook her head Harley formed a one-word question, "Fairfax?"

"Yes. And, something more. Mum, I need to talk to you. Actually, I need to show you something."

"We were just about to eat. Is it really that urgent?" Flora wanted to know, looking from Harley to Xanthe and back again.

"Well, lassie?" Harley put down his fork at last.

"Mum, I'm really sorry to drag you away from your meal, but I need you to come home with me. Now."

"But Annie's cooked supper. . . ."

Harley put in, "Don't worry about that. We'll do this another day. You should go with Xanthe," he insisted.

Flora noticed the look he gave her daughter. "Annie, I'm so sorry. . . ."

Annie sat down again, replacing the lid on the casserole pot in the middle of the table. "It looks like Xanthe needs you, Flora. Don't worry about supper. We'll do it another time."

"You are so sweet, after all the trouble you've gone to. . . ."

"It's stew, really, it wasn't any trouble. And Harley will happily eat your share."

"Leave it to me." Harley nodded seriously.

Flora got up. "Well, I'm sorry, but I need the loo before we set off. Is that OK with you?"

"Of course it is, Mum. I'm sorry . . . I'll explain everything when we get home."

While Annie helped Flora to negotiate the cluttered hallway that led to the bathroom, Harley spoke to Xanthe in an urgent stage whisper.

"Did you find him, way back when, you know . . . the time you traveled to. Was the bastard lying in wait for ye?"

"No, well, yes, but I had to come back."

"What? Why?"

With a sigh she explained, as quickly as she could. "Pie traveled back with me. She got out of the house and into the blind house just as I was spinning . . . I had to bring her home."

"Wait, she went and came back? No problems?"

"None that I could see. She was a bit tired, but other than that . . ."

"So, you could take someone with you!?"

"Yes!"

"Lassie, this is huge!"

"I know, which is another reason I'm here. I want to show Mum, to take her."

"What, right now?"

"I need her to see, just for a moment. I'll bring her straight back. I have a plan, and I need more things from here for it to work. More money too, really. Luckily, Mistress Flyte will help me. . . ."

"The old woman from before? But . . ."

"I can't explain it all, there isn't time. I've got to go back again, but . . . Harley, Fairfax is still trying to do things now, in my time. At the shop . . . he nearly killed me this time."

"What?!"

"He brought the chimney down. The whole thing. If I hadn't glanced up . . ."

"Christ on a bike!"

"I need to explain more to Mum. I don't want to frighten her, but, oh, Harley, I *want* to show her. Can you understand that?"

"Don't you think she believes you already?"

"Yes, but . . . I need to show her. I want her to feel it, to know what it is I feel. And maybe it will make her take the threat of Fairfax seriously too."

"I should imagine chunks of her house falling into her garden might do that. . . . Look, hen, the man's proving to be more bloody dangerous by the minute. If you're able to take someone with you, why not take Liam?"

"Liam?"

"You know I'd give my left . . . ear to hop through the centuries with you. Nothing would be more fan-bloody-tastic, but that would mean a lot of lies to the woman I love, and I cannae do that. But Liam, he's fancy free, apart from yourself. Take him with you this time. Let him help you. He'd look after you."

"I don't need looking after."

"But why tackle a man like Fairfax on your own when you don't have to? I am not happy about you facing him alone, hen, I'll tell you that now."

"I can't stop him from here, you know that. I'm going to take his astrolabe away from him. Destroy it."

"Oh, and you think he won't be expecting you to do that?"

Voices in the hallway told them the two women were on their way back. Harley gripped Xanthe's shoulder. "Hen, will you not tell Liam?"

"No. It's too much. Too soon. It's not an easy thing to share with someone, you know?"

"It's too damn dangerous to do it on your own."

"Mistress Flyte will help me. And I've thought about how to keep myself safe. I'll be OK. . . ."

"Right," Flora came back into the room, "I'm all yours, love," she said to Xanthe.

As they were leaving Harley tried one last time. Standing close he hissed into her ear, "Promise me you'll at least consider my suggestion."

She squeezed his hand. "OK, I'll think about it. But first, I need to show Mum. OK?"

"Aye, fair enough."

As they stepped out onto the chilly high street Flora paused to brush some of the dust off Xanthe.

"Where did this stuff come from?" she asked.

"I'll explain, but please can we wait until we get home?" As she spoke she was unable to stop herself glancing up and down the street. It was a small gesture, but an anxious one, and it was not lost on her mother. After that they walked the short distance home in tense silence. As they climbed the patched stairway Pie could be heard squeaking and scrabbling.

"Oh, poor little thing, did you miss us?" Flora opened the door to the sitting room.

"Leave her in there, Mum. And leave your coat on. I need you to come outside. I need to show you two things." She nipped into the kitchen and fetched a torch and then led her mother downstairs.

When Xanthe opened the back door she felt the sharpness of the night air and that the temperature had dropped noticeably, threatening a frost. When Flora went to step out into the garden Xanthe stopped her, switching on the torch and pointing its beam on the rubble on the lawn.

"What is that?" Flora asked.

"Our chimney."

"What? But how . . . ?" Instinctively Flora looked up, searching the dark sky for the silhouette of the chimney stack that should have been there but wasn't.

"The dust, the stuff I was covered in," Xanthe explained. "That lot missed me by inches, and only because I sensed something and stepped back."

Flora looked at her again now. Even in the low light of the garden with its borrowed illumination from street lamps beyond the boundary wall, Xanthe could see the shock on her face.

"You could have been killed," her mother whispered, hardly daring to form the words.

"He means business, Mum. That's what I need you to understand. Come on, watch your step, there are broken bricks everywhere."

She led Flora over to the blind house.

"I have to tell you, love, it doesn't look much like a time machine. Just a damp old stone shed."

"Stand here a minute." She stepped over to where she had tucked her bag and took the wedding dress out of it. Immediately it began to set up its song and the fabric felt hot in her cold hands. She showed it to Flora. "This is our ticket, Mum. Are you ready for this?"

"I . . . am not entirely sure what you're asking me to do?"

"If we step in there together, with this, if you hold onto me, I will show you. I'll show you how it works. What I do."

"You mean . . . we'll travel back in time? Together? Right now?" Again she looked skeptically at the blind house. "In that?"

"The blind house doesn't go anywhere. Just us."

"And where . . . *when* will we end up?"

"I don't know the exact date but I'm thinking it's around 1815. I didn't know I could take someone with me, but Pie followed me earlier."

"Pie?"

"Yes, and she was fine. I brought her back and, well, you've seen her. She's OK. I can take you, Mum. I can show you. If you want?"

Flora swallowed hard, processing what she was being told, finally facing the possibility that she might just be about to do the impossible. "Well," she said at last, "I always did like Jane Austen."

Xanthe smiled, yet again impressed by her mother's bravery.

"It'll be OK, Mum. Promise. If that means anything anymore."

Flora threw her a look as she stick-stepped past her through the door of the blind house. "Move to a small town in the country, they said. It'll be a quiet life with no drama, they said. . . ."

Once inside Xanthe switched off the torch. She had not considered how frightening the dark, musty interior might be for her mother. She reminded herself that only she could hear the high notes of the singing wedding dress and the myriad clamoring voices that now called to her. She squeezed Flora's hand, pulling her closer, recalling what Mistress Flyte had said about the risk of a non-Spinner being set adrift while making the journey through time. "Hold on tight to me, Mum, OK? Whatever you hear, whatever you feel, don't let go. That's really important, OK?"

"Will there be flashing lights, or something . . . I don't know what?"

"Nothing really, not for you. You might feel a bit dizzy." As she spoke she felt her mother pressing closer to her, her grip on her hand tightening. The voices only she could hear grew louder as with her free hand she held up the wedding gown, so that some of the tiny pearl buttons on its bodice were caught by a slice of light that fell through the still open door.

"What was that?" Flora asked.

"What? What can you hear, Mum?" She wondered if some of the voices, some of those lost and desperate souls, would be able to make Flora hear them too. Their entreaties were now so loud in her own head she found it hard to make out what her mother was saying to her.

"Outside," Flora explained. "I thought I heard someone call your name."

"It's OK. Just hold my hand," Xanthe repeated as she began to feel the now familiar giddiness that signaled the start of her journey. She was aware of her mother's breath against her cheek as she seemed to fall forward toward her and then the transformation was underway and together they tumbled through time.

{ 10 }

THE FIRST THING THAT STRUCK HER WHEN THEY COMPLETED THEIR JOURNEY WAS THE brightness of the light. So often she had materialized somewhere dark, such as a loft or a cellar hoard house, but this time as her surroundings came into focus she found she was outside, in strong sunshine, in a large walled garden. She was kneeling on the grass, not because of her own unsteadiness, but because of Flora, whose hand she still held, and who was slumped on the ground beside her.

"Mum! Mum?" She was relieved when her mother moaned and then opened her eyes. She slipped an arm around Flora's waist to steady her and help her to her feet. "Come on, up you get. Take it slowly. You're bound to feel a bit woozy."

"My sticks . . . ?"

Xanthe cursed herself for not ensuring the essential crutches had traveled with them. She glanced around to make sure they were unobserved and then spoke gently to her mother.

"Don't worry, you don't need to walk anywhere. We're going straight back. I just need you to look." She helped her mother stand steady and gave her a moment to draw breath. "Take a look, Mum. It's beautiful."

And it was. They could see the upper floors of the great house beyond the wall of the garden. It was definitely Corsham Hall. The place where the wedding dress had found Xanthe. The place where she had had her vision of the pretty, dark-haired girl among the roses.

The place where she would return again very soon, on her next trip, once she had helped her mother understand. Watching Flora take in her surroundings and make sense of them was like watching a child discover its first rainbow. There was so much to process: the fact that they were in an entirely different place to the one where they had stood only moments before, the fact that this pointed to everything her daughter had told her being true; and the sheer loveliness of the exquisite garden beneath the warm summer sun.

At last Flora found her voice. "Xanthe, love, it's all completely wonderful."

"This is where I get to say I told you so." She grinned, elated at finally being able to share the astonishing truth of what she could do, enjoying her mother's obvious delight. "And just in case you were in any doubt about the era, take a look over there." She pointed to the far end of the garden where there was a wrought-iron gate in the wall. Through the gate a stretch of the long, curving driveway to the main house was visible, and along it, at that moment, came an elegant carriage pulled by four smartly turned-out chestnut horses.

Flora gasped at the sight of it. "Look at that! The horses, the coach . . . look at the footman clinging to the back! Oh, I so want to go and see who gets out of it."

"And to do that we would have to run the risk of someone seeing us. No, sorry, Mum. We have to go home now."

"So soon? But that house . . . imagine all the treasures!"

"Here, hold on to me, like before. Don't let go. Not for a second, OK?"

"But, we're not in the blind house. And . . . you don't have the wedding dress. How will it work?"

"I told you, we use the locket you gave me, remember?" She fished it out from under her dress. "Think of home, Mum," she said and then closed her eyes, ignoring the whispers that filled her ears as the magic worked again, carrying them back to their own time and place.

She was not surprised that her mother found the return journey more difficult than the outward one. She knelt beside her on the floor of the blind house, holding her close, whispering reassurances to her, giving her time to adjust and recover. What did surprise her, however, was the sharp light dancing against the dusty stone walls. Surely they had left the sunshine behind and returned to nighttime? There should be no light, save for that borrowed from the street lamps some way off. Confused, she blinked, shielding her eyes against the glare. Her heart lurched as she realized what it was. Torchlight. Someone had stepped into the blind house and picked up her torch. And that someone was still there.

"Hey!" she said, turning her face away. "Can you point that thing somewhere else?"

There was a mumbled apology, which was still sufficient for Xanthe to be able to recognize the speaker as they retrained the beam of light onto the floor.

"Harley?" She peered forward, her eyes recovering their night sight so that she could make out Liam standing next to him.

Beside her, Flora was regaining her wits. "Liam? Harley? Why are there suddenly so many people in our shed?"

Xanthe tried to process what their presence meant.

"How long have you been standing there?" she asked.

"Oh, a wee while," Harley replied.

"How much did you hear?"

"Oh, enough," he said, glancing sideways at a clearly stunned Liam, who at last found his voice.

"No, not enough. Not nearly enough. What the fuck just happened?"

Flora retrieved her sticks from the gritty floor and casually stick-stepped her way past the shocked spectators.

"It's perfectly simple, Liam," she said. "Xanthe and I just did a spot of time traveling."

"And I'm green with envy, hen," Harley put in with a smile, ignoring Liam's open-jawed expression, "I don't mind admitting."

"Xanthe . . . ?" Liam put his hand on her arm.

She turned to Harley. "What are you doing here? You knew what I was going to do, that I was going to show Mum . . ."

"I hoped you'd change your mind about telling Liam. That you'd decide it would be better, safer to have some help."

"Help with what?" Liam wanted to know.

"Wait a minute . . ." Flora frowned. "Harley, you knew about this?"

Xanthe leapt to his defense. "Harley understood about ley lines, about the Spinners . . ."

"Before you told me anything you told him everything?"

Liam was becoming exasperated. "Everything being *what?*"

"But it was you I showed, Mum. You're the one I shared it with. Please tell me you understand," she said, brushing a wayward hair from her mother's eyes.

Flora gave a small sigh. "How can I not, after what we've just done, after where you've just taken me." She smiled then, the connection between them reinforced.

Harley addressed Flora. "You are a lucky woman. I'm jealous as hell, Flora, I don't mind telling ye."

"I'm glad you were able to help Xanthe. I'm glad she wasn't doing it all on her own." As she spoke, Flora teetered, catching hold of Harley's arm to steady herself.

"Mum? Are you feeling OK?"

"Just a little wobbly. A small price to pay for such an experience!"

Liam had had enough. "Right, just stop! OK? None of this is making any sense. The only thing I'm sure of is that everyone else here knows more about what the hell is going on than I do. Will you please tell me, before I lose my mind, where did you just go and how, in the name of all that's bloody sensible, did you go there?"

Xanthe took his hand and stepped toward the entrance. "Come

on, let's go somewhere we're not all standing on each other's toes, shall we?"

"Aye," said Harley, hauling the door open a little wider, "and I for one could do with a drink."

"I'll put the kettle on," Flora promised as she headed back across the lawn.

Harley mumbled something about tea not being quite what he had in mind and Xanthe found herself explaining the bricks and rubble they had to walk around on their way back into the house. She led them into the kitchen, pausing to release Pie, who bounded excitedly from person to person. Five minutes later coats had been slung over the backs of chairs and they were all sitting at the narrow wooden table sipping hot drinks, the fumes from Harley's mug giving away the tot of whiskey he had persuaded Flora to add to his. A slightly stunned silence had descended until Harley said, "Well, lassie, it's your story to tell."

She looked at Liam.

"It's quite a lot to swallow," she said. "And to be honest, I'm not sure how to start."

"OK," he said, glancing at Flora, "let me see if I've understood so far. Harley called me up, said you needed my help, met me at the door of the pub and brought me round here. He was gabbling on about some dangerous bastard . . ."

"Aye, Fairfax," Harley put in.

". . . and about how this guy was the one that started the fire."

Flora nodded. "Xanthe told me what she thinks happened. It's a lot to get your head around, but once you do it sort of makes sense."

Liam went on, "And then Harley starts telling me this guy lived hundreds of years ago, and that's where you have to go to sort him out. At which point I think I might have used some bad language . . ."

"Understandable," said Harley.

". . . but Harley insisted he hadn't been drinking . . ."

"Well, no more than usual," he confirmed.

"... and that the best way for me to believe him was to talk to you. To see the blind house, and to hear about the wedding dress and the time travel directly from you. Only he wasn't completely sure you wanted to tell me."

Xanthe sipped her tea, frowning through the steam at Harley. "I wanted to show Mum. She had ... *has* a right to know. This all affects her directly."

Harley looked sheepish but determined. "I'm sorry I took it upon myself, lassie, but I did it out of concern for your safety. You know that."

"I only wish you'd told us both sooner," said Flora.

Liam spooned more sugar into his tea. "Yes, if it was OK to keep us in the dark about all this ... time traveling—wow, doesn't sound any less crazy when I say it—if it was OK before, why tell us now? I mean, by the sound of it you've been managing without me," he pointed out, a note of hurt to his words.

Xanthe said, "That's exactly what I've been telling Harley. He wanted me to share all this sooner, but I didn't want anyone else taking risks. The found things sing to me; the people who call out for help call to *me*."

"You are the Spinner, lassie."

"A Spinner?" Liam needed clarification

"That's what we are called," Xanthe told him. "We spin through time."

"Logical. I think."

"My point is, it's for me to do," she went on. "Only now ..."

"Now?" Liam waited.

"Now Fairfax is reaching my time, my home. He's threatening not just me but, well, anyone who matters to me. He said as much to my face, just a few short steps away from here, sitting at one of Gerri's tables."

"He was that close?" Liam's expression darkened. "That's when you should have come and got me!"

"He didn't stay long. His position in the modern world is pretty weak, really. I mean, think about it, modern technology, the way everything works, he'd be like an innocent. And I got the impression it was a fleeting visit. Where he's chosen to live—the early eighteen hundreds—from what I've found out he has money there, and some influence."

Flora asked, "And that's the time you think he's causing all this damage to the house? You think he's doing it somehow from there? From then?"

"Somehow, though don't ask me how it all works. Which is why I need to go back to that time, which is when the wedding dress began. It's connected to Fairfax and calling me back to deal with him. Not for my sake, but for the poor girl he's supposed to be marrying."

"OK." Liam rubbed his temples slowly. "Let's say I get the whole time-traveling thing, which you might still be trying to convince me of if I hadn't stood in that stone shed and watched you disappear and reappear . . . let's go with that. And obviously this Fairfax is a . . ."

". . . dangerous bastard," Harley put in.

Liam nodded. "Yeah, that. The fire, the chimney . . . OK, that's a given too, then. And he needs dealing with. What I don't get is, why? Why is he bothering? I mean, he's a time traveler, you say he's pretty well set up in his own time . . . what's he want from you?"

"I think it's the Spinners book," Xanthe explained, daunted at the thought of how much Liam didn't know about. How much she would have to try to help him understand. "It's a book that contains all their wisdom and secrets."

"Aye." Harley's eyes brightened as he spoke of it. "'Tis a wondrous thing! Like an instruction manual for your time traveling, though a wee bit more cryptic."

Xanthe smiled. "Sadly. I wish it was more straightforward."

"Where did it come from?" Liam asked.

"It was here, in with a bunch of old editions of poetry and local history. Part of Mr. Morris's stock. I nearly chucked it out, before I knew what it was."

Flora beamed. "It was waiting for you!"

"It does sort of feel like that."

Liam shrugged. "I'm sure it's great, but, really? Fairfax is going to all this trouble for a book? If he's already time traveling, isn't that enough?"

"Nothing is ever enough for Fairfax," said Xanthe.

Harley was quite indignant. "It's not just any old book, laddie. Make no mistake, this would be powerful hoodoo in the wrong hands. And they don't come much more wrong than yon Fairfax. Assuming, that is, he can read it."

"It's in a foreign language?" Liam was confused.

She put it as simply as she knew how. "You can only see what's in it if you are a Spinner."

"Yes," Flora confirmed, "I've seen it. It only shows me blank pages, but when Xanthe touches it, the stories start to appear! Because it only reveals itself to a Spinner."

"Or sometimes a trusted helper," Harley piped up, unable to hide his glee at this fact, showing as it did how important he had been in helping Xanthe with her tasks.

"So?" Liam shrugged again. "Isn't that exactly what Fairfax is?"

"Yes and no. There are different types. Different levels. For instance, he needs a special object to travel. An astrolabe."

"You're going to tell me what that is, aren't you?"

"It's a device for plotting the movement of planets and stars."

"Your astrological pocket watch, kinda thing," Harley suggested.

"Anyway," Xanthe went on, "I don't think it's what it was made for that really matters. For some reason it works for Fairfax. No other astrolabe will do. Other Spinners, well, we can use lots of different objects, if they call to us. And I come home using something that's precious to me and rooted in my own time," she explained, taking her gold locket out from beneath her dress again and showing it to Liam. "Fairfax has his limitations."

"Though not," Flora pointed out, "when it comes to destroying our home."

Xanthe reached over the table and squeezed her hand. "It'll be OK, Mum. I promise."

"I might be missing something here," Liam went on, "but if there's a chance he wouldn't even be able to use this . . . time traveler's bible . . . why would Fairfax go to all this trouble, presumably risking his own neck when he came here . . . I mean, if he can't see what's written in it . . . ?

". . . he'd need to make sure he had someone with him who could," Harley said.

Liam gave him a sharp look. "He'd need Xanthe?"

For once, nobody spoke. Each was processing the importance of this fact. Each silently coming to realize now the true extent of the danger. At last, Liam voiced their collective fear.

"So if you go back to where he's well established and surrounded by people who would support him, if you try to get this gadget off him, chances are not only will he want to get that book from you, he'll want to keep you there. Forever."

Xanthe shifted uncomfortably in her chair. "He's tried before. I didn't let him."

"He came close, hen," Harley reminded her. "Which is why I'd feel a whole lot better if you took Liam with you when you go back again."

"Wow!" was all Liam could manage to say.

"I agree," said Flora. "If you must confront him, and I can see that you will, please don't do it on your own, Xanthe, love. Not this time."

Harley leaned forward on the table, the weight of his arms causing the wood to creak. "Listen to your mother, lassie. We've seen what this fella can do. Liam can help you."

Flora nodded. "I understand that you have to go, really I do, but . . . not alone."

"I've managed on my own so far," she pointed out, but in truth her resistance to the idea was fading. Pie had traveled with her without suffering any ill effects. It wasn't going to be easy taking Fairfax's beloved astrolabe from him. And seeing Flora's face now, the worry there, wanting to make up for the secrets and deception . . . "OK," she said finally. "Yes, if it'll put your mind at rest, Mum, Liam can come with me."

Liam made a small noise beside her and she realized that she had not actually asked him if he wanted to go with her.

"Oh, Liam, I . . ."

He stood up, taking his shearling coat from the back of his chair. "Xanthe, do you think I could have a word, in private?"

"Of course," she said, following him out of the kitchen and down the stairs. When they got to the back door he pulled it open and invited her to sit next to him on the step, so that they sat, side by side, gazing out at the darkened garden and the shadowy shapes of the ruined chimney on the lawn. There was no frost, but still the night air was cool, and Xanthe was not wearing a jacket. Liam took his sheepskin coat and wrapped it around both their shoulders, gently pulling her closer to him and keeping his arm tight around her waist. She could feel the warmth of him still in the woolen fleece inside the coat. After all the excitement of the evening, all the joy, in fact, of sharing her secret with those who mattered to her, it was good to feel calm for a moment, snug and safe.

"I suppose it's a lot to take in," she said quietly. "Time travel. A murderous stalker."

"Actually, I'm kind of relieved."

"You are?"

"Yeah. Well, you've been quite secretive, on and off, and that gets a person thinking, you know. Wondering. What with trips away, and ex-boyfriends . . ."

"Marcus? I promise you, I'm completely done with him."

"I wanted to think that, of course I did."

"So it's a relief to find out I've been traveling to a distant time and am being pursued by a man who most recently made a large chunk of my house fall off?"

"Well . . . now that you put it like that."

"You don't have to come with me, you know."

"I know. I can stay here and just think about you being trapped in time a couple of hundred years ago with some lunatic."

"I can do this on my own."

"I don't doubt it."

"And it's not as if it's my idea, actually, you coming with me. It'd just make Mum feel better about me going, and I do owe her that, I think."

"I know you're not asking me for you."

"I don't want you to feel pushed into it."

"The way you've been pushed into asking me?" he replied.

She found she had nothing to say to that. For a moment they sat as they were, a distant ambulance siren striking a discordant note in their tense little silence. She felt wearied by having to make difficult choices yet again. How could she be sure Liam would be safe with her? How did she know taking him would even be the right thing to do, assuming he agreed to go at all? Did she have the right to ask him in the first place?

As if sensing her confusion, her doubt, he turned and nuzzled her hair, kissing her ear softly.

Xanthe allowed herself to relax and let her guard down just the smallest bit.

"This is a great jacket," she said. "Super cozy."

"It's nicer with you in it."

"It's a nice place to be."

He paused and then said, "I tell you what wouldn't be nice; you not being here. Not nice at all."

She pulled away a little and turned to study his face. His expression was, for once, serious, and she saw in it such genuine affection that it pulled at her heart.

"You'd have to wear breeches," she told him. "You know that, don't you?"

"And fulfill a lifelong secret ambition," he insisted, hugging her close again.

Harley went home and Flora, still slightly drained from her journey to the past, went to bed. Liam and Xanthe stayed up long into the night making plans for their trip. She found a notebook and they made a careful list of everything they might need. This time there would be no room for mistakes and no possibility of playing things by ear. They would have a meticulously thought-through strategy and stick to it. One of the most important aspects of this was their cover. Two young people could not simply appear with no family, background, or status. If Xanthe was to find her way into the Wilcox family and befriend the bride-to-be in order to get at Fairfax whilst enjoying the safety of that friendship, she would have to be *persona grata*. That meant a plausible background, possible connections, and a reasonable grasp of the etiquette of the day. Xanthe was confident she could behave accordingly, having had to modify her mannerisms and speech and body language when visiting the seventeenth century. She also had a fair grasp of history, learned through growing up in the antiques trade. Liam, on the other hand, had far less knowledge and experience to build on, and precious little time to do anything about it. They decided he would have to affect a taciturn and moody personality, not given to speaking unless absolutely necessary. This in itself would be a stretch. While they continued their plans, Xanthe dragged him into the sitting room and put historical dramas on the TV, hoping that he would pick up some of the cadences of the way people talked and their formal, reserved manners. She also searched the internet for a song or two that was popular at the time, knowing that young ladies were expected to be accomplished. If she and Liam could sing at least something it would be a great help. At last she settled on a song from *The Doctor and the Apothecary* by Storace, who had been a contemporary of Mozart. She printed out the music and lyrics and showed it to Liam.

"'The Sailor's Lullaby'? Really?" He was not convinced.

"Trust me, we don't want anything contentious. Nothing bawdy, nothing maudlin, nothing too moralistic—this is ideal. It's short, so we can both memorize it. And look at the key and the tune. I should be able to sing it well enough, and you can figure it out on whatever keyboard we're faced with."

There was no time to go in search of a keyboard or fetch one of Liam's guitars, so they practiced a cappella until they had a reasonable grasp of the thing. It was nearly two in the morning when Liam called a halt, insisting they get some sleep. There was a lot to do in the morning before they could leave. And a great deal depended on the success of their journey. They needed to be rested. They needed to be at their best.

She knew what she had to do. Since her conversation with Mistress Flyte a plan had begun to take shape in her mind, and the more she thought about it, the more she believed it could work. She would not return to Bradford as some lowly traveling minstrel, who after all would have no place in smart Regency society. Instead, with the help of Mistress Flyte, she would present herself as the daughter of a well-to-do family, newly arrived in the area, who also happened to be a particularly accomplished singer. She would find a way to engineer an encounter with the young Wilcox girl and befriend her. That way she could get close to Fairfax but have the protection of the very family he planned to marry into. To be convincing she would need more clothes and more money. She knew there was not much by way of suitable coins among the shop stock, so she would have to find something to sell. It had to be easily transportable and of obvious value, but could not, of course, have anything about it that made it obvious it had originated in an era after the one she was visiting. To make matters more complicated, it must not be too near the time she was going to or it wouldn't make the journey with her. She was still uncertain how much latitude she had regarding the date of things, but she knew two versions of an object could not exist side by side. She unlocked the glass display cabinet in the corner of the shop and searched for suitable items. There was a nice pair of silver berry spoons, probably late Georgian, so the date was about right. She held them to test the weight. It was good quality silver, hallmarked with an anchor, meaning it had originated in Bristol. She ran her thumb over the indented designs, beautifully worked, depicting small bunches of blackberries and their leaves. It was a start. Further hunting yielded a silver snuff box, quite plain but in good condition, and an eighteen-inch gold chain. The necklace was most likely twentieth century, but the link was an old style known as Byzantine and there was nothing to say when it had been made. It was heavy, and would certainly fetch a good price. With mounting guilt at how much she was taking from the shop, she added a plain gold band and a pretty cameo to her haul. She needed something to put them all in. She took a handful of tissue paper off the walnut desk that served as their counter and wrapped the precious pieces into a secure bundle. Her leather and canvas satchel had served the purpose well for the seventeenth century but would not do now. She cast her eye about the shop, delighted to find a carpetbag with a brass clasp. She had a vague memory of Flora having bought it at an auction a few weeks back.

"You will do very nicely," she told it, undoing the sturdy clip and carefully placing her loot inside. It shut with a reassuring snap, and the plum-and-gold carpet felt both soft and strong. It would not look out of place, and there was room in it for more of her traveling necessities.

Once back in the vintage room she set about putting together a new outfit. Liam was going to get what he could from a costume hire shop, but she would need a change of clothing. She needed one that looked a little finer, but also was better suited to the warm summer weather. She would have to spend a good portion of her money on new clothes when she arrived, which would at least give her the perfect excuse to go back to the dress shop. If the bride's wedding gown—*her* wedding gown—was being made there, it was a good place to have in common with the young woman. Xanthe could only hope the proprietor would regard her more favorably if she had no dog with her this time, and money to spend. With increasing frustration she realized there wasn't much that would look more authentic than the pieces she had already found. She took some strings of fake pearls that should pass as there wouldn't have been such convincing imitations at that time. A chiffon scarf would do as an insert to another low-cut cotton narrow-striped maxi dress in cream and peach, with another silk one cinching the thing in just below the bust. She tried it on and studied her reflection in one of the remaining mirrors. She experienced a brief shudder at the memory of Mistress Merton emerging from her reflection to terrify her. Could that all have happened only a few months ago? So much in her life had changed since then. So much about herself. There was no time to dwell on what she might have done differently. Remembering how important gloves would be, even in hot weather, she rifled through a box of accessories and found two leather pairs, one white and the other pale blue with buttons at the cuffs. As she secured the final items in her bag she decided she would leave her other one behind, transferring everything into the more convincing carpet bag before she entered the blind house. There was one further thing she had at last decided about: She would take *Spinners* with her. She would need it now more than ever. She felt that she had only just begun to understand its workings and to be able to learn from it. The thought of being parted from it was dreadful. It was so much a part of who she was now. She knew there was a risk, taking it to within Fairfax's reach, yet that too seemed to be necessary. If the Spinners book was what he was after—and she was increasingly sure this was the case—better that she draw him closer to her, not send him back to her own time in search of it while she wasn't there. She would take the astrolabe from him and destroy it. Beyond that, she would have to assess the situation and think on her feet.

The following day Liam went to Devises to the costume hire shop they had found on the internet the night before. The plan was that he should get them an outfit each, with some extra bits and pieces for authenticity. Already Xanthe was blessing the fact that she did not have to do everything by herself and in secret anymore. In the kitchen she filled Flora in on the details of the tactics she and Liam had devised. She had scrambled some eggs and set the plates of food on the table as her mother poured strong black coffee.

"Here you go, Mum. Try not to completely smother it in brown sauce." She sat down in the chair opposite and ground black pepper over her breakfast. "You will eat properly while I'm away, won't you? You'll have to break the habits of a lifetime and go to the supermarket. There's not enough in the fridge to last until market day."

"Xanthe, love, I am a grown woman living in a town that exists largely to persuade people to eat. I won't starve in a few days."

"I don't know how long I'll be gone. How long *we'll* be gone. It feels so strange to be able to say that."

"Strange but good," said Flora, gently pushing Pie's paws off her lap and passing the wagging dog a toast crust to nibble. "It's so much better that there will be two of you. He'll be such a help."

"I hope so. It takes a bit of getting used to, being in a different time."

"You don't have to tell me. I felt that and I was only there a few minutes."

"I need him to be less, well, less Liam. He's a bit exuberant for the era."

Flora laughed. "Bet he's never been called that before!"

"We are going to stay at the tearooms and put it about that Mistress Flyte is our aunt. We've come to Bradford-on-Avon to escape the heat and stink of London in the summer. Maybe take the spa waters at Bath."

"I'm surprised Liam agreed to you being brother and sister. Thought he might prefer you pretending to be husband and wife."

"He did suggest it."

"You weren't keen?"

She shook her head as she ate her breakfast, ignoring the questioning expression on her mother's face. "I need to get close to Fairfax's fiancée. It's easier for me to do that as an unmarried woman. We'll have more in common, be in similar circles, wear the same sorts of things. Lots of that changes once you're married. The etiquette is a minefield."

"Oh dear, how will you remember it all? I'm sure I'd get it wrong."

"My tactic has always been to follow the lead of others, watch what they are doing and copy that. And try not to draw attention to myself. Which didn't really work when I was presenting myself as a minstrel," she added, thinking of her performance at the birthday celebrations of

Clara Lovewell. On that occasion, a few months and several centuries earlier, she had used a rousing, bawdy song which had proved hugely popular. It had upped the tempo of the evening, kicking off dancing, which Xanthe narrowly escaped. To be found unable to join in the popular dance of the day would have marked her out as strange indeed, particularly given her cover story of being a player and a minstrel in a theatrical troupe.

"But you're not going to be a singer this time?"

"A well-brought-up young lady from a prosperous family wouldn't be making money doing anything, but . . . and this is the helpful thing really . . . all girls were encouraged to be accomplished. They had to be able to sing, play the piano, paint, do needlework . . ."

"I hope nobody asks you to sew anything," said Flora, feeding Pie another bite of toast.

"It's unlikely. But I can offer to sing. So can Liam, if it comes to it. Or he can accompany me. He's pretty competent on the keyboards, after all. I found a song we can use and we've been practicing it every chance we've had."

Flora was thoughtful for a moment and then said, "I envy you both. Such an adventure."

"You've been so brilliant about all this, Mum. So trusting, after all the times I've lied to you . . . and you believed me when I told you the whole story, I think, even before I took you through the blind house."

"Antiques have been singing to you since you were eight, love. You've been able to tell me things about their history that no one else could have known any other way. Maybe, after all, it's not such a leap for me to make to imagine those same objects drawing you back to their own day and the origins of their story."

Xanthe studied her expression. "I don't want you to spend the time I'm away worrying about me. That's why I didn't tell you sooner."

"My magical daughter? With her trusty sidekick? Why would I worry? Any more toast going? Pie seems to have eaten most of mine."

After their meal Xanthe went downstairs to open the shop and look for a couple more valuables to take in lieu of money. She had been reluctant to take more good stock, but Flora had insisted, saying it was better to have too much than too little, and that she could always bring it back if she didn't need it. As she hunted for suitable pieces she served customers and chatted to browsers, all the while pondering the madness of doing such normal things when she was about to do something so extraordinary. There were one or two early browsers and three customers who bought a set of four flower paintings, a Royal Albert china trio of plate, cup, and saucer, and a small wooden milking stool. When the doorbell rang again Xanthe turned with her professional smile already in place only to find Gerri elbowing her way through the door, a pile of vintage clothes over one arm and her hands full with a tray of chocolate flapjacks.

"Morning!" She kicked the door shut behind her with a perfectly polished Mary Jane shoe, her full 1940s skirt swirling as she did so.

"Gerri, you are a vision. Nailed the vintage look again, new clothes for the shop, and treats. I don't know how you do it."

"My mother always told me I was a hectic child who had to be doing three things at once. I suppose I've never lost the habit."

"Please don't, it's our gain. Here, let me help you with those." Xanthe took the flapjacks and followed Gerri through to the vintage clothes room.

"You've managed to get rid of the smell of smoke," Gerri said, setting down the things she'd brought. "It's really fine in here. It's a wonder there wasn't more damage. Are you any closer to finding out what caused it?"

Xanthe hesitated, then said vaguely, "Oh, they think probably an electrical fault. We're getting someone in to check the wiring out. Wow, that's a lovely jacket you've found there."

"Isn't it?" Gerri held up the garment of soft green silk, beautifully tailored and slim fitting. "It's small, but will look fabulous on the right person. And there's a midi skirt to match, see? Emporio Armani."

"Wherever did you find it?"

"A friend of my mother's is downsizing her house and was having a clear-out. It gave me an idea: Why don't we advertise a sort of wardrobe clearance service?"

"You mean, house clearance but specifically for clothes? D'you think people would go for that?"

"Decluttering is all the rage. People get daunted by the stuff they've collected. Not to mention embarrassed about all the impulse buys they've never worn. If we offer a small payment for the good pieces they'll feel better about the whole thing."

"You might be onto something. Mum could put an ad together for the local paper, maybe some fliers in the shop and on the town notice board."

"Shall we tell her about it over a flapjack? My mum's watching the tea shop for ten minutes for me."

"Actually, I'm a bit pushed for time. Can we talk about it again when I get back?"

"You're going away again? Looks like you'll be moving back to London at this rate, all these gigs."

"What? Oh, no. Just a couple of days up north. Another antiques fair . . ." She trailed off unconvincingly and was relieved to be interrupted by the sound of the doorbell.

She was about to go back into the shop when they heard brisk footsteps and Liam called out, "Xanthe, you there? Wait till you see what I found. The boy done good. Plunging neckline for you and the tightest of tight breeches for me. Oh, hi, Gerri." He stopped in the doorway, costumes held aloft.

Xanthe opened her mouth to say something but Liam beat her to it.

"We're going to a fancy dress party," he blurted out.

"Oh? That's . . . lovely. Xanthe, you're full of surprises today. Is it before or after the antiques fair?"

To which Liam answered "before" and Xanthe answered "after" at exactly the same moment.

Gerri laughed, taking one of her own flapjacks from the tray and shaking her head as she moved toward the door. "Well, well, well. Seems like you two have got lots going on." She grinned, giving them a knowing look. "I'll leave you to it then. See you when you get back," she said with a wave.

"Bye, Gerri, and thanks!" Xanthe called after her.

"Ouch," said Liam as they heard the shop door close.

"Now she thinks we're off on a romantic mini break that involves dressing up," she groaned.

"It was all I could think of. I'm not used to having to lie on the spot like that."

"Welcome to my world," she said, helping herself to a flapjack and biting into it hungrily. "At least I don't have to lie to you and Mum anymore."

"It must have been tough. Never mind. You've got me to help now. And you are going to love the gear I found us."

"Plunging neckline?"

By lunchtime all preparations were in place and there was just one thing Xanthe needed to do before they could leave. Once she had finished packing, she headed for The Feathers. She found Harley in the kitchen. When he saw her he hurried forward.

"Come away upstairs, lassie. They can manage without me for five minutes," he said, ignoring the stern look from Annie that said otherwise.

"No, it's OK. You're in the middle of the lunchtime rush. I just wanted to see you before I left."

"Did you bring me the book to look after? I've been thinking about a safe place to put it ever since you said you'd like me to guard it for you."

"Actually no, I've changed my mind. I'm going to take it with me."

"Are you sure that's wise? If you're right and it's what Fairfax wants, it's a big risk to take it to his very door."

"It is, but I think it's a necessary one. I need it, Harley. I feel . . . uneasy being parted from it. And the times it has shown me most is when I've been back in the past with it. I can study it there more effectively than here. I need its help. And, well, it might just be I can use it to trap Fairfax somehow."

Harley let out a low whistle. "It's up to you, lassie."

"You think it's the wrong thing to do?"

He gave a shrug. "Maybe you should keep it with you. Keep it close. Just promise me you won't let Fairfax get his filthy hands on it."

"I promise. Thanks, Harley. I couldn't do all this without you, you know that?"

"I know nothing of the sort, but I'm happy to play my part, however small."

Xanthe gave him a hug, laughing at the thought of such a bear of a man ever doing anything in a small way. She gave him a quick peck on the cheek and left, feeling that with both Harley and Flora working as the home team while she and Liam were traveling, they were all a little bit safer.

$$\{\ 11\ \}$$

LIAM STOOD IN THE KITCHEN, ARMS AKIMBO, EVIDENTLY DELIGHTED WITH HIS COSTUME.

"Well, what d'you think?" he asked.

"I think it looks like fancy dress because that's what it is."

"Not impressed, then?"

"It'll do until we can buy something better."

"Looks fine to me," he muttered, smoothing down the velvet of his cutaway red jacket. "What's wrong with it?"

"For a start, the color," she told him. "The Napoleonic wars had just finished. People had got beyond celebration into a bit of somber realization that half the country's male population and half its wealth had gone into years of fighting. France and America, according to my intensive googling. Most men wore dark blues, blacks, and browns. Also, that . . . *thing* at your neck."

"My spotty cravat?"

"Should be white. And starched. And your breeches are more eighteenth century than nineteenth, with those bows, dear God."

"I promise you, it was the best Devises had to offer. Does the hat at least meet with your approval?" he asked, briefly raising and repositioning his black hat. It had a deep crown and a narrow brim and was not hugely different from the one Samuel used to wear.

Xanthe tried to reassure him. "Don't worry, we'll get to the dressmakers and tailors as soon as we arrive. We'll stick to our story that our trunk was lost on the journey up from London, so we need new clothes while we are visiting our aunt."

"It's great we've got a place to stay with your friend."

She nodded, trying to ignore the persistent thought that Mistress Flyte was not going to approve of her taking Liam. She'd just have to persuade her it was a sensible idea and hope that, when it came to it, she would support them in their plan.

Flora came into the kitchen and held out a silver chain. "Here, love, take this one too. It's pretty good quality and an easy thing to sell, I should imagine."

"Mum, I already have so much stuff. . . ."

"Just take it," she repeated, closing her daughter's fingers around the cool links.

Xanthe gave Flora a long hug and then quickly pulled away, not wanting to make parting more difficult for either of them. She nodded, smiled, and left the kitchen before either of them had time to get emotional. They both knew this trip back was likely to take some time, though neither knew exactly how long.

Liam paused as he passed Flora, taking a moment to say a few reassuring words, until Xanthe called from the bottom of the stairs, urging him to get a move on.

At the entrance to the blind house they quickly ran through a checklist of everything they needed to have with them. As she held it, she felt the wedding dress tremble and heard its song, high and clear above the whispered entreaties of the souls that called to her from distant times.

She looked at Liam. "Ready?" she asked.

"As I'll ever be," he said.

She took his hand and led him into the darkness.

"Do you know where we're going to end up?" he asked, a slight catch in his voice giving away the nervousness he was otherwise successfully concealing.

"That's the one thing I can't be a hundred percent sure of, but I'm working on it," she told him.

"Reassuring," he muttered.

"Hush now. I need to concentrate. I'm going to try something slightly different."

"Again . . ."

"Liam . . . Here, come closer." She let him encircle her with one arm while she held his other hand, the wedding gown clasped between them, the carpet bag over his shoulder. "Close your eyes," she said, reasoning that he would be more likely to keep quiet and stay focused that way. She ignored the cries and pleas of those who felt her presence in the blind house. She wondered briefly at what point Fairfax would detect her traveling and whether or not he would be able to sense Liam also. As she let the dress pull her she recited the words she had learned from *Spinners*, adding a request that she be taken to Mistress Flyte and none other. Over and over she said the words, softly but firmly, her mind set, her will strong. Moments later the sensation of falling became noticeable. She squeezed Liam's hand and together they plummeted down through the centuries.

Liam was still holding her hand tightly when they found themselves standing on a narrow cobbled street with sharp sunlight affording them no hiding place. Xanthe saw a young couple walking away from them and was thankful for the way love made the pair oblivious to the sudden appearance of two people only a few short strides away. She motioned to Liam to remain silent until the strangers had turned the corner out of sight at the end of the street.

She looked at him then. "Are you OK?" she asked gently. She knew him well enough to be certain he would play down any unfamiliar and disorienting feelings he was experiencing. She also knew how unsettling and alarming time travel could be. Watching people she cared about experience it was new for her, and she felt the responsibility keenly.

"I'm good," he insisted, even though she could detect a slight tremor in his voice and noticed that he was a little unsteady on his feet.

"Take a moment," she said. "You might be a bit . . . dizzy."

He managed an unconvincing but nonetheless brave smile. "You don't say?"

She studied their surroundings. This was not the alleyway she had arrived in on her recent journey, but it was familiar to her. There was something about the curve of the little street, the windowless walls of the backs of the buildings that ran along it, the unevenness of the cobblestones. Suddenly, unexpectedly given the warmth of the day, she saw the scene beneath a light covering of frozen snow. Now she knew it for the place where she had once found Mistress Flyte, beaten near to death and left to perish. Which she would have done, had not Xanthe and Edmund found her. "This way," she said, leading Liam toward an old wooden door that was set into the wall on their right. She had her hand on the latch when it was abruptly pulled open, startling both of them.

Mistress Flyte stood in the doorway. For a moment her elegant early-nineteenth-century attire threw Xanthe, who had just been recalling her dressed for the 1600s. She realized she was staring at her. The old woman frowned.

"I have been waiting for you," she told Xanthe. "I had not, however, been expecting a fellow traveler. Who are you, sir? Miss Westlake, was it your wish to be accompanied?"

"It was. Mistress Flyte, this is Liam."

Liam held out his hand before remembering what he was supposed to be doing. He executed a clumsy bow. "A pleasure to meet you, madam," he said.

"Liam who? What business has he here? How do you know him, that you would trust him with the secrets of a Spinner?"

"For our current purposes," Xanthe told her calmly, "he is Liam Westlake, my brother. And we are both grateful to our aunt for inviting us to escape the unpleasantness of a summer in London by offering to accommodate us for a few weeks here in Bradford," she explained.

"Indeed," said Mistress Flyte. There was a pause in which Xanthe thought that she might just refuse to play the part, and then she stepped back, holding the door open. "Family are, of course, always welcome," she said.

They followed her through the rear yard behind the tearooms, through the back door and the main part of the café, threading their way quickly between the little tables with their white linen covers and colorful china. Xanthe was aware of Liam's astonishment as he took in the real people in their real clothes inhabiting the real nineteenth-century world he now found himself a part of. She knew he would need time to adjust and adapt, but time was not on their side. He would have to learn fast.

Once upstairs, Mistress Flyte rang for Polly and asked her to fetch tea, letting her know that their guests would be staying for a while. Beds would have to be prepared. Liam would take the spare attic bed-room. Xanthe would have the daybed in the sitting room. The maid looked flustered at the thought of so much extra work, so that Xanthe felt compelled to reassure her that she would help and that they would be dining out often. As soon as they were alone and seated, Mistress Flyte began to speak, expressing her concerns with some vigor.

"You have overstepped the bounds of behavior expected of a Spinner," she told her. "Plainly put, it is not for you to decide who might and who might not traverse time. This . . . person . . ." Here she waved a hand dismissively at Liam.

"My good friend," Xanthe put in, noticing the minute reaction from him.

". . . that is of no importance! To trust a non-Spinner with your gift in such a way is ill-advised and quite possibly reckless."

Xanthe was taken aback. She was unaccustomed to Mistress Flyte criticizing her actions and decisions in such a way. She had hoped for support from her friend.

"I disagree," she replied, firmly but calmly. The old woman was silenced by this declaration long enough for Xanthe to put her case. "As a Spinner I am charged with using my gifts to their best advantage. I have tasks I must carry out. I have to use my wits and good sense to do those tasks. In this instance, I must face Fairfax."

"Which you have done on a previous occasion and with success. Alone."

"I was not, actually, alone," she said, remembering how Samuel and his family had risked so much to help her. "Nor was I particularly successful. If I had been, he wouldn't still be threatening me, would he?"

"He has been using his own talents as a Spinner to attempt to achieve his goals. How will an ordinary person be able to confront him and come off unscathed by that encounter?"

"Here, in the time he's chosen to settle, to make his name for himself, to gain that position in society and the influence and security he craves, he has to be seen to be acceptable, respectable, behaving within the laws of the time. He won't be able to actually use his Spinner talents here. Not directly, not to stop us. I need Liam's help to take the astrolabe from him. It will be well guarded, and he will be watching my every move. I might be able to do it on my own, but what if I fail? No one I care about would ever be safe again. I'm not prepared for them to pay the price of my poor judgment. And, aside from that, I won't allow Fairfax to get his hands on *Spinners*."

"He must not have it!"

"Well, we agree on that, at least. It's possible, of course, he won't be able to read it, but I don't want to rely on that, do you?"

Mistress Flyte shook her head. "The risk is too great."

"Exactly. Which is why I have brought someone I trust to help me stop him. And, there's another aspect of him having the Spinners book that makes it more important that he can't get what he wants."

When Mistress Flyte waited for her to continue, Liam spoke up.

"He might need Xanthe to read it for him. He might keep her here just for that. He could threaten her family if she didn't cooperate. She would be his prisoner. I'm not going to let that happen. No way."

"Whilst I applaud your devotion, young man, allow me to harbor doubts that your abilities will match your ambition."

"Xanthe is very important to me, Mistress Flyte. I will do whatever it takes to protect her."

The old woman considered this for a moment. "Yes, I can see that you will. And you are correct, child," she said, turning back to Xanthe, "when you say that Fairfax remains single-minded in his desire to further his own cause regardless of the harm he may cause. He has no respect for the laws and morals which guide and govern a Spinner. After your last visit he came here."

"I worried that he might. I met him on the bridge. I can't imagine he was happy about the way I left."

Mistress Flyte allowed herself a small smile. "He was, shall we say, displeased at being thwarted. He spoke plainly of his intentions, knowing that I would relay his words to you."

"He mentioned the book specifically?"

She nodded. "Have you brought it with you?" she asked, her ordinarily inscrutable expression allowing an iota of anxiety to reveal itself.

Xanthe's hand went to the bag at her shoulder in an instinctively protective gesture. "I have this time. I think I might need it."

"What I still don't get," Liam leant forward on the narrow gilt chair, "is why he wants it so much. I mean, he can do the time traveling thing, as long as he has his astrolabe. Sounds like he's pretty well set up here already, marrying into a good family . . . Why risk going to Xanthe's time? He's really vulnerable there. Why go to all the hassle of trying to get her and the book here, and keep them here . . . what for?"

Mistress Flyte folded her hands neatly in her lap. "The truth of that, young man, is something we have yet to discover. What is clear, however, is that if you are not to be considered a foreigner here—and quite possibly a madman attracting unwelcome attention—you must guard your tongue and attend to your manner."

"I'm sorry, did I just say something rude?"

Xanthe shook her head. "You just don't sound very nineteenth century. We talked about this, remember?"

"OK." He held up his hands in a gesture of submission. "I know, I have to be the mysterious and moody type. All dark stares and grumpy silences."

"Silence will suffice," Mistress Flyte told him. "For there is not time enough to school you. The wedding gown called you here, Xanthe. Its story will play out, and Fairfax's part in it also."

"Do you know when the wedding will be?"

"The date is fixed for the last Saturday of July. Two weeks hence."

Xanthe got to her feet. "In that case," she said, opening the carpet bag and taking out her cache of silver, "we need to go shopping."

Mistress Flyte, unsurprisingly, turned out to be capable of highly effective haggling, so that Xanthe was given a good price for the pieces from the silversmith in the high street. It was strange watching things she had found and bought in her own time in the hands of someone living two centuries earlier. She felt a momentary stab of worry that these things did not belong where they had ended up. That by bringing them here she had somehow upset a delicate balance that was beyond her understanding. As if sensing her concern, Mistress Flyte spoke quickly to her as she took her arm upon leaving the shop.

"It is not for you to question, child. You have answered the call as a Spinner. You are where you are meant to be, at the time you are required to visit. If you stay true to your task you will not do anything that is not already expected of you."

"Thank you. It helps to hear that. Especially from someone who knows what it is to be a Spinner."

The three of them made their way to Pinkerton's. They had earlier decided that Mistress Flyte should present her niece, establishing her bona fides, and then take Liam to the tailors at the other end of the street. The proprietor was delighted to see Mistress Flyte, who had spent good money in his shop over the years. He did his best to mask his surprise at seeing Xanthe again, the businessman in him evidently overcoming any doubts or qualms he might have had the moment she began listing all the items she would need to buy from him.

"The mail coach lost our trunk and even my small valise," she explained. "My poor brother and I have nought but what we wear. We have a busy social program ahead of us and we must be properly attired. It was such a relief when our dear aunt informed us Bradford boasts a very fine dressmaker. Though, hearing how in demand your gowns are, I was concerned you might be too taken up with other customers to help us."

"Fear not, for you have come to the right place, Miss Westlake," he assured her. "Here at Pinkerton's we pride ourselves not only on the quality of our gowns and accessories, but on swift service, catering to the every need of our patrons. We have had the honor of providing many exquisite dresses, chemises, redingotes and spencers for Miss Flyte, as I am sure she will attest . . . we shall be equally honored to meet all the needs of another family member. You say she is sister to your mother? Are the Flytes, then, a large family? A London family, if I have it right?" Mr. Pinkerton was a slender twist of a man, whose beautifully tailored clothes were deliberately understated, presumably so as never to outshine his patrons. His face was not unattractive, but had over years worked itself into the habit of appearing attentive and refined, and the lines of that effort were etched into it. Xanthe thought he was probably in his forties, but he had a dryness and a spareness about him that somehow made him look worn down. She wondered if he secretly loathed spending his days pandering to the whims and fancies of wealthy women. She wondered if he had a wife of his own or was happy to retire to his apartments upstairs and be free of females. He certainly had very little patience to spare for the young shop assistant, Constance, who wordlessly obeyed his every instruction.

Mr. Pinkerton picked up his order ledger from the high counter at the back of the shop. He took a pencil and began writing down the items that would form Xanthe's new wardrobe.

Mistress Flyte ushered Liam, who had successfully remained silent so far, toward the door, calling over her shoulder as she did so. "Cut no corners, Mr. Pinkerton, but be circumspect. My niece's trunk may yet be found, and my sister would not countenance undue spending."

Xanthe shot Liam what she hoped was an encouraging smile as he left. She had been impressed at how quickly he had recovered from the shock of his first stint of time travel. She found that already she was beginning to lose her concern for having brought him, the sense of responsibility lessening, so that instead she felt glad he was with her. Felt supported and reassured by his being there. She became aware Mr. Pinkerton was waiting for her to speak.

"Well now," she said, doing her best to play the part of a young woman excited at the prospect of new clothes, "let me see. I shall need two day dresses, one lighter for warmer days, perhaps a muslin, the other cotton, I think. Have you cotton prints? Yes? Excellent. And a gown for the evening, something elegant and simple."

"May I suggest something from the new French range, direct from Paris?"

"Alas, time is against us, Mr. Pinkerton. I must fall upon those items you have made that might be altered for most of my clothing, certainly the small clothes, chemises, hose, and such like, and the day dresses. Might there be some to suit, do you think?"

"Undoubtedly, Miss Westlake," the dressmaker wrote quickly as he spoke, "and we have some finely stitched shawls to complement your choices. And there are two long coats I am certain will suit very well indeed. And a short spencer, naturally, perhaps in velvet?"

"Lovely. Will I be able to take something with me today, do you think?"

The next half hour was spent in discussing the details of what was needed, with Constance sent back and fore to the stockroom, Mr. Pinkerton scurrying up and down the wooden ladder to the high shelves of fabric, trimmings, and lace, and Xanthe enjoying the surreal experience more and more by the minute. It was decided she would be fitted out with one ensemble from stock, the small alterations being undertaken that very afternoon. She would then return later in the week for a second fitting of the dresses that had to be made, having chosen fabrics in stock, rather than wait for them to be shipped from London or Paris, however desirable those alternatives might be. When the shop owner held out a box of lace for her consideration she experienced a shudder of recognition, for it was the very one that formed the bodice of the wedding dress. She touched it gently, feeling it warm quickly beneath her fingers, its singing picking up at once. It was a powerful reminder of why she was there. Of the fact that, however diverting and pleasant the dress shopping might be, there was a serious reason for it.

"That is a little elaborate for me, I think," she said. "But it is very beautiful. I imagine it is popular."

If Mr. Pinkerton remembered her asking him about it the first time she came to his shop he showed no sign of it. "Indeed, it is the most fashionable and most requested of all our laces, for it has been chosen by none other than Petronella Wilcox for her wedding gown. You are, of course, familiar with the residents of Corsham Hall?"

"Naturally. Though the groom-to-be is not a Bradford man, is that right?"

"Benedict Fairfax, dear me no. He hails from the other side of the county. A queer fellow, if I may venture, but wealthy. They say he has more than ten thousand a year, though no one here knows his family. Indeed, little is known about him at all."

"And yet he is to marry a local beauty from the finest family in the region. Is that not a little . . . strange?"

Mr. Pinkerton seemed about to gossip further but then checked himself, perhaps remembering that although Mistress Flyte was a regular customer, he did not know this strange young woman at all. He could not risk speaking out of turn.

"I am sure Miss Wilcox's father is most happy with the match," was all he would say on the matter, carefully steering the conversation back to dresses and ribbons.

Xanthe knew she had to make as much use of the dress shop as possible for reaching Petronella. It was the thing they had in common. It was, she believed, her best chance of meeting the young woman and forming a quick friendship with her.

"Tell me, has Miss Wilcox completed the fittings for her dress yet? There must be a great deal of work for you to do, to produce something that will surely be the talk of the town for months to come."

But Mr. Pinkerton's tongue was not to be loosened by flattery. Running a tape measure along her arm he said flatly, "A fashion house must guard close the privacy of its patrons. Loyalty is all," he added, as if concerned that he had previously been too forthcoming with his opinions about the betrothal. After recording measurements in his ledger he moved to the counter and opened a larger, leather-bound record. "Let us arrange your appointments for fittings. We can have the dresses ready for you to try tomorrow morning. Shall we say eleven?"

Xanthe interrupted him. "Oh, what charming braid that is."

He looked up from his page. "Braid?"

"That one, up there on the top shelf. Such lovely gold stitching on the blue background. I would very much like to see it."

"But of course," he said, striding on silent shoes to the ladder which he deftly repositioned beneath the appropriate shelf.

As he climbed, Xanthe stepped over to the counter and quickly scanned the pages of the appointments book. The flowing copper-plate handwriting took some deciphering, but then she spotted the name she was looking for. Petronella Wilcox was due in the shop for a fitting the following afternoon.

"The two-inch wide, or the three, Miss Westlake?"

"Oh, the three, I think," she replied with a smile, casually moving back to the center of the room.

Mr. Pinkerton handed her the card of braid. Xanthe fancied he was viewing her with a little suspicion. Had he noticed her studying the appointments?

"Yes, it's very lovely," she said, hoping to distract him with the promise of another sale. "I should like it stitched onto the navy velvet spencer. Would that be possible, do you suppose?"

"But of course. The military look in a jacket is most becoming and highly popular after our country's recent victories. A wise choice, if I may say so. We can see to it at your fitting tomorrow morning."

"Oh," she pretended to stifle a yawn, "I am so very fatigued, I do think later in the day would be a much more sensible time. Might I alter my appointment to, say, two o'clock?"

And so it was settled. Twenty minutes later Xanthe left the shop with a neatly wrapped bundle of clothing and a fitting booked for the next afternoon. One that she would make certain overran so that she would still be at the dressmakers, happily engaged in the harmless occupation of having a garment altered, at the exact time Petronella Wilcox was due to arrive.

"LIAM, YOU ARE NOT SERIOUSLY SUGGESTING YOU GO TO THE PUB!" XANTHE SPOKE IN A stage whisper as they stood at the foot of the stairs in the tearooms. The last of the customers were just finishing their cinnamon cakes and custard pastries. The smell of the delicious treats reminded Xanthe it was a long time since she had had anything to eat.

"It makes sense. The local inn is where all the gossip is. I can buy a few pints of ale, loosen a few tongues. . . . I bet I'll find out more about Fairfax and the Wilcoxes than you could any other way."

"I'm going to meet Petronella at Pinkerton's tomorrow."

"And that's great, but she's not going to tell you sensitive stuff in your first conversation, is she? We need to find out exactly where Fairfax is living, how many staff he has, how well guarded the place is. And what sort of thing he's made his money from, or at least, what he's *telling* everyone he's made it from. If he's got rich through his time travels he's still going to have a legit cover for his wealth, isn't he? And what's his plan once he's married into the Wilcox family?"

"The man is obsessively ambitious. Always has been. Which is why he wants the Spinners book."

"Exactly. So the more we know, the better. Don't worry, I'll watch my words. And anyway, drinkers don't notice details like that so much, not after a few pints. And if they do think I'm odd they won't remember that tomorrow morning, will they?"

"I'm still not convinced it's a good idea. . . ."

"Xanthe, you brought me here to help. Let me do this. Besides, I'm all dressed up with nowhere to go," he pointed out, smoothing down the front of his newly acquired chocolate brown jacket.

His outfit was a huge improvement on the fancy dress it replaced, and there was no denying it suited him. The long jacket fitted perfectly, showing off his lean, strong build, cut away to accentuate his narrow hips. He wore a starched white cravat and black waistcoat with horn buttons. Even the dark brown breeches and long leather boots looked good on him. Although his hair was at last touching his collar it was still unfashionably short hair for the time, but even this did not undo the effect of the whole outfit; he looked convincingly Regency. Xanthe noticed that his new garb seemed to make him stand a little straighter and walk just a little prouder. He had also had a professional shave so that he both looked and smelled like a fine, well-groomed gentleman.

"OK," she said at last. "Just be careful."

"Don't worry about me," he said, turning to leave, placing his neat new hat firmly on his head. It was completely of the moment, its simple shape replacing the tricorn of a decade before, its crisp narrow brim quite flattering, particularly when worn at a slight angle.

"Liam . . ."

"Yes?" He turned back to her, blue eyes sparkling beneath the brim of the hat.

"You look . . . good," she said, reaching out to touch his newly smooth cheek. "Suits you."

"Thanks," he grinned, briefly putting his hand over hers.

She watched him walk confidently through the tearooms, pausing to touch the brim of his hat and make a small bow to those ladies who acknowledged him as he passed. She needed to trust him. He was personable and resourceful. He would be fine.

❋   ❋   ❋

Xanthe's appointment at Pinkerton's the following afternoon passed in a flurry of activity. Mr. Pinkerton himself oversaw the fitting, though it was the seamstress, Betty, who was tasked with the job of pinning and measuring and making minute adjustments to the dress that was to be altered that very day. Betty was a woman in her middle years, whose knees creaked as she knelt to pin a hem or when she rose again to check a cuff. Her spectacles were so thick Xanthe wondered she could see through them at all, and were evidence of many years spent stitching in low light. The working life of a seamstress, however illustrious her clientele, would have been limited by the quality of her vision. Betty's time at Pinkerton's was likely nearing its end. Once again, Xanthe was reminded of the harshness of existence in the past. For all its romance and glamour to those gazing back at it, the truth of living its reality was quite different for most people. While the lives of the upper classes were indeed often luxurious and decadent, nobody would wish to endure the existence of someone at the bottom of the social heap.

"Oh yes, indeed." Mr. Pinkerton was pleased with the results of the alterations and nodded approvingly at the way the skirts of the dress now swept to the floor from the tight gathers below the bust line. "An elegant silhouette, Miss Westlake, and the color suits you well, if I may venture to say so."

Xanthe turned slightly this way and that, enjoying the way the light muslin flowed to follow the movement. The fabric was the palest mint green, with darker green at the bodice and the capped sleeves, where a little deep pink embroidered braid had been sewn in for definition and contrast. It was a small detail but gave the dress more structure and interest. It was a far more girly dress than she would have worn in her own time. Or at least, she might have given it a bit more grit by adding chunky boots or an oversized man's jacket. But in 1815, delicacy, femininity, softness, these were all desirable attributes in a woman. No hint of the masculine would have been allowed, with the exception of, perhaps, a short jacket, beautifully fitted, with military style trimmings as a tribute the country's brave soldiers.

"It's lovely," Xanthe said. "Betty, you have worked wonders in such a short time. I am so grateful."

The seamstress smiled back. "Just a little more taken in at the back, miss, and an inch let down at the hem. This design looks very fine on a tall young lady such as yourself."

The proprietor clapped his hands. "Come, come, Betty. Time races from us and we have yet to fit the redingote. This spell of warm weather may not continue. Miss Westlake will need a long coat should the chill return." As Betty hurried to help Xanthe down from the stool on which she stood and lead her toward the screen at the rear of the fitting room the doorbell in the shop could be heard ringing. For a moment, Xanthe experienced a flashback to her own shop, with its clunky brass doorbell. She wondered how Flora would be coping without her. At least this time she had the comfort of knowing that her mother knew everything now, and that Harley would be watching over her.

Mr. Pinkerton glided out to the shop, where his assistant could be heard greeting the new customers. Betty gasped.

"Dear me, there's Miss Wilcox arrived and us not yet finished. Mr. Pinkerton will be in a fret! We cannot keep her waiting."

"Don't worry, I have plenty of time. Why don't I change into my own clothes and go and wait in the shop while you attend to Miss Wilcox?"

"What? And interrupt your own appointment?"

"I would be happy to browse through the ribbons and shawls. There are so many to choose from and I have new outfits to match. It will be no hardship for me," Xanthe assured her, turning so that Betty could help her out of the dress.

Mr. Pinkerton appeared in the doorway. "Betty, make haste!"

"Miss Westlake wishes to step into the shop a while and select ribbons . . ." Betty was too flustered to explain further, dashing away to hang up the dress.

Xanthe spoke over the top of the screen. "I am happy to take a break. Standing for fittings can be a little tiring. Miss Wilcox is welcome to have her fitting now. I shall resume mine when she has finished."

The proprietor needed no second bidding to take up the idea and was soon ushering his important client into the changing room, just as Xanthe stepped out from behind the screen. The sight of the bride-to-be gave her a jolt of memory so vivid that for a few seconds she forgot what she was supposed to be saying or doing. Here was, as she had expected, the beautiful young woman she had seen in the walled garden of Corsham Hall in her vision. She was every bit as stunning now that she met her, face-to-face. She was slender, with pale, clear skin and wide blue eyes. Her fair hair was elaborately curled and pinned beneath the bonnet she was now removing. On seeing Xanthe she broke into a natural smile that would melt the stoniest of hearts. Xanthe wondered anew what was compelling this lovely creature to marry a man like Benedict Fairfax. Only on looking closer did she register the significant difference between the girl she had seen the first time and the one who stood before her now: There was a deep sadness emanating from her now. The smile, however lovely, masked a sorrow that was palpable. Gone was the girlish laughter that had been so spontaneous and so charming. It was clear to Xanthe, even in that short moment, that Petronella Wilcox was a painfully unhappy girl. The fact that she still managed to be thoughtful and kind was testament to her character.

"But you must have your appointment," she insisted after Xanthe had been introduced and the situation explained. "I cannot be the cause of your having to wait."

"I am here only for everyday things. How much more important is a wedding gown? I should so very much like to see it."

For a second, Petronella's expression faltered, allowing a glimpse of her true feelings. She quickly mustered another polite smile, however. "Then you shall, for it is the very least I can do."

Betty reentered the room, the gown draped over her outstretched arms. Xanthe had to resist putting her hands to her ears, the singing of the lace was so strong. She fought panic at the idea that she would have to flee the room if its call got any louder, but, as if sensing that it now had her attention, the high notes softened to a manageable hum.

She reached out tentatively and touched the pristine fabric. "Oh, it is gorgeous. May I see how it looks on you? I know it will suit you so very well. I would dearly love to see."

"Of course, come, Betty. Miss Westlake, you will need patience aplenty, for there are so many buttons!"

Xanthe sat on a small pink cushioned chair while Petronella went behind the screen. She knew she only had a short time to strike up the sort of connection that would lead to a friendship. She had to hit on something that would cut through the polite small talk that could otherwise swallow up all conversation.

"Will the wedding be held here in Bradford-on-Avon?" she asked.

"Oh no, all the Wilcoxes wed at the chapel at Corsham Hall. Papa has such fond memories of his own wedding there, and with Mama having been lost to us so many years ago, I would not deny him that small pleasure," she said.

"I am sorry to hear your mother is no longer with us. I imagine you will miss her keenly on such an occasion."

"I am accustomed to her absence, and I have fond memories to sustain me. It is harder for my little sister, I believe, for of course Evangeline never knew her mother. And it will be arduous for Papa because he has never stopped loving her. Anyone who has known true love knows it cannot be replaced," she said quietly.

Xanthe bit her bottom lip, thinking hard, hoping to steer the chat onto more cheerful ground. Happily, Petronella did so herself.

"But there," she went on, "we have reason to be cheerful, for it is high summer, and Papa has agreed to my request to hold the wedding breakfast outside. Imagine! He told me, 'Nell, my dearest, how can I refuse my little flower the chance to celebrate her special day among her beloved blooms?' for he knows I am nowhere as happy as I am in my garden."

"I have heard," Xanthe said brightly, "that the gardens at Corsham are delightful. Of course, many large houses have beautiful parks, but I believe your own garden has something a little different . . . ?"

"You have heard of my roses? Ha! Evangeline teases me for spending so much time in the rose garden. I have tried to explain to her how I find their scent and their delicate beauty both soothing and uplifting, but perhaps she is too young to understand."

"As we live in town we have only a small garden," Xanthe said, imagining the little walled space in Marlborough but allowing Petronella to assume she was speaking of a London residence. "No grand parks or topiary for us. My mother and I have planted one or two roses, however, and we do enjoy them."

"Oh, what varieties have you there?"

Knowing very little about gardening Xanthe decided there was no point in attempting to be some sort of expert. "Alas, I know only there is a cheerful yellow one with full and fragrant blooms and another with tiny double pink flowers that scrambles all over the wall."

"How charming! My favorite is an old white rose that was among the first in my garden. The head gardener at Corsham planted it when Papa was a boy and of course he took no interest so the name is lost in time. But what do names matter? It is the joy these flowers bring that makes them memorable."

"I could not agree more." Xanthe took a breath and then plunged in with, "I wonder . . . I don't suppose it would be possible . . . no, I cannot ask."

"What is it? Please tell me."

"I only thought, well, my brother, Liam, and myself, we are here for a few weeks only, visiting our aunt, but even now I miss our little garden. How I would love to spend just a short time among your wonderful roses. Might it be possible, do you think?"

"But it is a splendid idea!"

"You are not too busy? Your schedule too filled, with the wedding to prepare for . . . ?"

"The wedding will happen whether I am ready for it or not. The preparations are mostly left to others, in point of fact. I should be delighted to share my garden with someone who loves flowers as I do. You and your brother both must come. We shall have tea in the garden, so as not to waste a moment. Oh, I feel quite cheered by the thought!" And she looked, just briefly, as if the shadow of sadness had been lifted from her.

Betty emerged from behind the screen. "There you are, Miss Wilcox. All buttoned up. If you would step out and onto the stool I will see to the hem once more, for I fear it does not yet fall as it should. Do you have your silk slippers with you?"

She offered her hand and helped Petronella the few steps across the fitting room floor and onto the stool.

The young woman held out her arms and looked at Xanthe.

"Tell me," she said, the sorrowful note returned to her voice, "will I be a bride to make my father proud?"

"You will be the most beautiful bride in all of Wiltshire," Xanthe assured her, and it was not a difficult promise to make. The gown, even in its unfinished, tacked and pinned state, was every bit as lovely as the bride, and together they were breathtaking. The lace of the bodice was so much brighter than the centuries-old version of it that Xanthe had found. Its every detail stood out crisply. The neckline was modest, quite high, and sweetheart shaped. The long sleeves of the altered Edwardian version were not there. Instead Petronella's pale arms were bare, save for the lace and voile caps. The lengths of the skirt were of

softest silk, so fine that it showed off the bride's slim curves underneath
it. Xanthe wished that the girl could look happier in it, for no amount
of beautiful fabric and exquisite dressmaking could make a bride radi-
ant if she was unhappy. She needed to be certain the visit was fixed, so
she turned the conversation back to the garden. "You will have your
homegrown flowers for the wedding; how lovely that will be," she said.

"Oh, it will be such a solace to me!" Petronella exclaimed. It was
a strange choice of word, given the occasion, but the girl seemed not
to care. Did everyone know she was an unwilling bride, Xanthe wondered? "I am to have lilies of the valley for their fragrance, with sprays
of gypsophila for its delicacy and of course some of my beloved roses."

"I am so looking forward to seeing your garden for myself."

"Then come tomorrow. Oh, say you will! It is looking particularly
fine just now, though too much more of this heat and some of the
more tender plants may begin to wilt. Would two o'clock suit?"

And so it was decided. Xanthe stayed on at Pinkerton's after Petronella had left, so that by the end of the day she had one complete new
outfit, all the small clothes she would need, a matching shawl, various
ribbons, a workaday bonnet, a pair of shoes, and a short spencer jacket.
The redingote and second-day dress would be ready for her by the end
of the week, as would the lovely evening gown and two pairs of gloves.

The following afternoon the Wilcox landau carriage and four arrived at the tearooms to collect Petronella's guests. She had insisted on
sending it, knowing that their aunt had none of her own to lend them.
Liam let out a low whistle at the sight of it.

"Impressive," he muttered, as the immaculately liveried footman
jumped down from his seat on the back of the vehicle and opened the
glazed door for them. Liam helped Xanthe to step up and into the
carriage. She had yet to master the art of elegantly getting about in
her new dress. While the stays were not madly tight, the narrowness

of the skirt and their full length forced her to take small strides and frequently lift the hem. Despite these handicaps, she was delighted with the printed cotton dress Betty and Mr. Pinkerton had chosen and made for her in such a short time. The tiny forget-me-not flowers printed onto a moss green background gave the dress a freshness and prettiness that she loved. She had even forgone her beloved boots for a pair of kitten-heeled shoes, which looked perfectly the part.

The interior of the carriage had plush red padded seats, set facing one another across a spacious footwell. As the door was closed Liam tapped the roof with his cane. "A soft top. I didn't know they had convertibles way back."

Xanthe signaled to him to keep his voice down but the driver had already cracked his whip, sending the horses forward at a smart trot, so that the noise of their ironclad hooves on the street and the rumbling of the wheels meant any conversation inside the landau could not be heard outside.

"It is a beautiful thing," Xanthe said, running her hand over the velvet cushions, peering out through the window that afforded a neatly framed view of the little town as the driver adeptly navigated the cobbled streets. "The Wilcoxes can't be short of money to keep something like this."

"This does feel a bit more special than your average family vehicle," Liam agreed. "Fantastic suspension, can you feel it? I'd have thought anything like this would have been a bone shaker, but it's a pretty smooth ride. Amazing. And it shifts too!" He beamed as they left Bradford and picked up speed along the open road heading west. "Only four horsepower and it's got better acceleration than my MG."

"It's a bit more comfortable than the stagecoach I traveled in when I was here in 1605."

Liam shook his head slowly. "The stuff that comes out of your mouth."

"I know, it all takes a bit of getting used to. But it's real."

"Yup," he said, pushing his hat a little farther back on his head, "and that is what makes me feel more than a little bit crazy."

"It gets easier," she assured him. "Which is when you have to be even more careful. Don't let your guard down. Remember . . ."

"I know, quiet and moody, no chatter, no jokes . . ."

"How did you get on at the inn last night? I heard you come home late."

"They don't seem to have a chucking-out time. Luckily the beer is pretty weak, otherwise I'd have been snoring under a table in there still. Quite the drinkers, the locals round here, and, well, I had to match them."

"Of course."

"But it was worth it. The barman was either busy or cagey; didn't get much out of him. There were a few snooty types who sat at tables and didn't go near the bar, just waited to be waited on and kept themselves to themselves."

"It was like that even a couple of centuries ago. Spies and traitors everywhere, was what people thought. Everyone suspected everyone of either being treasonous or being about to denounce them as treasonous. The chocolate house was one of the few places people felt they could talk freely. Things should be calmer now, though. The wars are over. From what I know, the Prince Regent might be unpopular but he is accepted as ruler."

"He's your party animal, by all accounts. Throws money around, endless balls and fun and more clothes than he can ever wear, and mad vanity building projects. Not popular is right, but I get the feeling people are more interested in just getting their lives and their businesses back on track."

"Wars always hit the poorest hardest."

"Looks like. But, gossip is free, and every pub has its resident talker. In fact, the Rose and Crown Inn has two, and they compete with each other to tell the most scandalous tales."

"Excellent!"

"It was. Though a lot of it wasn't anything to do with what we're here for. I had to sift through a fair amount of tabloid stuff. Remind me to tell you about the lonely farmer and the white donkey when we have a moment."

"Can't wait."

"So, what I learned about Fairfax and the Wilcoxes. First up, despite this awesome, high-spec set of wheels, Mr. Wilcox is practically broke."

"Things are that bad? But they are such an old family, and the estate is huge . . ."

"It's also falling to bits. Partly due to lack of workers, with so many of the men lost to fighting Napoleon, but mainly due to bad investments. Seems Wilcox loves to entertain, hunting parties, shooting, having loads of people to stay . . . and this was all funded by the family wealth, which took a severe hit when the treasury changed taxes and stuff to fund the war. Looks like he was badly advised, put money in the wrong places to try and increase his income, and practically lost the lot."

"So they need a wealthy husband for Petronella, and Fairfax was just waiting right there. How handy. Makes you wonder if he played a part in those ill-fated investments. I wouldn't put it past him."

"It gets worse. Not content, so Bob Darrington told me after his third pint, with marrying into high society and then waiting for his new bride to give him an heir to inherit the family pile, Fairfax gets Corsham Hall as part of Petronella's dowry. Once they are married Mr. Wilcox will hand it over to him. And, just to keep an eye on his soon-to-be new home, I guess, he's currently living in the dower house on the estate."

"That is good news! Now we know where the astrolabe is. And the closer to the Wilcoxes the better, for us, if I can manage to build on this friendship with Petronella. Well done, Liam!"

"Might not be as helpful as you think. Apparently, Fairfax never invites anyone to his home, is fiercely protective of his privacy when he's there, and keeps three burly footmen who look like they were chosen for their size and their handiness with their fists."

"Damn."

"Fairfax does have a bit of a reputation as an oddball around here. He's from off, and no one has ever heard of his family. All they know is he has a lot of money."

"Which will buy you status, if you know who's selling."

"Like Mr. Wilcox."

"Like Mr. Wilcox."

"Comes to something, when you have to sell your daughter."

"It wasn't uncommon. Making a good marriage was sometimes all a young woman could hope to do to restore the family fortune. She couldn't inherit anything herself. She couldn't earn any money. With no brothers to inherit the estate, it would have gone to some distant relative anyway once her father died."

"Well, I don't believe any half-decent father would marry his daughter off to a man like Fairfax if he knew what he was really like. At least we can tell him, warn them."

"It's not that simple," Xanthe explained. "If they were to call off the wedding, what would they do? The money's got to come from somewhere. She has to marry someone."

As the reality of the poor girl's situation hit home, they continued their journey in silence for a while. Xanthe held on to a tiny hope that somehow she would be able to find a way to help Petronella beyond ridding her of Fairfax.

"Wow," said Liam a moment later, leaning close to the window to lower it and get a better view. "That is some house."

Corsham Hall, revealing itself in glimpses as they sped along the avenue of lime trees, did indeed look impressive under the warm summer sunshine. The grand Georgian facade, with its handsome classical proportions, clean lines, and generous windows, looked very much to

Xanthe as it had when she had attended the sale there. The trees along
the driveway were smaller with no gaps in their number, having not
yet weathered so many storms. There were, of course, no electricity
wires or cables to interest the view, and no cars. Instead the parkland
was dotted with sheep, the gravel approach bordered with low box
hedge and some splendid topiary, and the sweep leading on toward
the east side of the house where the stables were. The driver pulled
the puffing horses to a halt outside the front entrance and the footman jumped down from his perch to open the carriage door. Xanthe
and Liam had barely stepped down when a maid in spotless apron
and mob cap scurried out from the front of the house and nimbly
descended the broad steps. She bobbed a curtsey to the guests.

"If you please, miss, sir—Miss Wilcox asked that you be brought
to the garden directly." With that she turned for the side of the house.
They followed, Liam twisting this way and that to try to take in the
house and grounds as the maid led them quickly through the formal
parterre and across to the iron gate that opened into the huge walled
garden. Xanthe felt a pang at the memory of bringing Flora to this very
place, and of watching the wonder on her face as she had taken it all
in. Although she still worried about what Fairfax might do in her own
time, she felt so much better now that her mother knew where she was
and why. As the maid let them through the gate they were spotted by
Petronella, who at once put down her trug and hurried to greet them.

"Miss Westlake! How happy I am you are here. Come, Evangeline!" she called to the slender girl who at that moment was enjoying
the swing seat beneath an arbor of white roses. Her sister looked to
be about twelve years old, with delicate features, lighter hair than her
sibling, and abundant energy.

Xanthe bobbed a slow curtsey and Liam managed a good bow,
remembering to remove his hat. "Thank you for inviting us," she said.
"This is my brother, Liam."

"Miss Wilcox." He succeeded in looking quite somber until Evangeline leapt off the swing with a giggle and came running over. Her glee was infectious and Xanthe watched as he smiled broadly, took her hand, and kissed it lightly, executing another impressive bow as he did so. "Miss Evangeline, I believe. Delighted to make your acquaintance," he said carefully.

Petronella reached out and straightened the sash on her sister's dress, the bow of which had become crooked. "Evangeline shares my passion for the garden," she said, "though less for love of flowers, and more for the opportunity to run wild."

"I am pleased to meet you, Mr. Westlake, Miss Westlake, and I am not such an unrefined creature as my sister would have you believe," she insisted, performing a wobbly curtsey with a determinedly straight face, which she only maintained long enough to make Petronella smile, before falling into giggles again.

"Fortunately," Petronella said, "we do not stand on ceremony here at Corsham. Without the civilizing influence of a mother all these years we are shockingly casual in our habits, and Father has always encouraged us in activities that take us outside the house. He was disappointed not to have boys, d'you see?"

Liam shook his head. "I do not believe any father could possibly be disappointed with two such delightful daughters," he said.

If Xanthe could have nudged him without being noticed she would have done so, hoping to remind him to keep quiet whenever possible, rather than venturing into the risky business of paying compliments. It was already becoming clear that their plan for him to be the moody, mysterious type was never going to work. His efforts were well received, however. Evangeline looked at him closely.

"What uncommon hair you have," she said.

"Evangeline!" Petronella hissed at her.

Liam lifted his hat again and gave a shrug. "I confess I am not much bothered about my hair," he said, adding, "there are so many better things to be doing, don't you agree?"

"Oh yes!" Evangeline nodded. "I swear I would sooner cut all my hair off, it is such a nuisance with rags to be tied in at night and pins to tame it by day. How much easier it would be to climb a tree or scramble down a riverbank free from the fuss of ringlets and coils."

"Do you often climb trees?" Xanthe asked.

"Only when Petronella is not looking," she replied.

Her sister corrected her, "Rather, when you think me distracted. I always know what you are about, Evie, you cannot have it otherwise."

Evangeline frowned a little. "Then you will know I have set up the pall-mall on the far side of the delphinium beds. Let us play before tea!"

"Our guests have just this minute arrived. . . ."

"And will be stiff from sitting in the carriage and in need of activity if they are to enjoy their cake and sandwiches. Mr. Westlake, you will have a game, won't you?"

Liam opened his mouth and closed it again, uncertain as to what was being asked of him. He shot Xanthe a look, brows raised.

Xanthe scanned the garden for clues and was thankful to glimpse two croquet mallets propped up against a far wall.

"My brother would be happy to play. He thinks himself quite the expert," she leaned closer to Evangeline and whispered, "only he has a shameless disregard for the rules, so see he does not cheat!"

"Indeed he will not!" Evangeline laughed, taking him by the hand and leading him at the run toward the flat piece of grass beyond the flower bed.

Liam looked back at Xanthe with an expression of mild panic but she was reasonably confident he would do a good job of keeping Evangeline occupied while she talked to Petronella.

"There," Petronella took Xanthe's arm, "my sister is happy and I have you to myself. Come, I have so looked forward to showing you the roses. Now, you must not mind that some are not at their best. July is a hard month for them, with the spring and early summer varieties over and the August blooms not yet come. But here, my favorites are lovely still, see?"

"Oh, yes, these are beautiful." She touched the nearest flower, a blowsy white rose with the most delicious scent. "You will have plenty to choose from for your wedding," she said, watching closely for the girl's reaction to mention of her upcoming nuptials.

Petronella gave little away. "They must not be picked a moment sooner than is necessary or they will wilt terribly in this heat," was all she said.

Xanthe tried again. "Such an exciting day. Your father must be very proud; I hear your fiancé has a fair fortune," she said, fighting against the modern British reserve that made her uncomfortable even mentioning money, particularly when linked to the choice of a husband. She told herself these were different times. To be marrying to secure the future of the family was a thing to be applauded, an achievement, not a reason for sadness or embarrassment.

Petronella turned away from the roses for a moment to watch her sister, her face showing a mixture of love and sadness. "We do what we can for those who rely upon us. It is a simple matter, when the way forward is so clear," she said.

Xanthe asked as gently as she could, "Forgive me, but you are a young woman, do you not yearn for love?"

Petronella turned back to her roses. Even in profile, Xanthe was able now to detect the sorrow in her expression. "Believe me when I tell you I have known great love, Miss Westlake. I was engaged, you see, to Edward Steerwell. He was an officer in the King's Lancers, which is a noble and wonderful thing to be. Alas, in time of war, it is also a perilous occupation, and one he did not survive."

"I'm . . . so very sorry."

"Do not pity me. I have known love, which is more than many can say, it is not?" She looked at Xanthe then, the composed, stoic smile back in place.

Xanthe was thrown by this admission of heartbreak and at a loss for a reply. She was still trying to find the right words when the sound of fast-moving horses interrupted the moment. The others heard it too. Evangeline broke off her game and ran to the second gate in the far wall, Liam following on. Petronella muttered a small sound of disappointment under her breath but then recovered herself.

"Here is Father and his party home from their ride, and sooner than expected. He will be pleased to meet you both. Though, I confess I am disappointed not to have more time with you, Miss Westlake. I should so like to know you better."

"Please, call me Xanthe."

"I shall!" she said, taking her hand. "And you must call me Nell, for it is my family name, and I feel we will be firm friends, you and I. Come, let us meet the men before they take it into their hot heads to bring the horses into my garden!"

As they stepped through the gate and onto the expanse of lawn they had a clear view of the park as it flowed away from the house, and three riders approaching at speed. The horses' flanks were foam flecked and their necks glistened with sweat from fast riding on a warm day. The front rider of the trio was an older man whom Xanthe took to be Mr. Wilcox. He carried a little more weight than was healthy and his complexion betrayed a love of port wine and good food, but he looked vigorous and strong. The second man rode a showy black horse which still fought for its head even after a long ride. The man appeared completely untroubled by his mount's antics, looking as at ease in the saddle as if he had been born there. The third member of the party was not such a natural horseman yet exuded an air of confidence and seriousness, and even at a hundred paces his demeanor and his eye patch meant Xanthe was able to recognize him at once.

⟨ 13 ⟩

"FATHER!" EVANGELINE RAN TO GREET THE RIDERS, MAKING A FUSS OF HER FATHER'S horse, not in the least concerned about getting her hands or dress dirty. Xanthe could tell she was a child who longed to be active, outdoors, and generally engaging in things that were considered unseemly for a young lady. She did not envy her the constraints of her life. "We have this moment begun a game of pall-mall; say you will join us."

"Let us at least dismount before you pester us, child. Nell, can you not teach your sister patience?"

"I fear she has not the capacity for it. Much like her father." Petronella smiled.

"Ha! As ever, I am to blame, I see." He lowered himself somewhat heavily from his horse as grooms appeared, hurrying from the direction of the stables. "Yet, I know my daughter has manners enough to introduce our visitors," he said, looking first at Liam and then at Xanthe.

"Father, this is Mr. Liam Westlake and his sister, Miss Xanthe Westlake. Mr. Westlake plays pall-mall very well, but not so well as to be able to beat me."

"I would not dare," Liam said, bowing. "I am pleased to meet you, Mr. Wilcox."

"Hmm, Westlake, you say?"

Xanthe stepped forward. "We are staying with our aunt, Miss Lydia Flyte, in Bradford."

Petronella took her father's arm. "I found Miss Westlake at Pinkerton's. We fell to conversation over a fitting and have become friends already."

"What? More dresses?"

"Only my wedding gown, Father," she said, glancing at Fairfax, who took the opportunity to present himself.

"I am delighted to make the acquaintance of a new friend of my fiancée's. Benedict Fairfax," he said, smiling, taking Xanthe's hand and bowing over it before gracing Liam with a nod of his head. Xanthe felt Liam tense as he stepped closer to her. "How pleasant to see brother and sister traveling together," Fairfax commented.

"I am happy to be at Xanthe's side," Liam said flatly. "She no longer need face any difficulties alone."

Mr. Wilcox, for all his appearance of a man unbothered by petty quarrels or the subtler details of etiquette, was astute enough to pick up something in this exchange that was surprising. He looked closely at Liam then. If he had been about to question him on his background the moment passed as his second riding companion swung his leg over his horse's withers, jumped down, and all but bounded forward to greet the newcomers effusively. He was tall, red haired, and flamboyant in both dress and manner.

"Henry Anstruther, at your service, Mr. Westlake, Miss Westlake. A fast ride through excellent parkland and now charming company. I tell you, Wilcox, you keep a fine house and live a fine life here. Capital!" he exclaimed, slapping his friend heartily on the back.

Evangeline giggled. "Henry is a Corinthian!" she exclaimed. When both Xanthe and Liam looked blank she went on, delighted to be in possession of knowledge they were unaware of. "Oh, you surely have heard of the Corinthians! Father would be one himself, of course, but he is too old."

"Evie!" Petronella tutted at her little sister but Henry was enjoying the joke.

"We've made your father an honorary member of our society, Miss Evie. Why, he can ride, shoot, hunt, and fish better than any man I know. And that's what we Corinthians are all about, don't ya know?"

Mr. Wilcox turned to Liam. "And you, sir, do you ride to hounds? Do you call yourself a passable shot?"

Fairfax put in, "I think Miss Wilcox's new friends are of the city, not given to country pursuits. Do I have it right, Miss Westlake?" he asked, giving Liam a disdainful look and happy to take the chance to put him down in his host's opinion.

Xanthe resisted snapping at him. She knew what he was trying to do, but she had to be cautious. She couldn't make claims for Liam he might fail to live up to. Liam, however, was quite capable of standing up for himself.

"I love to ride, though I don't get much chance for it in London. And yes, I can shoot well enough, though I prefer a rifle to a shotgun."

Xanthe stared at him.

"Capital!" declared Henry. "We shall find a gun for you, shall we not, Wilcox?"

"Certainly, Henry, but after taking tea. I see Petronella has a table prepared in the garden, and I know better than to disrupt my daughter's arrangements when they involve her beloved roses. Come, Fairfax, you will stay awhile longer for a little refreshment. And then we will fix a time for shooting, Henry. Fear not, I shall not ask you to sit still all afternoon."

As he spoke the grooms led the horses away and maids and footmen appeared from the house bearing more trays of food and tea. There were in fact two tables set beneath an apple tree in the corner of the walled garden. More chairs were hastily fetched and all accommodations made for the expanded party. On their way to the tables, Fairfax dropped into step beside Xanthe, touching her arm to signal she should slow her pace so that he could speak privately with her. While she recoiled at his touch and hated the thought of doing anything he might consider agreeable, Xanthe had come there to deal with the man once and for all. Better to make her position clear as soon as possible.

"Tell me," he whispered, "have you brought the book with you?"

"So, finally we have it. It is *Spinners* you want."

"It is here? You have brought it?"

"I have brought it with me, but for my use only. To help me do what I have come to do."

"You have only to give it to me and your troubles will be at an end. I will have no further interest in you, or your home."

"I'm here to put an end to your abuse of your Spinner's gifts, not to add to them. And don't think you can frighten me with your threats any longer. You've pushed me too far, Fairfax."

"If you imagine bringing your beau with you will make any difference you are seriously underestimating my determination. I will have that book."

"Do you really think it will reveal its secrets to you? If you understood half of what *Spinners* is you would know it is not to be misused. It will not be. You will never have it!"

"Xanthe," Petronella called to her, "do sit by me. I will not let these men rob me of my time with you. After all, you are my guest. Let them speak to each other of dangerous gallops and struggling fish and fallen deer. Such things will not add flavor to our tea, I think. Come, take this seat," she insisted, patting the cushion beside her.

Liam sat on Xanthe's left and as he did so she whispered urgently to him. "For heaven's sake don't talk yourself into going hunting with them!"

"Calm down, it's not hunting season yet. And anyway, I can ride. Quite well, as it happens. And I'm not a bad shot, either," he whispered back.

"How did I not know that about you?" she asked, looking at him slightly incredulously.

"Summers spent pony trekking in Wales as a child, and rifle-range shooting with my dad when he retired," he explained before turning to accept the offer of milk and sugar in his tea.

There was delicious food on offer, and both Xanthe and Liam made the most of it. They were aware that Mistress Flyte, though happy to help them, could hardly spare Polly to cater for their needs all the time when she was needed in the tea shop. At Corsham, however difficult the truth of the family finances might be, entertainments were evidently always on a lavish scale. There was strong Indian tea served in beautiful china, the pots topped up from heavy silver water jugs with hinged lids. The teacups and plates were pale blue with a delicate fluting to the edges, set off by a slender line of gold. Cake stands and platters offered a variety of savory and sweet temptations. There were small cakes, or dainties, smothered with fondant icing; thin slices of cold ham, beef, and venison; pastries of all shapes, some filled with lemon cream, others with salmon mousse. A huge plate of glazed fruits shone like jewels, and another platter supported a tower of snowy white meringues. That this had been a simple tea in the garden for four people, now stretched without difficulty to feed seven, spoke to a life of excess and expense. It seemed the information Liam had gleaned in the tavern regarding Mr. Wilcox's lifestyle was not merely baseless gossip after all.

Petronella poured more tea for her father, who had drained his first cup before settling in his seat. "Xanthe shares my love of roses, Father. It is delightful to find a friend with whom I can share my passion. She had suggestions for my wedding bouquet."

"I am indebted to you, Miss Westlake. My daughter feels the absence of her mother keenly at this time, as any bride-to-be would."

"I'm happy to help in any way I can," she told him. "I am without acquaintances here in Wiltshire, so it is a pleasure for me to have company too. My aunt is quite taken up with the tearooms, alas, so does not have much time to spend with us."

"Then you must come here as often as you can," Petronella said.

Henry spoke through a mouthful of cake. "Wilcox's hospitality is quite legendary, don't you know? No guest of his will ever go hungry, thirst for wine, nor spend a dull minute at Corsham Hall, I guarantee it," he insisted, enforcing the point with a wave of a freshly selected pastry. "Even out of hunting season there are coneys to shoot in the woods hereabouts."

Evangeline bounced on her seat. "Why do they not come and stay? Oh, Father, say they can! It is so long since we have had any guests to entertain us, aside from Henry, but he doesn't really count . . ."

Henry gave a squawk.

". . . only because we know you so very well and you are here so often we think of you quite as a member of our family," Evangeline hurried on. "Petronella, is it not the best idea? Then Miss Wilcox can assist you with preparations for the wedding, and Mr. Wilcox can improve his game of pall-mall when he is not taken off for shooting and riding!"

Fairfax leaned a little across the table to address his fiancée. "My dear, whilst it is a charming idea, might it in fact be a . . . distraction, to have guests so close to the wedding, rather than being helpful? You are your father's daughter, indeed, so I know you will wish to be the finest of hosts. And yet, while there are such demands on your time . . . ?"

"Nonsense!" put in Wilcox. "Never let it be said there was not room at Corsham for friends, old or new. There's space aplenty, and we share what we have. Petronella will benefit greatly from the company of a woman at this important time, of that I have no doubt."

Petronella turned to Xanthe. "Can your aunt spare you, do you suppose?"

"Oh, I'm certain she will be very happy with the new arrangements. We would be delighted to accept your kind offer, wouldn't we, Liam?"

"We would indeed. How very generous," Liam agreed.

"Capital!" declared Henry.

And so it was decided. Xanthe and Petronella would take the carriage into Bradford for another fitting at Pinkerton's, after which they would call upon Miss Flyte, explain the change in plans, and collect what few belongings the Westlakes had brought with them. Liam was to accompany the men on an hour's shooting, once they had found him a gun and suitable boots.

Evangeline had complained that she was not included, so it was decided she should go on the Bradford trip. In addition, Xanthe promised that at the very first opportunity, she and Liam would help her practice the song she was preparing to sing at her sister's wedding.

It was nearly seven o'clock when Xanthe and Liam saw each other again. They had returned to the house after their excursions and activities and each been shown to their rooms so that they might change for the evening. Xanthe answered a knock on her door and found Liam, dressed in more formal dinner clothes, his cravat in his hand.

"For God's sake help me with this," he begged as he stepped inside. "I had a valet dressing me but he got called away to do something else. The one from the costume hire was sort of sewn into shape. You got any idea how to tie one from scratch?"

"Come here, let me have a go." She took it from him. "Sit on that stool so I can reach," she said, directing him to the little dressing table by the window.

"Wow," he said as he sat down, "I thought my room was grand but yours is even more amazing. Difficult to believe the Wilcoxes are short of money."

"A beautiful house is one thing, having the funds to keep it going is another. But yes, it is a gorgeous room. Look at that bed, for a start. Can you imagine what that would fetch up in London in the modern day?" Xanthe peered over Liam's shoulder into the mirror on the table and marveled again at the splendid four-poster behind them. The canopy and posts were of the finest burl walnut, all carved to slender pillars and finials, hung with glorious duck egg silk bearing a print of exotic birds and flowers.

"It's a step up from Mistress Flyte's place," said Liam. "I bet she was secretly pleased we weren't taking up more of Polly's work time. She must be relieved that we were moving out, or at least that I was."

"She knows we need to get closer to Fairfax, and that this is probably the safest way to do it. The more the Wilcox family includes us in their day-to-day life the better. Though I already feel I should have ordered more clothes from Pinkerton's."

"Henry lent me some of his. The man actually has several types of everything and he's only staying here a couple of weeks."

"The etiquette surrounding how people dress is pretty demanding. Did you know, for instance, that, however posh you feel right now, you are in 'half dress'?"

"I am?"

"What you wore this morning was 'undress,' believe it or not. If you get to go to a ball, that'll be 'full dress.'"

"It's exhausting, all this changing and eating. The shooting was easier."

"Please tell me you didn't actually kill any bunnies."

Liam smiled. "Luckily, they are super fast! And, I thought it was tactful not to show off. Plus, I discovered a nineteenth-century shotgun is a little bit different from a twenty-first-century rifle."

"You managed not to do yourself or anyone else an injury. And I'm sure Mr. Wilcox and Henry think more of you for going with them."

"They were patient with me, actually. You'd expect lots of bluster and bravado, but they were kind. Fairfax, on the other hand . . ."

"He surely didn't risk doing anything to you with them watching."

"Let's just say being close to him while he had a loaded gun raised is not something I'm keen to repeat."

"You think he might have shot you?"

"Not 'deliberately' but, well, an unfortunate shooting accident . . ."

"Oh my God."

"Don't worry, we're going riding tomorrow."

"No guns?"

"No guns."

"There." She finished tying the stock. "That's the best I can do. Stand up, let's have a look at you. Hmm, not bad. Maybe you should take to wearing this lot when we get home," she said, trying to play down the horror she had felt at the thought of Fairfax shooting Liam. It had been his decision to take this dangerous journey with her, but that didn't mean she didn't feel responsible for whatever he might have to face.

Liam took a long, slow look at Xanthe. "I will if you will," he said. "You look . . . stunning."

She stepped back and did a twirl, enjoying the feel of the muslin against her skin as she moved. "It's one of Petronella's. We had fun choosing from her incredible collection. It is beautiful, isn't it?"

"You are beautiful," he said quietly.

"Don't look at me like that, brother dear."

"Sorry. Difficult to remember, sometimes."

"Try to keep it in mind. And remember tonight, there'll be more eating, and some drinking. Watch that, you still sound like a madman every time you open your mouth."

"Is it really that bad?" he asked with a smile.

"OK, not every time, but if you get tipsy . . ."

"I'll be careful."

"And there will be singing. At least we are on safer ground there. We can sing the song we practiced. Petronella said she has a piano, which will be easier than a harpsichord."

"I can manage a keyboard."

"I'm counting on it. And we can help Evie with her song. Play to our strengths."

"What did Fairfax say to you, out in the garden? He looked so damn smug, so sure of himself. After all he's done to you, after his threats. Couldn't I just have five minutes alone with him?"

"Thumping him might make you feel better but it's not going to help. He wants the Spinners book."

"Does he realize he might not be able to read it? That he might need you?"

"I think his ego won't allow him to contemplate that. At least, not to admit it to me. Anyway, the gist of our <u>very</u> brief conversation was that if I give him the book he'll leave me and mine alone."

"He must know you won't give it to him."

"He's used to getting what he wants. He's not going to give up without a fight."

"I know someone else like that," said Liam, pushing a wayward lock of hair out of Xanthe's eyes. Her curls had been smoothed and coiled into an elegant up-do which involved leaving ringlets hanging loose to soften the style. She was one of the very few people who didn't need curling irons to achieve the look.

"Before we go downstairs," she said, "there's something I need you to do." She went to her bag and took out *Spinners*. "This needs to be hidden. I don't trust Fairfax not to come looking for it, and my room is too obvious. Can you put it somewhere clever in yours? Somewhere we can get at it when I need it."

"Sure, I know just the place," he said, holding out his hand.

For a moment Xanthe hesitated, the very thought of passing the book into someone else's care sending a shiver of anxiety through her.

Liam read her expression. "It'll be safe, I promise. Henry has lent me a pair of riding boots. They came in a beautiful wooden box, lined with red satin. I'll lift the lining and put it in there. OK?"

She smiled, nodding, needing to trust him to help her. Knowing the book would be safer there.

"Let's keep it there while we are at dinner, in case he sends one of his servants looking for it. I'll collect it on my way to bed. I need to study it tonight. Also, we have to think of a way of getting into the dower house when Fairfax isn't in it," she told him. "Can you find out if he's definitely going riding with you tomorrow?"

"I am not happy about you trying to, well, steal the astrolabe on your own. He's bound to be expecting that. One of us ending up in jail is not part of the plan."

Xanthe paused and gave him a light kiss on the cheek, touched by how much he cared, happy to have him on her side. "Let's just take one thing at a time, OK?"

The evening was a true test of both of them in a variety of ways. At dinner, although it was supposedly a simple supper, there were curious habits to observe and copy in an attempt not to be seen as uncivilized. Xanthe found herself slowing down everything she did so that she was forever one beat behind her fellow diners. This gave her the chance to study their behavior and imitate it, whilst also, she hoped, making her look both relaxed and refined. She was seated at the opposite end of the table from Liam, but when she was able to catch his eye he appeared much as she was, tense, alert, focused, but on the whole confident and successful. One of the most unnatural things, as far as Xanthe was concerned, was the polite and completely sham conversation she was obliged to make with Fairfax. However well behaved he was in public, she knew the man too well to forget for one moment what he had done, and what he could do. She pitied Petronella anew as she watched the stoic and resigned way the young girl interacted with her husband-to-be. It was clear, even if she thought him respectable and trustworthy, there was no affection between the couple at all. In either direction. What a cold and artificial marriage it would be.

After dining, the party withdrew to the music room, where Henry,

Mr. Wilcox, Fairfax, and Petronella made up a four for bridge. The piano turned out to be a beautiful grand pianoforte, made of walnut and decorated with intricate inlay. Xanthe found herself admiring the craftsmanship and knew how much Flora would admire such an exquisite piece. Evangeline was eager to show them how she could play, though her enthusiasm rather outweighed her skill. She stumbled her way through the piece she was to play at the wedding, with Liam giving her tips for the trickier parts. At last, Petronella suggested she stop and let someone else have a turn.

"Mr. Westlake," she smiled at Liam, "won't you play something for us? I can tell from your patient instructions to Evie you are quite the expert, do not try to be modest and pretend otherwise."

"I play best when my sister sings," he told her. "We have a favorite song, if you would like to hear it," he added.

"Very much!" Petronella replied.

Evangeline leapt up from the piano stool to make room for Xanthe, who took her place beside Liam. They had not sheet music to help them, and had not had much time to practice, but at least they had one piece he could play passably well by ear as they had rehearsed it so recently. They elected for Xanthe to sing it once through solo, and then they would sing it again as a duet. The melody was gentle and soothing without being melancholy, and the tunefulness of the score was well suited to her clear, agile voice.

Liam played the introduction and nodded to count her in. She remembered to sit up straight and smile as she sang.

Peaceful slumb'ring on the ocean
Seamen fear no danger nigh;
The winds and waves in gentle motion
Soothe them with their lullaby.
In the wind's tempestuous blowing,
Still no danger they descry.

The guileless heart its boon bestowing
Soothes them with its lullaby.

As soon as she started to sing the atmosphere in the room changed. Evie stopped her fidgeting and sat on the window seat, leaning against the closed shutters, utterly entranced. Petronella laid down her cards to give the singers her full attention. Fairfax remained politely silent. Henry rose from the card table and moved to stand at the end of the piano, beaming at the duo. Even Mr. Wilcox left off puffing on his cigar to listen. Singing with Liam, despite their unusual audience, was a familiar comfort for Xanthe. Following the swooping and soaring of the music, feeling the lyrics shape in her mouth and take flight as she sang, listening to his harmonies and light playing of the piano, gave her joy, made her feel she was, after all, still herself. It was a meditative moment, a break from the tension of what they were trying to do, and it was hugely welcome. As they came to the end of the song she turned and looked directly at Fairfax. She held his gaze. She was not frightened of him, and she wanted him to know it. She was not alone. She was not some feeble girl he could terrifying and subdue. She was a Spinner, and she would crush him.

14

TIRED AS SHE WAS, XANTHE FOUND SLEEP IMPOSSIBLE THAT NIGHT. THE HEAT OF THE day had left even her high-ceilinged bedroom uncomfortably warm. She had thrown the tall windows wide open but there was no breeze to cool the air. She sat up in the enormous bed, imagining how snug it would be in the winter months with the heavy drapes drawn around it creating a snug room within a room. There was a plump moon high above the house, throwing a silvery light through the windows, giving the interior a soft, pearly glow. Xanthe decided it was pointless to chase sleep further. She leaned over to the white painted table beside her bed and used the flint and stone to light the candle. It was a simple task, but required practice to master properly, and she felt clumsy and impatient. At last she created sufficient spark to ignite the waxy wick. She positioned the candle so that when she sat up against the heavy feather pillows its light fell on the Spinners book she held in her lap. She and Liam had decided it would stay with her when possible but otherwise be in its hiding place in his room. She had collected it on her way up at the end of the evening and felt a thrill of anticipation when she held it in her hands again. She needed its wisdom now. Needed to be shown how she could best achieve her goals. On the matter of helping Petronella she was conflicted. On the one hand, she wished to warn her of Fairfax's true nature and save her from a cold and loveless marriage. On the other, she knew Petronella had agreed to the match for the sake of her family and no other solution to their financial difficulties presented itself. On the issues of stopping Fairfax from getting the Spinners book, threatening her and her family, or abusing his power as a Spinner, however, she felt clear in her mind. The *what* was plain enough: The *how* was more difficult.

"Show me, then," she muttered. "Tell me what I'm supposed to do." Despite the stillness of the night, Xanthe's hair moved slightly as if disturbed by a zephyr as she slowly turned the pages. She heard soft whispers, some laughter, the sound of carriage wheels, of the ocean, of rain. Unconnected sounds and snatches of speech fluttered out of the book, just as flashes of images appeared and then disappeared. Maps, astrological charts, portraits, pictures of houses or drawings of arcane objects and devices all floated across the stiff, pale pages before fading into nothing again. Xanthe had in mind a vague idea that she could somehow use her talent as a Spinner to gain access to the astrolabe. Perhaps she could outwit the servants in the house by observing their movements and then traveling back in time to an instant before they were somewhere between her and where it was kept. Could she do that? Could she move through tiny bursts of time within a time? It was, after all, similar to what she had done with Fairfax when she had taken him to the very moment of his walk to the scaffold. She recalled how nervous she had been then, how unsure of her ability to do such a thing. "I need to make time work for me," she thought aloud. "I need to bend it so that I can..." She stopped suddenly, the words swallowed up by a terrible screech that came out of the pages. She gasped, recoiling against the pillows as a fearsome face, or at least a pair of eyes, leapt forward at her, the screeching continuing for a full, terrifying ten seconds before it ceased and vanished. She sat very still, her heart pounding, waiting to see if the shocking apparition would reappear. When it did not, she resumed turning the pages, carefully, warily. "OK," she muttered, "not that then. I get the message."

The air around her seemed to calm and settle a little, though the whispers continued. Then, without anything seeming to change otherwise, she turned a page to find one covered in words. She could not be certain, but she thought she recognized the handwriting as being the same as the one that had revealed to her the story of the boy escaping his abuser. As she began to read, she heard a voice telling her the story. The voice was that of a young man, his accent shaped with the rounded vowels of the West Country, a soft lilt to his sentences, the tone rich and mellifluous.

I had reached a decision that was to put me in danger, and that danger would likely come from many I had, to that point, counted friend. I set down here what happened so that others who come after me may understand. We form our allegiances through serendipity, through the path life bids us tread, and through the giving and receiving of trust. It is a hard truth to learn that those allegiances, however hard-won, however close, must alter at the behest of our conscience. To see those whom we admired and trusted be corrupted by their gift is to know true sadness. All that is left for us to do is choose the right way, the moral direction. I knew I must leave. Must put distance between myself and those I had come to regard as my kin, lest I had to act against them. It was only as I made my way out of the house that I was discovered. At the door I turned. She descended the stairs.

She: Once over that threshold you will have put yourself beyond the point of ever returning to us. You must know that in your heart.

I: It is for the best.

She: How is it you have developed such a pious conscience?

I: Do not, I beg you, ask me to stay.

She: Is it so easy to leave me?

I: It is the lesser thing. If I were to stay, that conscience you criticize me for would have me take more drastic action.

She had reached me by then and put a gentle hand upon my arm. She had the most elegant, delicate fingers of any woman I have ever met, before or since, all these long years. Her touch at that moment was exquisite torture. When she saw I would not be turned she let her hand drop and I felt the absence of it keenly. She smoothed her skirts but did not step away. How easy it would have been to take her in my arms once again. I could smell her scent and it called to my memory our shared passion.

She: You have made your choice, then.

I: You made it for me! When you chose to spin time you put yourself forever beyond my reach.

She: But, Erasmus, you too, are a Spinner!

I: No longer.

She moved to touch me again.

I: Do not, I pray you, for if I am ever to lay hand upon you again it will be to end your life.

And so, I left. I stepped away from the life I had known. Stepped from the people who had been all and everything to me. Stepped out of my Spinner's skin, for I could stand to inhabit it no longer.

The words disappeared. The voice fell silent. Xanthe waited, hoping there would be more, but nothing came. Outside an owl broke the quiet of the night with its shriek.

"Dammit, just for once could you be a bit more straightforward? What has this guy got to do with Fairfax? With the wedding dress? With me?" She was about to give up and put the book away but decided to turn one more page. For a moment she thought her eyes were just tired, as the surface of the thick paper seemed to wobble. She squinted, trying hard to focus, longing for something helpful to show itself. What emerged from the nothingness made her gasp. Slowly an image formed. It was a painting of a young woman. The clothes were not of the 1900s, though she was unable to accurately date them. All she knew was that they were earlier by a good few years. The woman was seated on an iron garden seat, straight backed and poised, her hands clasped in her lap. All around her were small fruit trees, and behind her a high stone wall. The garden could be the one at Corsham. It looked a little different, but then, if the picture had been painted decades earlier than the point in time Xanthe had come to know it, differences were to be expected. What had caused her to utter such an expression of surprise was that, despite being shown in her youth, the woman in the picture was easily and unmistakably recognizable as Mistress Lydia Flyte.

It had been agreed that, the next day, the men were to go out riding, while the women would take a walk. As a means to locating and sizing up the dower house, Xanthe had expressed a wish to see the estate, and after explaining that she was a poor horsewoman, Petronella had happily agreed that they should go on foot. Xanthe had expected they would make an early start to avoid the heat of the day, but she had not taken into account the morning routine, or, in fact, the altered version that her request for a long walk had brought about.

A maid brought tea to her room at about eight o'clock and said she would return to help her dress at half past. Much as Xanthe would have liked to have been independent and avoided putting the maid to extra work, she did not want to refuse a kind offer, nor upset the accepted way of doing things. On top of which, the cotton day dress she had purchased from Pinkerton's had small buttons at the back which she could never have done up herself. The maid returned punctually and explained that Mr. Wilcox and the Misses Wilcox would be pleased to see her in the dining room for breakfast directly. She went on to say that the family did not normally take breakfast, or at least, not until much later in the day. Ordinarily the ladies of the house would go on their morning visits, or receive callers, who would only stay for half an hour at most. By the time Xanthe descended the grand staircase she was concerned that she had overstepped the mark as a guest and put her hosts out unnecessarily. She was relieved, then, to be greeted warmly by Mr. Wilcox as she entered the dining room.

"Ah, Miss Westlake, a glorious morning for your walk! I trust you slept well. You will need to be in fine fettle to keep up with my daughters. They walk apace and never tire. I recommend the deviled kidneys, for they set you up a treat."

Evangeline was already cleaning her plate with a piece of bread. "Father would like to chide us for being unladylike in our walking habits but he is too engaged galloping about the estate to notice most of the time!"

"Hush, Evie." Petronella leaned over to adjust her sister's collar, which was not as straight as it might be. "You know full well Father allows us more freedom than any of your young friends."

"That is because he knows I should kick against endless dances and visits. I can think of nothing more tedious than to sit quiet on a chair and exchange talk of dresses and gossip regarding people I scarcely know."

Mr. Wilcox gave a harrumph. "You will change your tune as you grow, young missy, mark my words. You will have to, if we are ever to find a husband for you."

"Father, I don't want a husband! I shall never marry, but stay a wild girl, running through the woods, and never care that any call me mad."

"You may not care," said Petronella, "but we might. Fortunately, we have a few years before you must curb your wildness. Ah, here is Mr. Westlake." She smiled at Liam as he joined them at the table.

Pleasantries were exchanged and everyone ate large quantities of kedgeree, sausages, kidneys, and ham. Xanthe wondered briefly how a vegetarian would have survived the diet. She couldn't imagine living on a meat-free regime in Britain with no imported vegetables or salad, and tropical fruits and nuts a rare and madly expensive thing. More pressingly, she wished she could speak to Liam on his own, but the opportunity did not present itself. At least the plans had been made with everyone present on the previous evening, and she knew he was astute enough to work out the real reason for her wish to tour the estate. After breakfast they were joined by Henry—who always rose late and preferred not to eat until after exercise—and Fairfax, who rode over from the dower house on a fine grey horse. Xanthe waved at Liam as he set off with the others and felt a mixture of relief and pride to see how comfortably and confidently he sat on the lively brown mare that had been provided for him.

Petronella lent Xanthe a straw bonnet, declaring that she could not set off without one as the sun would soon be hot, causing her little sister to gleefully imagine their brains boiling in the heat. The three left the house not along the driveway but striding down across the great sweep of grass that led away from the western side of the gardens. It was only as they were almost on top of it that Xanthe saw the ha-ha that separated the lawn from the field beyond it. This walled drop was invisible from the house, so that it created an uninterrupted vista, whilst preventing livestock from wandering into the gardens. It added to the feeling of grandeur and space that the parkland provided so well, with its enormous oaks, beech, and chestnut trees planted at considered random, with small woodland areas on the rising slopes of low hills to either side, leading the eye to the lake in the distance. It looked as if the builder of Corsham Hall had happened upon the perfect spot for the house, but the truth was that the landscape had, late in the previous century, been carefully constructed to give the appearance of a natural, rural idyll. The little hills, the woodlands, even the water course, had all been constructed to provide arcadia for the residents of the great house. When they reached the side of the lake the scale of the thing became apparent. To one side there was a stream, cascading down a narrow, fern-filled gulley that fed the large expanse of water, which must have been almost an acre in size. The far shore had a small jetty with a rowing boat moored to it. Willows stooped low, their delicate leaves offering shade beneath which irises and bulrushes thrived, fringing the edges of the water. In the sunnier stretches, broad lily pads floated upon the silky surface, their oriental blooms opening to bask in the sunshine. It was what stood at the other end of the lake that really caught Xanthe's attention. Rising out of the water as if it were in fact a moat was a tall tower that closely resembled a partly ruined castle. Instead of the smooth gold of the big house, this was constructed of rough, grey stone, and had crenellations on the top.

"Goodness!" she said. "That is a curious building."

"Ah," Petronella explained. "That is Grandfather's folly. I do not remember meeting my father's father, for he died when I was younger than Evie is now, but he loved to make improvements to the grounds at Corsham. Father says it is from him I get my love of flowers and plants, but I confess the majestic landscape he was set upon creating does not please me half so much as the intimacy of my own little rose garden."

"So, it is a folly? Just for show?"

"The notion was that it gave something romantic to the lake. The house itself is, you will have noticed, designed along classical lines, all symmetry and order and restraint. This scrap of castle is here to represent something altogether more stirring."

"Was it built exactly as it is now? Half ruined? I thought perhaps something had happened to it."

"Oh no, for there is beauty in decay, is there not? I think I understand what my grandfather tried to do. There are times when I consider a faded rosebud more beautiful than a bright bloom. Such intimations of mortality speak to our souls, don't you think so?"

Evie ran past them, calling as she went. "Come along, do! I will be first to the top of the tower!"

"Evie, have a care!"

"Oh, Nell, I know well . . . the stairs are steep and uneven, the wall broken in parts, the drop long, and the water deep. When have I ever so much as stumbled?" She ran on, quickly disappearing through the doorless archway at the base of the building.

"She is so reckless," Petronella observed.

"Is the folly unsafe?"

"Oh, not really. It appears to be crumbling but is firmly built. Only my sister's haste makes it dangerous, for the fall into the lake would indeed be perilous."

Once through the entrance Xanthe could see that the structure was, for the most part, a facade, with very little by way of rear walls or interior. There was part of a keep—which had a small room set into the wall with a gate of iron bars closing it off, putting her in mind of the blind house in Bradford—and then spiral stairs leading up to the turrets, all covered with carefully planted and nurtured ivy. The effect was convincing. If she hadn't been told otherwise, Xanthe could well have believed this was a remnant of an ancient building. The climb was steep and not made any easier by the long skirts of her dress, nor the tight stays of her bodice that forced her to take shallow breaths. They could hear Evie, already at the top, teasing them for their slowness. Xanthe looked up, shielding her eyes with her hand against the fractured sunlight that sliced between the castellations of the uppermost wall. As they emerged from the shadows of the stairs they were rewarded for their climb with an astonishing view.

"Isn't it splendid?" Evie demanded, bouncing with excitement.

"It certainly is," Xanthe agreed. From their vantage point, the landscape flowed away in all directions. To the south lay great swathes of pasture where sheep and cattle grazed. To west and east were further meadows, along with the hillocks and small copses that broke up the more exposed nature of the lower reaches of the parkland. North of the folly sat the house, though partly obscured by trees, the wall of the garden, and the quadrangle of stables and coach house to the rear. From such a perspective, Corsham Hall was reduced in scale, somehow, seen in such an expansive setting, yet still retained its grand presence.

"Such a drop!" Evie exclaimed, leaning over the low wall of the parapet.

"Evie!" Petronella pulled her back. "You will have my hair turn white before you are grown, I swear it! Step back, child, I beg of you."

"But, Nell, is it not thrilling, to be so close to danger? Do you not love it?"

"Indeed I do not! It is the least appealing aspect of the folly, and I do not believe it is the purpose of the building to terrify."

Xanthe was not so sure. Given what Petronella had said about the beauty of decay, and taking into account the broken nature of the construction, it seemed to her that everything about it spoke of ruin, of mortality, of death, even. It was, she knew from what she had learned of paintings and literature of the era, what the Romantic movement was all about; to move people to feel strong emotions by reminding them of the frailty of life. She peered over the edge of the wall and experienced a burst of giddiness brought on by the vertiginous drop and the thought of the dark water below.

"Is it very deep?" she asked.

"Father has always said that it is deep enough to save any who might fall in from the folly tower. Happily, no one has put it to the test."

Evie shook her head. "One might survive the fall," she said seriously, "but the snatching weeds at the bottom of the lake are so thick they would take hold of you and pull you down until you drowned!"

"Oh, Evie, what morbid thoughts you harbor. Miss Westlake does not wish to have her head filled with such gloom on such a sunlit day."

"I nearly drowned myself once. Not on purpose," Evie insisted. "I fell from the rowing boat and those deadly weeds twisted about my ankle. Father jumped in and fetched me out, else I should not be here to tell the tale," she explained with relish.

They stood awhile, taking in the spectacular view, pondering the ever-present chance of fatal accident, letting the heat of the July sunshine slow their thoughts. Suddenly, Evie cried out, pointing into the distance.

"Look! There is Father, and your brother, Miss Westlake. Do you see?"

"Oh, yes," she said, squinting against the sun to better make out the two riders. She recognized the brown horse Liam had been given. It was moving swiftly, in front of his host's heavy chestnut cob. "And there are the others," she said, noticing Fairfax on his grey, and Henry, out in front, unsurprisingly, galloping hell for leather on his highly strung black thoroughbred. They were all moving fast, going in the direction of a dark, dense wood at the far edge of the estate.

Petronella sighed. "Must men always be in such a hurry? Would that they could learn caution to temper their fearless youth," she said wistfully.

Xanthe turned back to look at her then, thinking of how painful it must be for her to see a young man living his carefree life while her fiancé had given his for king and country. She was, in that moment, so clearly a heartbroken young woman, not an eager bride, and Xanthe felt a new rush of pity for her.

They left the folly and continued their walk, which took them through a patch of woodland that afforded welcome shade. The last of the bluebells added a shimmer of blue to the ground as dappled light fell through the broad-leafed trees. Two wood pigeons called to each other and a short way off a woodpecker could be heard hammering against hard bark in search of grubs. Even with her hat, Xanthe was glad of the protection of the woodland canopy, as the midday heat was a trial in so many layers of shift, petticoat, and dress. At least the fabric was light and cool, and however tight her stays, the fashions of the day did not call for the sort of corsetry that would, in a few short decades, practically render the wearers handicapped for lack of breath and movement.

After a further thirty minutes' walking they left the woodland and emerged onto an area of smaller meadows with a lane tucked against one side of the shallow valley. This they followed, rounding a corner in a few hundred yards to see the dower house directly ahead of them. Xanthe had been expecting a modest home, perhaps with a fancy fa-cade and pleasant garden. In reality, the dower house was only mod-est when compared to Corsham Hall. It was constructed of the same glowing, honey-colored stone, three stories tall, each with long win-dows, the width allowing six of these and suggesting plenty of rooms for residents and servants. She recalled that such places were, after all, given to the dowager of the big house, and had to be seen to reflect the status of the owner. If the resident had once been the lady of the Hall, she would not happily downgrade to a meager cottage just because the next generation had taken over her previous home. A dower house had to be elegant, imposing, charming, and large. The other thing about it that struck Xanthe, and made her bite her lip with frustra-tion, was that it looked practically impregnable. There was a huge front door beneath a classical portico, and the scale of the home sug-gested there would be quite a number of servants living inside it. It would never be completely empty, and its treasures and privacy would be well guarded. She chided herself for ever imagining she would be able to somehow just gain entry, sneak about, find the astrolabe, and take it. Even if she could get inside unnoticed, Fairfax was unlikely to leave the thing anywhere other than locked up somewhere secure, and she wasn't a safe breaker. How had she thought she would be able to steal something so precious? It was an impossible task. As that realiza-tion hit home she had to accept that she must find another way to take the astrolabe from Fairfax, and at that moment she was at a loss to see how it could be done.

After dinner the same day, Xanthe claimed a headache as an excuse for going up to her bedroom early. On leaving, she signaled to Liam, who interpreted the gesture and arrived at her door a little while later. He was holding a small bottle of liquid and a spoon.

"I asked Petronella for a remedy for your headache and volunteered to bring it to you myself," he told her. "I explained you often get these and it helps to have someone to talk to you gently as you sit in the dark."

"You'd make a great nurse," she said, taking the bottle from him and letting him into the room. She held up the liquid to the candle-light. "I wonder what it is?"

"God knows. Glad you don't have to actually drink any."

"I'll have to pour some away or they'll notice," she said, stooping to pull the chamber pot out from underneath the bed. She tipped a little of the medicine into the empty pot, which she then slid back into its place. She replaced the cork stopper in the bottle and set it down on the dressing table. Liam sat in the armchair near the fire, wincing as he did so.

"Wilcox has a wonderful stable of horses but he could do with spending a bit of money on his saddles," he said. "I ache in places that have never been called upon to do anything before."

"You looked like you were managing just fine. I saw you galloping into the woods."

"Actually, the riding itself was fantastic! Who'd have thought single horsepower could be such a buzz? Just needed more padding . . ." he added, adjusting a cushion in the chair.

"We have bigger problems to deal with than your saddle sores. I've seen the dower house."

"Ah, me too. We rode past it on the way home."

"What did you think?"

"That we won't be nipping in and relieving Fairfax of his bloody gadget anytime soon."

"We need to find another way, and I think I've come up with a plan."

"OK . . ."

"I'll offer him a deal. I'll trade him *Spinners* for his astrolabe."

"What?!"

"You don't like the idea?"

"Let me see . . . no! How can you think it'd work? For a start, you have told him pretty definitely that he will never get his hands on that book. That it is yours, it is special, it is powerful, and you'll never let him have it. So he probably won't believe you are actually going to give it to him."

"He might if I let him believe that I don't think he will be able to use the book without the astrolabe; that way it would make sense for me to give it up. Don't you see? It will play to his ego, if I let him think I can see no other way, that he has defeated me. So, I give him the book because it's what he wants and then he will leave me alone. But I don't think he'll be able to use it without the astrolabe. Then he'd be an ordinary person living in this time and he'd have to make a go of his marriage with Petronella, so it's better for her too. He knows I care about her. So, he would believe that I think I'm not giving him the power of the book, only he has such an inflated idea of himself he's bound to think he can find a way to unlock its secrets for himself."

"Now I have a headache."

"It's quite simple, really."

"OK, let's assume he buys that part of it. Let's pretend he believes you are going to give him the book you said you'd never give him."

"Yes . . ."

"If I were Fairfax—and thank God I'm not—I wouldn't risk giving up my astrolabe. It might be the only way I *can* use the book. He's not going to give away the very thing that might make all the power in the Spinners manual his. Particularly if you have just told him you think he won't be able to use it without the astrolabe. You're shooting your own idea in the foot."

"I don't think that's physically possible."

"You know what I mean," he said, sitting forward in his chair, trying to make her see. "It won't work. In fact, the only reason Fairfax would agree to a trade would be to lure you into a trap."

"Which is what I would be doing to him."

"And then what? You meet somewhere, he's standing in front of you with the astrolabe and you're standing there with the thing he wants most in the world. You aren't really going to let him have it, are you? I mean, after all you've said about *Spinners* and not being able to trust him to use the gift as it should be used, you're not going to risk him being able to use it."

"To be perfectly honest, the thought of parting with it at all is truly awful. The thought of giving it to Fairfax makes me feel sick. But, and this is the point, it wouldn't be forever. I will get it back. Right now, I need to stop him, and that means taking the astrolabe. I know I'm a better Spinner than him, even without the book. I'll figure out a way to get it back. That's a promise I've made myself."

"OK, well then what about the fact that he's not going to risk letting go of the astrolabe. So, tell me, how do you see that going?"

"Well, I think you're right, he'll have a plan to trick me out of getting it from him."

"A plan which might well involve violence. He could bring a knife or a gun with him, or a henchman. How are you going to stop him just overpowering you to get what he wants? Is it me? Am I your back-up plan?"

"There's no way he'd agree to meet me unless I'm on my own."

"I could get hold of one of Wilcox's shotguns."

"He has his own shotguns, and muskets, and swords and, as you put it, henchmen. No, I have to be cleverer than that."

"I came here to help."

"Look, if we were going to resort to shooting at people and getting shot at we might just as well have a go at breaking into the dower house, holding a knife to his throat, and getting him to give us what we want."

"It's beginning to sound like a better idea than the one you've just told me about!"

"Except that we are not Special Forces, and if we succeeded we'd probably end up arrested and hanged for burglary." She walked over to the chair and knelt on the floor in front of him, taking his hands in hers. "Liam, I'm not going to risk you getting shot."

"And I'm not going to let you walk into a trap that could get you killed," he replied, reaching forward to stroke her cheek. "Seriously, why don't you just let me shoot him."

"Because you are not a murderer. Crazy as all this is, it's real, and we don't kill people. I will find a way to use my gift to outwit him."

"You think you can find the answer in the Spinners book? Gotta say, it's been pretty cagey about giving up its secrets so far."

"I know but it's showing me stuff all the time. More and more now that we're here. I just have to make sense of it."

"How long do you think that's going to take? The longer we stay here, the worse things get. The wedding is in less than two weeks. Then Fairfax moves into this place, and we have to leave."

"And Petronella becomes his wife."

"You still think the wedding dress called you here to stop the marriage going ahead?"

"I don't know. She doesn't realize what he is, what he's capable of, but, well, what will she do if she doesn't marry him? Do I have the right to doom her whole family to a future of poverty? Maybe that's not what I'm supposed to do. I don't know. All I can do is press on with putting a stop to Fairfax's spinning. Maybe everything else will come out of that. Somehow." She sat back on her heels, rubbing her temples.

Liam gently kissed her brow. "You want me to get you some of that headache medicine?"

She smiled and shook her head. After a moment she said, "I will find the answers. You have to let me do it my way."

"I came here to protect you. Promised your mother I'd get you home safe."

"Did you? I promised Harley the same about you," she said, making him laugh. Then, more seriously, she told him, "I'm really glad you're here."

"Honestly?"

"Honestly. But you have to trust me, OK? Tomorrow, I need you to help me get the chance to speak to Fairfax alone so I can offer him the deal."

"Xanthe..."

"Please, Liam. I need you to do this for me."

He looked at her with so much tenderness she felt awful for putting him in such a position. She knew he was frightened for her. If he had been the one putting himself at the mercy of Fairfax, she would have felt the same. At last he managed a small smile and a shrug.

"OK," he said. "After all, I know you better than he does. He's the one who should be worried."

She leaned forward and gave him a grateful hug, relieved that she had his agreement and support, but still uncertain exactly how she was going to make her risky plan work.

15

IT WAS LATE THE FOLLOWING MORNING BEFORE XANTHE SUCCEEDED IN BRINGING ABOUT the opportunity to talk to Fairfax on his own. Liam had challenged anyone willing to a game of pall-mall, and the Wilcox sisters and Henry happily agreed. Fairfax, who had arrived at the house to take morning tea, condescended to watch the game, in preference to actually playing it which, Xanthe felt certain, he considered a little beneath his dignity. While the players were busily engaged in their sport at one end of the walled garden she invited Fairfax to join her in walking to the other to enjoy the roses. He politely agreed, and Xanthe caught a glimpse of satisfaction in his expression as he did so. It was aggravating to think he believed himself to be so in control of the situation. That, she decided, was about to change.

As they strolled along the grassy paths between the flower beds the pair must have presented, to anyone who cared to notice, the picture of two acquaintances engaged in pleasant conversation, however far from the truth this was.

"Your companion," Fairfax started, flicking a dismissive hand in Liam's direction, "appears to enjoy his role rather too well. He may develop a taste for traveling through time and demand more of it from you."

"We are friends: We don't demand anything of each other."

"Indeed. I myself regard a friend as an equal, not a . . . let's see . . . puppet?"

Xanthe continued to walk, admiring a bed of delphiniums, refusing to let Fairfax rile her. "You must know," she said, smiling for the benefit of anyone watching, "that I don't wish to spend a minute longer in your company than I have to, so I will come to the point."

"Something you have, in my experience, ever been adept at."

"I'm here to stop you tormenting me, and to stop you misusing your power as a Spinner. I believe that power, for you, lies with the astrolabe. Therefore I suggest a trade. Give it to me, and in exchange I will give you the Spinners book."

This brought Fairfax up short. He stood staring at her, as if doing so could show him exactly what it was she was planning. After a moment's further thought he spoke, his voice still calm, but a noticeable tension giving it an edge.

"You swore never to let me have it."

"To give it up would be . . . very hard. It is a precious thing," she said, "but I believe I was sent here for a purpose, and it's my task to discover what that is and to fulfill my duty to the best of my ability. Nothing I have learned from *Spinners* condones the way in which you use your gifts, so I believe stopping you is what I have been charged to do. I know you cannot travel without your astrolabe."

"But if I had the book . . ."

"The book only reveals its contents to those it considers worthy."

He frowned at her, his brow beneath his hat but above his eye patch creasing with displeasure. "Are you so filled with your own importance you place yourself on a higher tier than me? On what evidence?"

"Well, for a start, the evidence that I can travel without needing a talisman to do so."

"Objects have to call to you."

"I can return to my own time without them. And I believe they will continue to call to me."

"Your argument is self-defeating. If, as you say, it is your destiny to come here and therefore to give me the book, am not I, then, the one chosen to have it? Has not my own worth therefore been recognized?"

"If you believe that, then you won't mind giving up the astrolabe. What have you to lose, if you think *Spinners* is finding its way to you? If you are right, you surely won't need anything else to enable you to travel."

"Why would I take the risk? Mayhap I shall need both to be free to travel as I please. Why would I give up the astrolabe to you when I can merely force you to give me the book?"

Xanthe walked on, which meant he was compelled to do so too.

"I don't believe you would do anything to risk your standing in society here. You have always craved acceptance and recognition of your status and wealth. You need this marriage. You need the approval of those whose opinions matter to you. And, as you have pointed out, I have Liam with me. I'm not helpless and defenseless."

"And yet, you left your home and your mother to come here. . . ."

It was Xanthe's turn to stop and glare now. "I'm still trying to work out exactly how you do what you do to things in my time without traveling there, but know this. I have not left my mother unprotected, and I won't give in to your threats."

He smiled at her, offering her his arm. "Come, come, Miss West-lake, it will not do for us to be seen quarreling."

She took his arm, though touching him cost her dearly, and they continued their walk.

"As to the fire," he said calmly, "it was a necessary move to bring you to me."

"Tell me how you did it. I know you're keen to show me how clever you are."

"More clever than you give me credit for," he said. "You will recall, a little while back, there came into your shop a clumsy young couple. There was a mishap. A piece of china was broken. Was it Minton?"

She stopped, removing her hand from his arm, turning to look at him in astonishment.

"Wedgwood," she said quietly. "It was a Wedgwood plate."

"Quite so. And you were so very understanding, and they so very ready to pay the cost of their clumsiness."

She recalled the thick fold of money the young man had pulled from his pocket.

"You sent them?" she asked, still not fully understanding.

"Not them. It was the other young woman, just a customer to you, she was the one I sent. You will remember she showed an interest in your clothing, which is, is it not, located in a room at the rear of your establishment. A room next to the stairs?"

Xanthe did remember, picturing the tall woman in the long, heavy coat. "She set the fire? But how?"

"A simple device for transporting fire that has been used for centuries. A hot coal, or slow-burning piece of charcoal. Even close to your modern day such things exist, I am told, for those of an inclination to camp in wild places. They can be used to heat a pot or a pocket, set into the appropriate container. Such a hot coal, placed beneath a loose stair, will take several hours to ignite the wood around it."

"And leave no trace," Xanthe muttered, understanding at last why the fireman could not find the cause of the fire.

"Such a plan had the added benefit of putting in your mind the notion that I had somehow influenced the future without traveling to it. Which, alas, I do not have the ability to do."

"You were still there? After I saw you outside Gerri's tea shop, you stayed?"

"Come, come, you yourself know it is not, for us, an insurmountable challenge to travel back and fore for short times. And you must not be so arrogant as to believe that you are the only Spinner to be able to travel with a non-Spinner as your aide."

"And the young couple?"

"People of any era can be bribed, I find."

"You wanted me to think you could harm us from your own time."

"Was it not a terrifying prospect? Did it not bring you, and the book, to me all the quicker?"

Xanthe walked on, pacing quickly to help take in what he had told her and order her thoughts.

Fairfax wished to turn the conversation back to the book.

"Let us suppose," he said at last, "that I agree to your trade. I will give you the astrolabe if you give me the Spinners tome, and that will be the end of our association. You will not hear from me further, nor will I visit any further injury to you, your loved ones, or your home."

"That would be the deal."

"I assume, also, that I would receive no further visit from you or your . . . agents, but be free to continue my life as I see fit, with Miss Wilcox as my wife, and Corsham Hall as my home, yes?"

Xanthe hesitated, the thought of Petronella having to submit to being Fairfax's wife causing a tightness in her chest she could not ignore. And yet, would meddling in their arrangement be beyond her duties as a Spinner? Would it be wrong for her to stop the marriage, even if she could?

Fairfax put his hand over hers as she held his arm. "Know this, I will not agree to your bargain until after I am wed. Upon that point I will not be moved. The marriage must take place first. The exchange after. Do you agree?"

Slowly, she withdrew her hand, feigning interest in a rose that climbed over an iron archway which spanned the path. She tilted one of the pale pink blooms so that she could breathe in its sweet scent. Without turning to him she said, "Agreed. The day after the wedding, meet me at the folly on the lake at midday."

"You will be alone?"

"As you must be."

"Agreed," he said.

Xanthe found she could maintain the pretense of civility no longer, bobbed him a shallow curtsey, and walked briskly back to join the others at their game, her heart beating hard and fast. It took her a moment to shake off the agitation she felt, so that she had to be careful to mask her mood when Petronella left the game and came over to her.

"Shall we sit awhile on the swing seat?" the young woman suggested, taking Xanthe's arm. "I am so very grateful you consented to stay here, you and your brother. New friends bring such diversion, such energy to our little society. Your company has lifted our spirits, particularly my sister's," she observed, smiling at Evangeline's obvious glee at sharing a game of pall-mall with Liam.

"It saddens me," Xanthe said carefully, "that you should need cheering when you are soon to be married. Surely a bride should be happy. . . ."

Petronella leaned back on the seat, enjoying the motion of the swing, her gaze falling upon her fiancé. "You know that ours is not a love match. People accept a proposal of marriage for many reasons. I believe mine to be good ones."

"I understand, really I do. Only . . . I wish you could be happier."

"It is easier for me than you might think, to commit myself to such a union. I have not, I know, fully explained . . ."

"You don't have to. It's not my business, I'm sorry . . ."

"You see, as I told you, I have known love. Oh, such a love! Edward and I would have been the happiest of couples, I am certain of it. It was here, in this very garden, that we made our promises to each other. I promised that I would love no other, and nor shall I. Do you see? I could never marry for love now, not after Edward, not after that promise. So, for me, an advantageous match, one that will help those I hold dear, that is the very best outcome I could wish for."

"And yet, your spirits needed raising?"

"It is unavoidable that my thoughts should turn to Edward, to what might have been, as I prepare for my wedding, do you not think so? He must occupy Evie's mind greatly too, for she was fiercely fond of him, and has no affection for Benedict."

It was the first time Xanthe had heard Petronella use Fairfax's first name and it brought her up short. She studied him anew. Could he change? Could it be that, once he discovered his days of being a Spinner were over, he could settle for the fortunate life he had constructed for himself, reform and be a good husband? Was it possible? She found it hard to believe. Petronella noticed her scrutinizing him.

"You do not find my future husband . . . agreeable?"

"Oh, I hardly know him." She shook her head. "Not sufficiently to form an opinion."

"I am aware he can seem a little cold. Aloof, perhaps. It does not trouble me, for I believe it indicates a nature able to allow me my own life, without placing demands upon me I would be unable to meet. He does not expect me to love him, only to be a respectable wife. I am content that I will be able to do that. Father will not suffer the disgrace of losing Corsham. Evie may continue her childhood here and, one day, be free to marry whomever she chooses. I have no doubt my husband will run the estate with crisp efficiency."

Xanthe nodded, her respect for Petronella's stoicism growing, while her disquiet at Fairfax ruling her life increased at the same rate. She was glad to have the opportunity to speak to Liam about it when he slipped away from the game. When they were sure they could not be overheard he asked her about her conversation with Fairfax.

"Well? How did he react?" He waved at Evie as she celebrated setting back Henry's winning streak with a fine shot.

"He agreed to the swap."

"He did? Wow, he's really going to part with his precious device?"

"He's adamant he won't do it until after the wedding, though."

"I don't trust him. He just wants to get his hands on the book. I don't believe he has any intention of giving you the astrolabe. What I do believe is that, if he thinks he needs you to see what the Spinners have written, he'll do whatever it takes to keep you with him."

"I don't really care what he plans on doing, I just have to get hold of the astrolabe."

"It's too dangerous."

"I'm not stupid, Liam. Don't you think I might be prepared for his tricks?"

At that moment Henry came over to them, throwing down his mallet. "That's me done for. Never again shall I let Evangeline thrash me at pall-mall. It is not good for a fellow's soul to be bested by a child. I'd sooner step into the boxing ring, hopelessly outgunned, and be flattened. At least there is honor in that."

Evie came running along behind him, laughing. "Oh, Henry, you could win if you only tried."

"Nonsense. I am fair done in. Take mercy on your victim and find ale, I beg of you," he asked as he flopped dramatically onto the grass.

Petronella shook her head. "You shall have lemonade and be thankful for it. Evie, run in and ask for some to be brought out to us."

The shadow of Fairfax fell across Henry's recumbent form. "I trust you will recover quickly, Anstruther, for I am planning entertainments you would not wish to miss."

"Capital! What's it to be? More shooting? Fishing, perchance?"

"A ball," Fairfax told the assembled company. "What say you, Petronella? Is there a better way to welcome our new friends into our society, and to begin the celebrations leading up to our wedding day?"

While Petronella mastered her surprise and started to agree with Fairfax that a ball would be a splendid thing, Xanthe was fighting panic. There was no chance she and Liam could successfully explain why neither of them could dance. There had not been time when preparing for their trip to learn any of the complicated steps and phases of the many popular dances of the day. She had to find a way to change the plan to something that would not arouse people's suspicion and reveal herself and her supposed brother to be frauds of some sort, for every well-bred person should know how to dance. She remembered a scene in Jane Austen's *Mansfield Park* when a picnic was suggested as a less formal, more fun summer occasion than a ball.

"Nell, I wonder," she began, "as the weather continues so hot, would you not prefer to continue our entertainments outdoors? My brother and I have so enjoyed our time spent outside in your delightful gardens and wonderful parkland. Could I suggest, instead, a picnic?"

"A picnic?" She looked surprised that Xanthe would not be more delighted at the idea of a ball.

Xanthe watched the receding figure of Evie as she ran toward the house and wished she had her there to support the idea. She imagined she would be a ready ally.

"We could make it such a lovely occasion and of course invite others to make it a party. And there would be games for Evie. A ball would be rather stifling in this heat, don't you think?"

Whether or not Fairfax guessed the reason behind Xanthe's resistance to a ball she could not be certain, but he was quite determined to take control of the situation.

"A picnic might be far better," he agreed, even managing a smile. "After all, our guests should be the ones to choose, and Miss Westlake is right in what she says; the weather is too warm for crowds and dancing. How much more pleasant to be somewhere charming and shady out of the house. Why, would not the lake be the perfect spot? There could be boating or fishing for those who enjoy it, and the folly presents such a delightful setting, don't you agree, my dear?" he asked of Petronella, who was only too pleased to say yes to something that so obviously made her fiancé and her new friend happy.

Liam whispered into Xanthe's ear as they turned for the table to take their lemonade.

"What's he playing at now?"

"He's taunting me. Don't worry, it won't work. A ball would have been a nightmare for us. The picnic will be fine. Let Fairfax try all he wants to unnerve me, it's not going to work. Now, come on." She took his arm, her voice returning to a more public level. "Petronella and I have another fitting at Pinkerton's and it is thirsty work!"

That night, as had become her habit, Xanthe sat up late delving deep into the Spinners book, searching, listening, hoping. Again it revealed to her the painting of Mistress Flyte and she promised herself that at the first opportunity she would return to the tearooms to talk to the old woman. She was convinced that there was much she knew that she somehow wasn't telling, and now was not the time for her to be kept in the dark. She still had to find a way to be certain she could outwit Fairfax when the time of the exchange came. She did not trust him any more than Liam did. In fact, she would be expecting him to try to trick her somehow. She had to be ready for him. She had to find a way to take his power from him, protect the book, and keep herself safe. Somewhere, hidden among the ancient brittle pages in front of her, lay the answer. All she had to do was find it.

❧ 16 ❧

THE DAY OF THE PICNIC WAS, IF ANYTHING, EVEN HOTTER THAN THE PRECEDING WEEK. Xanthe was astonished at how much activity the occasion sparked in the Wilcox household. For three days, servants appeared to do everything at the run, and deliveries arrived almost hourly, it seemed. When she questioned Petronella about how such elaborate preparations could be necessary her hostess merely smiled and told her that her fiancée was not a man to do things by halves, and that a certain number of guests would always merit a certain amount of work. Invitations had been sent out at once, and letters of acceptance arrived with even greater frequency than carts bringing food, drink, and other necessities for the party. Xanthe chose her new muslin dress, which was the coolest garment from her limited wardrobe. As the maid helped her get ready she felt a small thrill of excitement. The fabric was whisper light and would have been entirely transparent without the cotton chemise and petticoat beneath it. She instructed the maid to tie the stays of her corset as loosely as possible, earning a look of pursed-lipped disapproval from the middle-aged woman, who clearly had an opinion about what was the proper way for a young lady to dress, even if she was not allowed to voice it. Xanthe submitted to a lengthy bout of hairdressing, where the maid brushed and twisted and pinned her long curls into a tight, high bun, with loose locks at the sides to soften it. The end result was too severe for Xanthe's liking, but she knew she would be keeping her hat on anyway, so there was little point in protesting. The bonnet itself was newly purchased on a trip to Bradford with Petronella. They had visited a milliner at the top of the high street and enjoyed girlish glee trying on a dizzying selection of hats, boaters, bonnets, and fascinators. In the end, Xanthe had settled on a small straw bonnet, shaped so that it tipped slightly upward at the front with sides that were not so big as to make her feel as if she were wearing blinkers. The crown was made of beautifully woven straw, the pattern of the weaving needing no further decoration save for the narrow ribbon that held the bonnet in place by tying at the nape of the neck beneath her hair. She found this a far more flattering style than a bow beneath her jaw, which always made her feel faintly ridiculous and became quite uncomfortable after an hour's wearing. This one, she felt certain, she could wear all day, not feel as if she were in fancy dress, and be glad of the way it kept the sun off her head. The dress had a matching shawl which would also keep the sun off her bare arms and the back of her neck if necessary. Petronella had encouraged her to buy a new pair of light slippers. They were the one element of the outfit Xanthe was sure she would never be fully comfortable with, she was so used to her heavy boots. But they were light, and although she would have to wear stockings, she could at least kick them off when no one was paying attention.

At eleven o'clock she went downstairs. They were all to meet at the front of the house so that everyone could be allocated space in a carriage. She found Liam on the steps.

"I thought we might just stroll down to the lake, maybe carrying a rug and a hamper," he said quietly to her. "Seems I hadn't quite understood what a picnic was." He waved a hand at the almost manic activity going on around them. "Will you look at those beauties!"

Xanthe knew him well enough to know he was referring not to the prettily dressed female guests who were arriving, but the carriages they were being conveyed in. There were already six at the house, their drivers vying for space in which to wait for further directions, and others could be seen moving swiftly up the long driveway. There were more different types of traps and carriages than she knew existed at the time, some more easily identifiable than others, and each, no doubt, reflecting the wealth and social standing of their owners. Just as in her own day, it appeared, a vehicle, besides being a mode of transport, was a status symbol. There were fully covered carriages, large and grand, pulled mostly by at least four horses and suggesting a particularly well-off family. There were smart landaus with their tops folded down, the better to display the finery of their occupants. There were fast cartouches, high-wheeled and precarious, mostly drawn by two racy horses harnessed in tandem. The ones pulled by a single horse fell into two types. There were the ones driven by extravagantly dressed young men, practically standing in the driver's seat, traveling at daring speed, their horses fighting for their heads and looking fit to bite anyone and anything. The second group were the entirely more workaday contraptions pulled by smart but humble ponies. The space outside the house was quickly becoming overcrowded, and footmen and grooms were sent hither and yon to direct the traffic. The drivers were told to unload their passengers and then park at the stables. There was a general air of excitement and good humor, on which Mr. Wilcox, in particular, seemed to thrive.

"Ha! A fine day for it. Miss Westlake, will you walk to the lake? Those who wish to ride will be conveyed in the smaller carriages to the end of the lane, from where it is a shorter distance."

"Oh, I should be happy to walk from here," she told him. "We enjoy walking, don't we, brother?"

"Indeed," Liam agreed, tipping his hat to Henry, who was already mounted on his favorite horse, which fidgeted, unused to being made to stand for so long.

"Good morning!" he called to them, raising his hat in a flamboyant gesture. "Capital day! Capital!" he declared before wheeling his mount on its haunches to go and greet what looked like two fellow Corinthians with their caped coats and fast conveyances.

Xanthe turned to Mr. Wilcox. "I wonder Henry has the patience for a picnic. He can't surely expect that horse of his to stand quietly tied to a tree."

"There will be riding for those who have a taste for it. See, he is calling the ostlers to help his friends unharness their horses. Shouldn't be surprised if they have their guns with 'em. Never miss out on the chance for a spot of shooting, in season or out, these types."

Liam took Xanthe's arm and they began to walk toward the lawns, taking care not to be in the way of any of the carriages. They caught up Petronella and Evie, who were attempting to reach the picnic spot ahead of most of the guests.

Xanthe commented on the scale of the event. "We're used to picnics being small affairs, just a few friends and family, a rug on the grass, sandwiches," she said.

"Oh." Petronella was surprised. "It's funny how when one lives in the country one imagines everything in London being so much grander and finer."

"Not picnics," Xanthe assured her.

She smiled. "There, we do not have the poorer version of everything here in our little backwater," she said. "Evie! There is no necessity to climb over the ha-ha." She tutted at her sister as she attempted to scramble down the sunken wall and its drop to the sweeping lawns below. "Do use the steps, or you are certain to snag your muslin."

Liam muttered, "Poor little backwater?" under his breath, raising his eyebrows at Xanthe.

She knew he was determined to keep her upbeat about the day's event. Given its location, and the fact that Fairfax would be there, the upcoming exchange would be on her mind. They had agreed he chose the venue specifically for that reason. It would be hard to avoid thinking about it, particularly as she was still unsure how she was going to prevent Fairfax ending up with both the astrolabe and the book, and what he might do to her to keep them both. She needed to decide on a plan of action soon. The wedding was only a few days away. As they neared the lake they were able to see the preparations that had been made for the picnic.

"Good heavens!" Xanthe said, taking it all in as Evie bounded off to race around the lake, heading for the small footbridge at the lower end which crossed the stream that fed into the body of water. "How has all this happened overnight? It's as if an army of elves have been working away in the dark to get it all ready."

Petronella laughed. "I'm sure Cook and Mrs. Mason, our housekeeper, would be most grateful for such assistance! Alas, they have only the belowstairs maids and the footmen. Though I noticed the gardeners were absent yesterday afternoon, so I suspect they too, were pressed into service. Mr. Fairfax was adamant that this was his idea so that he must oversee it and we were not to be troubled by the arrangements. I think he has done rather well, don't you agree?"

It would have been churlish not to. On the far side of the lake an open-fronted marquee had been put up, providing ample shady seating for at least twenty people. Tables were set with spotless white linen cloths and the finest silverware and glass. There were even vases of flowers and carafes of wine and water. On either side of this central point, further canvas canopies had been stretched between trees, and beneath these were wicker seats and low tables. On the sunny grass there was a game of quoits complete with chalk and scoreboard. A little way off there was a row of archery targets, with bows and quivers of arrows ready and waiting. Three more rowing boats had appeared on the lake to add to the solitary one which was permanently moored there. On the banks sat rods and fishing paraphernalia. Liam let out a low whistle.

"Are we up to this?" he asked Xanthe quietly.

"It's better than a ball. If someone turns up with a fiddle, just refuse all suggestions of dancing. Stick to things we're good at."

"Fixing cars?"

"I mean, we might have to sing. Come on, it'll be fine."

Petronella enjoyed making the introductions, leading her new friends through the thirty or so guests as they arrived, presenting them to a succession of faces that blurred into so many fancy bonnets and refined smiles by the end of thirty minutes that Xanthe could not recall a single name. She and Liam were both quick to offer to take Evie out on the lake. A footman appeared as if from nowhere and held the little boat steady while they climbed in. Liam picked up the oars and rowed them out onto the silky water. Evie leaned over the prow, searching for sight of minnows or frogs. Xanthe trailed her hand through the cool surface of the lake, doing her best to enjoy the beauty of the place and not think of Fairfax. Liam, as if reading her thoughts, nodded back toward the throng of guests.

"He's enjoying playing lord of the manor already," he said, earning himself a curious glance from Evie.

"It's an impressive event. Looks like he's invited all the great and the good from the area. Do you know everyone here, Evie?"

"Most of them. Father loves to entertain, but I'm not allowed to stay up if they are dining late. He makes me eat in the nursery like a child!"

"Imagine," said Xanthe.

"But I always sneak down to the stairs and watch as the guests come into the house." She looked up from the water for a moment to study the crowd. "I can see two earls, a countess, and four baronets. I fancy Mr. Fairfax would have been happier had he found a duke, but there aren't many left in Wiltshire during the season; they are all up in London."

"Your family doesn't like to spend the summer there?" she asked.

"No. Father says he prefers entertaining here, and he likes his hunting and shooting. He is always impatient for August and then we shall scarcely see him for days on end and every meal will be pheasant or grouse."

"Not good?" Liam asked.

Evie pulled a face. "I like fish!" she said firmly, going back to peering into the lake in search of some.

Xanthe looked with her. "Are there lots in this lake?" she asked.

"Oh yes. I'll catch one later, you'll see. You have to know which fly to use, because the lake is very deep, and the fish hide down in the weeds, which are all over the bottom. Can you see?"

Xanthe narrowed her eyes against the glare of the sun, forcing herself to focus below the surface. "Yes, yes I can. It looks like seaweed, and it's moving."

"That's because the stream flows in one end and out the other, underground. It looks like a real stream, but it isn't. It's built to flow in a circle. The water pulls at the weeds as it goes. You have to take great care if you decide to swim in there, or you will get tangled. One of our distant cousins drowned because he did not watch out for the weeds."

"Oh, I am sorry to hear that. Do people swim in it much?"

Evie laughed. "Not when there are so many people watching!" she said, reminding Xanthe that there was no such thing as swimming costumes for men at the time, so most people who bathed out of doors did so naked.

"There is a trout!" Evie exclaimed. "Did you see?"

"No, I don't think so . . . wait, is that it?" As she spoke she watched a dark shape moving far down in the depths, beyond the reach of the sun's rays. Slowly it began to rise, so that it emerged into the lighter level of the lake. As it did so it became paler, more distinct, so that she could soon see it was not a fish. It was a face. Suddenly it was near enough to recognize. Now she could see the whole person as he fought to swim to the surface, his hand reaching up toward her, his expression one of panic. As she stared at the apparition the figure began to sink again, his hand dropping, his body receding into the depths, farther and farther until he was lost to the darkness. With a cry Xanthe leapt back, causing the boat to rock wildly.

"Steady on!" Liam warned.

"Did you see a very big fish?" Evie asked.

"I . . ." She struggled to speak sensibly. "Yes, just a glimpse. Gave me quite a start." She closed her eyes to try to blink away the shocking vision she had glimpsed but it was there, haunting her mind's eye too. She opened them again, blinking away the shocking image of the drowned face.

"Are you all right?" Liam asked. "What scared you?"

"Nothing. I'm fine. The fish just . . . made me jump," she said, for how could she tell him the truth? How could she tell him that the figure she had seen drifting away beyond her reach, beyond saving, was him? She took a deep breath. "Is anyone else hungry?"

"Me!" cried Evie. "Let us have lemonade and cake. Petronella will tell me I must eat meat, but she will be too busy to notice. And Cook has made such puddings! See how people are crowding around the table? Oh, do please row faster, Mr. Westlake, else it will all be gone before we get there."

Xanthe was aware of Liam watching her closely as he worked the oars. She did not meet his eye. The image of him pale and drowning was so distressing she needed to distract herself from it, so she chatted lightly to Evie about what other food there would be for them to enjoy. They returned to the bank and Liam eventually helped Evie onto the little jetty. The girl ran ahead to find lemonade. As he helped Xanthe out of the boat he whispered to her.

"What is it? Is Fairfax up to his tricks?"

"No, it's nothing. Just this damn corset in the heat and leaning over the side of the boat. Made me woozy."

"You sure?" he asked, unconvinced, letting go of her hand to touch her cheek, searching her eyes for the truth.

"I'm fine, really," she assured him, concerned about how his gesture might look to anyone watching them. His expression and his concern went beyond the brotherly to anyone who cared to see it. "Come on, let's get something to eat."

They left the jetty and made their way toward the food. They had almost reached the marquee when Fairfax stepped out from the shade of a towering oak, glass of wine in hand.

"How quaint to see brother and sister so affectionate toward each other," he said, his words dripping spite. "What would the assembled company make of the truth of your relationship, I wonder? To masquerade as family whilst in point of fact being . . . let us say *friends* . . . well, it would call into question everything about a person, I should imagine. Wilcox is a genial host but even he has limits to what behavior he expects of his guests. Scandal is not to be tolerated."

Xanthe opened her mouth to respond to this but Liam acted before she could speak. With a glance over his shoulder to check they were not observed, he strode forward, taking hold of Fairfax by the lapels, and forcing him around the back of the tree. Xanthe lifted her long skirts and scurried after them. Liam had all but lifted Fairfax off his feet and had him pinned against the ancient bark of the oak. The older man had dropped his glass and clutched at his assailant's hand, his scrabblings having no effect on Liam's strong grip.

"Just so you know," he growled, keeping his voice low, "you only have all your teeth left because that suits Xanthe right now. You do anything, *anything*, to hurt her, and I might just forget my manners and give you the payback you already deserve for what you've done."

Fairfax spoke through his twisted, tightened collar and a furious scowl. "I had thought Miss Westlake more discerning than to bestow her affections upon a thug. It seems she had a use for you in mind after all."

Xanthe hissed at Liam. "Stop it! For goodness' sake, what if someone sees?"

Reluctantly, Liam let go, Fairfax dropping to his feet and folding at the stomach, coughing and holding his bruised throat.

"Just so you know," Liam repeated before offering Xanthe his arm and leading her on toward the marquee.

"That was reckless!" she told him.

"I know."

"What if somebody had seen what you did? How would we have explained it? Liam, we have to be more careful."

"I know," he repeated, the contained rage inside him still evident through the tension Xanthe could feel in his arm as she held it. They had almost reached the refreshments when she saw a figure a few paces to their left. "Wait a minute, look who's over there," she said, pointing toward the woman she had noticed.

"Mistress Flyte!" said Liam, before quickly correcting himself in case they were overheard. "Aunt! How nice that she was invited."

"Let's go and speak with her."

Mistress Flyte was wearing a fine cotton dress in a style which suited her well but was a touch old-fashioned for the time. Xanthe thought at first this might be because she had to watch the pennies and make things last, but then realized it was more contrived than that. A woman of mature years would, unless extremely wealthy and modern in her outlook, wear styles that harked back to her own youth and did not attempt to compete with the young girls of the day. Respectable older women invariably wore heavier fabrics, more elaborate corsetry, and covered themselves up. Even so, and despite the heat, she looked, as ever, poised and elegant. She greeted her niece and nephew affectionately, which meant allowing Liam to bow and kiss her hand and Xanthe to curtsey and kiss her cheek.

"How lovely to see you here, Aunt."

"Mr. Fairfax sent an invitation. A rather insistent one."

"It is unlike him to be quite so . . . considerate," said Xanthe.

Liam frowned. "He must have had his own reasons. I can't see him doing anything that could be considered kind."

"No doubt," Mistress Flyte agreed. "Whatever his motive, I am pleased to be here and to have the opportunity to speak with you."

"Let's walk together," Xanthe suggested, taking her arm. "Liam, would you mind fetching us something to drink?"

"Oh, of course," he said, understanding that she wished to speak with the old woman on her own. He bowed again. "I will catch you up bearing refreshments shortly," he promised.

Xanthe took them in a direction that led away from the main party. Other couples were strolling, and some were sitting on the grass, but there was sufficient space for a conversation to be private as long as they kept their voices low.

"I have been concerned at your silence," Mistress Flyte told her. "I cannot imagine being in such close proximity to Fairfax is either comfortable or safe for you. Has he approached you about the book?" she asked.

Before coming to stay at Corsham Hall, before what the book had revealed to her, Xanthe would have trusted her friend with everything she found out. With all the details of her plans. Now, though, she had been set wondering. Why had the Spinners book shown her a young Lydia Flyte? And what was the connection between her and the Spinner whose story she had heard? Was she the woman conversing with him, and if so, what on earth had she done to warrant a threat of death from him? Once again, her mind went back to how she had felt when she and Liam had arrived at the tearooms: how she had had the sense of glimpsing another side to this refined, elegant woman when she had been so against her having brought Liam with her.

"He has made his intentions very clear," she said carefully. "He wants the book. If I give it to him he says he will leave me alone and not cause any more trouble for me in my own time."

"And you trust him?"

"Of course not. I am . . . trying to find a way to take the astrolabe from him. That is my main concern at the moment. That and . . . well, I have been having visions, and hearing things from the book. It's hard to know what is connected to Fairfax and what isn't."

"The book has been speaking to you as well as showing you what is written? I recall it doing this in the past. It is a sign of the urgency and importance with which it wishes to communicate its secrets to you. You are fortunate indeed, to be so chosen," she said, and for the first time Xanthe detected a note of jealousy in her tone.

Was that why the book had shown her Mistress Flyte? Was it warning her not to trust the person who had helped her so much, who had assisted her in learning about the book in the first place?

Whoops of delight from a lively trio trying their hand at archery interrupted her thoughts. It bothered her that she had to be wary of the old woman, but there was too much at stake to be wrong. If, some-how, Lydia Flyte was siding with Fairfax, she must be on her guard and reveal nothing of her plans. However much she resisted believing such an idea, she had to tread softly.

"It's not just the book," she said. "I've been seeing glimpses, flashes of things—I don't know what they mean, but they are frightening. And confusing."

"The more time you spend as a Spinner, particularly out of your own time, the more the gift infiltrates your life. Soon you will not be able to separate the person you are when you are not spinning, from the person you are when you travel."

"You are speaking from your own experience? From the time when you were a Spinner?"

"It is not always a simple matter to move away."

"Well, of course, you *are* still spinning, aren't you? I mean, you use your gift to live in different times. Even if you aren't answering any calls, you are still time traveling."

"As I say, it becomes harder to separate the two aspects of oneself. Which is why you are having the experiences that seem, to you, unconnected."

"I suppose I know there is a connection, that it all joins up somehow. I just haven't worked it out yet."

"Tell me what conclusions you have drawn thus far. It may be that I am able to offer some clarity."

"That would be very welcome, but . . . I suppose it's not surprising . . ."

"What is it, child?"

"Some of the things I see, I hear, I read . . . they involve you."

She felt the slightest tremor of tension pass down Mistress Flyte's arm as she held it. Other than that she gave no outward sign that this information in any way disconcerted her.

"Indeed. The book will show you many Spinners, no doubt. Perhaps it wishes to put those you have met in context. As you say, it is not, after all, surprising."

"Maybe not, and yet . . ." She paused and stopped walking. Still holding the old woman's arm so that she might gauge her reactions, she asked simply, "Who is Erasmus Balmoral?"

Mistress Flyte's sharp blue eyes widened and she snatched her arm away, taking a step back. For once her inscrutable expression and her unshakable composure were undone. Her face showed genuine dismay.

She seemed on the point of forming a reply when a shout went up from the main group of the party, followed by several shrieks and cries. Xanthe turned to see that Henry's horse had broken loose and was thundering blindly across the grass, scattering picnickers in all directions. Men tried to grab its bridle, or waved their arms to turn it away from the women and children. Henry ran after it, shouting alternately oaths and warnings. For an awful moment it seemed there would be casualties until a footman, dropping the silver platter of pastries he had been charged with, leapt in the horse's path and took hold of its reins, quickly turning it and bringing it to a halt. The danger passed, Henry retrieved his mount and led it away uttering heartfelt apologies.

Evie came sprinting up to Xanthe. "Did you see? Did you see? Lady Melrose was near trampled to death! Mr. Fairfax is calling for poor Henry's horse to be shot, but Father will not hear of it. I fear they shall come to blows. Oh, please come and bring your brother to speak to them both!" she begged, grabbing Xanthe's hand and dragging her back toward the marquee.

The remainder of the day passed slowly for Xanthe. Her thoughts were so focused on what she had to do, anything other than preparing for it was an unwelcome distraction. She needed to get back to the Spinners book but could only do so when the household had gone to bed. Up to this point, it would not have mattered if someone had interrupted her reading. To the uninformed observer she would simply be doing just that; reading peacefully in her room. Now, though, the time had come to go one step further. A significant step further. After turning over and over in her mind what she had seen in and heard from the book so far, she had formed an idea of how she might be able to outwit Fairfax using her talent as a Spinner. To be sure of success, she needed to try out the plan first. And that meant she could not risk being interrupted. It was gone midnight by the time the house was quiet. She had not even wanted to tell Liam of what she intended doing. While it was reassuring and helpful to have him at Corsham Hall with her, she needed to spin alone. To have him present as she did so would pull her in the wrong direction. Focus, clarity of intention and thought, would be vital.

Xanthe had allowed the maid to help her out of her day dress and into her nightclothes, but now quickly slipped her pinafore over the linen shift.

"Fail to prepare and prepare to fail. Or something," she told herself, knowing that she had to plan for both best- and worst-case scenarios. To this end, she also put a few essentials in a small bag and slipped it over her shoulder. There was no key in the lock of the door, so she jammed a chair in place to prevent anyone coming into the room. "Just in case," she muttered, trying to keep herself calm. She was pleased to realize that it was not apprehension but excitement that was causing her pulse to quicken. She picked up the Spinners book and set it down on the dressing table, a candle either side of it. She hesitated then, wondering if she should leave a note for Liam. She decided against, reasoning that nothing she could say in it would be useful, and nothing he could do—if her experiment went wrong—would make any difference. The thought reminded her that she and he would always have this strange distance between them; that she was a Spinner and he was not. It saddened her to think that distance could never be completely crossed. "Not now, girl," she told herself, quickly tying her hair into a loose ponytail to keep it out of the way. She slipped on her ankle boots and tied a shawl around her shoulders, not knowing what weather she was likely to encounter. Next she moved the little stool out of the way and stepped forward to stand before the book. She turned the pages, willing it to show her again the incantation she had used when taking Fairfax to find his astrolabe. How long ago that felt. How much had happened since.

"Show me," she asked. "I am Xanthe Westlake of Marlborough, Spinner, and I wish to travel. Show me the words I need."

For a moment there was nothing, then the whispers started. Whispers that put her in mind of the clamor she heard every time she stepped into the blind house at home. There seemed to be more than Spinners talking to her through the book. She detected the cries and entreaties of people who needed her. It was as if declaring herself as a Spinner out loud and with the book had allowed her presence to be detected not only by Spinners themselves, but by those who would be helped by her. She shuddered at the thought that, of course, Fairfax would be able to sense her activity. She pushed the thought from her mind in case it somehow summoned him.

At last words began to form on the page in front of her, hastily written, it seemed, scrawled almost. No voice read them, and she decided this was because it was she who was meant to say them aloud. Her voice that needed to be heard now. She took a breath.

> *Let the door through the fabric of time swing wide,*
> *May I travel through time's secret rift.*
> *Let the centuries spin at my bidding,*
> *May my return be sure and be swift.*

She repeated the lines. An unnatural breeze caused the flames of the candles to dance. The whispering voices fell silent.

Xanthe spoke again, directly to the book, to the spirits of the Spinners within it, and this time she did not ask diffidently. This time she instructed.

"Take me to a time, in this place, where I can see what I need to see, find what I need to find, know what I need to know. Show me something that will help me in my task. But return me here, to this very time and this very place." As she said these words she stamped her heel hard on the wooden boards. She knew she had to anchor herself to the time somehow. It didn't feel enough. She looked around for something she could take with her, something small yet intimately tied to the room as it was at that moment. The bed had been made for the house, its drapes and covers too. Quickly she took hold of one of the red tassels on the heavy bedspread and pulled a silk thread from it. This she tied through the buttonhole at the neck of her green cotton pinafore. She stood by the book again.

"Show me now!" she demanded. In her eagerness to make the request work she gestured with her hand, emphasizing her words, failing to take into account how close she was to the candle. Her hand swept over the flame. The sharp pain of it made her cry out, and the burnt line across the tender underside of her fingers continued to hurt as she quickly dropped her hand to her side once more. She dare not let the pain distract her. "Time-within-time!" she said, repeating the words that were now being all but shouted in her ear by a male voice she recognized. "Time-within-time!"

Suddenly, the pages of the book turned of their own accord, flipping first steadily, one at a time, then faster, more and more pages, an impossible number, so that they became a blur, until the air in the room was disturbed out of all sense. Both candles guttered and failed, the darkness enveloping her, the smell of smoldering wax accompanying her as she plunged through time.

The transition was swift. Xanthe felt no dizziness nor lessening of her senses at all. It was as if, being so much more active in the process, she was more able to withstand its effects. She found herself in the walled garden of the Hall.

"Yes!" She allowed herself a quiet expression of satisfaction. She might not be inside the house, but she had controlled the location of her travel point quite well. It was sharply cold and the thin layer of snow beneath her boots and bareness of the fruit trees spoke of deep midwinter. It was not yet fully nighttime; the sun was setting, painting the sky a brash orange, the heavy clouds a dusky pink. She heard soft voices. Not the whisperings of those in a distant time, but words being spoken there and then, in the garden. She must not be discovered. There was a dividing row of thick yew trees into which she quickly stepped, their evergreen branches providing excellent cover. From her hiding place she watched as two figures, a man and a woman, walked into view. They stopped only a few strides from where she crouched, so that even in the twilight she was able to see, and to recognize, their faces. The couple were unmistakably Lydia Flyte and the man Xanthe now knew to be Erasmus Balmoral. Their relationship was clearly one of intimacy and affection. The man turned his love toward him, encircling her in his arms, gazing into her eyes with a fierce intensity. Xanthe tried to pinpoint the date by studying their clothes, but the cold weather meant they were both wearing heavy coats that covered them from neck to ankle. The boots were not much to go on. Erasmus's hair, grown long past his collar and swept back, was salt-and-peppered with maturity but he appeared youthful and strong. Lydia wore no hat and her hair hung loose down her back. It was a surprise to see her golden tresses instead of the white-grey Xanthe was accustomed to. When the pair kissed it was with passion restrained and evident longing.

Erasmus stroked her cold cheek. "You understand me now?" he asked. "You truly accept what I must do?"

She nodded slowly. "I have made my choice."

"You will side with me on this? For I can take no other path."

"I will, I promise."

"That promise must be freely given," he told her. "For you will forfeit much and there can be no altering course once the decision is taken."

By way of an answer she kissed him again.

He took from the pocket of his coat a small sprig of white winter heather. He reached up and tucked it into the buttonhole of her lapel.

"For good fortune and for protection," he said. And then he kissed her again and added, "You have my heart."

For a moment they stood, her face tilted up to him, the strange sky lending them both a curious supernatural glow. Xanthe was moved by the passionate way he regarded his woman. Was that feeling returned? As she studied Lydia's face she noticed an unusual flare from her eyes, which she put down to the low sun and the awkward angle from which she was compelled to observe them.

"I must take my leave," he said. "Until tomorrow." He left quickly then, striding away, his boots crunching through the snow as he went.

Xanthe waited, not daring to move. Lydia Flyte watched her lover leave the garden. Once she could see him no more, she took the heather from her coat, crushed it in her hand, and threw the ruined flower onto the icy ground.

It was then that she turned and stared in the direction of the yew trees. Xanthe held her breath. She must not be found, not by her, not at that moment. Quickly, she fumbled at her pinafore until she had hold of the thread of silk.

"Time-within-time," she whispered urgently. "Return me to my time-within-time."

She closed her eyes, conjuring a clear picture before her mind's eye of her room at Corsham Hall, thinking of Petronella and the wedding dress and Liam in his fine Regency clothes. Anything, in fact, that would pull her toward that specific time and place. She felt rather than heard Mistress Flyte moving closer across the frozen garden, but in an instant she was spinning through time again, and in another heartbeat she was there, in her bedroom, snow melting off her boots onto the Persian rug.

{ 17 }

NOW THAT SHE HAD SUCCEEDED IN MOVING BACK THROUGH TIME AND RETURNING TO A time that was not her own, Xanthe dearly wanted to share her news with Liam. She needed to talk it through, to try to make sense of what she saw, to get his opinion on Mistress Flyte and whether or not she could be trusted. More urgently, she wanted to talk to him about how they might use her newly acquired ability to safely take the astrolabe from Fairfax. She was up and dressed early, taking a moment to wrap a strip of cotton over the candle burn on her fingers. She found his room empty and was told he had gone out riding with Henry before breakfast to avoid the heat of the day. She resigned herself to spending the morning with Petronella and tried not to be impatient. The bride-to-be was becoming increasingly subdued as the days went by, and Xanthe suspected the reality of her upcoming marriage was beginning to strike home. They went to visit a family who lived in one of the estate cottages, taking them produce from the garden, and then into Bradford to find new shoes for Evie, who had unhelpfully outgrown the ones she had planned to wear for the wedding. After buying a pretty pair of blue leather shoes, the three decided to stroll around the town for a while before returning home. Petronella took Xanthe's arm, while Evie skipped ahead, looking in windows or stopping to pet a passing pet spaniel out for its constitutional.

Petronella regarded her sister a little wistfully. "How lovely to be young enough not to care for anything beyond climbing trees and greeting dogs."

"Life is certainly simpler when you're a child."

"Which is as it should be of course. One day, Evie will grow up and we shall be planning her wedding."

At that moment Evangeline clambered up a short run of railings so that she could reach a caterpillar she had spied on the branch of an ornamental cherry tree at the edge of the park. Watching her, both women laughed.

"I think it might be a while yet," Xanthe said, pleased to see Petronella happy for a moment. "Do you feel ready for your own wedding? Only a few more days. Is everything in place?"

"All is prepared, I believe, now that Evie is shod! In truth, there is more to organizing a ball than a country wedding. It is important that the villagers and the estate workers witness our marriage, as they are to have a new master at Corsham Hall. Beyond that, there will of course be a wedding breakfast, but a modest one. This is not London, after all, and people are still mindful of so many years of war."

"And you will not go on a honeymoon?" The puzzled look on Petronella's face made Xanthe wish she could swallow her words. Only in that moment did she recall that such things did not exist at the time. "I mean, you will not be going on a holiday, with your new husband? A short trip abroad, perhaps?" she asked, merely to try to cover her mistake.

"Oh no, Benedict is eager to begin work modernizing the estate. He has great plans."

"I'm sure he does."

"And I shall do my best to run the house according to his wishes. Oh, look! There are the Miss Sullivans. I'm sorry to say but they are terrible gossips and I have no wish to be interrogated by them in the street. Come, Evie! We must go home," she said, turning around to walk quickly back toward the coaching inn where their carriage was waiting for them.

On their return to the Hall she found the men still out. She did her best to be a good friend to Petronella and cheer her up but she was horribly preoccupied with her own concerns. She was in the walled garden when she saw the riders return to the stables. As soon as she could she made an excuse to Petronella about needing to spend a little time out of the sun in her room, and hurried indoors.

Once upstairs, she checked that she wasn't observed and then quickly let herself into Liam's room, turning to close the door. From behind her, Liam's voice showed more than a little surprise.

"Well, come right on in. No need to knock, not like I might be taking a bath or anything," he said.

She spun around to see him lying in a huge copper bath that had been positioned in front of the fire. Steam rose from the hot water as he rested against linen cloths that had been draped over the back and sides of the tub. He pushed his damp hair off his face. His strong shoulders gleamed, the colors of his tattoos were darkened, the muscles of his arms showing their curves and fullness. Xanthe found herself staring at a water droplet that was running down his throat, past his collarbone, over his chest, and into the water. Fortunately, sunlight from the tall windows caused the surface of the water to be reflective, rather than transparent, at least from where she stood. Flustered, she kept her gaze on Liam's face. He grinned at her, raising a washcloth.

"Feel like scrubbing my back?"

"Sorry, can't," she said, showing him her bandaged hand.

"Oh, what did you do?"

"It's nothing. Burnt my fingers on a candle," she said dismissively. "Don't want to get the bandage wet."

"Come here, let me take a look."

"Er . . . no?"

He shrugged. "OK, I'll come to you," he said, placing his hands on the sides of the bathtub as if about to push himself up.

"No!" Xanthe strode forward. "Just stay in there," she said, kneeling beside the bath, giving him her hand, and doing her best not to keep looking at his nakedness.

Gently, he unwrapped the dressing and examined the burn. "Ouch. That must have hurt."

"Never mind that, it's nothing. I have so much to tell you!"

"Might have to put something on it. Can't risk it getting infected."

"Forget about my hand," she said, rather more curtly than she had intended.

He let go, raising his hands in submission and his eyebrows in a way that questioned her.

"Sorry, didn't mean to snap," she said. "It's just I've been dying to tell you . . . last night I traveled back in time."

"What? Why? And why didn't you tell me?"

"I needed to figure something out for myself. To work with more control. The thing is, I managed to go back, not sure how many years . . ."

"Oh, so, really in control then."

"I controlled the location, which was one thing I was determined to do. I landed in the garden."

"But you don't know when?"

"I can't be certain. The main thing is, when I wanted to come back, I did it, straight away, to *this* time. Don't you see how big that is?"

"Sort of, but didn't you do something like that when you were getting Fairfax his astrolabe?"

"Not the same." She shook her head. "Once we had it, the astrolabe acted as a found thing."

"But you sent him and it some . . . *when* else?"

"I still used it to send me back to Fairfax's time, and to where the chocolate pot was."

"That means, it could have been the wedding dress that brought you back to this present time, not anything you did."

"I don't think so."

"Why not?"

"Well, for one thing this was much more accurate. I had very little say in where I ended up when I traveled before. This time it was precise, bringing me back to the room I left, to the exact spot where I had traveled from. And for another thing, it was because I wasn't passive. I was directing things. I was in control. Only I didn't use the locket and go back to Mum and home. I came to here. To now."

"So, what did you use?"

"I took a thread from the bedcover. That bed was made for this house, and quite recently, according to the maid. And I used an incantation from *Spinners*. And then I just focused on Petronella, and the wedding dress, and . . ." She hesitated.

"And?" He waited for her to finish the sentence, picking up on it having a different significance.

"And you," she said, looking him in the eyes, holding his gaze, watching him watching her. "I thought about you, here, in your nineteenth-century clothes, waiting for me."

He was silent then, for once not responding with a flippant remark, not making a joke or keeping the mood light. Slowly he sat up straighter and then leaned forward, lifting a wet hand to touch her cheek. Xanthe felt herself stirring, her mood altering. She had sought him out to tell him about her important progress as a Spinner, but what she had explained to him highlighted something else. In that moment she was as certain as she could be that it was Liam, and her connection to him, that had drawn her back so accurately to that time. To him. As she looked deep into his pale blue eyes she felt that connection spark a fire inside her. Liam let his finger trace her jawline, then trail down her throat. His expression was serious, his voice low when he spoke again.

"Xanthe," he murmured. Just that. No smooth words. No suggestive remarks. No clever comments about her joining him in the bath, which, she realized, she might happily have done, there, then, in that charged moment. Instead, he just said her name, and filled it with such desire and such longing it made her blush. The force of her feelings, of her reaction to him, was unexpected and disconcerting. Now was most definitely not the time. Sensitive to her confusion and seeing that she was conflicted, Liam pulled back.

"Hey, you're the time traveler," he said, deliberately steering the conversation, and the focus, toward her task, and away from themselves. "I won't pretend I understood half of what you just told me, but, it's not the job of the sidekick to get it all. You're the brains of this outfit."

She stood up, plucking a towel from the chair by the fireplace and tossing it to him. "And don't you forget it," she said mildly. She walked over to stand at the window to allow him to get out of the bath and get dressed. And to allow herself to look firmly and pointedly somewhere else. Anywhere else, so long as it wasn't at his fine, freshly washed body.

"There's more," she told him. "When I went back, I saw a couple in the garden. They were lovers, making promises to each other, and he had to leave, and she . . . she was Mistress Flyte."

"Oh, really? Why would the book want you to see that? I mean, she must have been a beauty in her day, I guess she had more than one bloke keen on her. I don't see how it helps with what we're trying to do."

As he spoke she could hear water dripping as he climbed out of the bath. She tried hard not to picture it.

"It could have been something to do with what happened when he left," she explained. "While he was there she was promising love, loyalty, everything. As soon as he left she destroyed the love token he'd given her and threw it away."

"Sounds like she definitely had strong feelings for him, one way or another."

"I think maybe the book was warning me. That she's not to be trusted. Or at least, her actions are not to be taken at face value."

"But, she's been helping us . . . you said she was a Spinner once, and someone you could trust. A friend."

"I did trust her. I had to, the last time I traveled . . . it's hard to believe she's not what she seems, and not, well, good."

"And the man you saw, who was he?"

"Someone I've learned of in the pages of the book. His name is Erasmus Balmoral. He was a Spinner, who'd had a brutal upbringing, then joined the other Spinners, fallen in love with Lydia, then made a decision that sounded like leaving the group, and she agreed to do it with him. But looks like she was lying."

Liam, wearing clean breeches and a loose linen collarless shirt, stood next to her, leaning against the jamb of the window. He looked at her in the friendly, casual way he usually did. Xanthe couldn't decide whether she was relieved or disappointed.

"Nope," he said, "still don't see how any of this helps."

"Nor do I. Yet."

"Except we maybe don't tell Mistress Flyte any more about what we're planning to do."

"That. And somehow I should be able to use the hopping through short bits of time so accurately to help us."

"Well, you could hop back to an hour ago when Fairfax met us in the woods. He was on that beast of a horse of his. You'd know for certain he wouldn't be at home."

"He wouldn't be, but his servants would. And the astrolabe would still be under lock and key, you can rely on that. No, I can't see how yet, but I will. I just need a little more time."

"Which is, unfortunately, exactly what we don't have much of."

* * *

Although it was not to be a particularly grand affair, the remaining time before the wedding day saw a fair amount of activity at Corsham Hall. Guest rooms were aired and prepared. Deliveries of food came fast and frequent. Arrangements for guests, for their carriages and horses, and for the ceremony itself, all occupied the entire household. The ceaseless work made Xanthe wonder what a ball would entail, given what Petronella had said about her marriage celebrations being on a modest scale. At last the appointed day arrived. Xanthe dressed with the help of a maid and then went to the bride's room.

Petronella stood in front of the full-length mirror in her bedroom looking breathtakingly beautiful in her wedding gown. She appeared as gorgeous and as bridal as it was possible for a person to be, but her manner was anything but that of a joyous bride. Xanthe wondered, not for the first time, what she would have done had she been in her situation. She knew that nothing would have persuaded her to marry Fairfax, but Petronella did not know the man's history or his true nature. What mattered to her was her duty to the family she loved. Which was not to say her life choice had not cost her dearly. Xanthe tried to imagine how she must be feeling, dressed for her wedding, about to marry a man she had no affection for and barely knew, when it should have been her beloved Edward waiting for her at the chapel. To have known such love and have lost it, to have had happiness snatched away from her by the savagery of war, was a lot for a tender young heart to withstand.

"Oh, Petronella, you look so very lovely."

"Will Mr. Fairfax approve, do you think? I do want to be a good wife to him, and for him to have no cause to complain to Father."

"He is a fortunate man to have such a charming and accomplished bride. Mr. Wilcox will be the proudest father ever, I'm certain of it."

"I cannot help but wonder what my dear mother would have felt, to see her daughter dressed so, about to be wed . . . My parents were so blessed, for theirs was not only a mutually advantageous match, but one of love. What would she have to say about my choice of husband, do you suppose?"

"She would have known you were acting upon the best of intentions, with your sister's future uppermost in your mind, as well as security for your father, and yourself. She could not have asked more of you."

Petronella seemed content to hear this. She allowed Xanthe and her maid to put the finishing touches to her hair, adding tiny rose buds to the complicated chignon and ringlets. The creamy petals sat prettily against the rich dark brown of her hair. The maid fastened a double string of pearls at her mistress's neck. Xanthe had removed the bandage from her hand, but the burn was still sore and apt to make her clumsy, so she let the maid help with the trickier things. Petronella wore no other jewelry. The detail, the lace, and the beading of the dress were so decorative, nothing else was required. The final addition was the veil, which was made of whisper-light voile. Xanthe had to stand on a stool to pin the comb in exactly the right spot in Petronella's hairdo. The maid arranged the veil so that some of it fell forward over the bride's face while the rest cascaded down her back and onto the floor in a romantic train.

"Thank you," said Petronella to both her helpers. "I believe I am ready. Let us walk down together. Father will meet me at the chapel door." She reached out and touched Xanthe's hand. "Come now, happy faces for a happy occasion. I will not have anyone say I was an unwilling bride." To underline her point she smiled, her beautiful face even more lovely when she did so. The maid handed her the bouquet made of flowers picked from the garden earlier that morning. Petronella breathed in the sweet perfume of the roses, lily of the valley, and gypsophila.

Xanthe took her arm. "It will be a beautiful wedding for a beautiful bride," she agreed.

Together they made their way down the stairs and through the house, the maid holding the gossamer-light train of the veil. They walked to the east wing, beyond the ballroom and the music room, along a wide corridor where distant ancestors observed their progress from gilt-framed portraits. At last they went out through a side door which gave onto a narrow stretch of lawn, traversed by a gravel path. At the end of this, and a little forward from the door to the family chapel, stood the father of the bride. When they reached him his mouth opened in astonishment at the sight of his daughter but no words came. Instead, he offered her his arm. Xanthe stepped back to take up the train from the maid, and the trio made their way through the high arched entrance.

Inside, the organist struck up Mozart's wedding procession. The chapel was small, with everything on a modest scale, but all was lavishly decorated and of the very best quality, with a gilded altar, carved altarpiece and choir stalls, burnished oak pews and lectern, brass and marble nameplates set into the floor and walls, and even its own lofty stained glass window in the nave. There was seating for fifty or so, but only four pews were taken up. These were filled with family and close friends only. The vicar stood at the end of the aisle, a tiny choir of four boys, two men, and two nuns behind him.

There were flowers from the garden at the end of each pew and on the altar. Xanthe thought of how much care Petronella had put into choosing each and every bloom. She felt her stomach tighten at the sight of Fairfax standing tall and proud, turning to watch his bride approach. Liam was in the second pew, looking smartly turned out. He gave her a small smile of encouragement, knowing how much she hated being a part of such a charade, pretending that Fairfax would make a good husband, hoping that she would somehow be able to save Petronella from her fate and yet unable to find a way.

When the little procession reached the appointed place, Mr. Wilcox let go his daughter's arm and stepped back, and the vicar raised his eyes and his voice to begin the service.

It was a short and simple ceremony, with only one hymn and a short sermon from the vicar on the importance of obedience and trust in a marriage. In what seemed an almost disrespectfully short time, he had declared them man and wife, permitted the groom to lift the veil and kiss his bride, and the pair were walking back down the aisle, Mr. and Mrs. Benedict Fairfax of Corsham Hall.

Xanthe fell into step behind them, taking up the train again. The church bells were rung with gusto, welcoming the bridal party to their new lives as they left the chapel. She was surprised, as they emerged into the golden sunshine of the day, to hear a cheer go up and find a crowd had gathered. Looking closely, she recognized the family she and Petronella had visited a few days earlier, the gardeners, the grooms and stable boys and other servants, and people from the village. These were not grand society friends and acquaintances, they were local folk, people who lived and worked on the estate or in the house itself, villagers and farmers and schoolchildren, all invited to come and witness the union of the new master and mistress of the great house. They cheered and threw rose petals and rice, and Fairfax reveled in every second of their adulation and approval. The wedding party, with guests filing out of the chapel, then processed across the gardens, along the side of the house, and up the grand front steps. Here the newlyweds turned to wave more to the crowd. Fairfax handed small bags of coins to three footmen who walked into the gathered crowd, throwing money, causing children and adults alike to squeal and scramble. At last, the couple entered the house, followed by their carefully chosen guests, whom they led into the dining room where the wedding breakfast was to be served.

Liam caught up with Xanthe as they looked for their names among the place cards.

"I get the feeling this could take some time," he said, looking at the elaborate settings on the table. There were at least three glasses per person, and several sets of knives, forks, and spoons, suggesting large amounts of food to come.

"It's strange," she whispered to him. "Not like modern weddings. I mean, the food will be extravagant, yes, but everything else is quite small scale. I've never been to such a speedy service, and there can only be, what, thirty guests?"

"Just be thankful there's no dancing," he pointed out, moving aside to let a footman pull out her chair for her as they took their places.

"There will be singing later, though," she said.

"Evie has been practicing hard. I've volunteered to play so she can concentrate on singing. She's quite nervous about it."

"Hardly surprising," Xanthe murmured. It wasn't just that this was her big sister's big day, or the having to stand up and sing in front of lots of important-looking people, although both things were enough to make a girl nervous. She thought there was more to it than that. There was a tension about the whole occasion. It was not a warm, family celebration, romantic and fun. It had more the feel of a business transaction being made, with society people there to witness it. The formality was at odds with the prettiness of the bride in her dress and the personal nature of what was taking place, but it was unmistakable. However hard Petronella was trying to look, if not happy, at least content and willing, everyone present knew this was not a love match. Xanthe wondered how many of them also harbored doubts about Fairfax. He was a stranger to most of them, his background vague, and yet here he was, winning the hand of one of the most desirable girls in the county, and bagging an important house and estate into the bargain.

The feast itself was elaborate, expensive, and exhausting. Course after course was brought out by increasingly breathless footmen. Plates of game pies were followed by fish mousses which were followed by a clear soup, after which came stuffed fowl, and then hot slices of roast beef, all washed down with a different wine or port. The puddings and desserts when they arrived were spectacular and, to Xanthe's mind, triumphs of ingenuity given that the cook must work with an ice house rather than a refrigerator and no freezer. There were towering jellies and blancmanges, confections of spun sugar over tropical fruits that must have cost a small fortune in themselves, and syllabubs and sweet biscuits and all manner of nuts glazed, roasted, or pulped into pralines. There were no speeches as such, although Mr. Wilcox did rise to toast the bride and groom. After nearly two hours at table, the guests were invited to repair to one of the grander rooms, which had been set up for cards and singing. Fairfax and Petronella led the way. Once the party had settled in these more relaxed surroundings, the atmosphere became more convivial, helped in no small part by the amount of alcohol people had consumed with their meal. There was general chatter, some of it quite loud, and everyone was able to mill about and speak with whomever they wished to. As Xanthe circled the room she heard gossip being savored, family news being shared, and one or two risqué tales being recounted by the more exuberant men, most of whom appeared to be friends of Henry's and cut from the same cloth.

She was completely taken up with observing the fascinating interactions of so many aristocrats and high-society people who had let down their ordinarily impenetrable walls of manners and etiquette to allow a glimpse at how they truly lived their lives. She was so intrigued by them that she had not noticed Fairfax come to stand beside her. His voice made her start.

"Miss Westlake, I trust you are enjoying the celebrations."

"You have stepped into the role of master of Corsham Hall so easily, Mr. Fairfax, one might almost believe you deserved it." She glanced about to make sure they were not overheard before adding, "If, that is, one did not know you as well as I do."

"A lack of generosity of spirit in a woman is quite unbecoming. You might wish to consider that, if you aim to make your own way in society."

"The only society I am interested in is that of the Spinners. As soon as I have done what I came here to do I shall leave Corsham and return home. So, the sooner we make our exchange the better. You said it must wait until after the wedding."

"As you wish. Let us meet at the folly, as agreed, at midday tomorrow."

"You will bring the astrolabe."

"I shall. And you, little Spinner, will bring the book. Do not think to cheat me of it. I have defeated far more worthy opponents than you, and they did not live to talk of it."

"Save your threats, Fairfax. Tomorrow. Midday. Don't be late," she said, turning to smile at Evie, who was taking her place beside Liam at the pianoforte. She walked quickly away from Fairfax, choosing to stand beside Mr. Wilcox, willing her anger to subside so that she could put out of her mind what was to come the next day. For now, all she wanted to do was watch Liam play and enjoy listening to little Evangeline sing.

It was properly dark when Xanthe was finally able to speak to Liam. Many of the guests had left, their carriages being summoned to bear them away into the sultry night. The more hardy partygoers remained, mostly men, taking up residence in the music room or the larger of the drawing rooms. The level of conversation was of lower quality and higher volume. Evie had long since been sent to bed. The groom was making the most of every minute of the festivities. Petronella sat quietly with two maiden aunts and a cousin awaiting the moment when she and Fairfax would retire to their bedroom. Xanthe put a hand on Liam's arm.

"Let's step outside for a while. I can't bear to watch him crowing and her suffering any longer, and it is so hot and stuffy in here."

"An excellent idea," Liam agreed. "Just a second." He paused on their way out of the drawing room to help himself to a brandy decanter and two glasses.

They walked across the grand hall and into the main reception room, the windows of which had been thrown open. They stepped out onto the veranda, both sighing with relief at the cooler, cleaner air that greeted them. Liam led them to a low stone seat that allowed a good view of the vista from the front of the house. He took off his jacket and put it on the stone for Xanthe to sit on.

"Always the gentleman," she said.

He smiled as he poured two generous measures of brandy and handed one to Xanthe as he sat next to her. "Must be all these posh clothes and manners," he said. "Beginning to rub off on me."

"It'll all fall away when you get home. That's what I've found, anyway. All the strange mannerisms and stilted patterns of speech—you think they've become a real habit, but as soon as you are back in your own time, they fade away."

"Probably just as well. Not very practical gear for working on oily motors."

She sipped the fine French brandy. She was about to bring up the subject of her meeting with Fairfax when the sound of more carriage wheels distracted her. As they watched, a small but smart gig, pulled by one dappled grey, was driven around to the front entrance. It was something like a phaeton, built for speed and short distances, open topped and beautifully painted with polished brass fittings. The door of the house was opened by a footman and a figure emerged. Even in the low light provided by the torches placed around the driveway Xanthe recognized the man who trod heavily down the steps.

"It's Petronella's father," she said. "He must be going to the dower house. She said it is where he would be living now, but I hadn't expected him to leave so soon."

"Can't have two masters in one house," Liam pointed out.

Mr. Wilcox paused as the driver held the door of the carriage open for him. He turned slowly, a full circle, as if taking in the house that had been his, the home that he had been head of, the place where his wife had lived and died, for the last time.

"It will never be the same for him," said Xanthe. "It might still be home for his girls, but it belongs to Fairfax now. He will only ever be a guest."

At last, Mr. Wilcox climbed aboard and the driver shut the door and sprang up into his high seat. With a click of the tongue and a flick of the reins the horse picked up its hooves and trotted briskly along the drive, carrying its somber passenger away from his old life and toward his new one.

"Petronella's not the only one with adjustments to make. And what will it be like for poor Evie? She doesn't even like the man."

"She's a good judge of character."

"I feel like I've failed."

"You haven't."

"The wedding dress called me here. It must have been to help Petronella, and all I've done is sit and watch as Fairfax gets what he wants. Petronella. The estate. How have I helped her?"

"Your mission is to take Fairfax's astrolabe away and stop him abusing his Spinner's gifts. You can't fix everything. You have to concentrate on that."

She nodded, swirling the dark liquid in the deep, round glass. Liam put his arm around her, drawing her close, letting her rest her head on his shoulder. For a while they sat in silence, listening to sounds of increasingly raucous merriment drifting out from inside the house, and the distant call of young foxes exploring the summer night. She knew she should discuss their plan for what was going to happen the next day, but she felt suddenly overcome by weariness. It had been a long day, with too many people, and too much food, and more than enough tension. It was blissful just to sit, leaning on Liam, feeling safe, wrapped in the darkness, breathing in the scent of climbing jasmine as it surrendered its perfume to the moon.

{ 18 }

BREAKFAST THE FOLLOWING MORNING WAS ONE OF THE MOST AWKWARD MEALS Xanthe had ever had to sit through. Fairfax sat at the head of the table in what had been, until only the day before, Mr. Wilcox's place. To his right sat Petronella, subdued and pale, her lack of appetite obvious to everyone. Liam was doing his best to lighten the atmosphere in the dining room but with little success. Xanthe found herself eating quickly, keen to be anywhere but sitting among the sorry remnants of the family, finding the smug expression on Fairfax's face unbearable. Evie's chair was empty.

"Evie is late down this morning," she commented. "She's usually hungry as a hunter and keen to be attacking the day."

Petronella looked at her sister's vacant seat as if only just noticing her absence. "I imagine she is tired after the long celebrations of yesterday," she said quietly. "Let her sleep. There are no appointments arranged for today and she has no lessons with Miss Talbot, it being Sunday. We can attend evensong in place of morning prayers."

Liam accepted more scrambled eggs from the footman. "Nothing like a good breakfast after a late night, I find. Best cure for a hangover."

"What is a hangover?" Petronella asked. "It sounds frightful."

"Oh, a London expression," he explained. "It refers to suffering the aftereffects of too much drinking." Xanthe was impressed at how adept Liam had become at explaining away his anachronistic speech and vocabulary. Their plan for him to be the moody silent type and say as little as possible had never worked. She saw that she should have trusted him to be capable of finding his own way of being a Regency gentleman. He was really quite good at it.

"I see. Father takes raw egg with a dash of vinegar in it when he is similarly out of sorts." Her face brightened for an instant as she spoke of her father and then looked sad again as she glanced at the man who had taken his place as head of the household.

The lady's maid who attended both the young Wilcox girls entered the room looking more than a little flustered. She hurried over to Petronella as if to speak to her privately but Fairfax was having none of it.

"Elsie? Whatever is the matter that you should interrupt your mistress's breakfast in such a way. You look alarmed, and that in itself will alarm my wife."

Xanthe winced at the way he spoke of Petronella.

Elsie bobbed a curtsey and spoke quickly.

"Beg pardon, Mr. Fairfax, sir, but it is Miss Evangeline."

Petronella put down her spoon. "Is Evie unwell?"

"Not unwell, Miss . . . Mrs. Fairfax. Missing."

"Missing?" Now Petronella was truly alarmed.

"Not in her room, and, by the look of it, her bed has not been slept in."

Petronella rose from her chair, the sound of the wooden legs scraping against the floor echoing through the brief silence in the room. "Elsie, please ask the servants if anyone has seen her this morning."

"I will, ma'am. Shall I have them search the house?"

"Please do," Fairfax interrupted.

"She won't be indoors," said Petronella. "Evie loves to be outside." A sudden thought made her face light up again. "She might have gone to Father! Elsie, wait, have the gig sent round. I will go to the dower house directly."

Fairfax stood up. "As you wish, my dear. Mr. Westlake, will you join me in a search of the estate? I shall have Henry roused from his bed. Little Evie may have taken it into her head to go on a woodland walk. We three can cover a deal of ground mounted. Do not distress yourself, my dear," he said to Petronella, taking her hand. "We will find your sister, I am certain she has come to no harm."

Xanthe frowned at him, annoyed that he should put the idea in her head. "Shall I accompany you to the dower house, Petronella?" she asked.

"Oh, would you be so kind as to remain here? In the event Evie returns to the house I should not like her to find it empty."

"Of course," she said, registering the notion that if only servants were in the building it was deemed to be empty.

Fifteen minutes later, Petronella was already on her way to her father, and saddled horses were being brought to the front of the house for the three men. Xanthe spoke to Liam as he mounted.

"Petronella will be inconsolable until she is found," she said.

"Do you think she's gone to her father? She was sad about him moving out of the Hall."

"It's possible."

"I'm going to have a word with Henry about which route we're taking. Try not to worry too much," he told her, before riding his horse over to where Henry was having his stirrup leathers adjusted.

Fairfax was already on his grey horse. The weather was threatening to break, the sky heavy with the promise of a storm. Fairfax's horse was beginning to sweat in the clammy air. He maneuvered it to stand uncomfortably close to Xanthe, so that he was able to speak to her unheard by anyone else.

"It is a fool's errand we undertake, you should know that."

"You don't think you'll find her in the park somewhere?"

"Evangeline will not be found until I deem it opportune."

She stared at him. "What have you done with her?"

"She is quite safe. For now."

"But, why would you take her? She must be terrified. What can you possibly hope to gain by stealing her away and causing Petronella such anguish?"

"Let us say simply that I have her in my keeping against your being . . . impetuous. There is no reason to fear for her safety, as long as our exchange goes smoothly. Until noon, then," he said, touching his hat to her and then wheeling his horse about to lead the others off at a gallop, giving Xanthe no chance to tell Liam what she had just learned.

As she watched them disappear across the parkland her thoughts raced for a solution to this development. In two hours she would face Fairfax and try to take the astrolabe from him. She had turned the thing over and over in her mind and decided that he would not be satisfied with having only the book. He could not risk losing the device that might still be crucial to his time traveling. Which meant he would try to get the Spinners book from her and keep the astrolabe. Which was something she could not allow to happen. She had been prepared to use her Spinners gift of time-within-time to take him to another point in an earlier century and leave him there. It would not have been easy, but it was the only way she could be certain he would no longer pose a threat nor recklessly break all the Spinners' codes for his own gain. But now, with Evie hidden somewhere only Fairfax knew of, there was no way she could carry out her plan. She paced up and down in the walled garden, furious that he could have done something so awful. She could not risk Evie's life, not even for the Spinners. It seemed Fairfax had her trapped whichever way she turned. Somehow she had put herself in a situation where she would have no choice but to give him what he wanted. And then what? He would have the astro-

labe and the book, and her, if it came to it. All she had done by traveling to his time was to make him more powerful, to feed his craving
for power over other people and to make himself unassailable. At that
moment, more than anything she was furious with herself for allowing him to outwit her. She had no idea what to do next except give in
to his demands. She thought of going to Mistress Flyte and asking for
her help, but after what she had seen in her past, and the resistance
the old woman had offered to Liam's presence, she no longer felt she
dare trust her completely. There was no one she could turn to to sort
things out. It was down to her. A fierce determination grew inside her.
She would get Evie back; that was her first priority. And if that meant
giving Fairfax the book, so be it. She would get it back. She would
part with it only temporarily to ensure the girl's safety, and, hopefully,
to part Fairfax from the astrolabe. She wasn't totally reliant on the
book to do her work as a Spinner. She had proved that to herself. Fairfax might have won this point, but the game was far from over. She
would do what she had to do, even if it meant being separated from
the book for a while. In the end, she was cleverer than him. She was
more determined. She would get it back.

When Xanthe set off for the lake the lowering sky was still with-
holding the much-needed rain it carried. By the time she reached the
folly, however, it had released its grip, and the resulting downpour
was startling. The parched soil released its wonderful petrichor as it
drank in the long-awaited water. She was soaked through in minutes and thankful for the fact that she was wearing her cotton rather
than her muslin dress. The flowery print clung to her but at least it
was not rendered transparent. She had also kept the Spinners book
in its wrapping of cloth, so that it was at least protected. The pins
the maid had styled her hair with were no match for her long curls
when weighted with water, so that the shape quickly unraveled. She

climbed the stairs of the tower cautiously. They had been uneven but dry on her first visit. A wash of fast-moving rain had rendered them hazardously slippery. When she reached the turret she thought at first she had arrived before Fairfax, but then, looking over the edge, she saw his horse tethered on the other side of the wall.

"I am pleased to see you did not think to keep me waiting, Miss Westlake."

Xanthe turned slowly to face her adversary. He was still dressed in his woolen riding coat and long leather top boots complete with spurs. Rain fell from the brim of his black hat. She regarded him through a blur of water, having no hat of her own. She blinked away the rain that poured into her eyes, and held the Spinners book tightly, her arms folded across it.

"Where is Evangeline?" she demanded.

"Somewhere none of those devoted searchers will ever find her," he said with a dismissive wave of the hand. "Her continued safety lies with you now, my little Spinner. Give me the book."

"Give me the astrolabe," she replied.

Fairfax smiled, taking the device from his pocket and holding it up. "Such a wondrous thing," he said, turning it so that the rain coursed over its intricately worked surface. "And so very important to me. Why would you think I would ever part with it?"

"We had a deal. An arrangement."

"A necessary ruse to bring you to me, with the book. I had not imagined you would be quite so . . . recalcitrant. One would have thought having your home near burnt to the ground with yourself and your mother in it might have been persuasion enough. It seems not. The sham of a bargain, on the other hand, and here you are."

"Why?" she asked him, shaking her head. "Why do you want it all so much? You have money now, a beautiful wife, a grand house, the social standing you were always chasing. Why can't you be content? Doesn't it matter to you at all that your greed is hurting people?"

He looked as if he would give a terse response but for a second or two he paused and seemed to be casting his mind back. "I lived a simple life, once. I was not born into wealth or privilege and I had been content to live as a lowly merchant's son. My family sold all manner of goods; salt, fine rugs, glass, silk. My father would switch his products according to the demands of his customers. He was an astute man of commerce, yet we were ever only a single poor transaction or one bad debt away from penury or ruin. It was a precarious existence. After my father's death I became head of the business but had not any hope of advancement. I wished to marry, and would have done so, but politics at that time were apt to trample underfoot those who played only small parts. I lost the only woman I had ever . . . will ever love to the shifting tides of political powers. A monarch who took against her family religion. A nation thirsty for the blood of others to make themselves feel safer. Only my own cunning kept me alive. I vowed I would rise up and never again be so vulnerable to the whims and wishes of others. I would claw up the rocky face of society to a pinnacle from which I would not be moved. When I discovered my ability as a Spinner, and when I found my astrolabe, I saw the path to true power, the nature of which would never be challenged." He returned the astrolabe to his pocket and held out his hand. "Give me the book."

"And then you will tell me where you are hiding Evie?"

"I will. You have my word."

"That has not proved worth a great deal, now, has it?"

"It is all I am prepared to give you."

She nodded, her heart pounding. She knew she was taking a huge risk, but could see no other way. Her hand shook as she passed him the book, shaking away the whispered voices that had set up urgent entreaties, warning her not to trust him, counseling against the very action she was taking. At the point where they both had hold of it she said, "At least let me look at the astrolabe. One last time. I know you will only lead me to Evie if you have both it and the book, even so, I should like to see it again. It is, as you said, a wondrous thing."

Slowly he pulled the book from her grasp. For a moment it looked as if he would refuse her request but pride overruled his caution, just as she had hoped it would. He took out the astrolabe again and handed it to her. He pulled the book to him, hunching over it in a way that was both possessive and protective, as he could wait not a moment longer to look inside. He unwound its wrapping and opened the book, his stooped body shielding it from the worst of the rain. Xanthe took a step backward as she watched his expression change from eager anticipation to shock and rage.

"What trickery is this? There is nought but empty pages!"

"You knew this might happen. I warned you. You were just too arrogant to accept that the book wouldn't trust you," she told him calmly. "It will only share its secrets with those who will use them well."

"I need the astrolabe to see them! That is all."

"That might work," she agreed, taking another small step back. "More likely you need someone who can read what is there. Someone like me. But then, why would I help you?"

As she spoke she reached under the collar of her dress and pulled out her gold locket. Fairfax, realizing what she was about to do, lunged forward. Before she could make the transition toward home he had grabbed hold of her. She knew there was every chance he would travel with her unless she could shake him off.

"Let me go!" she shouted, twisting to free herself, the rain still beating down upon them both, the noise of it louder now. Fairfax had her arm in a grip so tight she could feel his nails digging into her flesh through the cotton of her sleeve. She kicked him smartly in the shin, making him shout out, the sharp pain briefly diverting his attention from the book, which she batted from his grasp. He cursed as he dropped it and she seized the moment to try to free herself, but still he held firm. She wrenched her arm backward, fighting to get away from him, causing him to lean forward to maintain his grasp. Which was what, ultimately, caused them both to topple over the top of the low wall. His weight, pushed against her smaller, slender frame, unbalanced her, so that together they tipped over the castellation and plummeted toward the lake.

The fall was so sudden and so disorienting Xanthe did not have time to register fear. Instinctively she tightened her grip on the astrolabe in her left hand, but falling headfirst confused her, making her reach out for the water she knew was coming, so that she let go of her locket. It was still fastened to the chain around her neck, but she must have hold of it to return home. She took a deep breath the instant before she plunged through the surface of the lake, hearing Fairfax cry out as they did so. She felt herself free of him then. The height of the drop meant that she continued down, down, down to the very bottom of the lake, landing among the long, grabbing weeds Evie had warned her of. She swam for the sunlight, fighting against the water as it dragged at her sodden clothes. Beside her, Fairfax was also struggling, the weight of his boots and spurs and thick jacket greatly hampering him. Even so, he reached out and grabbed her ankle. She kicked wildly, aware that she had little air left, little time to escape. He pulled at her, dragging her downward when she needed desperately to be going up. He reached over and clawed at her hand, trying to take the astrolabe. She saw then that he would never let it go. She took hold of her gold locket again, knowing that she was not strong enough to free herself and reach the surface in time. Her only hope was to spin home. Fairfax's grip on her ankle was impossible to shift. He looked at her then, his face contorted with fury, determination, and hatred written in every furrow, every line that bitterness had drawn over many long years. The device meant everything to him, for he could not imagine life without it.

Xanthe wrenched her hand away from him and with all her strength flung the astrolabe away. Away from herself, and away from him. The weight of the brass caused it to fall deeper at once. Fairfax let go of her and plunged after his treasure. As Xanthe clutched the locket and thought of Flora and the blind house and home, her vision faded, and with it the disappearing figure of Fairfax swimming away from her.

The transition was abrupt, as if affected by the heightened danger and very real peril from which she was escaping. Xanthe arrived in the blind house gasping for breath and coughing up water, her sodden clothes heavy against her shocked and chilled body. Without a moment's hesitation, she felt around the gritty floor for the wedding dress, which lay exactly where it had been as she left it to travel back before. She took hold of it, her voice trembling as she said aloud, "Take me back! Take me to Petronella and Liam!" There was a brief cacophony of shouts and cries, accompanied by the shrill whine of the wedding dress, and suddenly she was there again, on the bank of the lake, where the torrential rain still fell. She had returned as quickly as she could but still had no way of knowing how much time had passed. The fact that the storm was not yet spent gave her hope that she not been absent long at all. She scanned the lake, looking for sign of Fairfax, but he was nowhere to be seen. She heard shouts. Someone calling her name above the shimmering sound of the rain stinging the surface of the lake.

"Xanthe!" Liam came running from the folly toward her. "Xanthe!" he shouted again. As he reached her he fell to his knees beside her. "Dear God, look at you! What happened?"

She sat up, struggling to find her voice, seeing now that her wet clothes had picked up the loose dirt from the floor of the blind house. Her hair hung free and matted, and there was weed from the lake tangled in it.

"I'm all right," she said, still coughing. "Fairfax . . . where is he? Have you seen him?"

"No. He gave us the slip while we were out looking for Evie. I knew you'd arranged to meet him here but I didn't know when. When I got here I saw his horse. I found the book at the top of the tower."

"Is it safe? He hasn't taken it?"

"It's here, look," he said, pulling it out from beneath his jacket. "Here, see?"

She snatched it from him, holding it close, overcome with relief that it was still there.

"Xanthe," Liam asked gently. "What the hell happened?"

"We fell . . ."

"Both of you? Did that bastard push you?"

She shook her head. "He was trying to get the astrolabe. I was trying to take it home. . . ."

"You've been back? To your house?"

"Yes, but, I had to let it go . . . in the lake." She pointed toward where she and Fairfax had fought. To where she had thrown the astrolabe into the deep, knowing it would lure him away from her. "Where is he?" she asked again, struggling to her feet. "We have to find him."

"We should get you back to the house, you're in no condition to stay out here. You're shivering. You were lucky you didn't break your neck, a fall like that."

"No!" She stepped away from him, desperate to make him understand but too shaken to make sense. "I have to find the astrolabe and I have to find him! He took Evie. He's the only one who knows where she is!"

"Shit! OK. OK. We'll look for him together. Come on."

"I'll go this way. I can use the bridge to circle the bottom end of the lake. You go around the folly." As she ran, all she could think about was that if he had drowned they would never find Evie and it would be her fault. She kept her eyes on the water, slipping on the newly wet bank more than once. There was not a sign of him. The only thing that disturbed the surface of the lake was the pitiless rain. She worked out she could only have been back in her own time a matter of minutes. Enough time for Liam to get to the folly. Plenty of time for a person to drown. Or to swim to the bank, haul himself out, and . . . what? His horse was still where he had tied it. More tellingly, the Spinners book had been where he'd dropped it up on the parapet of the folly. By the time Xanthe reached the little wooden footbridge that spanned the point where the stream entered the lake she knew Fairfax must be dead. He would never have left the book he had risked so much to possess. The only other possibility was that he had managed to catch the astrolabe and, as she had done, had traveled through time in order to save himself. She stood on the bridge, leaning over the handrail, squinting through the rain at the lake. She half expected to see his body, facedown, floating lifelessly upon the water. What she had not expected, what caused her to cry out, was the sight of Fairfax looking up at her from no more than three feet below the surface. His pale hair spread out and floated behind him as the gentle current tugged at it. His eye patch was still in place and his one good eye was open, bulging, staring in horror. His hands were reaching up, drifting slightly this way and that, having failed to pull him up to that vital air. Xanthe peered down further into the depths. Now she could see that the long, sinuous weeds had wrapped themselves around his heavy boots and snagged upon his silver spurs, catching him in a deadly trap. Of the astrolabe there was no sign. Had he reached it he would have been able to save himself, so she concluded it must be lost in the silt at the bottom of the lake.

She stood up slowly, exhausted now by her experiences, appalled at the thought that she had put Evangeline in such peril. Suddenly, as if acknowledging the somber moment, the rain stopped. A silence replaced it that felt as heavy as the storm clouds that were now lifting and moving away.

"Liam!" She called to him, signaling, bringing him running from the far end of the lake. "He's here!" she shouted. And then, more quietly, as if telling herself something that she was finding hard to take in, "Fairfax is dead."

❧ 19 ❧

LIAM RODE TO GET HELP AND RETURNED QUICKLY WITH HENRY, THE CARRIAGE DRIVER, A groom, and a footman. They brought with them a small cart. Henry, Liam, and the young groom stripped to their breeches so that they would not be hampered by heavy wet clothes. Henry held his hunting knife and the trio swam over to Fairfax. Henry dived down and cut him free of the weeds. Together they floated his body back to the side of the lake and the others helped to haul his body out. They lifted him onto the back of the cart and covered him with the horse blanket they had brought for the purpose. Xanthe could not help thinking it was an inauspicious end for someone who had cared so much about how he appeared to others and what they thought of him. She did not feel sadness at his death. On the contrary, she felt relief. They were all safer with him gone, and he could no longer twist and misuse his Spinner's gift. The inescapable fact that tormented her, however, was that now she could never make him tell her where Evie was. It was up to her to find the poor, blameless girl, who had become another victim of Fairfax's ruthless ambition. She had to find her and return her to her family.

Henry pulled on his shirt and boots. "Pity poor Petronella," he said. "A bride but for a single night, and now a widow."

"And Evie . . ." Xanthe started, unsure how to finish the thought.

Liam put his hand on her arm. "We will find her. We will. Get onto the cart. There's room in front."

"I can walk back to the house."

"No, you can't. For once, just do as I tell you. I'll help you up."

Still holding tight to *Spinners*, she took the seat next to the driver and the cart set off on its slow journey back to the house.

When they reached the house they discovered Mr. Wilcox there. A messenger had been sent to tell him the news. Petronella was on his arm, standing on the broad steps, looking shaken. The little cart pulled up at the front entrance. Grooms appeared from the stables to take the riders' horses and Liam helped Xanthe down from the front of the cart.

"You're shivering. You need to get out of these wet clothes."

"I'm all right, really."

Mr. Wilcox left his daughter to walk down to the cart. He lifted the blanket, shaking his head at the sight of his late son-in-law. "A sorry end for such a strong fellow. What made him go near the lake in such a storm?"

"He was looking for Evie," Xanthe told him. "We both were. I . . . knew she liked the place."

She saw Mr. Wilcox shudder, the thought of his younger daughter meeting such a fate as Fairfax horrifying him.

"She wasn't anywhere there," Xanthe reassured him. "She will come home. I am certain of it."

He sighed. "She has taken herself on adventures before now. I pray that this is merely another, perhaps brought about by the . . . changes at the house. But tell me, how did Fairfax come to be in the lake? Did you see what happened? You too are soaked through."

"I saw him fall. From the top of the folly. The rain had made everything treacherously slippery."

"Riding boots have scarce any grip," Henry pointed out. "And are deuced heavy."

"I tried to swim to him, but my clothes . . . the water . . ."

Petronella let out a gasp. "Oh, my dear friend! You might also have been lost."

"I am so sorry, Nell."

"No, no. Do not reproach yourself. Why should you? I myself would not have had the courage even to try."

Henry put in, "Bad luck, I do say. And him such a strong swimmer."

Liam explained to them all. "His spurs caught in the weeds. It must have happened very quickly," he added, seeing the distress on Petronella's face.

Mr. Wilcox nodded solemnly. "The master of Corsham Hall will be afforded every respect and dignity, as befits his position. For now, our efforts must be entirely turned toward finding Evangeline. Come, Barnes, take Mr. Fairfax to the back parlor and send a message to the undertakers in Bradford. Have the servants gather in the yard. We must organize a search."

Xanthe took Liam by the arm and steered him toward the house.

"I need to speak to you alone," she said.

They went to her room and she set the Spinners book down on the bed. She asked him to undo the buttons at the back of her dress. The cold was beginning to take its toll so that she was shaking quite markedly by the time she took towels and dry clothes and went behind the screen to change. Liam stood by the window, watching the activity below.

"I must go and help them look," he said.

Xanthe pulled her wet dress over her head and draped it over the top of the screen. She was soaked through to her skin, so she began removing her shift and chemise too.

"They won't find her," she told him.

"What?"

"It's no use. They won't find her."

"My God, you don't think he killed her!"

"No, I'm sure he hasn't. But, well, it was something he said to me, up on the folly. He told me none of those searching for her could ever find her. It was as if he deliberately wasn't including me in that. He didn't say I could never find her."

"Meaning?"

"He hasn't hidden her in a place, he's hidden her in a time. That's how he could be so certain. He must have used the astrolabe to take her back."

"But . . . to when?"

"I don't know. He wouldn't have to make a big journey. To be sure she was secure he'd have to choose a time he knew about and a place that wouldn't be disturbed. He wasn't planning to keep her there very long."

"So, how are you going to find her?"

She emerged from behind the screen. She had removed all the pond-weed and pins from her hair and run her fingers through her wet curls. She had rubbed her body with the towels and felt the circulation returning properly to her fingertips and toes. She had put on a dry underdress. "Pass me the muslin gown from the wardrobe, please," she asked Liam. He fetched it for her and helped her into it, treating her with real tenderness. He picked up the fine blue silk shawl that was on the bed and wrapped it around her shoulders.

"Are you really OK?" he asked. "You've had a pretty terrible time of it."

She mustered a smile. "I will be fine once we've got Evie home. I need to go to her room and find something of hers. Something with a strong connection. Come on."

They made their way along the corridor, up a half flight of steps, and around the corner, to where Evangeline's room was on the west side of the house. It was a cheerful place, kept tidy by maids and as quickly untidied by Evie, with half-finished drawings on the table, a collection of pinecones on the windowsill, a shawl thrown care-lessly down on the floor. But, as the maid had told them at breakfast, her bed had not been slept in, her nightclothes lay untouched on the covers.

"What are you looking for?" Liam asked.

"I'm not looking, I'm listening. I need something to sing to me," she said, walking slowly around the room. She picked up a china doll in a sumptuous burgundy velvet dress, but could hear nothing from it. She found two little wooden horses, one with a repaired leg, showing that they had been played with often. She held them tightly, but felt no vibration and heard no song at all. None of Evie's clothes were able to provide the connection she needed. She scanned the room. "What does she love?" she asked aloud. "What is her favorite thing?"

"If you're asking me," Liam replied, "I'd say you're looking in the wrong place."

"Oh, why?"

"Evie is an outdoors girl. She doesn't like being cooped up inside."

"You're right. Of course!" Xanthe dropped to the floor and began searching beneath the bed.

"What on earth . . . ?"

She emerged seconds later clutching a pair of muddy boots. They were ankle length, brown, with laces to the top, their toes scuffed and low heel worn. "These!" she said triumphantly. "Evie's favorites. She was only wearing smart shoes yesterday because of the wedding. She lives in these." Excitedly, she held the boots to her, sitting on the floor, waiting, listening. For a moment she thought she had been mistaken, but then the high notes sounded, faint at first but growing in strength. The unmistakable song of a found thing. "Yes!"

"Can you hear something?"

She nodded. "These will take me to her."

"Wait, you're going now? Right now?"

"I have to."

"But, you don't know where, and how will you get back..."

"I'm traveling time-within-time, Liam. Just like I did from my room the other day. It'll be OK. Trust me, I know what I'm doing." She got to her feet. "I will be back really quickly."

Liam took a long breath and let it out slowly. "It's not easy, you know, being the one to watch you do all this. Just being left to wait. I feel bloody useless, to be honest."

"I need you," she said, taking hold of his hand. "I couldn't have done all this without you. Right now I need you to just go along with the search. I don't know where Evie is, but I don't think it will be far. Like I said, Fairfax had to be sure wherever and whenever he put her was secure. He couldn't have someone from another time stumbling across her. Having said that, I can't just reappear here with her, so, well... I need you to watch out for me. For us. And then go along with whatever tale I tell, OK?"

"OK," he said, kissing her quickly.

Xanthe hesitated and then pulled him close for another kiss. This time it was she who gave it. They embraced, and she breathed in his warmth, closing her eyes, drawing strength from him.

"Thank you," she said. "Now, I need to go."

She returned to her own room with the boots, waving Liam off as he headed back out to join the search. She hurried over to the bedcover and tugged out another silk thread. She wound it around her finger, tucking in the end so that it was secure. Next, she opened the Spinners book. Taking a moment to steady herself and focus, she tucked the singing boots under her left arm so that her right hand was free to turn the pages. She spoke to it calmly and confidently. This was no time for nervousness, no time to doubt herself.

"Take me to Evangeline," she said. "I must travel time-within-time. Take me to her." As she watched, the words of the appropriate incantation appeared, racing across the page. She read them out clearly, keeping Evie to the front of her thoughts, feeling the vibration of the boots against her heart. "Where are you, Evie?" she asked, closing her eyes. "Where are you?"

She traveled with a jolt this time, lurching forward, surprised by the violent movement, putting it down to the urgency of her mission. When she arrived at her destination she saw there was another reason for the unsettling nature of her transition. She found herself back at the folly, and for an awful moment thought she had taken a wrong turn. She was not up on the turret, but at the foot of the stairs. Looking more closely, however, she realized this was winter. The evergreen ivy still twined its way up the stone walls, but the trees around the building were bare, and the temperature jarringly cold. She turned this way and that, searching for any sign of the girl. Seeing nothing, she began to mount the spiral stairs. She had got no more than two steps up when she heard soft moans. Turning, she realized that they were coming from behind a low door she had not paid much attention to before. When she reached it she heard sobs from the other side. The door was worn oak boards with a small iron grille near the top, reminding her of the original lockup in Marlborough, where Alice had been incarcerated.

"Evie?" she called through the bars. "Evie, are you in there?"

There was no answer, but she could definitely hear whimpering and the occasional cough. She tried the door, fearing it might be locked, and was relieved to see it was kept closed by nothing more than a heavy iron bolt. It was stiff but she succeeded in pulling it back and releasing the catch. The door creaked open. Evie lay on an old mattress, huddled in a pile of blankets and pillows. There was a chamber pot in one corner of the room, a stone water jar beside the makeshift bed, and nothing more. She felt rage growing inside her at the thought of Fairfax leaving the child here, alone, trapped, in the dark, cold and terrified. It was a salient reminder of just what the man had been capable of and how well rid of him they all were.

"Evie, it's me, Xanthe." She crouched down and pulled the blankets off the girl, trying to wake her. She saw now that she was in the grip of a fever and barely conscious. Had she come a few hours later it might have been to retrieve a corpse. "Come along, little one, let's get you back where you belong." She sat Evie up gently. She took off her shawl and wrapped it around the girl, pulling her onto her lap and holding her close. "Stay with me, Evie. Just a small jump down the rabbit hole, you'll see."

She had thought of arriving back in Evie's proper time somewhere in the woods so that she could claim she had found her there, but the child was in no state to walk anywhere and Xanthe doubted she would be able to carry her far. She decided to trust to all the servants being involved in the search outside the house. She would return to her own room and play it from there.

"Take us back," she called out firmly, holding the red silk on her finger against Evie's cold hand. "Time-within-time . . . take us back to Petronella!"

Again the transition was swift and uncomfortable, as if the perilous condition of Evie's health affected it. They arrived as if falling from several feet onto the floor of Xanthe's room. Xanthe lifted her carefully onto the bed, smoothing her hair off her clammy brow. She pulled the cover up and tucked her in and then ran, shouting as she went. "Come quick! Come quick. Miss Evangeline is home! She is found!"

She had been right in thinking most of the servants would be out searching, but Cook and the upstairs maid were still in the house. After much in the way of exclamations and expressions of shock, Cook hurried to the kitchen to fetch hot water and broth, while the maid was sent to find someone to ride for the doctor, and someone else to find Mr. Wilcox and Petronella. As she and the stout woman tended to Evie, Xanthe explained she had heard a noise on the landing outside her room and opened her door to find the child half conscious in the hallway. They agreed that whatever had befallen her, she had taken a chill and used her failing strength to find her way home. They removed her filthy clothes, washed her with warm water, and made her comfortable in Xanthe's bed.

Within the hour, the doctor had arrived and the search party returned. Petronella took up vigil at her sister's side. Doctor Maynard tried to reassure her.

"Miss Wilcox is young and vigorous," he said, "and well equipped to fight through the fever, which I am happy to say is already showing signs of abating."

Xanthe was confused by what he called Evangeline and then remembered that now Petronella was no longer the oldest unmarried daughter, her sister was the default Miss Wilcox. She put a hand on Petronella's shoulder.

"Evie will be running rings around all of us again by the end of the week. Try not to worry."

"I feel responsible for her condition," Petronella said tearfully. "I was too much taken up with the wedding, or I should have noticed her absence sooner."

Doctor Maynard handed Xanthe two small bottles. "When she is able to sip again, give her two spoonfuls of this one. The other is a tonic for Mrs. Fairfax, to help her rally from her own loss. Can I trust you to see they are administered? Excellent. I will call back in the morning." He bowed somewhat creakily and left the room.

Xanthe took a chair the other side of what had been her own bed.

"Oh." Petronella looked up. "You must be so weary. I will have a bed made up for you in another room."

"Don't put anyone to the trouble, for I will sit up with you tonight. We will watch over Evie together."

Petronella thought to protest but then nodded. "Thank you."

By the time darkness had fallen Evie's face no longer looked flushed with fever and she was able to take the remedy she had been left and even a few sips of Cook's broth. Her eyes had regained their focus and she smiled weakly at her sister. She was made comfortable and fell into a peaceful and restorative sleep.

Xanthe saw how completely exhausted Petronella was. She stood up and took her hand. "Come and sit by the fire," she said. "You will be more rested, and Evie can sleep while we talk."

Even though it was high summer, the storm had brought about a drop in temperature, so a fire had been lit in the hearth. They each took one of the comfortable chairs in front of it. Xanthe insisted Petronella take some of the doctor's tonic, and a maid brought up hot milk laced with rum and ginger. When they were alone again, she took the opportunity to talk privately with her friend.

"Nell, I am so sorry about what happened to Mr. Fairfax."

"Such a cruel way to die, and when he was searching for Evie . . ."

Xanthe chose her words carefully, seeing no point in adding to Petronella's distress, and knowing she could never tell her anything approaching the truth.

"To lose a husband in such a shocking, sudden way must be hard to bear."

"It is difficult to reconcile myself to the fact that he lost his life trying to help me by searching for the sister he knew I adored. Even though she had no affection for him."

Again she had to bite her tongue, maddened by how far Petronella's idea of what he had done was from reality. The truth was he had brought her sister close to death and not cared one jot about it.

"Evie is home safe," she said at last. "And we are all thankful for that."

"Benedict would have been gladdened to know she returned to us and will regain her health fully. We may never know where she wandered to, for the doctor told me patients who suffer such fevers often lose their recollection of events. All that matters is that she is home." She was silent for a little while then, warming her hands on her comforting drink as she gazed into the fire. When she spoke it was with a calm voice that belied the enormity of how her life had changed in a few short hours. "I will not pretend to you that I loved him, for you know I did not," she said. "Whilst I would never wish any person ill fortune, it is the case that my husband's sad fate has left me in a favorable position. As a daughter, I could not inherit Corsham. As a widow, however, I will receive my late husband's estate in its entirety. He was a successful man of commerce; I shall be amply provided for. His fortune means our family's future at Corsham is secure. It also means that one day, should she choose to, Evie may marry for love, for she will never want for anything hereafter."

"Then some good has come out of a calamity," Xanthe agreed. She thought then about how the wedding dress had called her to help Petronella. She thought about the complicated train of events that had led to this; to Nell being free and her family saved, without having to endure Fairfax as master of Corsham Hall. Mistress Flyte had always maintained that being a Spinner meant ensuring that history unfolded as it was meant to do. It was a great deal to take in, to understand what that truly meant. If she hadn't chosen to meet Fairfax at the folly; if it hadn't rained so heavily; if she hadn't been able to kick herself free of his grasp—each twist and misstep and stride forward had led to where they were, and she had played her part in it. She wished she could talk it all over with the old lady. She badly needed so many things to be clearer. And yet, she could no longer trust Mistress Flyte with all her thoughts and fears. There were still things the Spinners book had showed her that she did not fully understand, and most of them related to Mistress Flyte's own history.

The next morning, Evie was sitting up in bed pleading to be allowed outside. Her father had sternly forbidden her from leaving her bed for at least another day. Petronella was already dressed in the widow's mourning that she would wear for at least six months and all the servants were wearing black crepe armbands. She had undertaken to make sure that her sister ate three meals and was entirely free of her cough before she would be permitted to venture out of doors. They had questioned her gently on the whys and wherefores of her disappearance but it was as Doctor Maynard had suggested: She could remember almost nothing at all. Xanthe was relieved to hear this, having worried that the child would suffer nightmares and flashbacks after her traumatic experience. The fever had done its work and erased painful memories. Mr. Wilcox returned to live at the Hall, at his daughter's insistence. He was at first reluctant, but she convinced him she sorely needed his help in organizing her late husband's funeral, and thereafter could think of no greater balm for her grief than having her dear father close at hand.

That afternoon, Xanthe made a point of visiting Petronella while she was in her bedroom. There was something she needed to be certain of.

"Would you mind," she asked, "if I took one more look at your wedding gown? It was so lovely, I should very much like to see it again. But of course, if to regard it brings you sadness..."

"Not in the least. More than anything it will remind me of our friendship, as you were so kind and so attentive during all the long fittings and alterations, without which we might never have met."

As she watched Petronella retrieve the dress from the box in which it had been placed, Xanthe felt a pang of guilt and sadness. She knew something else that Nell did not, something she could never explain to her. That she and Liam would soon leave, and would vanish from her life as mysteriously and quickly as they had arrived in it. It seemed a cruel end to what had become a warm and genuine friendship.

Petronella laid the dress upon the bed. "It was very beautiful," she murmured.

Xanthe stepped closer to it. Slowly, she reached out her hand and touched the fabulous lace of the bodice, holding her breath as she did so. Nothing. No vibration, not so much as a shiver. There was no calling, no connection, nothing more coming from it. The found thing had ceased its song. She let out a long, thankful breath.

"My sister has moved back into her own room," Petronella was telling her. "Please do take up the one she so abruptly took from you. It has such a pretty aspect."

"Oh, thank you, Nell, but there is no need. Liam and I must return to see my aunt tomorrow."

"Tomorrow?"

"Yes." She nodded slowly. "It's time to go home."

{ 20 }

LIAM STRAIGHTENED THE BRIM OF HIS HAT AGAINST THE STRONG SUN AS THEY STOOD on the step of Corsham Hall for the last time. Xanthe was at his side and they watched as the footmen loaded their belongings onto the carriage. He turned to her.

"If feels like only five minutes ago we were arriving here in that, but so much has happened since then."

She looked at him. "Will you be sorry to leave?"

"The Wilcox family, yes," he said, waving up at Evie, who had been allowed to sit in the window of her bedroom. Another day had made all the difference to her recovery, her dangerous fever now a distant memory. "This place too. I think I could have enjoyed a life of riding and hunting and fishing. Might have got quite good at it."

"And eating," she said, playfully prodding the tight waistcoat over his tummy.

He smiled. "They do like their food. And booze! I think I was a bit drunk practically every time I got on a horse. And then Henry would pass around a hip flask full of something lethal each time we stopped to let the horses have a blow, and I'd be even more drunk when I got off."

"I'm sorry to leave Petronella," Xanthe said. "I wish there was some way . . ." She let the thought go. They both knew this was to be a final goodbye.

Mr. Wilcox satisfied himself that what luggage there was had been properly loaded. The driver took his place and a footman held the door open. As it was another warm day Xanthe had asked the top be lowered. She knew it would please Liam for them to ride in the landau open topped.

Petronella, the black crepe of her dress shimmering in the sunshine, took both of Xanthe's hands in hers.

"My dear friend. How I shall miss your company."

"And I yours."

"Do send word the moment you arrive safely home in London. Will you spend long with your aunt in Bradford?"

"Only an hour or so. There is a stagecoach leaving at midday which will suit us very well." Abandoning etiquette, Xanthe wrapped her arms around Petronella and pulled her into a heartfelt hug. "Be happy," she whispered into her ear. Then, not wishing to prolong the emotional moment, she beckoned to Liam and they stepped up into the carriage. As the four strong horses stepped into a steady canter down the drive, she twisted in her seat for one last look at Corsham Hall as it had been, raising her hand in farewell to the small gathering on the steps. Liam slipped his arm around her waist, drawing her close. The miles through the beautiful countryside passed swiftly in companionable silence as they made their way back to Bradford-on-Avon.

When they arrived at the tearooms, Mistress Flyte came out to greet them.

"Polly has a lemon cake put aside for you," she told them.

"We will be in directly," Xanthe told her, stepping to the front of the carriage. She and Liam thanked the driver and the footman and tipped them both generously. They were the pair who had helped retrieve Fairfax's body from the lake, and Xanthe doubted anyone had properly rewarded them for their pains. As the carriage pulled away and turned to cross the bridge, she felt the last of her connection with the Wilcoxes of Corsham Hall disappearing.

"Come." Mistress Flyte held open the door. "We shall take tea together upstairs and you must tell me all that has occurred up at the the Hall."

Liam took the luggage to his room, partly to be helpful, but also so that Xanthe could talk to the old woman on her own. She had told him she did not want to stay any longer than was necessary, but there were questions she had for Mistress Flyte that required answers before they left. The two women settled in the small sitting room, where Polly had placed a tray of tea and thick slices of sugary lemon cake. Mistress Flyte poured as she spoke.

"News has reached me, of course, of the demise of Mr. Fairfax. Am I correct in my assumption that you were not unconnected to the events that led to his death?" She picked up a fine china cup and saucer—white with pink rose buds—and passed it to Xanthe.

"He drowned in pursuit of something that would have been useless to him," she replied, taking the cup and placing it on her lap to steady a slightly nervous hand.

"He was ever a person in pursuit of anything that would make him stronger."

"He fell, from the folly tower into the lake. I fell with him. He wanted the Spinners book."

"And you kept it from him?"

"We agreed, didn't we, he wasn't a fit person to have it?"

Mistress Flyte finished pouring the tea and regarded her guest levelly.

"You answered the call of the wedding gown. You did whatever was required of you, as a Spinner."

"I believe so. It's interesting," she added, "when Fairfax opened the book, all he saw were blank pages."

"Ah, so it would not reveal itself to him?"

"It makes sense, when you think about it. I mean, it will show itself only to those it thinks worthy. And not all of them Spinners. Did I ever tell you that my friend, in my own time, the one who helped me unravel some of the tangled truth behind the blind house, he can see some of what is in it?"

"I do not recall your mentioning such a friend."

"So, some non-Spinners can see what's there. Some Spinners cannot."

"It would appear so."

"Would you say, in your experience, that there are not only different people who are Spinners—some good, some not so good—but different *types* of Spinners?"

Mistress Flyte took an unhurried sip of her tea. "I am not entirely certain I see your meaning?"

Xanthe tried a different tack. "When we were at the picnic I asked you about Erasmus Balmoral. . . ."

Mistress Flyte returned her cup and saucer to the table. For a short while she was silent, as if weighing up what to share with Xanthe and what to keep hidden.

"I wondered," she said at last, "how long it would be before the book began to reveal more of the history of the Spinners to you. I confess, I had rather hoped it would not find it necessary to put me at the center of its story."

"But you were at the center of things, weren't you? And was he?" When Mistress Flyte did not answer she went on. "I saw you, together. I traveled time-within-time," she said, noticing the old woman's minute reaction to this information. "Oh yes, I have learned how to do that. I've learned quite a lot. I've seen quite a lot."

"Have a care you do not form hasty opinions of others."

"I know what I saw. Do you remember the moment, I wonder? It was winter. I can't tell you the month or even the year, but I'm sure you will know the exact hour that you stood in the walled garden of Corsham Hall and lied to your lover."

"If you knew the whole story you might not be so quick to judge."

"So tell me."

Again she hesitated before deciding precisely what she would speak of. "Erasmus was a principled man, and those principles cost him dearly. He and I met centuries ago. We both had our origins in the reign of Henry the Eighth. I believe, among Spinners, sharing a birth point in time carries significance. It adds resonance to a friendship. But it was as Spinners we met, when engaged in the business of answering the call, of righting wrongs, of standing for those who were victims of injustice. In short, of ensuring that history unfolded as it was meant to do. In the course of our work we traveled, together and separately, through the centuries, where we witnessed many acts of bravery and as many of wickedness. As you learned with Fairfax, a gift such as we have lends its holder great power over others. At times we needed to wield that power with force, in order to achieve our goals."

"Is that all you think Fairfax was doing? Wielding his power with force? Do you think the way he behaved, the things he did, were acceptable?"

"No, I do not. But I will not pretend there weren't times when other Spinners, myself included, were not compelled to push the boundaries of what we did. At times, we did indeed move those boundaries. And, as ever when one promotes change, there are those who resist it. Those who disagree."

"So you and Erasmus disagreed about how Spinning should be done? How it should be used?"

"We all of us wished only to do our work most effectively. What we disagreed upon was a matter of methodology."

"You fell out about the 'how' and not the 'what'?"

"In essence."

"What I read, what I heard, what I saw . . . there has to be more to it."

"Ultimately, we each had to choose where we stood."

"And you and he chose different sides?"

"As I said, he was a man of principle. He was not to be moved upon it."

"But what was it that he found so unacceptable?"

"You must understand, Erasmus was not the only one. Others left the family of Spinners. They established themselves under a new name. They called themselves Time Steppers."

Xanthe knew with complete certainty that Mistress Flyte was doing her best not to reveal everything. Erasmus had spoken of having to kill her if he saw her again. There was more to the split of the Spinners than she was prepared to admit to. It occurred to Xanthe that it might be wise, safer even, not to show the old woman how much she knew. She would have to be content with getting her answers from the book. As casually as she was able, she helped herself to a piece of lemon cake. As she ate it, enjoying the citrus tang contrasting with what would have been ruinously expensive sugar, she could not help comparing it, slightly unfavorably, to the one Gerri made. It was a good thing, she decided, that her thoughts were turning to home. Her work was done.

Mistress Flyte, however, had questions of her own.

"You still have the book, of course?"

"Of course. I never intended to part with it for more than the briefest time. I would never have left without it."

"And Fairfax's astrolabe?"

"At the bottom of the lake up at Corsham, I'm sorry to say. He died for it, and now it's lost."

"It is strange to think of him gone. He strove to make himself unassailable."

"Which was, in the end, what got him killed."

"Did you kill him?" she asked, the directness of the question after so much prevarication catching Xanthe a little off guard.

"No, I did not. I told you, he fell from the tower and drowned in the lake."

"And you did not cause him to fall?"

"He took me with him!"

"But you did not drown."

"I used my locket. I used my Spinner's gift to save myself."

"And he . . . ?"

"Chose to go after the astrolabe."

Mistress Flyte was quiet then, digesting this information, her face inscrutable. It felt to Xanthe that they had reached an impasse. It saddened her that their friendship had faltered. The old woman had helped her so much when they first met, and there was so much she could still learn from her. But to learn she would have to trust her, and after what the Spinners book had shown her, that trust was gone.

Xanthe got to her feet. "It's time we left. I must take Liam home," she said simply.

Mistress Flyte nodded. "From where do you wish to travel?"

"I think the point we arrived will do nicely. It's a quiet street. We should not be observed. But first, I need to change." Much as Xanthe would have loved to have taken some of her beautiful new clothes with her, she knew it was pointless. Once in her own time they would slowly crumble. It would be hard to leave them, but harder to watch them disintegrate. She asked Mistress Flyte to see that they went to someone who needed them, though to make sure they would not be seen by Petronella or Evie. She went up to the attic room where Liam had already changed back into the costume he had hired in Devises.

"I see what you mean about this being way off," he told her, shaking his head at the outfit he was wearing. "Look at these colors . . . this silky stuff . . . what were they thinking?"

"Listen to Liam the historian!" She smiled at him. "You look fine. You can take it off as soon as we get home."

"I might need some help," he said, grabbing her around the waist as she went to step past him. "You got any buttons need unbuttoning?"

"You can help me out of this," she said, turning her back to him.

"I can manage the hire costume easy enough. It wasn't designed with servants in mind."

He undid the long row of buttons that followed the dip of her spine and then busied himself folding his discarded clothes while she dressed.

"It'll be weird being back in overalls," he said. "Though I am looking forward to a decent pint. And to get back to the band."

Xanthe laced up her boots, casting a wistful glance at the dress she had taken off, wondering if she would ever again have something so lovely made for her. "Time travel has its rewards," she said. "But yes, it will be good to get home."

Liam gave a short laugh. "I can't wait to tell Harley what we got up to. He's going to be so jealous!"

"I think it might have been harder to pass him off as a Regency gent, somehow, don't you?"

She finished dressing, picked up her bag, double-checked that the book was in it, and turned to Liam.

"Ready?" she asked.

He nodded and opened the door to the steep stairs.

"Liam . . ."

He paused, waiting to hear what she had to say.

"Thank you."

"My pleasure." He grinned.

"No, I mean it. It was such a leap of faith, coming here with me. That sort of trust . . . it matters."

"Are you trying to say you couldn't have done it without me?"

She pulled a face, playfully pushing past him. "I wouldn't go that far."

"Didn't think you would," he said, following her down the stairs.

"I would have managed," she insisted.

"Course you would," he agreed.

Outside, the little alleyway at the back of the tearooms was, as

Xanthe had predicted, empty and quiet. The sun had moved beyond the midday point, so that the high wall of the yard cast a deep shadow down one side. She led Liam to stand in that cool shade. At the door, Mistress Flyte stopped.

"I will bid you farewell and safe journey," she said, executing a perfect curtsey, which Xanthe returned and Liam answered with a bow. The old woman went through the yard door, closing it quietly behind her, her footsteps on the cobbles of the yard dwindling as she returned to the tearooms.

"Right." Xanthe stepped closer to Liam. "You remember the drill?"

"Let's see, hold you tight and never let go, no matter what?" He encircled her with his arms, pulling her gently but firmly against his strong body. "I think I can manage that," he said, the desire obvious in his voice.

"And now you have to be quiet," she told him, attempting to be stern, but unable to hide her smile. She gripped his arm with one hand and with the other took the locket from beneath her blouse, closing her fingers over it to nestle it in her palm, feeling the smooth gold against her skin. "Close your eyes," she told him. "Think of the blind house, think of home." She had barely spoken the words when she felt the spinning begin. She was accustomed to the sensations it brought but was conscious of how strange it was to Liam, and how unsettling it could be. She tightened her grip on him and felt herself thrown backward in a way that she had not experienced before. Abruptly, she landed on the floor of the blind house. The darkness of the small space was sliced through with sunlight falling through the half-open door, illuminating small areas. She gasped, surprised that yet again, as with the time she had gone to Evie, the transition was quite violent. She thought it curious, as she had explained the unpleasant nature of her traveling time-within-time to rescue the child by the fact that Evie was so unwell and in such distress. There was nothing dangerous or upsetting about going home with Liam. She found she had arrived kneeling on top of the wedding dress and quickly got to her feet, stooping to pick up the dress as she did so, shaking the dirt from it, registering the fact that it was silent.

"Well," she said into the gloom, "that was a bit of a bumpy landing. Sorry if you've picked up any bruises, Liam. Liam?"

A coldness swept over her.

She was alone.

"Liam!" she screamed. Mistress Flyte's words of warning came back to her, about how a non-Spinner traveling could be lost in time. Set adrift in a limbo between times. Panic making her feel sick, Xanthe rushed outside into the garden. Blinking against the spring sunshine she searched the garden frantically. "Liam!" she called again.

"Xanthe?" Flora came hurrying out of the house, stabbing the lawn with her crutches, Pie bounding ahead of her. "What is it, what's the matter?"

"Oh, Mum! It's Liam. He hasn't made the journey! We were travelling back together . . ."

"But, you had hold of him?"

"Yes, of course! And he had his arms around me. I told him not to let go! I told him, just before we traveled. He knew he had to hold on."

"He wouldn't have let go of you, love. Just calm down." She reached her daughter and put a hand on her shoulder. "Calm down and think. Did anything happen just before you left? Look how Pie managed to go with you just by jumping in the blind house that time. . . ."

"There was nothing. We were on our own. It all felt exactly as it should have before we started, and then . . ."

"And then?"

"I knew something wasn't right. The spinning felt . . . rough . . . difficult, I don't know."

"Did anyone see you go?"

"No, I told you, we were on our own. Mistress Flyte said goodbye and went back indoors." She stopped, a thought forming in her head.

"What is it, Xanthe, love? What have you thought of?"

"I don't know . . . I'm not sure." She looked at her mother then, try-ing to draw on her calmness and strength so as not to descend into blind, lurching panic. "I have to go back," she said.

"Yes."

"Right now. The rate of time is different wherever I go to in the past, and it's not fixed." She started to move back toward the blind house. "Ten minutes here could be almost the same then or a day, I've no way of knowing. I must go straight back to where I left him."

"You've got the wedding dress, go on, I'll grab hold of Pie," said Flora.

Xanthe stopped in her tracks. "No! No, the wedding dress won't work anymore."

"What?"

"I've done what needed to be done. It's not singing anymore, Mum. It won't work."

"Oh, Xanthe . . ."

"Wait, it's OK. I've traveled time-within-time before without us-ing a found thing. I can do it from here. Of course I had Evie's boots when I went looking for her, but when I asked the book to show me something I needed to know . . . I just used the book and an incanta-tion. And a candle! Without a found thing I need a candle."

"There's one in my workshop. I took it out of a silver candlestick." As Xanthe sprinted from the house Flora called after her. "There are matches on the shelf above the sink!"

When she returned, breathless from running, her hands were shak-ing as she set the candle on a flowerpot inside the blind house.

Flora took the matches from her. "Let me do that," she said, strik-ing one and setting it to the wick. A timid flame took hold. "What else do you need? Can I help?"

"Just this." She placed the book in front of her so that the light from the candle fell on it. Kneeling down, she held the book, steadying herself. "It's OK, Mum," she said, calmer now. "I'll just go straight back to the exact place where I left him, and the exact point in time. You take Pie and go back in the house now. OK?"

"OK, love. Good luck," she said, picking up her sticks and stepping out through the old door, calling Pie as she went.

Xanthe waited until she heard the back door shut and then opened the book, trying her best not to rush. She must get the words right, the place and the time. Liam's life could depend on it.

"Show me," she asked the book, but it was already ahead of her. As if sensing the urgency of what she needed to do the pages flipped over in a blur, an impossible number fluttering open until it chose the one she needed and stopped. The words that appeared on the worn paper were slightly different from those she had used before, for a moment making her wonder if they were the correct ones. Then she remembered that she was not traveling time-within-time, so they would be different. Nor was she using a found thing. She had never done this before, so she should not expect to see instructions she had used before. "OK," she said aloud, as much to herself as to any listening Spinners. "I get it. I trust you." The other thing that struck her as peculiar was that there were no whispers from disquiet souls, no cries or entreaties. It was as if these were triggered by the special objects she took into the blind house, not the traveling itself. "So much to learn," she muttered, leaning closer to the page to make sure she could read the words accurately.

Let the door through the fabric of time swing wide,
May I travel back safe and swift.
Keep my course straight and true, my task to be done,
Lest wickedness pull me adrift.

As she finished the incantation she straightened up and stared into the flame.

"Take me to Liam!" she called out, his name barely out of her mouth when she was flung back, falling decade over decade, generation flashing past generation, years upon years, until she stopped in breathless silence. She had not properly experienced darkness this time, so that she arrived in Bradford, in the alleyway she had only minutes before left, neatly standing in the shadow of the yard wall. She kept very still, checking that she had not been seen. The alley was empty. No startled witnesses, and no Liam. She raced to the door in the wall but found it bolted from the inside. She rattled the handle, pulling on it desperately.

"Mistress Flyte!" she shouted. "Polly? Let me in!" She waited but there was no reply from the other side of the door, no footsteps suggesting someone hurrying to answer her calls. Leaving the alley, she ran into the street and around to the front of the tearoom. As she went she reminded herself she did not yet know how long had passed since she had left. She had not taken any notice of the time before traveling. The sun appeared to have sunk a little lower, the shadows lengthened somewhat, but it wasn't much to go on. She flung open the front door, the tinkling bells announcing her arrival, as she charged through, drawing surprised looks from the ladies taking tea. Polly appeared with a tray of china.

"Miss Westlake! I thought you had left for London. Was there a problem with the stage?"

"What? No. I . . . My brother came back for something he left behind. We seem to have missed each other. Have you seen him?"

"No, miss."

"Not at all?"

"No, miss. Not since you left."

"How long ago was that?" Xanthe asked.

Polly frowned and looked up at the grandmother clock on the wall. "I should say an hour."

"I need to speak with Miss Flyte. Is she upstairs?"

"Why, no, miss. My mistress has gone."

"Gone? Gone where?"

"She didn't say. Only told me that I was to shut the tearooms at five, and then not open again until she returned."

"But, when will that be? How long will she be away for?"

"I'm sure I don't know, miss. Miss Flyte didn't think I needed telling, is all I can think. Not for me to ask. Is there anything I can help you with?" she asked, setting the tray down and wiping her hands on her apron.

Xanthe felt a cold dread take hold of her. It was as if she were in a nightmare. Liam was missing and Mistress Flyte had left suddenly and unexpectedly with no explanation. The two things had to be connected. Somehow. The thought that the old woman might interfere with their journey through time, putting Liam at such risk, tricking them so completely, filled her with rage. The one small comfort this theory gave her was that it meant Liam was most likely not lost in a timeless nothingness. For whatever reason, Mistress Flyte had taken him or sent him somewhere. And if he was somewhere, he could be found. And to find him, she would have to start from *his* time.

"Thank you, Polly, no. I must find my brother," she said to the maid, backing toward the door. She was on the point of leaving when something else occurred to her. "One more thing, how long after we departed did Miss Flyte leave? Do you recall?"

"Why almost the same instant, miss. She came through the tearoom with nothing but a small valise, delivering her instructions to me as she went without so much as breaking her stride. Then she was out the door and gone."

"Did you see which way she went? Did she hail a hansom cab, or walk across the bridge? Did she go around to the side of the building? Into the alley, perhaps?"

At this, Polly finally lost patience. She put her hands on her hips.

"I'm sure I have more things to do than gawp after my mistress to see where she chooses to set her feet. Considering I'm left to do all and everything here there's plenty to keep me minding my own business, miss. If you pardon my saying so."

Xanthe nodded, muttering a thank-you as she went. She slipped around the side of the building, pausing only briefly to check no one had seen her, and then took hold of her locket and traveled swiftly home.

When she stepped out of the blind house she almost walked straight into Harley.

"Hey, lassie, have a care! Your mother called me with the news. I came straight over. What's happened, hen? What the hell's going on?" He held her arms gently, looking into her eyes with very real concern.

She dearly wanted to let him give her a friendly, reassuring hug. To let him tell her everything would be fine and not to worry, they would sort it out together. But she dared not, fearing she could all too easily give way to tears if she let anyone be too nice to her at that moment. She needed to stay strong, for Liam. She thought then about what she had seen on the lake when she had been boating with Liam and Evie. She had looked into the silent depths and seen not a fish, as she had told the others. She had seen Liam, reaching out to her but unable to be saved, being taken by the cold, suffocating water. Was that a warning of what had happened? Was Liam lost in a timeless purgatory she would never be able to retrieve him from? She remembered the time he had startled her outside the shop, creeping up on her unexpectedly. She had turned around and seen an unnatural shadow over his face. Seen him appear death-marked and in great danger. Why hadn't she heeded those warnings? Why had she taken him back in time? She knew how dangerous it was. She shouldn't have asked it of him. Forcing herself to focus, she took a breath and tried to explain to Flora and Harley what she had to do next.

"I need to go to Liam's flat," she said. "I need something of his that will sing to me. You've got a spare key?"

"Keep it behind the bar. Come away over. I'll fetch it for you and take you up there."

"I'm coming too," Flora said from the steps to the house.

Xanthe was about to tell her there was no need but she recognized the look on her mother's face. It was the look that said you are my daughter and I'm not going to let you do this alone.

Flora clipped Pie's lead on and the little dog led the way, happy to have an unexpected outing. Xanthe plucked a duffle coat off a peg in the hall as they passed through it, shrugging it on over her costume, more against the cold of the fading March day than the strange glances she would garner. It was a little after five, so Flora turned the sign on the shop door to CLOSED and locked up as they left. The walk through Marlborough was an assault on her senses, with the rush-hour traffic chugging through the high street, the market traders dismantling their stalls, last-minute shoppers bustling along the pavements, phones ringing, pedestrian crossings beeping—it all felt so loud and bright and brash after the relative quiet of the time she had just come from. Harley went through the main entrance of the pub to fetch the key and met them at the gate to Liam's workshop and yard. Xanthe fidgeted impatiently as he unlocked the padlock on the gate and then the door to the flat. She trotted up the stairs, leaving Flora to follow more slowly, as Harley flicked on lights. Pie darted past her, hurtling around the kitchen. It pulled at Xanthe's heart that the little whippet was also searching for Liam.

"He's not here, pooch," she said quietly, stroking her head and looking into her button-bright eyes. "He'll come home soon, I promise." She scanned the flat one room at a time, walking slowly, listening, picking things up and putting them down again. Feeling she was horribly intruding on Liam's privacy, but knowing she had to find something with a strong connection to him.

Harley caught her up. He watched her for a while and then asked, "Nothing, hen?"

She shook her head, pausing to pick up a karting trophy on the windowsill. It had his name inscribed on it. "Nothing," she replied, fighting mounting despair.

Flora sat at the kitchen table. "Perhaps that means he doesn't need you. I mean, not urgently. Maybe he's OK where ... when he is. And he'll send for you when he's ready. When the time is right?"

"It doesn't work like that, Mum," she told her, not meaning to snap. "I—I need to find something that mattered to him. Really mattered. That's what will sing."

Harley raised his hands and then let them drop by his sides in a gesture of helplessness. "If you'd asked me, hen, I'd have said that was you."

"I don't think people can work in the same way," she said, her heart tightening at the truth of what he had said.

Flora let Pie jump up onto her lap. "He wasn't home much, really. If you think about it, he was either practicing with the band, playing a gig, out with you, or working on his blessed cars."

Xanthe looked at her. "That's it! How can I have been so dim?" She hurried through the flat and tore back down the stairs, calling back to Harley as she went. "The keys to the workshop, Harley? Can you bring them?"

He puffed after her, sorting through the jangle of keys as he went, locating the right one as Xanthe all but hopped from one foot to the other waiting for him. With a rattle, they rolled up the broad shutters that closed off the front entrance to the workshop. Everything was neatly put away, cars he was planning to work on parked up at the back. More recent acquisitions and more costly models near the front under dust sheets or tarpaulins. Xanthe hurried from one vehicle to the next, lifting a corner of the covers until she found what she was looking for.

"Here it is!" she cried, throwing back the canvas to reveal Liam's favorite red sports car.

"Aye," Harley agreed. "That's his pride and joy all right."

She stood still, placing her hands on the shiny bonnet of the car, waiting, listening, hoping. Pie, with no sense of the importance of the moment, came bounding down the stairs and proceeded to snuffle around the workshop in search of biscuit crumbs. Flora caught them up, moving cautiously across the concrete floor, avoiding patches of oil.

"Anything?" she asked gently.

Fighting back tears, Xanthe shook her head.

Harley was incredulous. "You're sure? Not even from this?"

"Nothing," she told them. "Just . . . nothing."

The three of them stood in silence, letting the significance of that nothing sink in. It was Xanthe who broke the tension of that silence by voicing what all were thinking.

"Nothing is singing to me. For whatever reason, nothing is drawing me to him. It doesn't matter. I've traveled without a found thing before. I've just done it, for goodness' sake."

"You have," Harley agreed, "but you knew *when* you wanted to go to."

"And *where*," Flora pointed out.

"Aye," said Harley, "we don't have any idea when or where Liam has ended up."

"No," said Xanthe calmly, determination taking the place of panic now, a kernel of strength giving her the focus and courage she needed, "we don't. But I'm learning new things all the time. The way to find him, the answers to where and when he is, they will be in the book. It's up to me to find them."

Harley tilted his head. "It seems to me, hen, there's a heap of time to go looking in, and an awful lot of places."

"Places can be traveled to, and times can be traveled through," she said, looking from one to the other, needing them to understand, to believe in her. "I am a Spinner. It's what I do. It's what I am. Liam has been taken somewhere, because of me. It's up to me to get him back. I will work out where he is, I will find the way to spin through time to reach him. Whatever it takes, I will bring him home."

ACKNOWLEDGMENTS

As always, heartfelt thanks go to my editor, Pete Wolverton. His patience, attention to detail, and enthusiasm for my stories sustain me through the long, slow business of getting the book written. And this one was longer and slower than some, due to a veritable ark of circumstances and events. More than this, his continued belief in me and support of my work is something I value hugely and will never take for granted.

I'd like to say a big thank-you to the team at St. Martin's Press. This book has come into being through strange times, indeed, and I appreciate everyone's fleetness of foot and determination in getting everything done well and in good time.

Once again, I am particularly grateful to the art department team for the beautiful cover. I am always thankful that they listen to my various demands, accommodate them where they can, but hold out for what they know to be the best version of what the book requires.